The whole moment seemed eerie and like a dream. A very bad one.

He wasn't sure what he faced and needed to be as quiet as possible. He sat back and pulled off his boots. Not easy to manage, but urgency drove him. He bit back a grunt when his shoulder screamed with pain. He dare not make a sound until he assessed the situation completely.

Yelling again. He gently laid his boots on the deck and rose again to all fours, creeping up to the starboard side wall. Hugging the wall, he crept as close as he dared to the hallway leading to engineering. He figured whoever was hollering, they yelled to someone on the dock; the voice carried away from him.

"We intend to blow this garbage scow of a boat off the river, and if you don't want the girl to be on it, We suggest you step right up and take her place, Briggham. That is, if there is any nerve left in you!"

Well, that message was clear enough. The captain was here. And someone had captured a woman on the boat, and she was in trouble. Jeremy wanted to charge in, but pushed his feelings aside. He could not allow emotion to get in his way and meddle with his thinking.

He fell back to his pilot's training. First things first. Assess the situation. Then formulate the plan. Next, proceed and do what needed to be done. No matter what that might be.

He scooted up to get an idea of what circumstances waited at the end of the hall. The entrance to engineering was dark and murky. He didn't want anyone catching a glimpse of him, but he needed to see what was happening.

Slowly, he edged to the hallway opening, and peeked around, only allowing the smallest part of his face to show. Just enough to see out of one eye. Squinting against the sunlight pouring over his shoulders, he didn't see much. In the dark murk of engineering, a bundle lay, something heaped on the floor near the doorway at the end of the hall.

It moved. Unwrapped. A woman. He'd recognize her anywhere. Sarah.

Theater of Illusion

Kathy Steffen

MEDALLION
P R E S S

Medallion Press, Inc.
Printed in USA

Previous Accolades for Kathy Steffen's
First, There Is a River

"A supremely contemporary story in an authentically depicted historical setting. A novel that will ring true with women readers of all types."
—G. Miki Hayden, Edgar and Macavity winner, and author of *The Naked Writer*

"Set in 1900, Steffen's debut presents a captivating view of life aboard a riverboat a century ago . . ."
—*Publishers Weekly*

"The healing power of the river and the magic of love are explored in this emotionally fulfilling and beautifully written tale of good triumphing over evil. Readers will cheer for Emma."
—Barb Anderson, *Romantic Times Book Reviews*

"Kathy Steffen provides her audience with a powerful historical fiction that focuses on the lack of rights for women and the lack of protection for children. Emma is . . . fabulous as the only reason she remains with abuser Jared is their offspring, but once he sells them into child labor, she has no ties. The support cast including the river and the boat is strong as it brings out a bygone era. The romance is unnecessary though well written as *First, There Is a River* is foremost a character-driven deep historical tale."
—Harriet Klausner

Previous Accolades for Kathy Steffen's
Jasper Mountain

"This fantastic, powerful novel has an intriguing plot and well-formed characters. Steffen's prose captures the imagination from the first sentence."
—*Romantic Times Book Reviews*

Theater of Illusion

Kathy Steffen

DEDICATION

For my sister, Jane,
a most wonderful inspiration for Sarah.
From the moment you insisted on the title "drum major"
and on wearing pants like your male counterpart,
I knew you'd take the world by storm.

Published 2010 by Medallion Press, Inc.

The MEDALLION PRESS LOGO
is a registered trademark of Medallion Press, Inc.

If you purchased this book without a cover, you should be aware that this book is stolen property. It was reported as "unsold and destroyed" to the publisher, and neither the author nor the publisher has received any payment from this "stripped book."

Copyright © 2010 by Kathy Steffen
Cover design by Arturo Delgado
Edited by Helen A Rosburg

All rights reserved. No part of this book may be reproduced or transmitted in any form or by any electronic or mechanical means, including photocopying, recording, or by any information storage and retrieval system, without written permission of the publisher, except where permitted by law.

Names, characters, places, and incidents are the products of the author's imagination or are used fictionally. Any resemblance to actual events, locales, or persons, living or dead, is entirely coincidental.

Typeset in Adobe Garamond Pro
Printed in the United States of America

ISBN: 978-160542086-8

10 9 8 7 6 5 4 3 2 1
First Edition

ACKNOWLEDGMENTS

I owe everything to my family for their continued belief in me and my writing: my mom and dad, Eva and Ted Groft; my sister, Jane; and my dear friend Eddie. And my husband, Rob, who never wavers in his support, encouragement, and patience.

While I researched life on the river, the incredible men and women who lived and worked there came to life thanks to the Ohio River Museum in Marietta, Ohio, and the National Mississippi River Museum in Dubuque, Iowa. Special thanks to the *Spirit of Peoria* for my first riverboat ride and for allowing me to stand behind the wheel of an authentic sternwheeler.

My gratitude to Kevin Lamport for his friendship and critiques. A huge thank-you to Lori Devoti for helping me through the trials and tribulations of the writing life. Thanks to Christine DeSmet and Laurel Yourke for their constant encouragement and support. And finally, a huge thanks to all my friends at WisRWA Madison for their enthusiasm and wonderful, positive energy.

And a special thank-you to everyone at Medallion Press for their talent, hard work, and dedication.

Only by acceptance of the past, can you alter it.
—T. S. Eliot

Prologue

September 18, 1900
The *Spirit of the River*, Premier Riverboat on the Ohio River

Jared's eyes locked on his sinning, betraying wife. She stood on the deck of the riverboat, hands fisted around the handle of a skillet, knuckles white. She didn't have the grit to swing it.

Emma Perkins was not a woman of courage.

She didn't even possess the backbone to be a decent kind of wife, never mind raise his children. He'd been forced to take them from her. He had no choice. She coddled them, made their lives easy, filled their heads with foolishness from books. Taught them to read and draw and sing. Why, his son was growing up to be a nancy boy.

He'd have none of that.

Emma froze before him, like a timid, hunted animal. He grinned. She'd never escape him—he knew it sure as day. Now she knew it too. No matter where she ran, who she met, what she did, there was no place to hide. She was his. To do with as he saw fit.

And he saw fit to finish this lesson. Oh, he was gonna teach her good, all right.

Her whore of an assistant, Lilly, wriggled under his foot. He leaned more weight on her chest to stop her from squirming. Damn puny slut, he'd crush the life out of her right here. In front of his wife, the woman who promised to love, honor, and obey him.

Emma didn't obey so good.

"You gonna hit me with that thing?" Jared asked his wife, and laughed. "You didn't have the guts before in our bedroom."

Shock hit her face; fear spread in her pretty green eyes.

"Remember, Emma? I do."

"N-no." Her voice sounded far away. Weak.

"Y-yes," he mocked. "I seen you that night. I see everythin' you do, Emma. I seen you sin with the scarred man. Don't despair. I erased the blight upon your soul."

"Gage! He's kilt! Threw him over!" the little whore, Lilly, gasped out. He shifted even more of his weight on her, enough to shut her up.

"And your uncle. I saved you from his sins, too."

More shock spread. Her face became a comical mask, stretched white with terror. Next, her expression crumpled with pain. Loss. Served her right. He'd had to take care of her messes, and he'd done it. Killed her Uncle Quentin, and just throttled the life out of the scarred engineer, threw him in the river only seconds before. He'd cleaned up her life. Seemed he was always cleaning up her life.

Sure, it was nice of him, but his duty as her husband, the way he saw things. Emma caused him a load of work. She should thank him.

Instead, she stood frozen, a skillet clenched in her hands. Her brown hair had come loose, falling around her shoulders. Escaped its binding. Well, no escape from him. Ever.

He couldn't wait for this lesson. To teach her the way of things.

"I see it all, Emma. See and redeem you from your own sinnin' and damnation."

"No," she whispered. Fear ran off her and he took it in, like a wolf sniffing out its prey. "No, no, no," she continued. Each *no* came louder.

Her face changed and he saw something he'd never seen from her before. Not fear. Not cowering. Not her sickening, mousy, terrified look.

She was angry? How dare she! And after he'd gone to such trouble to fix her life.

"Who the hell do you think you are?" she ground out, as if she had the right to say such words to her husband. As if she had any rights at all.

He'd teach her to love, honor, and obey, starting now.

"I'm your husband," Jared answered silkily. "Your savior. I see all. And now, retribution for this whore." He settled his full weight on the foot holding the yellow-haired slut. Her eyes bulged and her tongue popped out of her mouth with a small gag. She curled as he crushed her in her final judgment.

Ah, he loved this. Teaching sinners the way of things. God would thank him for taking care of one more. The whore didn't deserve to live; she didn't even deserve the effort it took for him to rid the earth of her pestilence.

She owed him a little enjoyment, and he had to say this for her, she did perform. Her face took on a shade of purple he'd never seen. She didn't look so cute and flirty now, did she?

"Get away from her! I'm warning you!" His wife raised the skillet higher.

He laughed from the sheer pleasure of finding his calling. The Clean-Up Man. The fun of a job well done as he delivered sinners before the judgment of the Lord.

"I said, get away from her! Now!"

Jared Perkins. The hand of God. He wielded the power of the Lord. And now his wife saw this, knew it. The girl beneath his foot was about dead, exterminated while Emma watched. All part of the lesson. He laughed harder. The slut beneath his foot gasped for her last breath.

Iron impacted against the side of his head with a sickening, wet crunch, and the world exploded in a red haze of agony. His teeth blew out and he experienced the horror of his face collapsing. He staggered back. Pain dulled his senses; black wrapped around his head, shutting down the world. A spot cleared. Emma. There she was. Black around the edges, her face wavered, but he, in the name of the Lord, could see her.

The whore gasped. Emma stepped over her, got between him and the girl.

"You don't see everything," Emma said. "You're no savior. All you are is a pathetic excuse of a man."

Streaks of righteous rage shot through him. He was the eye of God. The hand of God. And nothing could stop him. Certainly not Emma Perkins. How dare she? His wife? His *wife*?

Red hot anger bubbled up. She gave him no choice. The time for vengeance, swift and true, was here. He snarled and reached for her. She swung again, the skillet smashing into his arm. A crack shot up to his shoulder and weakness waved through him. His knees crumbled.

He fell sideways, grabbing for the rail. Instead of stopping him, he took it with him as he crashed through and tumbled into the river.

Cool water surrounded him, washing away the blood, the hurt. He held on to the heat of fury, now his lifeline.

Something darted through the water, a thing, a black shape. The Angel of the Lord, come to save him. Eyes burning red, its powerful arms and shoulders flexed as it reached for him with long, gnarled fingers.

He opened himself to it, let the angel see his true heart and soul. He welcomed the glorious being to take him home. Steel nails dug into his tender flesh and the creature swallowed him in its grip, searing him with cold fire. Every fiber of his body screamed with holy torment, pure and sharp. Jared became one with the Angel of God.

Swirling black hair of the seraphim surrounded them. Jared let go of his physical shell, watched it sink to the river bottom. He needed it no more. His savior had come. The Messenger of God infused him with everything: strength, courage, fortitude.

Wrath, fury, revenge.

His soul embraced the darkness. He clung to it, with only one thought, one desire.

She couldn't hide from her lesson. From her final judgment. From him.

She was his wife.

He would return.

Chapter 1

September 18, 1910 (ten years later)

This time he'd do it.

Tobias Perkins' legs dangled over the two hundred-foot drop of Lost Soul's Cliff. The night clung to him, the last vestiges before dawn. He felt a little fuzzy, and more than a little guilty for stealing the bottle of whiskey from the *Spirit's* bar. At least he'd grabbed it from the top shelf.

"Nothing but the best for the *Spirit of the River*." He lifted the bottle in a toast to the riverboat where he and his family worked and lived. His mother, Emma, shared ownership of the boat and she insisted everything aboard be top-notch. Which suited the event of a man's first drink. Ironically, also his last.

He had to jump. Jared Perkins, his father, had returned. He haunted Toby. Lived inside his son, looking for an opportunity—a moment of anger—to explode out and destroy. Toby clutched the bottle to the center of his chest where a burn flared, his father's anger. Every time he felt the burn, Toby knew his father wanted out.

He raised the bottle higher to the amused moon. "Here's to my last few moments on earth. Hey, what was the nursery rhyme about the cow jumping over the moon?"

The silver orb gazed back, no answer.

"Don't worry, I'm not planning to jump very far. I'm just looking for the nerve to drop off this edge." He lifted the bottle and hesitated. He'd never tried this before. He swallowed. Whiskey scorched all the way down. He gagged. Choked. No wonder they called it "liquid fire."

"Cripes, why does anybody drink this junk?" He knew his reason; hopefully he'd find courage with his first swig. His friend Charley insisted time and time again, a good, stiff shot was all he needed.

Just down one. Quick like. Then you'll be able to talk to the ladies without gettin' your tongue in a twist.

Charley always focused on chasing after girls. Toby needed courage for a different reason. He raised the bottle to the bright disk in the sky.

"Thank you for your rapt attention, Moon. I needed a witness." He wondered if anyone would find his body, or if he'd sink and wash downriver and out to sea forever.

Despite the hideous taste, he gulped another swig and belched. Lovely. And still, no sign of courage. All the whiskey accomplished, besides causing a burp, was to make him nauseous. He took another gulp. And another.

"Aack!" This stuff was really horrid.

After the next gulp, he saw them. In the black, two tiny, red dots glowed from far, far down. Watching. Calling.

He flung the bottle into the dark in their direction. In the time it took for his heart to thud several times, the bottle smashed on the rocks below. The delicate sound of shattering glass broke the soft rush of the river. The red dots watched. Didn't waver.

"Hey there, dear Father, we both know that's not you," Toby whispered.

Legend explained the occasional sight of glowing red eyes to Tobias' murderous father reborn. Once human, the stories told, Jared Perkins had come back. Legend grew as legends did, and stories circulated of an angry spirit stalking the banks. The shadow of an insane minister. A creature from hell. Passengers and boatmen alike glimpsed glowing red eyes in the dark. Warnings sounded along every town: *stay away from the river, especially at night!*

Tobias laughed. Must be another explanation for the red dots. And not because he didn't believe in ghosts and hauntings. He believed. Heck, he lived one every day. In fact, he knew exactly where Jared's demonic presence lived, and he planned to take it over the edge and into the river.

Toby spread a hand over his chest, willing the burn beneath his heart to quiet. "Not now," he whispered. He couldn't risk any distraction or he'd never do it. He listened to the river rushing below, watched moonlight glance off rippling water and shatter into a thousand glittering pieces.

He only needed to lean forward and push off. And fly. He'd finally be free.

In his left hand he clutched the small toy bear he'd cherished as a child. Felt its soft, plush body. Monkey Bear. He'd loved the thing, clung to it through many nights, cried as its snuggling comfort helped him through the worst days of his life. Only fitting a toy should plunge with him to his final destiny.

Darn. He needed another swig of whiskey.

"Shoulda thought of that before I threw it away," he said, regretting his grand gesture. He couldn't even get this right. God, he'd miss Sarah and his mom. The boat. Charley. Gage. Even the captain. He swiped something away, something wet and on his cheek. Tears? "Cripes, can I get any more pathetic?"

At least only the moon and the mysterious red dots watched his last, pitiful moments.

The burn roiled in his chest again. "You aren't out there on the river, are you, dear Father? Nope, we both know where you are." Toby had to end his life before the thing within him did something terrible, some harm he wouldn't be able to reverse and would regret forever. Time to mash them both on the rocks below. End the evil for good. The only answer.

Be a man. Do it. Jump.

"Courage?" he asked the night. "Just for a second? It's all I need."

Lean forward. A little more.

Wind came up and tickled through his hair, reminding him of the loving hand of his mother. She had no idea of the monster she raised. It fell to him to end the Perkins family legacy.

Jump. Jump now.

The moon winked. He clutched Monkey Bear tight and leaned forward.

Sarah Perkins bolted upright in her bed and listened. In her cabin aboard the *Spirit of the River* she generally slept deeply, but something felt wrong. The night, usually hushed with nothing more than the sound of the river outside, sharpened with anticipation.

She pulled her blanket closer, fighting the chill in the night air. The heaviness of sleep melted away and she remembered. This day—soon to come—assaulted her with sour memory. Twisted her stomach. Wrong? Of course, something was wrong. No wonder she couldn't sleep.

She rose, mindful of Lilly, her roommate, sound asleep on the other bunk. Gloom wrapped through her room. She wondered about the time as she slipped a shift over her dressing gown. The shadows of night reminded her of watered-down coffee—weak and thin. Was it past midnight then?

Sarah made her way to the door and opened it with care despite the flicker of panic deep in her gut. She stopped and listened. Water lapped at the edges of the riverboat. A gentle, soothing resonance. Caressing. Beyond the sound, the quiet rush of the river. And Sterling City, a town built on the labor and money from steel, slept. Even the drunks were silenced for the night and the taverns closed.

Through the seeming tranquility, she sensed something watching. Eyes from the past. Her father, Jared Perkins, ten years dead on this day. A most terrible anniversary, indeed.

Or happy, depending on which way you looked at it.

September 18—the day Sarah and her family achieved freedom from Jared Perkins' oppressive wrath. No tears wasted on him; she was glad he was dead. He hadn't shown a shred of compassion for his family. Her father—the man who was supposed to protect them. All he protected was his own wrathful pride and warped view of the Bible. Both had been more important to him than her mother. Or her. Or Toby.

Realization hit her as warning again took hold. Her brother. Toby needed her. Now.

Damn it all anyway, why hadn't she figured out her brother needed her, today of all days, before now? The answer came back, accusing. Too involved in her own world, she'd been a selfish little ninny.

"Enough!" she said. Berating herself wouldn't help Toby.

Once outside, she struggled to shut the door slowly and not slam it closed. Moonlight spilled over the deck. Intruding through her worry over Tobias, a reminder bubbled to the front of her thoughts. Her test was today.

The riverboat pilot test before the River Board. Nine a.m. sharp. She'd practiced, she knew every part of the river, she was set to pass the damned thing this time around. If the River Board would approve of a woman pilot, she would finally realize her dream. Stand on her own. Pilot a riverboat.

One thing could conceivably get in the way. This year the board scheduled her test on the anniversary of Jared Perkins' death. On purpose, she suspected, to distract her from the task. The board had no use for a woman among them.

Well, she'd show them. She would not allow her dead bastard of a father to reach from the past and ruin her dreams. And she absolutely would not allow his memory to hurt her brother. Which circled her back to why she was out here in the dark. Toby.

She tiptoed down the corridor to his room. Toby shared quarters with Charley, a waiter onboard the *Spirit*. She pulled back her desire to kick the door in and rapped softly instead. A faint rumble came from inside. She creaked the door open. Moonlight glowed from behind her, illuminating Charley's bunk complete with his slumbering, snoring hulk. Toby's bunk stretched out, empty. Pristine. Blankets tucked, pillow smooth. Either he'd risen and made it, or not slept in it at all.

She shut the door, thoughts whirling through her mind. Where could he be?

"Oh, my God."

She flashed back to four years ago. Her brother, only thirteen, leaving a suicide note apologizing for throwing himself off Lost Soul's Cliff. He had no choice, the note insisted, he owed it to their father's victims. She arrived barely in enough time to stop him.

That's where he'd be. Again. She knew it, without a doubt.

Wait. Chasing him down? Insane. A wild goose chase at best.

"Don't be silly," she whispered to herself. She always jumped to conclusions—the worst ones. Toby was fine, most likely down in the galley, getting something to eat. Or unable to sleep, perhaps wandering the boat. What if she went all the way to the cliff and he wasn't there? After all, the cliff towered over the other side of the river more than five miles away.

No use pretending. He'd be at Lost Soul's Cliff; she knew it inside, deep and sure. Sarah didn't want him to be there, because it meant he was in trouble of the worst kind. Again. Being perfectly honest with herself, she didn't want to chance missing her exam either. Well, damn it all, she'd manage both, save her brother and become the first woman pilot on the Ohio River. After all, she was Sarah Perkins. She could do anything, especially the impossible. Sarah Perkins, indomitable. Tenacious. Unstoppable.

"Idiotic," she said aloud. "At times, apparently delusional."

Could she make it to the cliff and back in time? It didn't matter. The hell with becoming a riverboat pilot. Reaching her dream. Toby needed her. She returned to her cabin to gather her shoes and a scarf.

Chapter 2

The worst day of the year.

The massive paddle wheel of the *Spirit* waited, motionless in the river, water lapping around its edges. Emma usually loved daybreak, especially before the *Spirit* took off. This particular morning, however, Jared managed to sour the coming sunrise and the excitement of the journey beginning later today.

Emma pursed her lips, wanting to completely purge her memories of him. No matter how she tried, every year on this day, Jared Perkins barged to the front.

Thank heavens she had work to keep her occupied. Good, honest work saved her as she rebuilt her life and a home for herself and for her children. She smiled to herself. Yes, children. Tobias and Sarah might insist they were adults, but they would always be her babies.

Emma had begun the morning by going to Sarah's room to wish her luck. Lilly, Sarah's roommate, answered the knock with a groggy expression, curls corkscrewing from her head in a blonde explosion. Sarah had left before dawn. Today was her pilot test, which far eclipsed any other importance of this date.

"Nonimportance," Emma reminded herself.

"Talkin' to yourself again?" Arms circled her waist and lips brushed her neck. She melted back into Gage's embrace.

"I always know the answer. No surprises."

He chuckled. He always did, no matter how lame her jokes. Turning, she looked into the black eyes that frightened her the first time she saw him. Before she knew the compassionate, gentle treasure of a soul inside.

"I knew I'd find you back here," he said.

"This paddle wheel holds lots of good memories."

"We was right here when I got the gumption to kiss you for the first time."

"I remember." She touched his face, ran her fingers over his scars, and he pulled her closer. She caressed his cheek, the scarred side where burns, years ago, blistered then rehardened his skin, sculpting the most beautiful face in the world. She leaned in, and their kiss was filled with the emotion of two people who'd loved each other for years.

When they parted, Emma nodded at the wheel. "Even when it's not spinning there's something so constant about it. Reliable, I suppose. I always feel like the world is right when I see it."

Gage's voice took on an edge of concern, and he ran his hands up her arms. "Anythin' wrong?"

"Sarah's left already. I wanted to wish her luck."

"Can't fool me. You're pry more nervous than she is."

"I do wish I could take the test for her. Although I'd fail miserably." She laughed.

"Gotta let go, Em. Sarah's a grown woman." Gage blessed her with the half grin she loved so much. "This is a big day, and you're entitled to some worry for her." He spoke in his hushed scrape, his voice resembling a creaking cog. He had trouble talking, another way Jared Perkins reached out from the past. He'd tried to kill this man, but all he managed to take was Gage's voice.

"Big day in many ways."

He shook his head. "You ain't out here rememberin' *him,* are you?"

"No, I like to remind myself on this day every year how lucky I am, how happy. And if Jared's memory attempts to crawl out of the river and back onboard, I will grab a shovel and whack him back to hell." She gave him a wry smile. "Sounds like I'm a bit insane, doesn't it?"

"Not at all. Although, I owe the man a whole lot."

"What?" She stepped back from him. How on earth could he think such a thing?

"He gave me so much," Gage said. "While Jared Perkins lived, he made the most precious family on this earth, and then he left you all with me." He shrugged. "I can't hate him. Just pity him."

"Naturally you see him that way. You are so kind." Then anxiety clenched at her, deep inside. "Sarah is on her way about now. Maybe waiting in the pilothouse of that old broken-down boat. This is so important to her."

"It's up to her now, and that girl can do anythin' she sets her mind to. Only question is whether or not the River Board will be fair." He ran his hand up and down Emma's spine. "You know, I think you need a distraction. Otherwise you'll stand here and fret the entire time Sarah's gone. And it won't pay to send worry her way."

"I *do* have some time before I need to be down in the galley." Emma put her arms around his neck. He pulled her to him, and worry swirled away. His love always made her dizzy. She drew back a little to see into his eyes. Every time she looked at Gage, she saw the perfect heart and soul of the man she loved.

"Why on earth do you think distracting me is this easy?" she asked.

"Because it is. I'd like to start my day with a little distraction, too."

She took his hand, and he followed her up the steps. As they approached their cabin door, she felt someone watch her. She slowed and glanced over her shoulder. Saw no one around. Still, she felt something . . . wrong. She shuddered.

"What is it?"

"Nothing. I'm anxious for Sarah. And the boarding today. I'm sure it's nothing."

A shard of light breached the horizon. Sarah's heart sank practically to her toes. Toby's silhouette glowed in morning-shadow lavender. He sat with his back to her, his huddled shoulders and defeated posture reminding Sarah of the defenseless, fragile, frightened boy he'd once been.

She didn't want to startle him, considering he sat with his legs hanging over a cliff. She thought this very scenario through a hundred times on the way here, had to do this right. No room for error. She waited until she caught her breath.

"Toby?" she asked softly.

An almost imperceptible flinch revealed he heard.

Sarah hated heights, and being this high absolutely terrified her. Especially when her sweet brother sat with his legs dangling over the precipice. She approached, willing him to stay steady, not lean forward too far. The way he hunched over, only one small movement would send him careening over the cliff.

Please, God, don't disappear.

She crept as close as she dared, sat down and slid forward, her heart in her throat. Some survival instinct pushed against her, cautioning her not to get too close; if she did, he might take her over the edge with him. She did her best to ignore the warning. He was her brother, and here because of his constant struggle. Tobias insisted on bearing the sins of Jared Perkins.

She scooted all the way to the edge and dropped her legs over. Fear crawled up them and numbed her, all the way to her lips. Gads, she hated heights! Focus, she reminded herself. She would not let fear get the best of her. Toby's life depended on it, and they were in this together now. If Tobias Perkins was intent on ending his life here, he'd have to take her with him.

"What in heaven's name are you doing?" she whispered.

"Enjoying the view," he answered in the quiet and slightly wavering voice of a boy on the cusp of becoming an adult. The older he got, the more he looked like Jared. Instead of a hard, handsome, and powerful persona, Toby moved quietly through the world, slight, almost frail. His face, always gentle. Kind. He wore his engaging looks like a wistful echo, didn't wield his charm like their father had, casting it out like a net and dragging in victims.

Although at seventeen Toby was actually a young man, she'd always see him as her baby brother, an image made easy as he grasped his childhood toy.

If Jared Perkins weren't dead already, she would have killed him for this.

During their nightmare of a childhood, Sarah took care of Toby. She took her charge seriously, sharing her strength and courage, and finding refuge in caring for his fragile, battered soul. Part of the passages of growing up were the taunts of other children, spears of meanness thrown their way. Sarah protected them both, fighting, brawling, backing others down.

Not an easy life, growing up as the child of a murderer.

She kept anger out of her voice. "Difficult day for us."

"Yeah." This time his answer sounded stronger.

"Why don't you come away from the edge?"

"I told you. View." He held his gaze steady on the river rushing by, its power diminished from this great height. Up so far, Sarah felt removed from the realities of life, a spectator.

She understood why this place drew Tobias. Called to him. He'd grown up keeping to himself mostly, as if he deserved to exist only on the fringes of life. Like a moth flitting around the edge of light, hardly noticeable. Every so often he flew close, allowed himself his feelings, those buried so deep. By acknowledging them he risked destruction. Like now.

He sat balanced at the point where desperate, saddened people, believing the world would be better off without them, ended their lives. One of the most haunted places on the river, and now, thanks to their father, the Perkins name wove into the tales of ghosts and despair.

"Toby, come back to the boat with me."

He stared out over the river.

"This doesn't do anyone any good. Mother is waiting for us. The *Spirit* leaves this afternoon. Please."

Still no response. Time for another tack.

"Toby, please. I don't have time for this, not today. I'm a wreck as it is."

Now he did look at her, his watery blue eyes filled with pain so naked, she flinched. Then his expression changed.

"Oh, criminy, Sarah, I forgot. Today is your pilot's test!" He jumped to his feet and she shrieked.

Then everything happened, fast yet slow, all at once. Still gripping Monkey Bear, he lost his balance and wavered. She grabbed his arm with both hands, threw herself back, and he tumbled down and rolled over her to safety.

They both lay a moment, stunned at what almost happened.

He laughed. Giggled.

Everything, all the tension, the fright, the shadow of their father, all of it blew away with the sound. Sarah sat part way up and scooted back until the tingles of fear stopped racing across her skin. She flopped down, allowing all her strength to drain into the cool ground. Overhead, thin clouds like smears of milk streaked the sky, their edges lit with gold morning light.

"Runt, you are such an idiot."

He sat up. "Yeah, I know."

"Don't ever do that again."

"I won't. Cripes, this might have been serious. I almost lost my teddy bear." He held Monkey Bear up and wiggled it.

Despite the teasing nature of his words, the look in his eyes conflicted with his fading smile and told her his promise might be one he couldn't keep.

I bide my time. I do this well. Years of waiting in the past, only living as a memory. Soon, I will become real. I will have a body. Hands. A face.

The Offspring fights me, does not want me to come out. And yet I always win. The child is weak. Stares in the mirror, attempting to push me down into nothing more than a flicker. I cannot believe the Offspring is of my loins, flesh of my flesh, blood of my blood.

Spirit of my spirit.

Yet here we are. Bound together by blood.

How many parents are saddened, embarrassed, disappointed by their children? When babies come into this world, wriggling and screaming, they have every possibility. They are fresh, pliable things that need to be molded. Some, though, stay soft. Never find the spine, the metal that will forge a human being fitting of fortitude. A person who matters.

No, instead, some burrow into the coward's way.

How did the father of Jack McCall feel on hearing his son murdered the hero and lawman Wild Bill Hickock by shooting him in the back? Or the pathetic case of Angela Cooper, who poisoned her infirm grandmother slowly with cups of tea, so she and her mother would inherit money enough to leave sooner rather than later. How proud was her mother when she learned of her daughter's deed and had no choice other than to go to the authorities and give her over to the hangman's waiting noose? Or Jebediah Bailey, hiding in a barn while his family was murdered in their beds a few yards away. He held a shotgun in his hands, could have used it to save those he professed to love. Instead, he hunkered down and shivered in the hay.

Did Judas' parents realize he gave over the Son of God with a coward's kiss?

Thus it is with the Offspring. Cowardice claims my own. The saving grace is me.

My thunder booms in the Offspring's ears, aggressive, angry. Its fear whimpers beneath the pulse of my strength. Soon, I will quell its fright with my anger, my fortitude. My body is gone, yet my will burns strong. I will become its heart and courage.

The Spirit of the River. Indeed. They have done this to me. Rent my soul from me. Destroyed my body. Stolen my life, my memory. Soon, I will have all back again.

They will not realize I am here. Until I wish them to see.

I will give them a hint. It is only sporting.

And I, at least, am not a coward.

Chapter 3

Damn it all. Ten minutes late. Unforgivable.

Sarah ran across the stage of the *K.S. Lamport,* the riverboat brought out from retirement for her pilot's test. She tripped in her rush—the floorboards were so warped and uneven. Luckily, she caught herself and didn't land on her arse.

Damn. Damn. Damn.

She had to calm down. Taking a deep gulp of air before climbing to the pilothouse seemed like a good idea until she did. A wave of dizziness washed over her. Brilliant, trying to force her breath to slow after having run five miles.

Holding to a post, she willed herself to relax and allowed her heart to slow to a reasonable pace. Another minute wouldn't matter, anyway. She'd as good as failed.

Well, she'd make them hear her out at least.

Above, a group of men crowded around the wheel. The examination board. The men to judge her. Again. They'd failed her twice already for one reason, and one reason only. She was a woman. Now she handed them a real reason to fail her before even stepping up to the wheel. Still, she planned to explain, although at the moment she had no idea what she'd tell them. As she climbed to the next deck, excuses ran through her head. None sounded the least bit acceptable, except the true one.

My brother was intent on throwing himself off a cliff and I had to stop him.

No. This morning was between Tobias and herself. No one else. She had to think of something to explain her tardiness away. Not allowing herself any more hesitation, she climbed up the pilothouse ladder.

When she entered, the board turned, like one creature with many heads. Age spots speckled across domes, wisps of white hair, blinking eyes. They reminded her of ancient sea turtles. She almost giggled at the four elder board members, from amusement or her nerves—she wasn't sure. She clamped down on her ridiculous emotions; piloting was a serious business and everything about her needed to reflect solemn intentions.

The fifth board member stood away from the older ones. Although just one man, his presence filled the pilothouse. He owned every space he occupied and commanded attention without saying a word. He caused concern, and a lot of it. Especially for her. The constant thorn in her side, Jeremy Smith, the man who piloted the *Spirit of the River* along with Captain Briggham.

The love of her life. The boat, not Jeremy, she amended to herself. Never Jeremy.

Sarah and Jeremy had both spent hours side by side, taking turns at the wheel under Captain William Briggham's watchful eye. The captain bonded with the boy. Sarah learned early on she had to fight for any time with Captain Briggham at all if she truly wanted to be a pilot. Her goal became clear: to prove to the captain and Jeremy that she was every bit as good at piloting a riverboat. Except, not surprisingly, Jeremy beat her to a license. And more.

Jeremy's current status—a fully licensed pilot and also the youngest ever to be a member of the River Board—was due to a few reasons.

Like her, he learned his craft under the most revered riverman alive, Captain Briggham. Quite unlike her, he piloted the *Spirit of the River*, the premier riverboat on the Ohio and Mississippi Rivers. And he'd beat her to the pilothouse because of the most important qualification for becoming a licensed pilot. He was a man.

Not that she'd ever forget that part. Jeremy's powerful arms strained against his shirt sleeves as he crossed them; his hazel eyes carried a question across his arrogant—and, yes, handsome—face. He obviously waited in anticipation of her explanation. Every time he looked at her, she experienced a tiny jump in her gut. No doubt a leftover memory of the crush she had on him when she was a young girl.

Damn emotions anyway. All they ever did was get in her way.

Thank heavens she grew up and finally saw past his chiseled features to recognize him for what he truly was: an arrogant, aggressive, disagreeable male. Her crush finally flared into frustration when she watched the captain choose him over her time after time to pilot during a race, to take the wheel during a storm or when the river became rough. She dumped any tender feelings for Jeremy in the wake of the realities of her life.

Let other women swoon over Jeremy Smith. She reminded herself again and again what choosing the wrong man could do. Just look at her mother.

Along with the question in his eyes, Jeremy wore a frown of disapproval. With four other board members, Jeremy, and herself, the pilothouse was a crowded affair indeed.

One of the ancient heads wheezed. "Miss Perkins." With a liver-spotted, trembling hand, he pulled at the end of a chain nestled in his vest pocket. A watch popped out. He studied it and frowned. "Eleven and a half minutes late."

"I apologize, sir. I do have an explanation."

They all stared, blinking under their hooded eyes, almost in unison.

"I had to stop on my way, you see. Downriver." She pointed vaguely and the heads swiveled to look, all except one. Skepticism tilted Jeremy's eyebrows. Damn it all, he knew she was fumbling. She couldn't give the real reason for her tardiness. She had to protect Toby, even at the cost of her dream.

The ancient heads swung back to her.

"A woman fainted and needed to be taken to the doctor in town. With only one other present, a gentleman, I thought it only proper I accompany them. I couldn't very well leave her unconscious to fend for herself. You know, for propriety's sake. Not to mention the humanitarian reasons."

That certainly sounded lame, even to her. Why didn't she say a boiler almost exploded with passengers about to die, and she saved the day? The real truth had been a matter of life and death.

She clenched her hands, waiting; yet she knew the answer. Piloting must come first. Period. The only excuse allowed for tardiness was the safety and care of passengers. Even then, a good pilot still made the schedule.

All of the members of the board, except Jeremy, shook their heads.

"Miss Perkins, the very essence of piloting is moving passengers and cargo to a point, a specific point, at a specific time. The river itself might be fluid, but a schedule must be forged of steel," one said slowly, as if speaking to a small child. He turned his back on her and reached for the door. Opened it. Began his descent.

"There is no excuse for tardiness. No room for it on the river," another added and followed.

"This isn't some frivolous game, Miss Perkins. Piloting is serious business."

"Absolutely unacceptable."

Sarah's gaze dropped to the deck as her cheeks flamed. The elderly gentlemen filed out. One man remained. Sarah stared at his shoes. He didn't leave. Finally she raised her head to meet Jeremy's eyes. She made sure she looked defiant and not cowed or embarrassed. She would not show any weakness to this man. Or any man at all.

Jeremy spoke, his disappointment clear. "A woman fainted? Couldn't you come up with anything better?"

"It didn't matter. They'd failed me before I came aboard."

"Being late didn't sway them to your favor. A faltering explanation didn't help."

"They still would have failed me. I'm a woman."

Jeremy sighed. "Yes, Sarah, that has come to everyone's attention. Easy to use your female status as an excuse, but this time the failure is all yours. You were late. If getting your license is as important as you proclaim, prove it. Next year, get here on time."

She did not need a dressing-down from Jeremy Smith. Especially while he wore his disapproving expression on his face. The frustrations of the morning finally exploded in her.

"It's awfully simple from where you stand, isn't it? Easy for you to do everything right. You have no barriers or challenges to being exactly what you want to be, and certainly nothing else in your life for distraction."

"I'm a damned good pilot, Sarah. One of the best."

"So am I."

"You certainly didn't prove it today. You didn't even get the basic part, the first part of it, right. Piloting is keeping to a schedule, being conscientious. Responsible."

"Don't bother with the lecture. You don't know the first thing about responsibility."

"I managed to get to my test on time. I arrived for yours *on time*. That's the first step to proving responsibility. Showing up."

She wanted to scream. She wasn't sure which upset her more: his jumping to conclusions and berating her or the disappointment in his eyes. Frustration heaped upon frustration, crushing her. But she refused to let anything destroy her, not even this. She clenched her teeth. One thing was for damned sure, she wouldn't cry. Not in front of him.

As they stared at each other, Sarah didn't trust herself enough to answer him. Beneath her feet the vibrations eased as the boilers began shutting down.

Like her life, she thought.

"Going back to the *Spirit*?" Jeremy asked, his voice soft. He moved in closer. For a second he looked like he wanted to take her in his massive arms and hug her. She was tall, strong for a woman; yet somehow, she felt slight every time Jeremy came near.

She glared. He moved back.

Using silence for her answer, she turned to look over the wheel, out at the river. She planned to stare out until he left. Which, hopefully, would be any moment. She heard the rhythm of his breathing behind her.

"Sarah?"

Damn it all, why wouldn't he leave? "Just go, Jeremy."

The engines shut off. Quiet settled around her.

Finally the door opened and shut, and she realized Jeremy had stayed because of duty. As long as the engines were engaged, a licensed pilot had to be in a pilothouse. The rungs of the ladder clanged with his steps. She listened to his footsteps in the corridor beneath, then the cadence of his walk descending a staircase.

Up here she stood on top of the world, even though she'd dropped to her lowest point. She wasn't sure she would ever regain the footing lost today. Not for another year. If at all.

She squared her shoulders and reminded herself of the most important thing. Tobias was alive. And on sure ground again or, at least, not plummeting away from her. Toby trusted her, and she would never, ever let him down. No matter what.

"Toby, get up, we's gonna be late for work." Charley's voice sliced through his brain like a rusty saw. Toby wondered when the hundred-pound sledge hammer had hit him. His friend's voice grated through the cabin again. "Come on, or I'm goin' without you. I'm not gonna let Malcolm kick my wretched ass again for bein' late."

Noise. Charley rummaging through drawers. Sounds of liquid in a bottle, shaking. The clink of a glass and the glug of something thick being poured.

Toby opened one eye, saw Charley sideways, a glass filled with some sort of bubbling concoction in his hand. His friend bent over to look Toby in the eye. "Rise and shine."

"I'm gonna puke," Toby mumbled.

"Finally, he lives. I ain't never seen no one drunk as you, and in the mornin'!" Charley held the drink closer. "Guaranteed to make you feel yoreself again. Come on, sit up."

Toby swung his legs over the bunk and the room swayed. Charley handed him the glass.

"I'm never drinking again," Toby promised.

"Oh, the times I've heard that oath," Charley answered. "I poured lots of coffee down you, dragged you into the head for a cold shower, and you've been asleep for a few hours. Now, git your ass outta bed! It's time to perform!"

Toby took a sip. A host of flavors assaulted him. Bitter citrus and what tasted like liquid grass? Pickles, salt, and soda?

"Ack!"

"Gotta pay the price, my friend." Charley hopped up on his bunk and pulled on his socks. "You was pretty gone."

"Charley, I can't remember coming back to the boat. Or any of what you just said—the coffee, the shower."

Charley's blue eyes teased. "Not surprisin'."

A shaft of sunlight speared into the cabin, lighting Charley's hair, and for a moment he resembled a celestial being. A guardian angel.

Actually, all things considered, he'd been one for Toby this morning.

Toby took another sip. "This is hideous!"

"You can thank me later."

Toby and Charley became friends the moment they'd met, several years ago when Charley came aboard the *Spirit* to work. Both about the same age, both without a father—in fact, as an orphan Charley faced the world without a mother as well—they understood each other and forged an instant connection. Charley didn't like to talk about his parents. Considering Toby's illustrious heritage, the unspoken agreement of silence between them suited Toby. They were just two guys. Working together. Having fun. Although Toby didn't feel much like fun at the moment.

"Can I take aspirin with this?" Toby asked. Charley nodded, and Toby pulled Uncle Quentin's strong-man tin off his shelf, careful not to knock down his model of the *Spirit* or Monkey Bear. "Hey, you made it back too, little guy."

"You was a sight to behold, staggerin' around, holdin' your teddy bear. I got you in here afore anyone saw, though."

"Cripes. Thanks." Toby looked down at the tin.

It had formerly housed one of the many cure-alls Quentin bought, tablets filled with magic and promises. Quentin's silly expenditures on miracle cures used to drive the captain mad, but once his uncle was gone, the tins they'd found among his belongings became precious. They divided the little boxes between his mom, Sarah, himself, Briggs, and Gage.

Toby chose his favorite tin, the one painted with the figure of a strong, robust man flexing bulging muscles. Gold lettering proclaimed *NERVE AND BLOOD TABLETS*. Letters on the side insisted *Entire System Purifier* and *Blood Thickener*, and the other side *Muscle Strengthener*, and *Nerve Revival*.

Toby flipped open the tin, now housing plain, old aspirin. He loved to imagine Quentin opening it up, taking a pill or two to revive his nerves. Thicken his blood. Purify his system.

Toby sure could use something like that now.

He popped a couple of tablets in his mouth and downed them with a swig of Charley's magic concoction and gagged. Charley chuckled.

Toby was never going to drink again. Ever.

Sarah looked up at the *Spirit of the River*. The boat rose majestically, her four stories towering above all the working boats crowded around the docks. A magnificent queen, dallying among the ordinary. She glistened white, her oak and brass staircase cascading down to the main deck, her polished wood floor shining like satin. The *Spirit's* calliope pipes pointed up to the sky, glistening like a silver crown. Among the squat working boats and tugs, she stood out as royalty.

The pilothouse perched at the very top. The control center of the boat, the pilot's hands holding the destiny of the community beneath it. Tears stung behind Sarah's eyes. She wouldn't be standing in the pilot's position this trip. Or maybe any.

Tears transformed to anger. She stomped down the riverbank and over the stage of the *Spirit,* and the platform connecting the boat to the landing trembled with her fury. Anger was much easier than disappointment. The board scheduled her test on this specific day on purpose; she knew it in her heart. And they won. She failed. It simply wasn't fair.

Now the time had come to face everyone. Nothing like public humiliation. The captain waited for her in the pilothouse. Since she'd been a girl at the wheel with him watching over her shoulder, she'd wanted to make him proud.

And what did she have to report? Failed. For being ten minutes late.

"Oh, excuse me. *Eleven and one-half minutes late.* Idiotic, creaky-old bastards!" She didn't care who heard. Better she blast her anger at the board. She didn't want to aim it at the real reason why rage coursed through her.

This was all her fault. Her responsibility. Jeremy was right, although she'd die before she admitted any such thing to him. It would only notch up his arrogance, and that was something no one needed.

She hesitated at the bottom of the staircase and stared up at the ornate riverboat towering above her. The pilothouse had never seemed higher or more unreachable.

"Sarah?" a raspy voice came out of the dark of engineering.

She whipped around. "I failed," she said before Gage asked the question. "I've studied every aspect of piloting. I know every rule, law, every crook in the river. I know more about the mechanical operations of the boat than any of those board members! And I've been piloting for years." She thought of the captain, of how disappointed he'd be. "I've learned from the best." She let out a defeated sigh. "I still failed, Gage."

His scarred face and dark eyes filled with something she hated to see. Sympathy. With his look, meant to help, even more humiliation crashed down.

"What happened?"

As much as she wanted to confide in him, she couldn't chance it. Toby would be devastated if he discovered his morning escapade had pulled opportunity from her already tenuous grasp. As long as she kept her mouth shut, Toby would never guess. She could count on one of the river's unwritten rules: whatever happened at these meetings stayed between pilots. No one else.

"It doesn't matter. It's over for now. I can't take the test for a year. And I don't think I will try again. I'm sick and tired of the whole thing . . ." Her voice drifted away, heavy as the muddy current slogging downriver. Tears? Damn it all, anyway. Not over this. She stiffened her chin.

Gage blessed her with his half-sided smile. "I know you. You won't give up and you'll get it next year. Anyhow, you have an important job here."

"Oh, yes, boat's purser, such a vital position. Let's see, I wear pretty dresses, welcome people onboard. Fetch extra towels for Mrs. Comstock in 7-A. Most urgent."

Gage shook his head. "If I wasn't so filthy I'd give you a hug, Sarah-girl. You take care of everyone onboard, not only passengers. You know how necessary you are to the *Spirit*. No matter what capacity you happen to be in." He'd lowered his voice. "You might feel like givin' up right now. Everythin' will look better with time. You'll get another chance."

She kissed him on the cheek. "Thanks for your vote of confidence. Just what I need before I face the captain." She tossed, she hoped, a rakish expression over her shoulder and began climbing the grand oak and brass staircase.

She'd hoped to replace the somber pallor of the day with good news and make this a date to celebrate. No such luck.

Arriving on the main deck she looked into the huge windows of the stateroom. From behind the focal point of the room—an intricately carved enormous mahogany bar at one end—Tobias fixated on juggling three wine bottles. No sign of his early-morning melancholy. He'd buried that deep within him and out of sight as he often did. Clearly, he was tired around the edges, his face a bit more pale than usual. He concentrated on flipping the three wine bottles into a circle in the air, the juggling not his usual quick, snappy trademark. He usually told jokes and appeared relaxed, like his tricks took no effort, but now his face scrunched with concentration.

It might be the sunlight, she told herself, making him seem so pale. Several years ago, Captain Briggham ordered Gage to install a skylight over the bar at the end of the stateroom so patrons could watch the stars go by. The installation also lit the stateroom during the day, causing light to glance off cut crystal and tiny rainbows to dart around the room. The breathtaking effect never ceased to amaze her.

Now in the harsh light, the shadows etched deeply in Toby's face.

She planned to watch him carefully the next few days, which would be a trick once the boat filled with the controlled mayhem of passengers and events. She needed to be sure Tobias had moved past all inclinations or thoughts of leaving them for good.

Waiters set crystal and silver on tables covered in white cloths down the center of the room in preparation for the passengers coming aboard. The room resembled an anthill with all the workers scurrying about. Two other waiters, one of them Toby's friend, Charley, applauded when Toby caught the bottles in succession and lined them up along the bar. Her brother scowled and put his fist to his forehead and swiped back his hair, the move making Sarah think he suffered with a headache.

Tobias met her gaze and headed through the dining room in her direction, his eyes growing in anticipation. A wistful smile began on his face. She wished she brought him good news. They both needed it. He swung the door open and his smile faded as yet another expression of pity greeted her.

"Another year, huh?" he asked.

"No. I'm not taking the test again."

His light blue eyes lit with excitement. "You passed?"

"Absolutely not. I'm simply finished with all that insanity."

"Oh." His face fell. "Sarah, I'm sorry." Then, he shrugged. "You're giving up. Good plan. I would, too."

His words caused her skin to hurt. "It's not giving up. I'm finally coming to my senses. I've accepted the fact that I don't have a chance and need to move on."

"See. I told you it's best to have no ambition. All I want is to serve drinks, juggle bottles, and perform the occasional magic trick." He pulled a quarter from her ear, his favorite trick for children. "I'm never disappointed." Even though his words came lighthearted and teasing, an air of melancholy wafted around him and she remembered his slump-shouldered silhouette from the morning.

"Toby, honestly, are you all right?"

"Never better," he answered, opening her hand and pressing the coin to her palm. "Aw, those idiots on the River Board are a bunch of dried-up old mummies anyway. They'll die someday. Probably sooner rather than later."

"Jeremy'll be there for years. He won't pass me, ever."

"Well, that's because he's jealous. You're twice the man he'll ever be." She swatted his arm.

"Actually, I think Jeremy kind of likes you," Toby continued. "Perhaps some after-hours persuasion might be in order?" He wiggled his eyebrows.

"That doesn't even deserve a response." But she smiled. "I'd better go face the captain."

"He'll understand. Good luck. See you later."

"Toby—" she began.

"Seriously, Sis. I'm fine." He headed for the dining room, then stopped and turned. "Thanks. You know. For this morning."

"You don't need to thank me."

"Yes, I do. You saved my life. Such as it is." He gave her a hint of a smile. "Let me know if I can, well, not that you'd ever need anything from me. But if you do . . ."

She hesitated to bring up a bad memory so soon, yet she needed the reassurance. "Toby, there is one thing you can do for me. Please promise me, the next time you feel so . . . hopeless, you'll come and tell me. Talk to me. Don't try to deal with your feelings alone. We can get through anything together."

"Yeah. We always have, thanks to you." He full-out grinned for her, yet she saw the sadness through his brave, light façade. She watched him continue in, making his way through the scuttling waiters and white-, silver-, and crystal-clad tables. Prisms danced around him. All light. All sparkle. At least on the outside.

She sighed. Above, the captain awaited.

Sarah continued up, coming to narrow, steep, painted wood steps with a handrail. These steps were tucked along the side of the boat, providing a sharp contrast to the grand, sprawling oak and brass staircase for passengers' use. Now she climbed to the practical part of the boat, the business part. No fancy ornamentation, nothing designed to impress. Simply what was needed. What was real.

The steps took her to the next level: the hurricane deck housing the officers' quarters. The Texas deck and pilothouse perched above, with Captain Briggham on watch, reading charts. And now for the most difficult part. She didn't know how to find the words to tell the captain his star student let him down and failed before she even began. Sarah shored up her defenses and prepared to let down her mentor. The hero of her life.

"Sarah?"

Oh, no. She whirled around at the sound of Jeremy's voice. "Not another lecture, please. Save it for someone who cares to listen to your pontificating," she said and turned to leave him in her wake.

He grabbed her. "Sarah—"

She spun and yanked her arm away. "I don't care to stop and allow you to gloat, and I certainly don't need any more words of wisdom from you. What I do need is for you to have the decency to keep the details of this morning to yourself. This is no one's business."

"Will you please listen?"

"No Jeremy, I've heard quite enough from you today. Just leave me be."

He reached out and she lunged back, slamming her shoulder against the wall. The knot inside her exploded. "Damn it all!"

She steadied herself as Jeremy lurched back, stunned, palms raised. "Sarah, I'm sorry. I didn't mean for you to—"

"Don't touch me again, you jackass."

His face pinched down with a look of hurt and he dropped his hands. "Not very becoming language for a lady," he managed, softly.

Theater of Illusion

"If there were a gentleman anywhere about, I might curb my tongue."

His eyes sharpened and drilled into her. "Now there's something I'd pay good money to see. Sarah Perkins keeping her mouth shut." He took a step closer. "Don't worry. Anytime you want to pilot, let me know. I'll be happy to supervise."

She let a moment of silence answer for her. When she spoke, her voice tightened with barely controlled anger. "I bet. Well, don't waste any time waiting."

"That's what you do best, isn't it? Make people wait."

This time, the silence between them pulsed with anger.

His face melted to chagrin. "God, Sarah. I'm sorry. I went too far." He extended his hand again to touch her, but stopped short and plunged both into his pockets. "I knew this morning would throw you into a foul temper and I'm sorry it did. I'm sorry about everything." He glanced away, then back at her. "Sarah, you have next year. It's not the end of the world."

Maybe not the end of the world, but the end of her dreams.

"Besides," he continued, "you're much better off with the job you have."

"What on earth do you mean?"

"It's not simply a good time up there, Sarah. Piloting isn't so much fun when it's your real job. We've had too much rain; the river is rough this season and fights the whole way. Nights are long, no matter if weather is bad or fine."

Incredulity spread through her. "You think I don't realize that?"

"Until you have the responsibility, and you can't leave no matter what, then you'll understand. Piloting is tough. The lives of people rest in your hands. The whole experience can be a heavy burden. Purser is a much better job for you, Sarah. It's safer. More fun. Be happy with what you have."

"How dare you!" She fisted her hands at her side and spun around before she punched him. She headed to the front of the boat, her heels clicking. His words scraped against her nerves and followed her down the hall and through the *Spirit's* front office.

She stopped. "Jackass!" she spit out to the empty room. At least she hadn't punched him. She didn't want to give anything else over for boat gossip.

Nothing worse than public failure. Gage and Toby were only the start of the sympathetic looks and knowing glances. And her mother. Her mother would find out she failed. She pressed her palm to her forehead. "God, I've let down everyone," Sarah whispered.

Then there would be those agreeing, like Jeremy, that failure was good enough for her. She had everything a woman might want. Pretty dresses, parties onboard to plan and attend; she should act like a lady and keep to her place. Find a husband, start a family.

She knew where that path led and she'd rather die. She thought she might explode with frustration. If she were a man, she'd haul off and punch the wall in lieu of Jeremy Smith.

"Oh, the hell with it!" She didn't punch the wall. She kicked it instead. Pain reverberated up her leg, and she bit her lower lip to keep from all-out wailing. Tears finally spilled down her face. She swiped at them. More tears fell.

She couldn't face the captain, not now. Damn it all anyway.

Chapter 4

Sarah Perkins and her bullheadedness would be the death of him yet. Surviving the woman was next to impossible. Why the hell did she insist on being in competition with him? It never even entered Jeremy's mind, not in all the years they'd been together, to think of them as adversaries.

He crossed the office and yanked his notes of recent river travel reports from the clipboard on the wall. He'd add any cautions to the charts upstairs. He thought about adding one furious female cub-pilot, but reminded himself he was the professional. He planned to set the perfect example.

His pencil snapped.

Grabbing a new one from the drawer, he tried to handle it with more care, forcing himself to focus on the task. He strained, but didn't hear anything coming from the pilothouse above. Was she up there yet? More than anything, he wanted to eavesdrop. Hear her explanation. Find out why she really came late.

"Jesus, when did I become a gossip?"

Sarah Perkins always managed to bring out the worst in him.

In his own defense, his feelings were more than curiosity. He wanted her to trust him again, talk to him like a friend, like they used to be. Not a rival. He didn't understand why she constantly tried to prove she could handle anything a man could. Why wasn't she just happy with herself? Why wasn't she happy with him?

He glanced at the clock. She'd been up there twenty minutes. His skin threatened to burst with anticipation, and when he couldn't take another second, he grabbed his notes and stalked through the office. He glanced up to see the captain in the pilothouse alone. Sarah must have already come and gone.

When he climbed to the pilothouse and opened the door, Captain Briggham swung around to face him, hardened features asking a question. Although he was an older man, Briggs' life as a pilot kept him in excellent shape. In the years Jeremy had known him, the power in the captain's stance hadn't diminished at all; yet today, his bearing seemed less sure. Quite simply, he looked tired.

"Young Sarah practically stomped the boat to pieces coming onboard hours before she should have finished. What on earth happened?"

"I tried, Briggs," he admitted, and he spoke the honest-to-God truth. "I did my best to convince them to let her take the damned test anyway. Told them there had to be a good reason why she came late."

The captain's eyebrows shot to the top of his forehead. "She arrived late?"

Damn. Jeremy struggled to keep his voice light. "Oh, she didn't tell you?"

"She hasn't come up here yet." The captain sighed. "I knew to expect bad news when she returned so early." His stature crumbled a bit more. Suddenly he looked every one of his fifty-seven years. "She was late? *Late?*"

Jeremy shrugged. "I can't figure it out. She's been anticipating the test for months. She must have lost her nerve. That woman is usually nothing but nerve, but it's the only explanation that makes the least bit of sense. Or maybe she doesn't really want to be a pilot and this was her way out."

Briggs shook his head. "I can't believe it." His eyes drifted, seeming to search for understanding. Tardiness for a riverboat pilot was sacrilege. "There must be a good reason . . . Did she give one?"

"Something about a woman fainting, but honestly, Briggs, she was evading the truth. Even I could tell she made it up."

"Late," he continued, voice heavy, "and no good reason for it. Perhaps piloting isn't for her after all."

Jeremy hated to see the captain like this. And Sarah didn't even have the decency to come and face the man. He wasn't sure if he felt more disappointed or angry with her. He handed the captain his notes. Briggs took the sheaf of papers and bent over the small corner desk. He unrolled the first chart and notated it.

Jeremy actually agreed with the captain; piloting wasn't the answer for Sarah. He knew for a fact how much piloting demanded, how much physical stress the job caused.

Sarah could choose any number of ways to make her life happy, had a heap of opportunities, more than most women. Yet she persisted chasing something that wasn't right for her. Jeremy considered himself a modern man; he didn't mind women working, but some jobs were more suited to a lady than others. Riverboat piloting simply wasn't one of them.

Piloting was rigorous, physically demanding, sometimes dangerous. He didn't want to see Sarah setting herself up for such hardship. Or any hardships at all.

Briggs continued to read his charts and make notes on their course. Beyond the window, a field of tows and boats gently bobbed in their docks and past them, the river ran free, unencumbered by vessels. Jeremy knew the captain well enough to recognize Briggs was making some time to think through the news. Sarah's failure filled the space between them.

Jeremy grabbed the clipboard with the prelaunch checklist and went down the items, one by one. Starting with the steering levers, he began his inspection. He'd do it again closer to launch. It didn't hurt to double- and triple-check everything. The more times he went over specifics, the more in control he felt, and that he liked. Precision made for an excellent pilot.

He didn't know what he'd do if he couldn't be a riverboat pilot. At seven years old, he'd begun his life on the river working in engineering. But from the time he started, he'd been fascinated with the pilothouse and Captain Briggham. Dressed in his white uniform, his gaze steel, the captain seemed more than a man, piloting for all the people onboard the *Spirit*, leading them forward to their destiny. One night, when Jeremy couldn't resist any longer, he snuck up to the pilothouse, just high enough to peek over the edge of the floor. He almost fell back down the ladderlike steps when the captain's black, shiny shoes angled in his direction. He'd been found out.

Instead of being angry, Briggs brought the boy up and showed him the river from a pilot's point of view. Jeremy spent every waking moment from then on at the captain's feet. He'd finally discovered his place in the world. Found the man who could teach him all he needed to stand on his own.

Briggs had taught Jeremy about more than the river and the boat, though. The captain treated Jeremy like a son, teaching him about life, how to read, even how to speak correctly. He owed the captain a much larger debt than he could ever repay.

Jeremy jerked back to the present, knowing nothing in his life had ever been so important as piloting a riverboat, and making Briggs proud.

"Not a thing in this world would keep me from making the test," Jeremy said. "Maybe you are right. Sarah's not meant for this."

The captain's eyes snapped back to Jeremy. "Now that I hear those words coming back at me, I don't believe them for a minute. I'm not

sure what happened with Sarah this morning, but one thing I'd bet on. There must be a good reason. A damned good one."

"If there was, she sure didn't share any. I used every bit of persuasion on the board I could think of, but when she came in, she gave an obviously made-up excuse. I thought you might know what happened."

"I'm at a loss."

Jeremy shook his head. "Lordy, she sure is one angry woman."

"Actually, here's a lesson for you, and not about piloting, but about women. She's hiding behind a façade of anger. If she didn't storm around, she'd be in her quarters crying. Or worse, keeping her disappointment inside and languishing in a puddle of depression. Her anger is quite a healthy reaction, I should think."

Jeremy contemplated the captain and leaned against the rear rail. "Now how does a confirmed bachelor such as yourself know so much about women?"

Briggs watched Emma, crossing the boiler deck down below. His entire demeanor and voice softened. "Not as much as you think. They can be quite a mystery, can't they?" His eyes snapped back to Jeremy. "Mostly, I've lived long enough to gain a modest understanding."

"I hate to see Sarah this dejected. She can always pilot, long as you or I are up here."

"Would you accept that sort of situation?" Briggs asked.

"Never," Jeremy replied honestly. "So what do we do?"

"Let her be. She'll recover."

"I don't know, Captain. I've never seen her quite so upset."

"The test today is only a small part of it. This is also September 18. The day Jared Perkins died."

"Oh, shit-on-me, that's right." He'd forgotten, and had been a part in making a bad day a whole lot worse. He wanted to kick himself a thousand times over for his words to her. "God, I'm an idiot."

"I do believe Sarah might agree with you, at least for today. Leave her be. We have quite an afternoon; not only the wedding party, but Lionel Jeffries arranged for a theater troupe to come onboard and entertain. Trust me, from what I've seen and heard, they will be exactly the diversion our Sarah needs."

The moment Emma entered the galley, waves of anxiety hit, and not her own. Lilly, standing before the huge, cast-iron stove, dropped her stirring spoon. It sunk into a pot of chicken broth.

"Devil be damned!"

"What's wrong, Lilly?"

The cook looked up, her expression one of a trapped animal. "Dropped my dadburned spoon," she mumbled. Lilly couldn't keep her feelings inside. Emma knew her almost as well as she knew her own children. Clearly, the young woman's tears were close to the surface.

"Lilly, what's wrong?"

She didn't answer. Instead, she stared into the soup stock, spoon drifting at the bottom of the pot. Red spread through the cook's face like spilled ink over paper. She shook her head until Emma thought her blonde curls might fly right off. "Nothin'."

"You're a terrible liar. You shouldn't even try." Emma calmly approached. "Sweetheart, what is it?"

"Em, please. I promised I'd keep my big mouth shut."

"We both know you won't, and it is probably for the best. Please don't make me nag it out of you. Save us both some trouble."

"Oh, Em, Sarah failed her test!" Lilly began crying. Well, actually, wailing.

Emma didn't stop to console her friend. Her feet barely touched the deck as she flew out of the galley. Sarah shouldn't even be back. Not this early.

Emma crossed to the steps and ran up to the hurricane deck, heading to the crew quarters behind the offices. She tried to calm her thundering heart yet knew it wasn't possible. God, Sarah failed again. Her daughter must be devastated.

She stopped in front of Sarah's door, wanting to bash it in and take her daughter in her arms. However, Sarah was a grown woman now. Emma settled for knocking. The sound ricocheted off her heart.

She listened. No noise. Except her heart, racing in her chest.

She knocked again. "Sarah? Sarah, are you in there? Honey, it's Mom. Sarah?" She waited for a second, pressing her ear against wood. Nothing. She might be anywhere, up in the pilothouse talking to Briggs, in the stateroom with her brother. But no, Emma knew her daughter was on the other side of this barricade. Mother's intuition. Besides, when Sarah became truly upset, she retreated. Tried to handle any emotional upset herself. Emma straightened and flexed her palm, holding it up to the wood door. "Sarah," she said softly, but still loud enough to carry through. "I heard what happened this morning. Please, let me talk to you."

The door swung open. Emma dropped her hand. Sarah's eyes burned with a tangle of emotions—all the big ones. Rage, hurt, fear. "You know what happened? How? Did Toby tell you?"

She took her daughter into her arms. Sarah resisted; it felt like hugging a cord of wood. Emma held on to her anyway. "No, I knew something was wrong the moment Lilly came down to the galley."

Sarah pushed Emma away. "Oh!" She seemed surprised, then accepting. "Oh."

"Sweetheart—"

"Mom, please stop making such a fuss and let me be. I'm fine."

"You don't look fine."

"Well, I will be. You are making the whole thing much harder. Everyone will find out soon enough. You don't need to stand out here drawing attention. Just let me gather myself together. I have to talk to Briggs and there's scarcely time before boarding begins."

"Skip this boarding. I'll take your place for you. And, I'll go up and talk to the captain."

"I simply need a few minutes. I don't need you fighting my battles for me."

Her words stabbed, but Emma's feelings didn't matter right now. Sarah did. Her daughter put up the only front she knew how to use: the tightly controlled, in charge, nothing-can-hurt-me one.

"Not fighting your battles, Sarah. Only trying to help you out."

Her daughter turned her back and retreated into her room. "I don't need your help. I'm fine on my own." She couldn't realize how those words cut through Emma. "I'll see you later. I need to get ready." Sarah shut the door.

Emma stared at the closed door. She found herself torn between what she wanted to do and what Sarah wanted. Without a doubt, her daughter's needs won. Hard as it might be for Emma to step back, Sarah deserved to handle this whatever way suited her best.

Emotions welled up, all the pain, hope, fears, wants for her daughter. The love she held for her children often overwhelmed her, and frustration came with those feelings. Sarah and Toby both made it a point to keep their trouble to themselves. Who could blame them after their childhood? Toby was shy, but Sarah was a warrior, launching herself at any perceived attack, standing up for her brother, for herself. Even at times and whether she needed to or not, for Emma.

She wanted to help her daughter bear her burdens, but Sarah was hell-bent to prove herself strong and independent. She didn't seem to grasp that she would always be Emma's little girl.

Because of this same overwhelming love, Emma was able to form her next words. "I'll be in the galley. Please come and talk to me if you'd like. Today or anytime. I want to help you through this, but

I certainly respect your wish for privacy." She swallowed against her tightening throat. "I'm right here, Sarah."

Emma lowered her head, pressing her forehead into the wood.

Unable to tear my eyes from the mirror, I watch his presence within me grow.

My father is here.

He waits for weakness to overtake me, when he will rear up and force my hands to do his bidding. I must not let that time come.

My father is years gone. Dead. Not before he inflicted damage, took lives. Claimed souls, including, it appears, mine. I open my eyes and I'm not surprised to see him, looking back from my very own face.

I have lost. I am too weak. What is left to me is empty. Filled with so much hurt it overflows and becomes something ugly and not born of me or my soul, yet is intertwined in my being just the same. Fury so sharp, it must be freed.

The creature within spreads and takes, finally reaching my surface. I flex my fingers but do not feel them. They are no longer mine.

I fade. Something wet is upon my cheek. Tears?

I am tired. I want this to end. I do not deserve this fate, but am no different than so many abused, neglected children.

And I am a child no longer.

Nor am I good, although goodness was once mine.

I am not gentle, yet once I knew its sweetness.

There is no kindness now; it slips away as I am reborn.

I give over. My father wins, as he always will.

And We begin.

Strangely, the tears won't stop. They pour, unfettered now, as We destroy for no other reason than We must.

Chapter 5

"Thank you, Jeremy 'Jackass' Smith."

The only one who heard was Sarah's reflection in the mirror of her cabin, which was probably for the best. Her foot still throbbed, the only trace of her earlier tears or upset. She wiggled and rotated it at the ankle. Damn, but it hurt.

She returned her attention to her fussy ensemble. Waves of cream lace, edged with contrasting brown, cascaded down Sarah's dress, complementing the brown velvet ribbon circling her throat. Amber crystals, dangling from the ribbon, caught the light and flashed.

Determined to complete the costume and create the latest style, she swept her hair up and back, coiling it at the nape of her neck, making sure a few pieces escaped to soften the look. Gazing in the mirror, she smoothed out every wrinkle of her scowl until she wore a tranquil, slightly smiling, contented mask.

There. The illusion of feminine perfection was complete.

She resolved to put the entire morning out of her life for good. Move forward, not look back. Today's boarding would be grand; the

Spirit was running to full capacity. The last trip for the season was also an important one, the main attraction a wedding party for Lionel Jeffries' daughter, Henrietta. Although it might cause her to explode, Sarah planned to be civil to the sniveling ninny.

She and Henrietta took exception to each other the moment they met at school, ten years ago. Sarah arrived—the new girl from the country—her clothing simple and her education from a small one-room school run by a preacher. She'd been years smarter than Henrietta, the rich girl with the newest, most beautiful dresses, flaming red hair, and nothing other than a vast emptiness filling the head beneath her fiery crown.

Sarah thought of dealing with Henrietta for an entire, excruciating week and her stomach knotted tighter. At least a theater troupe had been hired to entertain. Sarah's job would be easier with so much distraction. She planned to stay out of Henrietta's way and throw herself into her job as purser. With a boatload of passengers to care for, Sarah would have plenty to occupy her time.

If only she gave a damn about parties and such. Squaring her shoulders, she reminded herself that the frivolous events hosted by the *Spirit* were its lifeblood. That knowledge made the celebrations tolerable, especially the ostentatious ones like this wedding. Lionel Jeffries didn't do anything in half measures, and the marriage of his daughter must be one of the happiest events of his life. He'd finally unloaded the spoiled nit on some poor fool.

"Now, now, no calling the passengers names," Sarah reminded herself. Her job was to ensure the comfort and enjoyment of all paying customers aboard the *Spirit*. Even a person—and she used the term loosely—as disagreeable as Henrietta Jeffries.

The last thing Sarah needed today of all days, was the spoiled, rich debutante. She sighed. "Time to put one's best foot forward." Unable to bring up the smile needed, she still managed to bury her disappointment. It was the best she could do.

"At least I'll be on time for this." She opened her door, hesitantly. Time to welcome passengers meant time to face the captain. She wanted, more than anyone, not to disappoint him. Yet again, the choice was not hers. When did she lose all control of her life?

Afternoon sun glinted gold off the *Spirit's* polished wood deck. Sarah made her way down the grand staircase to take her place and welcome passengers onboard. The landing teemed with people, horses, luggage, carts, wagons. Above the din, giggles erupted. Near the stage, a flock of young women clustered, pastel colors floating on slim figures shaded by huge-brimmed hats. The wedding party. And in the center, like a floundering figure of royalty, Henrietta Jeffries laughed too loudly and gestured with wide drama, vying for the attention of all those around her.

The captain would perform Henrietta's wedding following a week of revelry aboard the *Spirit*. This was going to be one very long week.

Notes bounced around the afternoon air as the *Spirit's* dance band played a rousing ragtime piece. Sarah admired her mother's fortitude. Emma had realized her dream and made this vessel into a major destination for miles around. In her heyday the *Spirit* worked hard as a packet boat, transporting both cargo and passengers. Now, fore and aft, she was fully decked out for the enjoyment of events and parties. Weddings, cotillions, birthdays, anniversaries, coming-out parties, the *Spirit* was the place to be and be seen. While many other riverboat operations shut down, bowing out to barges, tows, and the railroad, the *Spirit* floated on, recalling earlier decades of grand river travel.

Sarah knew exactly how the grand lady must feel. Once, having an important purpose, the *Spirit* had mattered. Now she existed for show. Sarah sighed and took her place next to Captain Briggham to welcome the passengers aboard. All she would ever be was a piece of decoration. She might as well get used to it.

"I feared we might need to forgo your presence this afternoon."

The captain kept his powerful voice beneath the surrounding din, in deference to her, she supposed.

"I thought you knew me better than that, Captain," she said.

"I thought so as well." His look drilled into her. He knew there was more to the story this morning; she saw it in his expression. "Jeremy informed me of the outcome of your test."

"How very kind of him."

"Someone needed to tell me."

"Captain, I do apologize. I was . . ." Not sure where to go, she decided the truth was her best course. Well, part of the truth anyway. "I was upset and planned to speak with you later about it. Once I'd thought the morning through. Jeremy saved me the trouble, I see."

"Absolutely he did not." The captain spoke just above the sound of the ragtime band. "You owe me a discussion." Again, Sarah dropped her eyes.

Suddenly a dazzling song began, and she lifted her head, trying to recognize the music. Exotic and wild. Instruments she'd never heard before, high, airy strains and rumbling low pitches. Beneath the woven fabric of sound, a drumbeat, deep and round and pulsing.

Sarah glanced over to the band. They'd stopped playing and were sitting back in their chairs, yet music swept through the air. From up Main Street, ribbons appeared, swirling above the crowd in slow, graceful arcs. Through people milling about the landing, three men flipped in circles, effectively splitting the crowd. Two more came hurtling behind, their circular motion dizzying. The mass of humanity moved like water around drops of oil, gathering to the sides of the landing as the tumblers spread. Everything stopped and the crowd watched.

Behind the flipping men a troupe of musicians came, bows flying over violins. Tambourines glittered in sunlight, ribbons spitting color around them. Musicians wandered while they played mandolins, guitars, and several instruments Sarah didn't recognize. Jugglers paraded forward next, dressed in wildly colored costumes, voluminous pants, and tight-fitting shirts. They chatted and joked with onlookers while tossing balls, loops, and plates, objects whirling in controlled mayhem. One man with long black hair and a moustache strutted through the center of the other jugglers and flipped jewel-crusted knives. The sun glinted off them as they spun dangerously through the air, threatening to bloody anyone in their path. He caught them again and again by the handle and flung them back up.

"What on earth?" Sarah asked, but the exotic music, delighted gasps, and applause from the crowd swallowed her voice.

Beautiful, graceful women skipped and danced around onlookers, some of the women sporting gossamer wings like fairies from an enchanted forest. The fairy costumes were scandalously skimpy, yet somehow their skin, painted in blues and greens, reds and golds, kept them to this side of risqué. Other women, still a shocking amount of skin showing with their arms bare, spun like tops, veils swirling around them. Gold coins sewn to their costumes clanked and jangled in accompaniment to their graceful movement. Tiny people on one-wheeled bikes whirled through the delighted crowd, bells ringing and horns braying.

A circus? Traveling burlesque show? No, something else using elements of these, but going beyond. The performers were elegant, exotic. Their costumes in gold brocades and jewel-toned velvet were not the garish brightness of a circus but the deep, sensual richness of a king's court. The players' fashions were from different times; the Middle Ages, Victorian dress, veils and silks from the Far East. Some cuts were quite strange—many revealing more than propriety allowed—and surely nothing ever before seen on the Ohio River.

Dazed, Sarah felt she observed a bizarre yet pleasant dream.

A man dressed entirely in gold waved his hand. The torch in his opposite grip burst into flames. He threw his head back and opened his mouth.

"Oh, heavens, no," Sarah said. Astonished sounds, like a flock of frightened birds flapping away, rose from the crowd.

Theater of Illusion

"Oh, heavens, yes," Briggs said, and Sarah heard something rare from the captain. Awe. And a bit of delight.

The man lowered the flame to his mouth. Sarah's stomach jumped when the fiery torch plunged down. How could anyone swallow such a thing? Yet he did and pulled back a smoldering stake. He twirled the extinguished torch in the air, triumph on his face. Applause, cheers, and whistles broke out. The man blew on the blackened stake and it burst back into flame.

Behind him on the shoulders of six half-clad men rode a pallet bearing a throne and what looked like an Egyptian goddess. The men wore Egyptian headdresses and gold bands around their arms. Their bare chests and bodies were stained dark bronze.

The goddess's skin glistened. Strands of gold and silver gemstones glittered throughout the long, dark, heavy hair falling to her shoulders. She wore a slim, gold gown that flashed in the sunlight. Her eyes, heavy with liner, focused straight ahead, ignoring the crowd.

From the far bank, fireworks boomed, drizzling stars across the afternoon sky. Sarah clapped her hands to her ears.

"Incredible!" The captain laughed.

"This was all planned?" Sarah shouted above the delighted roar of the landing crowd.

Captain Briggham's eyes glittered with mischief. "Well, you've been otherwise occupied the last few days. We are transporting *Le Théatre d'Illusion* for the wedding party. They are a traveling extravaganza. Even have their own damned train. They agreed to perform for the Jeffries party. So far they seem worth every dollar Jeffries coughed up, and that, dear Sarah, is not a paltry sum by any means."

Lionel Jeffries was a millionaire many times over and could afford such spectacle. As everyone knew, anything he did must be the best, the brightest, the most expensive. Which was good for *Spirit* business, Sarah reminded herself. Let the man open his pockets as far as he needed to satisfy his business associates, friends, family, and daughter.

The crowd collectively gasped. Several high-pitched screams piped through the air. The pallet with the Egyptian goddess moved to the side. The men carrying her walked ramrod straight, the pallet never tilting a fraction of an inch.

From the center of the revelry burst a prowling tiger. A diamond collar surrounded the huge animal's thick neck. The tiger padded forward, its enormous body moving with sleek, graceful power. Right behind the magnificent beast, holding the leash, came an impossibly elegant gentleman striding as if king of this fantasy court. Every bold step he took coursed with purpose and complete authority. His morning suit, cut from deep, rich brown cloth, glowed in the afternoon sun. His vest, ascot, and the band of his high hat glittered, shot through with threads of gold. Even his hair matched his ensemble—sable-brown with highlights of blond glistening in the sun.

From his expression, he savored the reactions from the crowd. Sarah stared, mesmerized. Even surrounded by this confusion of color and sound, he stood out, demanded attention. He swept off his hat and scanned the mass of people. His eyes lit on Sarah and locked.

Everything else dropped away. Something glimmered through her, something strange and wonderful, slightly dangerous. She shivered. With what, she wasn't sure.

He smiled, only for her, it seemed. Then he broke his gaze and bowed low. Behind him, another face—half black, half white—grinned, but not with good-hearted amusement. His expression reminded Sarah of a nasty child about to play a mean trick. The man was dressed like a harlequin, his body taut and muscular beneath black-and-white geometry. His costume appeared painted on. Only the wildness of the pattern kept him in the realm of decency. Barely. Sarah avoided looking anywhere untoward. The brash nature of his costume and his quick, winding movements made her task difficult.

What she saw looked enticing. And dangerous.

Jingling bells dangled from his hat. Instead of a delicate and delightful sound, they mocked the good nature of the crowd.

The authoritative gentleman with the tiger straightened, replacing his hat. The harlequin curved to his side.

As the tiger passed, squeals rose from the huddle of young ladies making up the wedding party, the biggest shriek coming from Henrietta. She reminded Sarah of a wounded pig. Henrietta tiptoed back from the beast, her face white under her huge picture-frame hat and overdone coiffure. She looked to have so much weight on her head, Sarah wondered how her scrawny neck didn't snap.

The tiger padded past the party and across the stage to sit at Sarah's feet, the gentleman following behind. An overwhelming urge to back away raced through her, but she held her ground.

The evil harlequin stopped to perform magic tricks for the giggling wedding party. The young ladies gave him quite the once-over, not bothering to appear modest in their appraisal of him. Henrietta's eyes widened as she stared at the harlequin's muscular . . . well . . . bum. Henrietta elbowed the girl next to her, and together they both gawked at the man's backside. Sarah found her eyes wandering there as well. She tingled in places she shouldn't. Although in the preposterous garb of a court fool, the man seethed with animalistic appeal.

Sarah's eyes snapped back to the gentleman holding the animal's leash. Younger than she first thought; his purposeful movement and confident carriage had fooled her. He took her in, then shifted his attention to Briggs as he reached out to shake the captain's hand.

"Captain. A pleasure." His voice flowed smooth, enhanced by a flair of exotic elegance. Chocolate laced with brandy. He wore a smile as though everything around amused him.

"Oscar Gévaudan," the captain said. "Quite the entrance."

"Always, Captain. Life is about the entrance one makes, don't you think?" He turned his attention once more to Sarah and her face warmed.

"Your reputation is well earned, I see," the captain answered.

The man looped the tiger's leash around his wrist and swung his arms wide. *"The purest treasure mortal times afford is spotless reputation— that away . . . men are but gilded loam, or painted clay.'"* He ended with a slight bow.

Sarah resisted rolling her eyes at his incorrigible attempt to show off. Wasn't he making enough of an impression with the extravaganza swirling around him?

The captain squinted. "Shakespeare. *Richard the Second*, if I'm not mistaken."

Oscar Gévaudan's face opened with surprise, shifting to delight. "Act one, scene one, in fact. My dear sir, it is not often I find a man well versed in the wisdom of the Bard."

Or a workingman on a river knowing who Shakespeare even was, Sarah thought, having the good sense to keep the comment to herself.

"One of my favorites, Mr. Gévaudan."

Oscar looked Briggs over from head to foot as though seeing him for the first time. "I look forward to spending some time with you, Captain, enjoying some discussion. I believe we might share some interests."

"Oh, you'll become quite used to the captain's width and breadth of culture and intelligence. He barely surprises us anymore," Sarah said, not able to contain her annoyance any longer. At least she kept her tone light and stuck her hand out for a shake. Despite the tiger.

Instead of scowling, the man's face lit with appreciation at her comment.

"Allow me to present our purser, Sarah Perkins," the captain introduced, darkening his voice in warning. For her, most likely.

The man's eyes bored into her. He lifted her hand and lightly brushed it with his lips, never dropping his gaze. Charm radiated from him in waves, warm and seductive. His eyes danced like they held

some magical secret, completing the storybook air he wove for himself.

Logic told her he calculated everything for show; still, her heart raced with barbaric insistence. She smiled, the expression genuine. He'd managed to melt through her annoyance. In all honestly, she wasn't sure how she felt about this man. Arrogant, showy, putting on airs—he completely captivated her.

"Welcome to the *Spirit*, Mr. Gévaudan."

"*Enchanté*, Miss Perkins. And believe me, the pleasure is entirely mine." He released her hand and clapped his palms together. The tiger stood and stalked forward as the troupe twirled, flipped, and danced across the stage.

Sarah laughed. The day's earlier disappointment dissipated in the riot of color, sound, and laughter parading past her. She found herself grinning. Until the harlequin came near. Her smiled dropped when he slinked by. His expression flashed, sardonic yet somehow intimate, as if he knew all the secrets she kept buried deep.

She trembled again, this time, not with delight.

Lionel Jeffries stepped up with Henrietta on his arm. The millionaire's carriage made it clear he was a man used to getting exactly what he demanded; the cut of his suit exuded the cultivated elegance only money could buy. Arched eyebrows lent his expression a look of constant irony, and his dark hair, moustache, and goatee made him appear a bit devilish and dangerous.

"Captain," he said, shaking Briggs' hand vigorously. The captain's white suit and close-cropped hair stood in complete contrast to Jeffries' dark and calculated sophistication.

Henrietta beamed at the captain. Although the two women knew each other, Henrietta completely ignored Sarah, which suited her just fine.

"It appears we are in for quite a voyage," Jeffries said.

"Indeed," the captain answered. "Please, let us know if there is anything at all we can do for you or your lovely daughter." He bowed slightly over Henrietta's offered hand.

"Captain, I do thank you. The *Spirit* begins the most important journey of my life," Henrietta said in her twangy voice, words sounding empty, devoid of meaning. Her tone sharpened. "I do hope your crew is ready to work with me. Every detail must be perfect." She stared pointedly at Sarah.

Resisting the urge to grimace or worse, Sarah remembered her purser position and kept a smile fixed on her face. "Miss Jeffries, anything you require will be my number one priority." Surprisingly, she managed to speak without choking.

"And we intend to make this trip not only perfect, but memorable," the captain answered.

Everyone on the boat watched the parade of performers, giving Emma her chance. She had a much more important way to spend her time. With the extravaganza going on port side, she knew she wouldn't be noticed taking the starboard steps.

She slipped past the stateroom, all the waiters currently on the other side, watching the parade. It paid to stay in the background, work behind the scenes. Besides, Briggs loved being in the limelight. Although they shared the business fifty-fifty, to everyone, Briggs and the *Spirit* were interchangeable.

She pulled off the chain she wore around her neck. Out popped her key. She unlocked the door.

The dark room gave away no hint of the secrets it held inside. She lit the stained-glass lamp on the table nearest to the doorway, and opulence sprang to life.

The captain's dining room. A place very few had the privilege of entering. Only three people held the key: the captain, herself, and

Gage. She held the skeleton key and chain out in her hand, and warm light stroked burnished silver. It had been Quentin's key. She looped the chain back around her neck and tucked it under her blouse.

She felt, with it there, she held Quentin near her heart.

The beaded lamp threw bits of sparkle around the room as she lit the other lamps. An enormous crystal chandelier hung in the center, the button for instant illumination in the wall. Beautiful, but too much light for her purposes.

She missed Quentin every day. Terribly. Here in this room, she felt closest to him. He hadn't paid attention to any budget and his personality glistened in every detail.

The rosewood dining table glowed in the warm lamplight, and she padded across thick, Persian carpet to the buffet. Muffled strains of music from the outside drifted in like a faraway dream. She felt safe in here, hidden away at the top of the boat, surrounded by luxury.

No, that wasn't it. Surrounded by Quentin.

She picked up his teapot, the prize possession he'd brought with him from his travels abroad. Made of jade and silver, the spout in the shape of a dragon head, mouth wide, eyes flashing ruby red. Jade scales felt rough in her hands, but she didn't mind. She placed the teapot on one open palm while she steadied it by the handle—or dragon's tail, to be more specific—and made her way over to one of the gold and red brocade armchairs sitting on either side of the serving buffet.

She studied the eyes of the dragon. They flickered like red flame.

"I wish you were here, Quentin" she said, her voice in a hush. "Ten years, and I miss you every day, like you left us just yesterday."

Movement shuffled out of the corner of her eye, and she leapt to her feet, holding tight to the dragon.

Nothing. She was alone.

A boom caused her to jump, then another. She started around the table, about to return the teapot to its place and dash out, when she remembered: the theater-ordered fireworks. Briggs set them up to be launched from a barge as it floated beyond the city.

"Silly," she said, and retook her seat. She glanced around the room, feeling . . . something. Someone watching? "Silly," she repeated. Far off music still sounded, a little closer now.

Movement again. She got an idea.

"As long as silly is the word of the hour." She replaced the teapot and lit one of the beeswax candles on the table, then extinguished the lamps.

The room fell to shadows, only a small glow on the table beneath the candle. Picking up the teapot again, she placed it on the table and sat down. She wished ghosts were real and she could conjure up Quentin. How she longed to share some time with him again.

"Quentin?"

Nothing. Of course. What on earth did she expect?

A whisper she didn't quite hear breezed past her ear. All the hairs on the back of her neck stood up. Chills prickled down her arms to the tips of her fingers.

"Quentin, are you here?"

She should feel foolish talking to an empty room, but she sensed another presence sharing the dark with her. Probably wishful thinking, but what was wrong with that?

"I need someone to talk with. It might just be this anniversary, but everything feels like it's unraveling. Sarah failed her pilot's test. She won't talk to me about it, trying to handle it the way she does everything else." Emma tried to penetrate the soft dark around her. She didn't see anything, no movement. No, wait. She sat bolt upright. When she turned her eyes to the left, she thought she saw someone sitting at the other end of the table.

Quentin's ghost?

No, perhaps she saw the effect of candlelight reflecting in the copper-hooded fireplace. The burnished metal played tricks with one's eyes.

This was no trick. Someone must be here.

"Gage tries to help. But I feel Sarah and Toby slipping away from me," she continued, trying not to look at the spot. Every time she did, nothing was there, yet if she glanced away, something formed. A human shape. Head, shoulders. She continued, hoping he'd come into sharper view. "I don't know; perhaps it's as simple as they are growing up. Need room to become adults. They don't seem to understand they'll always be my children—"

Her words caught in her throat.

She stared into the memory of Quentin's face, and a tear leaked down her cheek. God, she wanted him to be here so bad, she imagined him right before her.

At first, his murder enraged her. When anger fell away, guilt replaced it. Time dulled the anguish of loss until she could live with it. But now, remembering him this clearly sharpened pain into a stake and hurled it into her heart. "I'm so sorry."

Memory or ghost, he disappeared.

We enjoy the dark. There are many places of darkness for Us here, on the Spirit of the River. *The rest are all outside, in the center of the glitter and light and color of their flimsy celebration, not knowing how close they dance to the edge, how easily joy can be corrupted. They do not realize We are among them. That will soon change.*

We have reprieve here, in the dark. Let go Our defenses. Allow Our façade to drop. It is tiring to wear the mask, yet the mask allows Us to move among them.

There is a victim here, one who will give Us no trouble. Quiet. Away from the others. Helpless. This is a good place to start. A good place to bring Us to the attention of the Spirit.

Our hand folds around the cool wood handle of a knife. This victim is hapless. Defenseless. Flimsy.

Rip.

No fight, thanks to surprise . . .

Rip.

or challenge. Still, We enjoy the sensation . . .

Rip.

and they will know We are with them . . .

Rip.

and have joined them for their voyage.

Chapter 6

"You should have seen it, Mom."

Emma looked up from her stack of to-do lists and invoices, past Lilly butchering eggplants, to where Sarah leaned against the doorframe of the galley. Relief tumbled through Emma, seeing her daughter once again in good humor. Thanks to *Le Théatre d'Illusion*, this day took a most agreeable turn.

"I sure never seen such a thing in all my born days!" Lilly giggled. "And believe me, I seen plenty!" She whacked the top off an eggplant. The thought of public beheadings came to Emma's mind.

"I thought I'd never live to see such goin's on," Gladys, the assistant cook, added. Her gray hair, pulled back from her face, added to her entirely too severe expression. But the look suited Gladys' disposition. She was cranky. Suspicious. Pessimistic. And one of the best cooks Emma had come across in a long time.

Piles of paperwork had again buried Emma. Organized stacks, yet stacks just the same. The daily duty rosters were late, and she rushed to finalize the picnic plans for a day from now. At least she commandeered the end of the counter and worked in her favorite place onboard, the galley. The captain preferred her to work up in the office, but at every chance, she headed down here. Emma loved the galley best, felt perfectly at home surrounded by the savory scents of roasting and cooking, the heat from the stove, and Lilly's chatter. Even Gladys' dire predictions were welcome relief from the sunny, stark quiet of the office.

Most important, Emma reclaimed her life ten years ago in this very galley. Much more than a room, this place gave her the opportunity to become a woman who stood on her own, no matter what she faced. The galley meant more to her than anyone would ever know. Even though they'd remodeled and doubled the size, this original portion remained exactly the same, at Emma's insistence.

She smiled. "I'll bet it was something. I hear the theater involved the entire landing with their performance. Let's hope they do the same spectacular job this week. Mr. Jeffries' expectations are quite enormous."

A frown shadowed Sarah's face. "Mom, you really ought to have come out to see it. There was no need to slave away behind this pile of papers. Everything would have been here, waiting for you when you came back."

Emma chose not to answer her daughter and take the chance a disagreement would begin. It had been too emotional a day already and Emma had no desire to discuss why she chose to remain on the boat whenever crowds gathered.

Her headstrong daughter did not seem so inclined. "Honestly, Mom, you need to come out more. Such fun, and the crowds! I don't think I've seen this many people come down to the landing in ages."

Emma pushed back a strand of hair slipping from her French braid and thought it best not to reveal she'd attempted a conversation with a ghost. Gladys already thought her strange enough.

"Well, I almost have more to do than I can manage at the moment. I don't even have tomorrow's schedule posted for the staff yet. Enjoying entertainment is low on my list of priorities."

"How often do you get the opportunity to see a tiger strut over the stage?" Lilly asked. "I cain't imagine such a critter onboard." She whacked off the top of another eggplant with her huge butcher knife. "What if he gits hungry and decides to eat someone?"

"That will be the end of this boat. All we need is a tiger eatin' Lionel Jeffries' daughter," Gladys piped in. Always the bright spot.

"I'd imagine Henrietta is too sour for the tiger's taste," Sarah grumbled.

Emma clamped down on a grin. "Briggs assured me the animal is completely safe. The tiger has been mingling with the public for years." She rose to retrieve the top of the eggplant rolling across the floor. "The captain would never put passengers at risk."

"Well, Briggs certainly managed to stir up interest in town over this whole thing. Everyone came out to watch the theater parade come onboard," Sarah admitted.

"I still don't like that durn tiger," Lilly added.

"Apparently Mr. Gévaudan has raised the animal from a cub." Emma stretched, her hands at the small of her back. Perhaps Sarah was right that she was working too hard. She felt stiff and creaky. "He insists the tiger is gentle as a lamb, and she's traveled all over the country with him. The publicity we are getting from this theater troupe is in papers up- and downriver."

"Not to mention gossip. Ever'one is talkin' on it," Lilly said over her shoulder as she diced with such speed the knife practically became invisible. "Imagine such a thing—a tiger onboard."

"Lilly, gossip is for the ignorant with too much time on their hands." Sarah looked pointedly back to Emma. "Why didn't you let me in on any of this? There must be a hundred details I could have taken care of for you. You're always so busy, yet you keep things like this to yourself."

"The plans to include the theater just came together," Emma answered, trying not to sound defensive. "I believe I did mention them to you," she said softly, resuming her seat behind her mountain of papers.

"You did say a theater troupe was due to come onboard. I expected a few ragtag actors. Not such an extravaganza."

"You have been occupied with other matters, sweetheart."

She watched her daughter's annoyance with her melt like ice on the first warm spring day, and for a brief second she saw all the misery of Sarah's failed test on her face. Then her daughter steeled herself and straightened. Sarah was determined to be the perfect, strong woman, taking care of everything. Living her life to perfection.

Emma stood and approached, draping her arm around her daughter's shoulders. "There will be a next time."

Sarah shrugged away from her mother's touch. "There will not."

Undaunted, Emma faced her daughter, took both of Sarah's hands in hers, and gazed unflinchingly into her eyes. "You may not feel it now, but you are more than a capable pilot. The hurt will fade. You'll want to try again."

Sarah pulled her hands away. "How can you possibly know what I want?"

Emma flinched. She knew her daughter's frustrations from the test forced the words, but they still stung.

Sarah's expression softened. "I'm sorry, Mom. I am terribly cranky today. But you are so busy with all these wedding preparations."

So like her daughter to pull her feelings back to take care of others. Well, Emma was the mother here. And her daughter needed her. At the moment, Sarah had no door to hide behind.

"You can do anything you put your mind to. Sometimes it simply takes time," Emma said. "There's nothing wrong with feeling hurt about the way things went. But it's not the end."

"Happens to all of us," Lilly piped in. "Ain't no shame to what you're tryin' to do, Sarah. Ever'body knows you're gettin' failed on account you're a woman. Dadburned bunch of old goats."

"If we're votin'," Gladys said, "I say keep your job as purser. You look absolutely beautiful in your dress, and a hot, sweaty pilothouse is no place for a lovely young woman."

They all froze and stared at the cook. It was the nicest thing she'd ever said.

"Why, Gladys, thank you," Sarah murmured. "Sort of."

"Unless there's a big, gorgeous man like Jeremy Smith in the pilothouse." Lilly winked at Sarah. Sarah blushed and Emma couldn't help but grin.

"All right, enough. It's getting very strange in here," Sarah said.

"Nope. Jest girl talk." Lilly twirled her knife in the air. "Same kind of thing they do up in the pilothouse, only men don't have near as much fun. Besides, this is the day for strange. We had us a tiger walk across the stage and come onboard!"

Charley McCoy stuck his head in the door and ended their chat. His blond hair, always tousled, appeared even more so. His eyes darted around the galley, wide and urgent, his attention finally locking on Emma.

"We got trouble in the dinin' room. Miss Jeffries ain't takin' to the color of the napkins. And Malcolm ain't nowheres around."

Malcolm, the headwaiter in charge of the dining room, always managed to disappear when a confrontation occurred. Time to speak to him again. But Henrietta Jeffries would be difficult for anyone, even Malcolm, to handle. Emma sighed heavily and headed for the door. Sarah stopped her.

"I'll go, Mom."

"No, sweetheart, Henrietta is a handful at best—"

"Mom, I'll take care of this. Besides, it's about time I face our blushing bride-to-be."

Emma hesitated, then tamped down on the desire to take care of every tiny thing. Handling passenger situations was Sarah's job. Hard as it might be to send Sarah into Henrietta's line of fire, it was the best thing to do. She supposed.

Emma gave her daughter a quick nod, and Sarah fell in behind Charley.

"Hope there ain't more fireworks up there," Charley said as they exited. "The ones from the theater was enough for this boat."

As much as Emma wanted to, she couldn't protect her daughter forever. Sarah had a job to do, and Emma knew from experience the best way to jump back into the stream of life after a huge disappointment was to concentrate on work. Even a disappointment as big as a failed pilot's test.

Or a marriage. She shoved that thought away. Damn Jared Perkins.

"I ain't never seen such a duck fit," Charley said, climbing the back steps. "This shore is gonna be one long week."

"Charley, you always tell the god's honest truth." Sarah followed behind.

"My job, Miss Sarah. Take a look."

Through the beveled glass door of the dining room, she saw Henrietta Jeffries clacking away. Toby tried to speak, but obviously couldn't get in a word during the debutante's tirade. Her mouth moved faster than a clucking hen, and her gloved hands waved in the air. Toby kept pulling back to avoid an errant smack. One red curl came loose from Henrietta's overdone coiffure and bounced under her enormous picture-frame hat, the feathers atop waggling. Behind Henrietta, a young woman cowered. Her ladies' maid, Sarah remembered.

Charley stopped. "After you, Miss Sarah." His apologetic half smile made it hard for her to blame him for stepping back. She opened the door, reminding herself to show restraint. It would be bad business to kill the stuck-up little nit. After all, Henrietta was a rich and paying stuck-up little nit.

"These are not peacock blue; they are white," Henrietta proclaimed. "Can't you see this is white? As in no color. None whatsoever. Not what I asked for." She narrowed her eyes at Toby. "My specifications were for peacock. Now, I imagine a *rustic* boat such as this might not have any stylish colors. However, I am an understanding person. Even common blue would do." She straightened away from Toby and smoothed out her voice. "There, you see. I'm not difficult. Quite easy to work with in all actuality." Her voice rose again. "If there is any proficiency on your part. But these are white! White! I. Will. Not. Have. White!"

As Sarah approached the sputtering girl, Toby backed away to safety behind the bar, his eyes glittering and mouth scrunched in a grimace. He was trying not to laugh. Sarah opened her own expression, careful not to scowl. She didn't find a damned thing about Henrietta Jeffries amusing.

"Henrietta?"

The girl spun around, eyes snapping. Then she smirked. Years of resentment inflated like a nasty piece of gossip between them. "Does this"—Henrietta grabbed a napkin and jiggled it in Sarah's face—"look like peacock to you?" Henrietta scowled. "I'm sure Adele followed my instruction to the letter and ordered peacock blue."

She whirled around, and the dark-haired woman behind the debutante nodded so vehemently, her hat threatened to tumble off. Henrietta swung back to Sarah, triumph in her eyes. "This is white, Sarah Perkins. Mundane. Which, I'm sure, looks fine to you. You're as colorless as these napkins."

Sarah gritted her teeth. Temper. Temper. "We can certainly find a suitable blue for you, Henrietta. I'll take care of it myself."

Henrietta tilted her face up, and her eyes narrowed. "You wouldn't know the right color if it splattered across your ugly dress." She sighed theatrically, like a vaudeville actress. "You will run everything through my ladies' maid, as, if I might remind you, my father previously insisted in our contract. Adele, you will make sure this . . . person . . . gets the color right."

Adele bobbed her head up and down again. Sarah wondered how the girl kept from snapping her neck right off, all the nodding she needed to do.

Sarah glanced over to Toby, who shrugged, still wearing a slightly amused expression thinly covered by mock concern.

Henrietta flipped the napkin and it slapped across Sarah's face. "You have the breeding and grace of a cow! Pay attention. Peacock. I will have peacock!"

The slow burn finally burst through Sarah. Her hands clenched into fists. When she spoke, her voice slithered with deadly calm. "Don't you touch me again, you blustering piece of fluff."

Adele gasped and nearly pushed over a table as she backed away. Toby snorted and followed up with coughing, trying to cover it and not succeeding.

Henrietta's eyes almost bulged from her head. "What did you call me?" She narrowed her expression. "How dare you!"

Sarah prepared as Henrietta geared herself up to attack. Fine. Sarah could take this ridiculous spoiled ninny. Easy as pulling the damn hat over the girl's face and shoving her overboard into the river.

Instead of launching herself, Henrietta took a step back. Her eyes rounded. She squeaked, staring beyond Sarah. All attention in the room focused over Sarah's shoulders. The door behind her creaked and she turned.

Oscar Gévaudan and his tiger entered the dining room. Oscar wore his amused expression. The tiger seemed fairly bored.

"Oh, my dears, please forgive me. Daisy and I were on a walk. She gets restless and rather insistent on exercise. I thought a turn around this deck might be fun, but I had no idea how much excitement I'd find."

Henrietta's mouth dropped open. The debutante was speechless. For once.

Oscar walked across the dining room floor, the wait staff backing away to give the tiger plenty of berth. "This boat is so very grand and huge even once you are inside it. I thought I might feel confined; however, I see the norm here is to be anything but." He stopped before the two women, his intense gaze on Henrietta. "'*But, soft! What light through yonder window breaks?*'"

Henrietta blushed deeply, color spilling over her pasty cheeks.

"Miss Perkins, who may I inquire is this stunning creature you haven't introduced me to as of yet?"

Despite the urge to gag, Sarah was grateful for his flirtation. "Henrietta Jeffries, allow me to present Oscar Gévaudan."

He grasped Henrietta's gloved hand and raised it to his lips. Henrietta stood like a column of stone, stunned as if in the presence of royalty or someone holy.

"*Enchanté*, Miss Jeffries," he said, dripping his chocolate-laced-with-brandy voice. "I noticed you the moment I came onboard. I am beyond delighted you are one of the passengers with whom we shall share the week."

Henrietta gaped like a caught fish, much like Sarah did earlier upon meeting the tiger and the man. Sarah enjoyed a clearer, more remote view, feeling like a bit of an idiot for joining the ranks of those he swept away with his charm.

Oscar tucked Henrietta's arm under his own. "I do hope you will join Daisy and myself on our walkabout. It is a perfectly gorgeous afternoon. Well, just about evening, isn't it? Henrietta—will you allow me the privilege of calling you Henrietta?"

The girl nodded, her hat threatening to topple over.

"You are with the wedding party, are you not?" Oscar asked.

"I'm the bride!" she squeaked.

"Oh, no! '*I am fortune's fool!*'" moaned Romeo. "You have broken my heart, lovely Henrietta." He glanced over his shoulder and winked.

Henrietta, Daisy, and Oscar exited, Adele following a few steps behind, leaving a silenced dining room.

"That was disgusting," Toby said.

"With any luck, the tiger will do everyone onboard a favor and decide to enjoy Henrietta for dinner," Sarah muttered. "However, she's probably much too skinny to prove any sort of temptation."

Toby sniggered. "Well, at least he kept you two from ripping the face off each other." The grin he'd been containing broke over his face. "Although it was going to be fun to watch."

"Naw, woulda been over in a second," Charley McCoy said. "I'd place my money on Miss Sarah."

Toby nodded in agreement. "True, but attacking paying customers is bad business."

"'Specially rich ones, like Henrietta Jeffries," Charley added. "And the Frenchy, what a buffoon. But he shore puts on a good show."

Toby looked sheepish. "Charley and I came out and watched them come on."

"That's fine," Sarah said. "The captain likes passengers to see the crew when they board."

"Yeah," Charley nodded, "but Malcolm told us we'd best get this dinin' room in order and skip the boardin'. And he's the boss. Least ways of this dinin' room." Charley gestured out the window. "I saw their theater show last year when they was in Riverbay. I told Toby he should see for hisself; it was better than a circus. They sing and everythin'."

"Oscar Gévaudan knows exactly what he's doing." Sarah recognized admiration in her voice. "On stage and off."

"Aw, he's jest a gussied-up dandy," Charley added. "But I like his tiger."

"The man plays people like a maestro." She returned her attention to the roomful of waiters. All eyes were on her. "All right now, show's over. On to decisions with dire consequences. Surely we have hues of blue in our napkin selection. Anything at all close to peacock?"

Toby cleared his throat, no trace of amusement. "We have a problem, Sarah. White is all that's left."

"What? We have napkins in stacks of colors."

"I'll show you." Toby led her out of the dining room and she followed him around to the dining supply pantry. Only a small window lit the small, dusky room. Cubbies lined the walls, supplies for dining behind each. Another of her mother's organizational masterpieces. Toby opened the cubby where the napkins were stored. A slip of green fluttered to the deck. What should be neat stacks of napkins arranged by color and hue, lay in a bunched, mixed-up heap.

"Who jumbled these up? They'll have to be re-pressed." She grabbed a handful of color. Instead of napkins, shreds of fabric scattered, a few more of the scraps following the green one to the deck. All sheared into strips. "What on earth?"

"That's what I was trying to tell you. Someone ripped these to pieces. The whites survived because they were in laundry. Janine delivered them half an hour ago. I didn't know what else to do, so I set the tables with them." He shrugged. "I didn't realize white napkins were such a monumental disaster."

They were only piles of color, only torn napkins, but a chill shuddered through Sarah. "Who would do such a thing?"

"The real question is why would anyone bother?" Toby asked.

Behind Sarah, Charley whistled low. She jumped, not realizing he followed them. Charley shook his head. "Who might hate napkins this much?"

"Probably not napkins," Sarah said. "Who hates Henrietta is the real question."

"Get in line," Toby answered. Sarah shot him a look. "Hey, I'm just telling the truth. You were ready to deck her yourself."

Sarah closed her eyes, putting herself in Henrietta's place. Her empathy, when she allowed it, made her an excellent purser. "And I was wrong to let her upset me. Henrietta is not just a paying customer; she's a bride. This is her wedding. Naturally she wants everything perfect." She nodded. "All right, we have time to avert the great Napkin Color Disaster of 1910. Charley, please run up and tell Jeremy to hold off the launch until I'm back. I should make it in time, but let's be sure I don't miss the boat. I'll run to the mercantile and get more material. What other colors did the little nit—I mean Henrietta—request?"

"Blue for tonight," Toby said. "Black for the rehearsal dinner."

"Black sounds about right for the groom," Charley said under his breath.

"And rose for the wedding," Toby finished.

Time for her to step up and be the kind of purser the captain and her mother deserved. Maybe she couldn't get to her pilot test, but, by God, she'd make sure everything ran perfectly with the entertainment on the boat. "I'll get blue, black, rose, and bolts of a few more colors. Toby, tell Janine to get ready for a sewing circle. Lilly too, if she's available. We'll do the blue first for tonight."

"Peacock," Charley said seriously. "Jest make damned sure you bring back peacock."

"Well, here's a sight for my poor ol' eyes." Henry Dobson's red-tinged gaze lit up as Sarah burst through the door of the mercantile. Outside, a huge moan blasted through town, petering out into a nothing more than a sad wail. The *Spirit,* making ready to leave. Hopefully, not without her.

"Henry, I'd love to chat . . ." Sarah's voice dropped off as she headed through produce and hardware, back to the dry goods side of the store where neat bolts of material lined the shelves. She grabbed the first solid one she saw. Red. Good. Then another. Peach. Blue? Where was the blue?

From outside, another blast rattled the windows.

"Ain't you supposed to be onboard?" Henry's voice asked from behind her.

Sarah passed the bolts to him without looking, assuming he'd grab them. He did.

"The *Spirit* is pulling out any moment. We are in desperate need of material to make napkins." She grabbed another bolt. Turquoise. One might say, peacock. It would do. And another. Rose. She dumped those on top of the growing stack in Henry's arms. "I'm holding the launch. Henry, please cut me ten yards of each, or if there isn't ten, whatever is on the bolt will be fine."

Henry nodded. "Hey, that circus theater is really something. We watched them come down the street—"

"Please, Henry, now!"

The *Spirit's* stack bellowed in agreement.

Henry scuttled away to the front counter where Maggie, his wife, waited with a pair of shears. God bless the woman, before she'd married Henry the store had been little more than hard tack and nails. Now it stocked a vast array of food, material, lace, and aprons, and Maggie even bought dresses from local seamstresses on consignment. She added fresh produce from farmers to the front of the store. And now everyone came to shop at Dobson's General Mercantile.

Sarah grabbed another bolt—black. A striped pattern called to her—burgundy with thin black stripes. Quite elegant. She picked it up. Oh, and lilac. And a deeper purple, right next to it. Was that enough?

"Miss Sarah . . ." Henry's voice behind her again. She dumped more bolts into his arms.

"Quick, Henry!"

Another blast shook the air, rattling the mercantile windows.

"Jeremy isn't one for patience," she murmured to herself. Ironic. She was making him late. He must be in quite a lather.

"Well, if you asked me, she deserved it." A sharp female voice rose from the back of the store. "One less whore we have to worry about."

Sarah faltered, only for a second. Someone gossiping, that was all.

"Still, what an awful way to die," another woman said. "Her face ground into the very mud in the street."

Sarah froze, her hand touching the navy bolt. She pulled it off the shelf and hugged it to her. Someone died? Murdered? A woman?

A whore. Face pushed down in mud in the street.

Jared Perkins.

Sarah clutched the bolt of material. Impossible. Couldn't be. How silly that she let his name jump into her head.

Henry already stood at the counter, Maggie's shears flying as she cut and stacked material. Sarah glanced over to the two women in the back of the store.

"Well, she asked for it, I say. You reap what you sow," a heavyset woman said.

Sarah didn't have time for this. She returned her attention to the bolts. She needed to focus, didn't remember what she had. She glanced back to Maggie. Blue, green, red, burgundy stripe, rose, black . . .

Henry's eyes changed to worry as he made his way back to her. "You feelin' okay, Sarah? You turned white as a flour sack."

Sarah pulled herself back together. Everything from this morning, her thoughts of Jared, had finally caught up with her. That was all. She was fine. Fine.

"Oh," one of the gossiping women said, coming forward from the back of the store. "I'm afraid we might have upset the poor dear. We were talking about the gruesome killing."

Henry puffed out his cheeks. "Sorry business. Hasn't been a murder in town for quite awhile, and then this."

"What happened?" Sarah clutched the bolt to her, hugging it.

"One of the tavern gals last night. They're saying a customer followed her, a big man. Stranger. She left with him. They found her later; she'd been . . . well . . ." Henry's jowls trembled.

A blast ripped through the store and jolted Sarah out of her dazed state. "Here, this will do it." She stalked to the front of the store, not wanting to hear any more, and slapped the bolt on the counter. Maggie began unwrapping blue material.

"It's upsetting, it is," she said. "But not unexpected. Those girls go off with whoever. You can't tell who is dangerous and who isn't. It's just not smart."

The thin woman dressed in white and black stripes approached. Her spectacles pinched her nose, making her look like a bird. She stomped to the counter, a basket half-full. "Smart? It's not decent. Those tavern waitresses do more than serve drinks. Despicable. The law ought to do something."

The heavy woman sidled up to the counter. "My husband said he saw one in the alley, a few nights before, goin' at it with some man for a dollar. Can you imagine?"

Bird Woman stared at her, shocked. "Your husband told you that?"

"Well, the police came to question him. He'd been in the tavern last night and got a look at the stranger. The police wanted details, but Thomas couldn't give them any."

"Sounds like he had plenty," Bird Woman said primly.

"He goes to the tavern every Thursday night while I'm at choir. He has eyes. He sees what goes on."

Interesting. Thomas knew exactly how much the girls charged.

"The police," the woman said, "closed the Bluegrass Tavern, and good riddance! All sorts of, well, you know, *things* were going on there. Back rooms and gambling and such. About time they shut the place down."

Maggie folded the last piece of material. "What will Thomas do on Thursday nights now?" She met Sarah's eyes with a wry glimmer in hers.

"He can fix a few things around the house, that's what." The heavyset, pasty woman plopped her basket down on the counter.

"Are these written up?" Sarah asked. "I really have to go."

Another blast broke through the afternoon.

"He's goin' to break my windows if he keeps it up," Henry said.

"You're all set, Sarah. Good trip!" Maggie slid the pile of material across the counter, and Sarah grabbed the rainbow bundle up in her arms.

"Thank you, Maggie, Henry! See you two in a week!" She darted out the door.

Coincidence. A tavern woman murdered. Drowned in mud. In the street.

Jared. The very same thing over ten years ago. In another town, miles down the river.

Coincidence.

Still, the stranger. A big man.

Ahead, the *Spirit* glistened, the setting sun bouncing off her. Sarah made out Jeremy's silhouette at the top of the boat. Where she should be. Where she would have been if not for . . .

Jared Perkins. Would he never just rest in peace and leave them all alone?

And so it begins.

We walk among them, one of them, and even with Our clues, they have no idea We are here. But they are not to blame for their ignorant ways. They will learn their lessons soon enough. All of them who ever turned away, did Us harm. They will all pay.

And Our price is very steep, indeed.

We know much about riverboats, you see. How easily the engines become overtaxed. How fragile boilers really are. How too much heat or one small, tiny, unnoticed flaw will script a fiery death sentence for hundreds.

Theater of Illusion

The Spirit of the River *has lived long past her use. She is no better than a rotting corpse denied burial. She carries the spoiled and rich and self-centered down the river where onboard revelries are grotesque and obscene. Entertainment is immoral and perverse. Debauchery is allowed rein.*

She is here. They all are here.

Years ago, the Spirit *carried livestock on its boiler deck. Now the only animals onboard are those working to keep the floating malignancy alive and running.*

We will change all this.

Soon the celebrations will end, with such explosion of light and color as when they began. Only this time, instead of announcing a wedding celebration, this will announce the death of the Spirit, *long overdue.*

We will watch from afar.

Chapter 7

All things led up to this. The moment, in Jeremy's opinion, when his life came out of hold and started again. The launch of the *Spirit of the River*.

The occasion grew sour. He pulled out his pocket watch and set it on the sill in front of the pilot wheel. They had one minute, and the boilers were stoked, but the stage was still down. Waiting for, of all people, Sarah. Which meant they would be pushing off late.

Disaster, in Jeremy's opinion.

He wondered if she did this on purpose, trying to make him look bad. Events appeared too convenient—a last-minute flurry that took her off the boat. Napkins? A pretty thin excuse. Who gave a damn about napkins, anyway?

Briggs would have his head if he left Sarah behind. And his hide if they departed late.

He scowled, watching the town from this height. Brick edged the river, the landing for their riverboat. His eyes traveled up Main Street and settled on the mercantile where Sarah had gone. He glanced at his watch again. Then back to the street. The engines hummed patiently under his feet, waiting for the signal from him to fire up and explode into action.

"Poor choice of thoughts," he said to himself. Explosions were always the worry of the pilot and first engineer during launch. Jeremy trusted Gage and usually never thought of such a thing; he must be all worked up and fidgety thanks to Sarah's stalling antics.

Finally, relief. Sarah burst through the mercantile door and ran along Main Street, her arms full of piles of colored material. For a moment he allowed himself to enjoy her graceful weave around pedestrians—trying not to run yet doing her level best to hurry—and gently but firmly push her way through the crowd gathered at the landing to watch their departure.

As she drew nearer to the boat, he prepared himself. Sarah crossed the stage, the plank reverberating with her quick footsteps, one bolt of red trailing behind like blood. Jeremy frowned. What on earth made him think such a thing? Must be the tiger onboard, making him nervous. Trail of blood indeed.

The roustabouts raised the plank, their muscles straining with the weight as they cranked. Chain groaned and two of the huge men guided the stage up and over the rail. Another fastened the gate. River water dripped on the deck as the stage swung across and several hands with mops scurried behind to clean up. Water on the deck could mean a slip and a twisted ankle or worse.

The stage swung with excruciating slowness, and Jeremy willed himself to keep still and not do anything. He needed to wait until the roustys secured the damned thing. All the while, the engines hummed beneath him, impatient to burst into action. Jeremy knew exactly how they felt.

Tension crawled through his body, and he tightened his fists. Expectation and helplessness at the situation were driving him to distraction. He did the one thing he could do and stepped up to the wheel. Once he pulled the cord, Gage would release full power to the engines as they backed.

Roustys lined the side of the boat facing the shore, all holding large poles, like knights about to joust. One of the roustys, Skunk, finally gave Jeremy the thumbs-up.

Jeremy pulled the bell rope. It rang out, and with exact synchronization, one end of all the poles dropped into the water as the roustabouts speared the sand bottom. Roustys pushed their entire weight to shove the boat away from the bank. They drifted back, Jeremy waiting until the perfect moment.

The rope, the signal to release the *Spirit's* full power, dangled above his head, taunting him to pull it. Waiting until the ideal moment, he grabbed.

The gong rang out, and the engines answered by rumbling beneath his feet. Up here, four stories high, Jeremy saw the entire town spreading back and up the hills against a sky swashed with the orange and gold of a perfect fall sunset. Most launches happened in the mornings or, at the latest, early afternoon, but Lionel Jeffries specifically requested the boat leave as the sun went down. Sunset cruise—a romantic notion keeping in line with the silliness of a wedding. Even at this later hour, waving people speckled the bank. And Jeremy knew beneath him every man, woman, and child aboard the *Spirit* stood on one of the decks returning the gesture of good-bye. Passengers moved to the front of the boat since the roustys were done securing the stage, and hands waved from the decks below him, arms swinging back and forth in farewell.

The calliope burst into song, "Let Me Call You Sweetheart," a new number Sam practiced all week until Jeremy wanted to grab one of the push-off poles and break the calliope to pieces. The sappy tune had probably been chosen due to the wedding theme. Despite the festive nature of the moment, his attention riveted to the other boats docked around them and the river ahead.

He grabbed the rope again, signaling to the engineer, most likely Gage, to change directions. The boat responded to his command, slowing. He swung the huge wheel to the right with every muscle in his arms about to pop. He loved this feeling, being in complete control.

The river current grabbed the boat, swung it around until they faced slightly south—the direction they'd travel. He signaled "full ahead." The stack bellowed a warning to all other boats for miles around.

Once they were well on their way and headed downriver, dinner would start. One of the best parts of being a pilot and the captain's backup, Jeremy never attended the formal functions. Those events were the captain's duty, which suited Jeremy just fine. He'd never had any schooling other than learning everything about the boat and river at Briggs' feet, and found a pilothouse the perfect place to spend the dinner hour. People, especially genteel, overeducated, rich ones, made him nervous.

Jeremy knew, no matter whose shift, Briggs would be up here to pilot some of the first hours out. Jeremy understood completely. Both men were in competition for the same grand lady, giving her the attention she required. Nurturing as a mother cradling her children in her arms, reliable as a preacher on Sunday, beautiful beyond words was the *Spirit of the River*. He felt honored and privileged to stand at her wheel.

The *Spirit* become part of the river's central current when it grabbed the boat. One last part to the launch.

Jeremy signaled Gage to throttle back the engines. The rumble dropped to a nice, gentle hum, and Jeremy relaxed a notch. The engines were taxed on departures where trouble most often happened. Gage was the best engineer on the waterway, and no coincidence, the *Spirit* the oldest riverboat in existence. Not only because Emma changed her into a money-making excursion boat and kept her in business, but Gage had kept the boat safe and running at top performance for more than a decade.

His feet planted firmly on the deck, the riverbank slid by, outside of the life of the *Spirit*. He loved this moment, the river stretching before him, and the wheel in his hands. More than just her pilot, he became a part of the boat, connected to her by hands and feet, yes. But his heart belonged to her completely. He settled into the vibration of the engines and the movement of the boat.

Jeremy was almost lulled into a sense of well-being when a chill brushed over his shoulders. He looked around behind him. Danny, the *Spirit's* cub pilot, entered. The boy's small size, blond hair, and green eyes made him look like an elf. His slightly pointed ears stuck out, completing the picture. Fourteen and the kid looked no older than ten.

Danny was one of the people tossed aside by Jared Perkins' destructive wake. Perkins had murdered Danny's mother, and Emma had wanted to take care of the boy. But Danny ended up with Tom and Mary Billings, the farmers who took in Sarah and Toby all those years back. They opened their home and their hearts to the boy.

Like Jeremy, though, once on a riverboat, Danny was hooked. His parents agreed to his working as a cub pilot once he turned thirteen, as long as the boy kept up his lessons. He'd been their cub for slightly over a year. Danny was a smart kid, great student, and excellent pilot. And cute as hell. The passengers loved seeing a miniature pilot at the wheel with an adult behind, teaching, guiding. Jeremy had to admit—all part of the show.

"Hey, Danny." Jeremy returned to studying the river ahead, squinting.

Danny shut the door behind him.

"Hey, Jeremy." He plopped on the bench. "You seen that tiger? It's sure somethin', ain't it?"

An insistent shard of cold sliced through Jeremy. Again. He decided to stop ignoring his unsettled feeling. What the heck was wrong? Like all good pilots, he possessed a built-in intuition for his boat, and didn't like any sense of foreboding, especially when nothing caused it. Or did he see or feel something not yet registering in his consciousness? Or did his unease come from a tiger onboard and a late push-off?

"I never seen a theater troupe before, but I seen a tiger last year when the circus came through," Danny continued. "Never one this close up, though."

The silly, overdressed man in charge of the show—Oscar Something-or-other—insisted the tiger was harmless. He'd convinced

Briggs the animal was absolutely no danger.

Jeremy smiled at Danny. His eyes were huge with a question and Jeremy remembered the feeling of sitting behind Briggs, praying for a chance to take the wheel with the captain standing over him. Skipping meals, skipping playtime, anything to be in the pilothouse with the captain.

"You get dinner?" Jeremy asked.

"They're servin' downstairs; it's a party. There's all sorts of little fancy food." Guilt flashed across the kid's face. "I got some before Miss Lilly caught me. She made me up a plate. You want me to fetch you some?"

Jeremy shook his head. "Nope, I'm fine, but thanks." And now that he knew Danny was well fed, time for the moment the kid waited for. "Hey, Squirt, you want to take the wheel?"

Danny shot up with enthusiasm and Jeremy stood behind the boy as he hopped into the pilot's position. Jeremy watched the river for a few minutes and, once convinced they were good for a bit, scanned the boat beneath them. Went over every detail. Everything seemed business as usual.

Still, something niggled at him. Probably nothing more than his imagination.

Zelda Vashnikoff glanced around her first-class cabin. What a dump. Surrounded by walls close enough to almost touch without moving, the room was little more than a wood box. Exotic Cleopatra entombed. Oh, she supposed by river standards this rough-hewn cabin was considered a grand affair; nevertheless, it would take a fair amount of work to change this hovel into her lair laden with pleasure and delights. Oscar allowed her three trunks from their train, more than anyone else. She could get anything she wanted from Oscar, and she made good use of the extra space while packing.

Magic filled her trunks, brought the power of transformation to her fingertips.

The Egyptian wig hugged her head, causing a trickle of sweat to wind down the back of her neck. She longed to relax and drop the Cleopatra act, but it was important she keep her façade intact.

Oscar would come to her. Most likely, he'd be in the mood for a game or two. Showing off for crowds always inspired him, and she liked him inspired. Tireless. His passion aflame. He really was quite a marvelous lover, something she always appreciated, especially when her trysts brought such wonderful returns.

Sterling City presented them a fabulous turnout. Most likely, *Le Théatre d'Illusion* was the most excitement this dull place had ever seen. She'd seen the proof time and time again: Oscar Gévaudan and his theater brought life and sizzle to the dead, gray lives of the people living in the central parts of the country.

No such bland existence for her. Not anymore. As long as she kept Oscar happy. She not only had the chance to dress like a queen; he treated her like one. Small enough price to pay, these silly games. He especially enjoyed the Cleopatra–Antony fantasy. He never let a chance go by when she donned the persona of the queen of the Nile, and he cherished his role as the forbidden lover.

Or, perhaps today he would be the slave boy, if he were in the mood for some gentle humiliation and sensual torment. With Oscar, she never knew. He tended to follow whatever fantasy took his attention, in his theater as well as his lust. Actually, the slave-boy scenario was her favorite. She loved Oscar groveling at her feet. Even if it was only make-believe.

As long as she kept him happy—an easy enough feat to accomplish—her position with the theater stayed safe. Men were such incredibly simple creatures. Keep them satisfied, and a woman pretty much had whatever she wanted. And Zelda Vashnikoff wanted for nothing.

But, she insisted to herself, she earned everything that came her way.

She opened the first trunk and lifted a sparkling strand of gems, draping it over the end of the bed. It would work for tying one down, no? No . . . the beds were built-in, an alcove in the wall. No anchor to wrap the thing around. Too bad there weren't any four-posters on this boat. Oscar so enjoyed a round of gilded bondage.

He was, at the least, creative in his needs. Quite egotistical, yes, but not disagreeable. Fun. Energetic. Although Zelda preferred younger men, she did not dally with anyone from the troupe. Oscar's goodwill was more than her livelihood. It was her life. Her self. Her reason for being.

Next, she pulled scarves out of the trunk and swirled them above her head. Such a shame no one observed her grace of movement. Tossing them around, across the mirror, the bed, the chair, she began the magic of transformation. And she was an expert at changing the mundane into the exotic.

Look at her own transformation.

She left her husband far behind when she changed her name and joined *Le Théatre d'Illusion*. And boring, uninspiring, predictable Evelyn ceased to be, replaced by Zelda Vashnikoff, Russian beauty, burlesque entertainer, exotic lover, actress extraordinaire. She became an expert at making herself into someone else. She glowed with self-appreciation, thinking how she'd dazzle this boat of humdrum travelers.

She worried every year when they toured this uninspired part of the country. Concerned someone she knew from decades ago might remember her. When Oscar told her of this job, actually aboard a riverboat, she experienced a few seconds of panic. Her fear lasted only for a brief moment.

She hadn't worked on the river like her husband. No, he kept her at home, away from any kind of life, insisted she keep their small farm up for his return between trips. She worked alone, bored beyond reason, mired in the squalid details of her life, becoming one of the nameless, faceless, gray women with gray lives dotting the Midwest landscape. Not even the hired hands passing through town kept her satisfied, although she filled her lonely nights with the excitement of their newness until her husband returned. Sometimes she dallied even once he came home to experience the thrill of getting caught. He hadn't cared enough to notice.

And she took on deeper shades of gray.

No one, but no one would confuse Zelda Vashnikoff with the dowdy, filthy woman working a farm, oh, so long ago. She left that gray woman behind when she decided she'd shoveled her last pile of cow shit.

And, tragically, her husband died a few years after she'd left. Tragic, because if she had held on a bit longer, she would have been a widow and sold the farm. Started with some money. Ah, well. This way, by leaving, she'd freed herself completely. From him. From the farm. And, not to mention, all the attachments of such an unwanted life. Including her toddler. It was for the best; she'd been a miserable mother.

"Everything happens as it should," she said to her reflection. "Especially when you have the gumption to design your own life."

Evelyn never did, except for one moment, when she left her old life behind and never looked back.

But Zelda—she was another matter entirely.

Oscar didn't bother to knock. He slammed open the door. Ah, so Mark Antony, Roman politician and powerful general, came to call. Oscar closed the door. A wicked smile crossed his face and his milk-chocolate eyes melted into need. Her body tingled in all the right places. Oh, the next few hours would be good. She looked coyly through her lashes until she watched his eyes widen and his head lower.

"My queen." He dropped to his knees. "What do you require?"

She kicked his shoulder and pushed him down to the floor, planting her foot on his chest. "You dare speak to me, you who are no more than a piece of chattel?" She leaned her weight, crushing the air from him "Vermin? You do not answer?"

His hands slid up her leg. It was going to be the slave boy after all.

Chapter 8

The galley exploded with activity: steam rising from pots, mouth-watering smells wafting along with them. Preparations proceeded exactly as planned, and Emma loved this more than anything. Existing in the center of her galley, creating culinary masterpieces to amaze and delight. Thanks to an extremely late night, her paperwork—schedules, duty rosters, bills, and invoices—was finally done and out. And now, her favorite part of the *Spirit's* trip.

Cooking.

Gladys sliced beef in thin ribbons, getting a jump on tonight's dinner, while the sweet smell of baking tarts filled the air. Emma lifted the cloth off rising dough and poked it down, then scooped up the glob to shape it into a loaf. Despite the early hour there was barely enough time to let it rise again and bake for lunch. But to accompany cinnamon-squash soup, warm just-out-of-the-oven bread was a must.

At the counter, Janine spread napkins in baskets. Usually the laundress and part of the cleaning crew, Janine helped in the galley when they needed her, which seemed to be more and more often. Emma made a note to discuss hiring another cook with Briggs.

Lilly lifted a tray of golden apple-filled tartlets from the oven. "First ones up!" she yelled.

"I can hear you fine," Janine answered. "You don't have to holler."

Lilly scowled and flopped the tray down on the counter. "Get a move on. I got nine more of these. If one of them burns, you're gonna be the one remakin' these little pie-things."

"Tartlets," Emma said, lifting dough out of the next bowl.

"I'd just as soon eat the counter as stuff these critters again. *Tartlets*. They even have a fussy name. Dadblasted heap of work."

"And a passenger favorite," Emma said.

Janine grabbed her spatula and flipped tarts into the first basket. "Why so cranky this mornin', Lil?"

Lilly shrugged. Janine finished the first tray, and Lilly grabbed it, replacing the empty tray with one filled with golden baked tarts.

"I know," Janine said. "You need a date, is what you need."

"When a man's the answer to anythin', I'll not only eat the counter; I'll eat them cupboards, too. And the floor. And the—"

"We won't have a galley left by the time you're through," Gladys chimed in.

Emma laughed, remembering the Lilly of the past, a woman who hooked her self-worth to whatever man she happened to be with at the time. That Lilly was long gone.

Lilly sighed. "Maybe you're right, Janine. Lionel Jeffries has been a widower for years. Bet he's gettin' itchy. He's tall and good-lookin'. And he's rich!"

Then again . . .

Sarah burst through the door. "Bicarbonate?"

"Third pantry, second shelf," Emma called out. One thing she learned between drinks served and the effect of boat movement on some people—to have plenty of bicarbonate on hand.

She returned her attention to her loaves, covering them with clean towels. They were in the galley hot spot, and rising time should be minimal. She wanted to get them in the oven before the breakfast parade of waiters began: an endless circle of heaped platters up, empty platters and dishes down.

Sarah rustled around in the pantry.

"Right at the front," Emma said.

She peeked around the wood door. "It's not in here."

"'Course it is!" Lilly said, plopping down her tray and barging over to help. Lilly rummaged around inside the pantry too. Emma wiped her hands on her apron and headed over.

"Dadburn it! Someone's been messin' around in here!"

Emma peered past Sarah and Lilly into the pantry. Sure enough, items were shifted. Annoyance slid through Emma. She didn't like anyone rooting around in the galley without her knowledge.

"Pry one of them rich folks lookin' for a midnight snack," Gladys called over her shoulder "Think they own everythin'." She returned her attention to slicing beef.

"Here it is!" Sarah pulled out a bottle of bicarbonate.

"I always keep it in the front," Emma insisted.

"No harm done. I have it." Sarah grabbed a glass, filled it with water, and picked up a spoon. "The groom is a nasty shade of green. I have it on good authority Henrietta doesn't care for the color." She sped out the door.

"I woulda told her a shot of gin would do the trick," Lilly said. "Heard he got pretty soused last night."

Emma leveled her best prim look. "Enough gossip, especially about customers."

Lilly smirked, returned to the oven, and opened the door. "Not really gossip. Saw the boy stumble back to his quarters with my very own eyes. He swayed more than the boat, that much is the God's honest truth!"

"Can you blame him?" Gladys whacked off a chunk of meat.

"Oh, damnation!" Lilly said, standing up and holding a retrieved tray of black tartlets. "Emma, I burned 'em."

"Start by eatin' the counter," Janine responded. "It's gonna take you awhile to choke this whole galley down."

"Ah, here you are."

Sarah whirled around at the sound of Oscar's voice. Light tan waistcoat and trousers, morning sun glancing off his cream-and-gold brocade vest, the chocolate brown of his cravat matching his eyes and top hat. He must spend more time in a mirror than anyone else onboard. Perhaps even more than Henrietta.

And, of course, his fashion accessory accompanied him: the gold and black tiger.

"Oscar, Daisy, you two are a vision," Sarah said.

"No, my dear, the vision is you." He scowled at the bottle, spoon, and glass in her hand. "Whatever are you about? Looks like serious business."

"One of the passengers is ill. A tad too much to drink last night."

Daisy stretched out right in front of the steps. Sarah wasn't sure how she felt about stepping over a tiger.

"I'm sure there is an outbreak of the gastronomic queasies this morning; the wedding party had quite a time last night."

"I hope they didn't keep either of you awake."

"Not at all. Daisy and I can sleep through anything."

"Are you looking for something?"

"Actually, yes. The captain promised me a tour of the boat. I need to absorb my surroundings. I find such inspiration from the places where we perform."

"Oh. Well, I believe this is his shift, but he gets off soon."

"It is; he's busy captaining. I checked with him already. Although he tried to hide it, his annoyance was plain. Don't think he's used to having a tiger in the pilothouse."

"Oh, of course. I doubt the problem was you."

He laughed. "Sarcasm. I like that. You are a constant, surprising delight, my dear. He suggested I find you to fulfill my request and his promise."

She smiled tightly. Sick passenger, then a boat tour. While the captain and Jeremy piloted. Perfect. She grew more trivial every minute. However, she admitted to herself, Oscar would be a fun diversion. The man constantly entertained and enthralled.

"I need to deliver this. Can you wait a moment and then we'll start with engineering?"

"Delightful. We'll wait for you right here."

"Um, I need to get up the steps."

Oscar looked down at Daisy, who flopped her tail. "Not eager to step over a three hundred and fifty-pound tigress?"

"She's really quite beautiful. I didn't realize they had white bellies and spots on their faces. I always think of them simply as orange with black stripes."

He stroked Daisy's head. "There is no 'simply' about this beauty. She has many colors in her coat. Daisy, dear, Sarah needs to get upstairs, and she has no wish to step over you."

Daisy yawned.

"Never mind, I don't want to bother her," Sarah said. "You two wait for me here, and I'll take the front stairs."

True to his word, Oscar and Daisy waited patiently for her return.

"Engineering is right through here." She gestured to the front of the boat. "This entire deck used to be opened when the *Spirit* operated as a packet, transporting livestock and agricultural products."

Oscar followed her into a dark corridor. Her eyes were used to the bright sunlight, and she held her palm against the wall to guide her.

The hall opened to the front where the boilers stood. A blast of heat hit Sarah, and the mechanical thrum of engines ran under the roar of fire. Gurgles of steam rushed through the network of pipes above their heads, completing the mechanical symphony. A roustabout shoveled coal into the mouth of one of the boilers, the fire inside roaring.

Sarah glanced at Daisy, who stood, calm as could be. She wondered if Oscar gave her anything to keep her subdued; she seemed more like a large toy tiger than a beast of the jungle.

"This is magnificent!" Oscar spread his hands and strode inside, Daisy padding behind him. The roustabout eyed the tiger and gripped his shovel, shuffling back a few feet.

"Careful of your suit," Sarah said. Tan cashmere and coal dust didn't mix well.

"Oh, pshaw, who gives a whit about clothing when one has the fortune to walk through the sixth circle of Dante's inferno!"

"Whose inferno?" Gage asked, emerging from the almost dark in the back of the boat.

Oscar spun to face the engineer. "Ah, and here is Dante himself. The sixth circle, my good man—flaming tombs."

Gage's expression remained quizzical.

"Um—the heretics?"

"You speak plain English?" Gage asked.

"Not if I can help myself," Oscar answered, rather honestly, Sarah thought.

"*Dante's Inferno*," Sarah explained. "It's a book about a man touring hell. The underworld is sectioned off into rings with different punishment and sinners at each level."

Gage shook his head. "Now I know why I never bothered to learn to read."

"Are you serious?" Oscar asked. "You can't read?"

"Never found the need."

"That's a shame, Mr. Engineer. You might have risen to a much higher level of life, had you been prone to seeking an education."

"I'm perfectly happy here," Gage said.

"How can you be? It's horribly dark and hot and miserable down here; you must dread descending into the bowels of the ship day after day," Oscar said.

"Not at all. I love engineerin'. And this is hardly the bowels of the *boat*. We're above the water line," Gage answered.

"So tell me, how can you possibly love this desperate, filthy place?"

Sarah waited for the lambasting of Oscar Gévaudan. However, Gage never got upset; he usually got quiet, which often worked better than the loudest string of profanities.

"Engineerin' is the heart of the boat," Gage said easily. "Everythin' runs off the boilers. The heat for the stove to cook your food, the warmth in your rooms, the power for the lamps, the steam for the calliope. This is where food, music, and light begin."

Oscar gasped. "Mr. Engineer, your words are nothing short of sheer poetry."

Gage's lips drew down as he tried not to smile. "Well, enjoy your tour." He nodded to Daisy. "You too, tiger. I have my poetry—I mean work—to get back to."

"Oh, dear Sarah, this is simply marvelous. What a treasure trove of wonders on this boat. Where ever will you take me next?"

Gage flashed an amused smile back to Sarah as he disappeared into the shadows.

"Let's go up to the officers' quarters and office next," she said. With Briggs in the pilothouse and Jeremy probably sleeping, there would be no one up there this time in the morning.

Should be the safest place to let loose Oscar Gévaudan and his tiger.

"We're gonna be late. Come on!"

"I'm right behind you." Toby straightened his bowtie and followed Charley to the back steps. They dashed down the steps to the large dining room.

The burn in Toby's chest pulsed mockingly, and he wondered, if he plunged a knife in, would a parasitic worm with dear Father's face on it spring out?

"Yum."

"Huh?" Hand on the knob of the dining room door, Charley turned around.

"Nothing. Just entertaining myself."

Charley snickered and swung the door open. Emma planned continental breakfast on the outer decks, but Toby needed to man the bar. Folks liked their morning drinks.

"You two are late!" Malcolm barked when they scuttled into the room. "You don't get any special privileges, Perkins." Toby heard this warning from Malcolm at least once a day. No secret the rotund headwaiter had it out for him. At least he didn't call Toby "Mama's Boy." He hated when Malcolm used that nickname.

"Yes, sir," Toby said.

"And don't you mock me, boy. I won't stand for it."

"Yes, sir," Toby said as they moved out of earshot.

"I'll deck him for you," Charley whispered.

"Naw, it's not worth your job."

"Why you don't tell your ma to fire his ass?"

"Yeah, right. Let Mommy fight my battles for me. Didn't work in school, and it sure doesn't work once you're a man."

"You ain't really a man yet. Your voice still cracks."

"Shut up!"

"See what I mean?" Charley said.

"Don't need you two flappin' your gums. Git to work!" Malcolm yelled from across the room. His round face, squeezing out of a too-tight collar, blossomed into scarlet.

Charley scooted over to the side where crystal water pitchers waited. He made a face at Toby, grabbed a pitcher, and started filling the glasses on the tables.

"We don't need those filled, idiot," Malcolm said. "Get down to the galley to help carry breakfast up."

"What about the passengers who come in here to dine, sir?" Toby asked.

The look Malcolm trained on him should have incinerated him where he stood. Charley exited through the rear doors. Toby ducked behind the bar to get out of Malcolm's line of fire and stooped to check his stock as long as he was down there. Juices, water, and every liquor imaginable. He reached in to straighten the bottles. Funny, he usually lined everything up at the end of the night. Not surprisingly, however, he'd been so distracted lately. He must have forgotten. He realigned the bottles and stood, bringing up a stack of napkins.

Napkins. He couldn't get away from them.

At least he'd had a small triumph last night. He managed to avert the threat of Mount Henrietta erupting again by placing peacock blue napkins folded in the shape of a bird on every dinner place. Once Toby finished the sculptures, he'd laughed to himself. It looked like bluebirds swooped into the boat and landed, one on each plate. He had to admit—pretty nifty. Bluebirds bringing hope and happiness. An entire flock's worth. What could be more fitting for a bride?

Henrietta actually squealed when she saw them, then shook her bird into a flat piece of material to spread across her lap and catch crumbs. No one appreciated art anymore.

Toby grabbed the top piece of cloth and began folding. Time for a repeat performance, only something different, fitting for a new day of wedding revelry. He created a bootie out of the flat napkin and glanced around.

Sugared lemons heaped over a cut-crystal bowl, reflecting morning light as if they'd been caught in a glittering ice storm and froze in place. Next to them, sugared strawberries and blueberries also heaped, as well as celery, olives, and pickles. And a passenger favorite, an oversized jar of pickled eggs. Toby scrunched his face. He couldn't imagine eating one, but his mom had trouble keeping up with their consumption.

He grabbed some of the sugared lemons and filled the napkin bootie. Another boot folded, and this time, he heaped it with sugared strawberries. Cripes, these were cute.

The burn flared. He figured dear Father hated folded napkins. When his father was alive, he'd smacked every piece of whimsical out of Toby. The worst beating Toby ever got was over a picture he drew of his family. After Jared finished "teaching his son a lesson," he'd ripped the drawing to pieces and made Toby eat every bit. He'd been sick for days.

No son of mine's gonna be a nancy boy.

Toby first learned to fold the simple pieces of cloth into charming shapes from reading *Mrs. Beeton's Book of Household Management*. He'd studied the volumes a few years back while trying to find his place on the *Spirit*.

He'd also killed his endless days onboard by juggling and learning magic tricks, which he mostly did because it would have infuriated his father. He loved to monkey around and his antics entertained passengers. The final piece fell into place when Charley came onboard and the two boys became fast friends. Toby became a waiter too, and found a purpose beyond fiddling around. His juggling and magic set him apart. Enjoying the passengers, his days with Charley, and being a viable crew member gave him something he'd never had. Ambition. He wanted to do a good job, be one of the best. He delved into learning about domestic service.

And then he came across the book with a chapter on napkins.

Jared Perkins would have knocked such silliness out of his boy. So Tobias decided to become brilliant at folding napkins into shapes. He progressed from Mrs. Beeton's basic folding designs to create sculptures in cloth, building his plethora of useless skills. Every silly craft he learned and perfected was better than spitting on his father's grave. Not to mention, more fun.

He made another bootie. "Take that, dear Father."

His chest burned in protest.

"Okay, I guess enough with the booties. Open for business."

"It's about time." Henrietta Jeffries' voice came from nowhere. Toby whirled around. Other than Malcolm, down at the end of the room, he was alone.

Her red head popped up from the side of the bar. She plopped her elbows down. "I have been waiting for over twenty minutes!"

"What did you do, take a nap on the floor? Hey, were you down there spying?" He regretted his challenge the moment it slipped out. Her eyes narrowed to no more than slits.

"I didn't realize they paid the hired help to speak, *boy*. And why would I be spying? Nothing around here is the least bit important."

He clamped down on what fought to spew out. He was already in enough trouble with Malcolm. He tried to calm the burn but it flared bigger. Radiated into his neck. His cheeks warmed. Not dear Father. Not here. Not now. No time to disappear and keep the thing under control.

"Did you fall asleep back there on your feet, *boy*?"

He cleared his throat. "What can I get you, Henrietta?"

"That's Miss Jeffries to you, Toby-the-Waiter."

"Bartender," he said. He grabbed a bottle from under the bar and instead of smashing it over her head like he wanted to, he flipped it into the air, picking up another, flipping it, and then another. Three bottles twisted and twirled. He smirked. "I can make anything your heart desires." *Provided you have one. Which is questionable.*

Henrietta watched the bottles spin, a grin breaking on her face. He hated to admit it, but she was kind of cute when she smiled. She rarely did, but the expression almost made her human. She even had dimples.

"Where did you learn to do that?" she asked, nothing put-on or forced about her voice. She almost sounded, well, like a person. Maybe even a nice one.

Toby kept the circle going, his attention back to the gin, rum, and soda-water bottles twirling in the air. "Here and there. Oops," he said, and stopped the bottles, one by one, catching the last one behind his back and lining them up. "Flipping a soda-water bottle probably wasn't such a good idea."

Henrietta's amused expression broke into a giggle. "Just don't aim it at me!"

With her laugh, the dear Father burn quieted.

Toby smiled. "After calling me *boy*, I'd say you deserve it right between your eyes."

"That was pretty rude, wasn't it? I always think of you as a kid. I guess you are just about grown up."

"Yeah, but not as grown as you, old lady."

Henrietta was Sarah's age, five years Toby's senior. It seemed like Henrietta wasn't any older than him. With Sarah, those five years were like decades.

"So what can I get you to drink, or do you need your shadow?" he asked, surprised to see her without her ladies' maid. "I thought you didn't make any decisions without Adele."

Henrietta scrunched her face. "Ha, ha. My father hired her to keep me out of trouble. I slip away from her every chance I get. Drives them both crazy." She smiled again. "Do you have lemonade back there?"

He grabbed a glass. "I do. And a special treat and *Spirit* exclusive. I make it with soda water so it bubbles. One sugared lemon, or two?"

"I found out we're having a picnic tomorrow," Henrietta answered. "I hate picnics. No one will listen to me. I'm only the dumb bride. Fill the whole darned glass with lemons. I have a feeling it's going to be a long day."

"You should be enjoying every moment of this journey, Miss Dumb Bride."

Henrietta leaned closer. "Careful. My good humor only goes so far."

Toby pulled a flower from the air behind her head. She gasped in delight, and took it from his hands.

"How did you do that?"

"Magic."

She tucked the flower in her hair behind her ear. "Golly." She grinned and again he thought her awful cute. "You might be a nice guy, Toby Perkins."

"Don't tell anyone." He started making her lemonade.

The smile faded from Henrietta's face. "Did you see the shape Billy got himself into last night?"

The groom—Billy Barkenthal—was the receiver of numerous drinks the night before, each one bought with a jab from his friends at becoming Mr. Henrietta Jeffries. Toby didn't know who to feel sorrier for: Billy or Henrietta.

"Yeah, I was the one serving, remember?" He topped the glass with a sugared lemon. "Hey, it's his last few days of freedom. I'm sure he doesn't mean anything by it."

"His last few days of freedom? Why doesn't anyone ever say that about the bride?"

Toby crinkled his brow. "That's a good question. I guess it's assumed a bride is dying to be a bride."

"Well, trust me, nothing is further from the truth."

He pushed the lemonade to her, the sunny drink in direct opposition to the darkness in her expression. A few passengers straggled in, one man holding two plates heaped with pastries and tarts, a skinny woman trailing behind him. The few apple slices accompanied by a thin cube of cheese seemed lonely on her plate.

"Manhattan, two of them," the man called out without even a look at Toby. He dropped his heaping breakfast on the table and headed to the bar.

"Oh, no," Henrietta muttered under her breath.

The man nodded to Henrietta as he approached. "Miss Jeffries, good morning."

She turned and beamed. "Good morning, Mr. Dowell. I'm thrilled you and your wife were able to make our cruise."

"Well, I don't mind telling you, the missus is beyond delighted." He nodded to Henrietta. "And as you will learn soon, my dear, it's of the utmost importance for one to keep one's wife happy. I'm always in the market to put a smile on Martha's face. I dare say, she never stops glowing."

Toby slid the drinks to the man and with one in each fist, he returned to the table.

"Horrible man," Henrietta whispered. "Father insisted he and his wretched wife be included." Henrietta sipped her lemonade. "And she never smiles."

Toby laughed. "Well, at least the picnic ought to be fun."

"I hate the outdoors. Sitting on the ground, insects, stuff from trees falling in my hair, sun marring my alabaster complexion. If I turn red, I'm going to kill somebody. The picnic was Billy's idea. He doesn't like boats."

"Then why are you having your wedding on one?"

Henrietta's evil grin told him everything he needed to know.

"Cripes," he said.

"Hey, a girl's gotta have some fun."

"You are a hard woman, Henrietta Jeffries."

"Toby Perkins, you have no idea." She pushed the empty glass back across the bar. "Make the next one a double."

"And what is behind this door?" Oscar asked, rattling the knob. Next, he squinted at the gold eagle, lifted the knocker held in its beak, and tapped it against the base.

Daisy took the cue and sat at alert at his feet, waiting for the door

to swing open. Sarah knew it wouldn't.

"You have an incredibly curious mind, Mr. Gévaudan."

"Inquisitive, yes. Served me well in law school."

Sarah almost fell back. You're a lawyer?"

"Well," he admitted, "was. Became bored and *voila*! The actor's life for me! My legal background comes in handy if we fall behind with payments or members of my troupe run up against the law. I can talk my way out of just about anything."

"No doubt."

"Isn't it strange how you manage to coax the truth out of a person," he said thoughtfully. "Now, how about a return of favors? What is behind this most mysterious door guarded by an eagle?"

"This is the captain's dining room. Invitation only."

A look of annoyance flitted across his face. "Surely I can look in? I imagine I'll be invited soon enough," he said, hurt lacing through his voice. Then his demeanor completely changed as he slid his congenial mask in place. "I promise to be a good lad and not touch anything." Sarah stifled a smile.

He placed his palm against the dark mahogany door, and ran his hand down the carved, beveled grid work. "This wood feels like satin. I do love the touch of fine, beautiful handiwork." He tilted his head and smiled at Sarah. "And this eagle is positively frightening!"

There were only three keys onboard. The captain, her mother, and Gage each possessed one. If there were such a thing as a sacred place on the boat, this was it.

"I'd love to show you, but I don't have a way of getting in."

"You can't be serious. What is in here?"

"It's just a dining room."

"Nothing 'just' about it if it's off limits." He dropped his hand. "A locked door drives me insane."

She laughed. "The furnishings in there are quite opulent and, I imagine, expensive to replace. Perhaps impossible. Uncle Quentin, who used to own the boat, traveled extensively. The room was put together from his collection."

"Oh, I simply must see it. If not, I'll die of curiosity."

She laughed again, then turned when she heard someone coming up the steps, happy for some distraction. Until she saw who it was. Jeremy Smith topped the steps and crossed his arms. He didn't even look at Sarah, but eyed the tiger, his gaze finally coming to rest on Oscar.

"Can I help you?"

"Ah, good day, sir," Oscar said without hesitation, his eyes squinting as he evaluated the pilot. "Do I know you?"

"No." Jeremy took a step forward. He was much taller and bigger than the lithe and elegant Oscar, which took Sarah by surprise. Oscar Gévaudan's presence made him seem so much larger in stature.

"Upon reflection, I do believe I have seen you about." He pointed his finger down and twirled it. "You drive this little boat, don't you?"

"Pilot," Jeremy answered. "I pilot the *Spirit of the River*."

Daisy yawned and stretched out at Oscar's feet.

"My sincerest apologies. It takes me a day or so to pick up the local colloquialisms. You, sir, are to be complimented in giving me the complete understanding of another useless term."

Jeremy's face transformed to stone, and Sarah knew that beneath his surface he fought with anger. Then stone wrinkled with annoyance. "You need to get in here? This is the captain's dining room."

"So your purser has informed me. I want to go in."

"Wait here," Sarah said, deciding the only way she'd be able to finish the tour was to get him inside. "I'll get the key from Briggs."

"Invitation only," Jeremy said, arms still crossed over his chest. She swore he flexed a muscle. Always proving himself quite the he-man.

As much as she didn't care if she showed Oscar inside or not, it would do no harm and certainly make their guest happy. For some

reason, Jeremy chose the moment to posture off. Which instantly placed her on Oscar's side.

"The captain requested I take Mr. Gévaudan on a tour and show him every inch of the boat. As a guest of the captain, I'm sure he would allow us access."

Jeremy squinted, studying her. He reached into a trouser pocket. "Fine." He opened the door, keeping his eye on the tiger. "I'll leave it to you, then, to be sure everything remains safe. My shift starts in a few minutes. I won't be late."

Sarah's cheeks heated and not from the jab over being late. Jeremy Smith with a key to the captain's dining room? And not her? Although a seemingly small thing, it hit her with the force of shame. She never felt so outside of the *Spirit*.

"Exquisite!" she heard Oscar say from deep inside the room as he lit lamps.

"You have a key," she murmured. It slipped out before she thought to stop it.

"Because Briggs lent me his for this trip. He doesn't plan to use the room and didn't want to have to run around in case it needed to be opened." Jeremy almost sounded apologetic.

"This is an unbelievably exotic teapot. Where is it from? What is its story?" Oscar's voice floated from inside the room.

Sarah didn't want to say anything, didn't want to sound jealous or disappointed or hurt, although she felt all those things.

"You better get in there before he or his tiger break something," Jeremy said, and held out the key. "Lock up when you're done and return it to me when you can."

She waited a second, then opened her palm. He pressed the key into her hand, holding it there.

"Thank you," she said. She nearly choked on the words. She was anything but grateful.

Chapter 9

Sarah's laughter had cut through Jeremy like a hot knife. She actually enjoyed the company of the strange, silly man. Women were so easily led astray by a sparkly new toy. He stewed over the theater man for an hour. His neck crimped tight and popped every time he turned his head.

He concentrated on relaxing, but lost ground when his shoulders tensed at the sight of Sarah making her way to the top of the boat. What now? Then he remembered he'd given her the key. She was probably returning it. She'd looked so strange when he handed it to her, although, he had to admit, he liked to touch her, to hold her hand if even for only a few seconds.

Why did she have to be so contrary?

He admitted, to himself anyway, she looked awful pretty in her simple white dress and powder blue shawl draping over her shoulders. She reminded him of a schoolgirl. Naïve. Sweet. No hint of the murderous temper or sharp tongue hiding within.

He whipped around to look front, out at the river.

The door creaked open. Sarah's voice rang out. "We're slowing."

"Brilliant observation."

"What's going on?"

He kept his eyes on the river. "Why do you care?"

"I wondered why we are slowing down. Are we stopping?"

"Why the sudden interest in our schedule?"

She sighed. "You're still angry about the launch?"

No, more like jealous of the time she was spending with that flim-flam excuse of a circus freak. Other than his idiotic costumes, the man might look close to normal on the outside, but Jeremy had seen enough to realize he was a twisted, mean little cretin on the inside. He wanted to warn her what a man like that would do to her, how badly she'd be hurt.

"First time I've ever pulled out late," he said instead.

"Jeremy, we had a furious bride on our hands. I realize you don't appreciate the finer points of business, but her father is footing the entire bill. Even you can understand this—we need to keep Henrietta happy. No matter what."

"I can't believe pulling out late was our only option. Sure made me look bad."

"Believe it or not, Jeremy, my world does not revolve around you or how you look."

He didn't answer. Nor did he seem able to ask her what he really wanted to: what did she see in a man like Flim-Flam?

He heard the door shut, and she came to his side. "Do you honestly think I'd hold the launch on purpose?"

"I have no idea what you'll do anymore," he said softly and watched as she contemplated that announcement. She looked perplexed. "What happened to you, Sarah? Where's the girl who used to be my best friend?"

Damn, damn, damn. Why did he say that? He whipped his head back around to focus on the river. With any luck, she'd let his statement pass.

"So why are you slowing down?" Her voice came softer, no demand in it.

He pulled the bell to reverse engines.

"We don't have any scheduled stops," Sarah said. When he didn't answer, she cleared her throat. "Are you ever going to speak to me again?"

"Hold on," he said, and swung the wheel to the left. He knew his arm muscles bulged. He was blessed with powerful arms and shoulders and didn't mind Sarah staring at him. He knew he looked good. Let her be the one to admire, for a change.

The current grabbed the back of the boat and as soon as it faced the shore, he rang the gong for Gage to return to forward thrust. The boat headed for the bank. Next, bell twice, cut engines. Roustabouts, poles in hand, shuffled to the front of the deck as the boat drifted. It was up to them to secure her. His job was over, for the moment.

He turned back to Sarah. "We're picking up Andrew."

"Brinkstone?" Sarah's face lit with pleasure. Andrew was an old friend to most of the crew, a city-raised country doctor always willing to help out, with a meal and round of poker as payment. Everyone enjoyed Andrew. And it wasn't a bad thing to have a doctor around.

"The very same."

Her smile quickly changed to concern. "Why? We don't need a doctor, do we?"

Jeremy shrugged. "Orders from the captain. Guess he sent word the day before we left. I found out about the stop this morning." He scanned the bank. "No sign of him, I hope he got the message."

"We have the time; we aren't due to be at the picnic grove until late morning tomorrow."

Jeremy wanted to reply with a snotty comment about Sarah and schedules and being on time, but decided against it. He'd made his point.

"So," Sarah said, "I was your best friend? When? I think I must have missed it."

He glowered. So much for letting his comment pass. "Forget I said anything."

"Oh, come on, Jeremy. Honestly, when?"

"You remember when we were up here together, learning how to do this? Hanging on every word out of the captain's mouth?"

"We were always fighting over his attention, to be the one at the wheel. As I recall, you usually won." Her voice sounded wistful, almost melancholy. She brightened. "Remember when I put glue on the pilot wheel? Briggs finally tried to schedule our lessons apart."

Jeremy decided it safest to look at the floor.

"You never told on me," she said.

"Believe it or not, I didn't want you to get in trouble."

"Ha!" she said. "More like you didn't want Briggs to know you fell for such a stupid trick."

His mouth twitched as he held back his smile. "I wanted him to admire me."

"He does, Jeremy. Why wouldn't he? You've done everything brilliantly, pretty much followed in his footsteps. He has a soft spot for you," she said, her voice again gentle.

"For you, too. He gave you anything you ever asked for, no matter what." He returned to looking at her, and hoped she didn't see what rushed through his mind. He would give her anything she asked, too. Well, as long as she asked nicely.

She pursed her lips, like she was thinking. "You hated my crush on you. I can't say I blame you. I followed you around with my heart in my hands, and you acted like I was the most repulsive creature on the earth!"

She was partially right. He'd been embarrassed, yet proud she followed him, gazing at him like he was a god. Those days were long gone. His cheeks heated and he stared down again. "I was a dumb kid, Sarah."

"I was, too."

He snapped his attention back to her. "So having a crush on me was dumb."

A long sigh escaped. "Jeremy, your pride is showing. You were just a boy. You presumably wanted to die of embarrassment, me trailing you, a lovesick adolescent girl."

"I liked us learning together, side by side. Being with you, and Briggs teaching us. Those were the best days."

"You just liked to show off for me."

"Yeah, I did," he said. He hoped what he was thinking didn't show on his face. He wanted to take her in his arms, would give anything to see the look of undying love he remembered so well. But that was the heart of an impressionable, sweet young girl, not the efficient, hardened, often angry woman standing beside him now, a woman who never needed anyone or anything. Not even him. Especially not him.

An empty feeling grew inside, and it hurt around the edges. He missed the girl. Missed the friend. Terribly, he admitted to himself. How did this happen, how did he get here, cornered in the pilothouse with Sarah's unflinching amber gaze trained on him, distrust and distance foremost in her expression?

He flicked his glance over to her, and what he saw surprised him. She was looking at him with something like . . . he wasn't sure. Like she didn't hate him or wasn't mad at him.

He knew how fast that might change.

The boat slid along sand and came to a stop. On the bank, Dr. Andrew Brinkstone, cinnamon curls topping his cherubic face and cashmere-clad round body, waved excitedly.

Sarah broke into an excited grin and waved back. "I can't wait to hear what he's been up to!" she said, and reached for the door.

Just once Jeremy wished he'd have that effect on her.

She bounced down the steps without a glance back.

Theater of Illusion

The evening bustle of party activity filling the stateroom gave Sarah the opportunity to remain away from Henrietta Jeffries. The silly chick was so happy being the center of attention, she didn't once look at Sarah. Strangely, her husband-to-be didn't even speak to his bride or glance her way.

Rumor had it the son of Samuel Barkenthal was ill-equipped to take over his father's coal empire. Or, by the look of him, Henrietta Jeffries.

Sarah wondered if the young man had ever done a day of honest work in his life. His long, manicured fingers gracefully wrapped around a cigar as he gathered his tuxedoed friends and procured a tumbler of scotch. Blond hair topped a pale face and tall, lanky frame. He appeared almost delicate. Like a day of real work might cause him to expire.

The groom and his group hustled out to the back deck like a colony of penguins. When Sarah saw the clouds of cigar smoke dissipating in the night air, she was grateful they'd gone outside. Standing out on the aft deck in their evening finery, they resembled boys playing dress-up. Poor fool, with a future of contending with Henrietta for the rest of his life.

Watching the arrogant young man ignore his bride-to-be, Sarah felt a twinge of sympathy for Henrietta. Common knowledge insisted the wedding served to seal a deal between two business moguls. Sarah wondered if Henrietta had a choice. Sometimes, Sarah thought, it paid to be part of the working class.

As well as the guests, the dining room was dressed for the party. Beneath soaring arches, food and desserts piled high on tables down the center of the great room. Emma and her staff of cooks were out of sight, but dish after tempting dish emerged in the hands of waiters.

Invisible, Emma orchestrated every detail of the perfect evening from the galley. Sarah was all too aware of the cooks, waiters, and staff slaving away on the deck beneath their feet to create the reality of elegance and abundance filling the stateroom.

For the moment, Sarah had nothing to do but stand about, looking as if she was enjoying herself. With the captain mingling among the passengers, she knew Jeremy worked up in the pilothouse. He probably listened to strains of the party drifting beneath his feet as he concentrated on navigating the moonlight-dappled water. Exactly where she should be.

Thanks to Tobias, she was nothing more than a useless piece of décor.

She pushed the thought out of her head. Toby's angst wasn't his fault. He'd been through so much as a boy, how could he be anything other than damaged? He was doing fine, all things considered.

"Ah, Miss Sarah," came a familiar voice from behind her, and she gratefully turned.

"Andrew, I'm so glad to see you. I'm sorry I couldn't spend more time with you this afternoon, I had a napkin-making emergency on my hands."

"Oh, sounds like quite the heart-pounding adventure."

Henrietta's laughter shrieked across the room as she gestured wildly with gloved hands at the crowd around her. She wore a bejeweled ring on every gloved finger, and her wrists dripped with diamonds. Doubtless enough fortune on her arms to run the *Spirit* for an entire season.

"And it's a pleasure to see you," Andrew said, bringing her attention back to him, "although I thought you'd be up in the pilothouse by now. Won't Jeremy share?"

She glanced around to see if anyone listened. All those around her were deeply engrossed in drinks and conversations of their own. Sarah's smile changed to a forced one.

"Oh, have I put my foot in my mouth again?"

"Not at all. I don't have my license yet, and I've so much to do to see the wedding goes off without a hitch." She was surprised at her smooth explanation, and how good it was to have the situation not be a huge deal, only a conversation point.

"I imagine the Jeffries–Barkenthal affair is a full-time job."

110

"More than," she answered. "Andrew, now I hope I'm not the one with a foot in my mouth, but what are you doing here? Not that it isn't wonderful to have you onboard."

"If you are assuming I don't have an invitation to the wedding, you are correct. Captain Briggham asked me if I'd join the tour."

"Why?"

Andrew's serene expression didn't break. "Various reasons. No need to bore you with them. Nothing near as exciting as a napkin-making emergency." He laughed, brushing her question away.

Her curiosity was piqued. Andrew evaded her question. Why? Before she had another chance to ask, the captain trained his attention on Andrew and broke from Lionel Jeffries' group, heading for them. Andrew stuck out his hand and the captain grabbed it.

"Andrew, thank you for joining us. I'm sorry I couldn't break away and see you when you came onboard. How are you? How is life in the backwoods?"

"I am absolutely wonderful, Captain. As far as the backwoods goes . . . let's just say the lack of excitement sometimes outweighs my enjoyment of Nature's beauty. I do so appreciate the invitation. I'll do anything for a spin on this boat!"

Sarah looked around, wondering how to find out more. As she surveyed the crowd, she caught Henrietta's eye and the silly girl scowled and stalked in their direction, Adele the ladies' maid in tow. Time to ward off another "disaster." What put Henrietta in such a lather? Sarah wondered.

Before the bride reached her, the front doors of the dining room burst open and music thundered as *Le Théatre d'Illusion's* musicians strolled in. They played exotic scales, notes sliding up and down, reminding Sarah of the Orient. A man with three huge drums strapped to him came next, a heartbeat thundering through the music. The rhythm pulsed through Sarah's bones as the air shook with it.

Seven men stalked in. At least, Sarah thought they were men.

They wore skirts and draping robes in deep, rich colors, faces painted white, and black wigs. They burst into song.

"If you want to know who we are . . . we are gentlemen of Japan . . ."

"I'll be damned," Briggs yelled in her ear. "Gilbert and Sullivan! Excellent!"

Sarah wasn't well versed in music, but she was grateful for the strange chorus and the attention they paid to the wedding party. They sang and circled Henrietta, who, obviously delighted, clapped her hands along with the song. Even the fiancé and his rookery of penguins came in to rejoin the party.

One "Gentleman of Japan" looked familiar. Under the white face paint, Sarah recognized the harlequin. His muscular body, fully clothed and draped, seethed with provocative power. He trained his attention on Henrietta. Sarah would hate feeling his eerie presence so near to her. The debutante lapped it up like a drunk clutching a jar of home brew.

Sarah sensed someone watching her. She turned. Oscar leaned against the rear wall, arms crossed, relaxed. Dressed entirely in a black dress coat, trousers, and top hat. His vest and bowtie glistened with flecks of silver. For a change, Daisy was nowhere in sight. He smiled at her and gave a slight nod.

The men finished their song and moved back in unison, lining the room. Three women wearing Japanese kimonos, white face paint, and black wigs done up in high, geometric styles, flitted in. To the delight of the crowd, they bobbed around and sang, beautiful voices lacing through the room. The lead singer, a tiny slip of a girl, played a character appropriately named Yum-Yum. She sang with a voice of spun silk. Across the room and behind the bar, Toby seemed mesmerized along with the rest of the crowd. Sarah glanced back again, and Oscar Gévaudan appeared to be enjoying the entire thing. He should; the entertainment was dazzling and the passengers delighted.

The man knew what he was doing. He was an extraordinary showman.

Sarah faced forward again, sweat squiggling down her back. Her lace dress clung to her. Despite the wonderful entertainment unfolding before her, she yearned for light cotton, flat shoes, and the cool breeze of the river coming through the pilothouse. And the solitary and powerful feeling of a licensed pilot, alone and unwatched. Unencumbered. Free.

A moment that would never be hers to enjoy.

Healers. Doctors. Shamans.

They put back together the bodies of those who are broken or burned or sick or torn. They mend some, hold the hands of those who suffer, and ease those past help into the arms of death. They use any and every method they can; they observe, analyze, chant, use magic, pray, call upon the gods to help, poke, prod, stick, stab.

They employ drugs. Potions. Poisons.

They have been known throughout the world and history as shamans, priests, medicine men. Gods. Angels of mercy. Angels of death.

To some they are healers. Others call them murderers, their hands dipped in blood, their ministrations quite bizarre.

Now, one has blessed the Spirit *with his presence.*

He will come to know Us with intimacy. And who, We wonder, will heal the healer?

Chapter 10

"I don't want to leave," Billy slurred, stretching his arms wide. Sarah and Charley grabbed one arm each when he staggered, keeping him from falling on his face. Billy the Groom was the last guest standing. Although judging from all the alcohol he'd consumed, he should be flat on his back by now. And in his bed, exactly where she and Charley were taking him.

"Come along, Billy, we'll get you to your room."

He muttered as they walked him through the doors. "Twenty-A," Sarah said, and Charley nodded. They didn't bother lighting the lamp when they entered the cabin and deposited the young man on his bed. He fell, plopping like an overstuffed bag of laundry. His arms and legs flung wide. He abruptly began snoring.

"With any luck, he'll sleep soundly." Sarah fisted her hands on her hips.

"I hope. I'd hate to have to clean up after him."

"Ah! Good thinking." She slid the wastebasket next to the bed. "There. He might make it without wrecking the floor."

Theater of Illusion

"Naw, not much of a chance." Charley tugged off the groom's shoes, dropping them on the floor. "Least I can do, make the poor fella comfortable. I'd be drinkin' a whole lot more than this guy if I faced the rest of my life in close quarters with Henrietta Jeffries."

"Better than to spoil two houses with them," Sarah pronounced over her shoulder as she exited Billy's room. "Hard to say which of them is getting a worse deal. Thank you for helping me, Charley."

He came out behind her and shut the door. "Not a problem. I'll see you in the mornin'. I have a few buckets of confetti to get off the floor." He grimaced. "They might be entertainin', but damn, these theater-types shore make a load more work."

Sarah nodded, glad to finally see her job finished for the day. Most passengers were hours asleep, Billy the last one down. She descended the back steps and passed the galley, taking a peek through the glass in the door. Spotless and empty, Emma, Lilly, and their crew no doubt catching up on some well-deserved rest.

The entire boat slept. The only people left standing, the few left to clean up the stateroom and the nightshift in engineering. And, of course, the pilot.

Sarah yearned to go up to the pilothouse, but Jeremy might be up there now. Their last encounter troubled her. She wasn't sure how she felt about him. He possessed the power to infuriate her. He was an arrogant jackass. Yet her heart raced every time she saw him, and not with annoyance. Why he still looked so good to her, she'd never know. Perhaps women never got over their schoolgirl crushes.

"Doomed forever," she said to no one in particular.

Only one place for a Perkins to go to work out problems, the massive paddle wheel.

Not a soul hovered around to spoil the contemplative sound of water rushing over the wheel. She tucked herself under the ceiling, which also served as the floor of the deck above. No one, even if they came out from the stateroom to watch the wheel, would see her down here. The paddle wheel churned, and she concentrated on the sound of water to relax her.

So far, this was the strangest voyage the *Spirit* had ever undertaken. Everything felt slightly unreal. Toby and the cliff, her pilot's test, the passengers boarding along with *Le Théatre d'Illusion,* the tiger, and those shredded napkins added the final touch of unreality. And, not to forget, Oscar Gévaudan.

Light from the stateroom windows glistened on drops dancing around the wheel. The lightest of refreshing mists enveloped her. She breathed in cold, moist air. Finally, the strains of the day began melting away.

"Perfect place for solitude." Oscar Gévaudan appeared to materialize out of nowhere. He wore the amused echo of a smile she realized was second nature to him. She wondered if she was a source of amusement for him as much as everything else seemed to be.

"Fabulous show," Sarah said.

He came a few steps closer. "I thank you. I shall pass your appreciation on to the performers. It is my job to simply observe while they weave magic."

"Oh, I think you do more than observe, Mr. Gévaudan. You are obviously the force behind *Le Théatre d'Illusion.*"

"Me? I am no force."

"I don't believe it for a moment." She leaned against the rail. "Captain Briggham was thrilled you chose Gilbert and Sullivan. He got a chance to see *The Mikado* in New York."

"Wonderful show, one of my favorites," Oscar replied, "and appropriate, don't you think? Musical numbers about an upcoming wedding."

"From what I understand, the bride is not willing and the groom is a buffoon. In the play, that is."

Oscar gave a slight nod. "As I mentioned, quite appropriate. And I simply love juxtaposition. The themes of death and cruelty running throughout. The notion of suicide as a laughing matter."

Lost Soul's Cliff shot through her.

The lines of Oscar's slightly mocking look softened into the first real expression she'd seen on his face. "I'm sorry, my dear Sarah. Too much dark humor? Please, smile for me once again." He touched her face. "I should know better than to be indelicate with a lady, but there is something about you that invites a man to speak his mind," he said, voice quieting to gentleness. His mask of charm slipped back into place. "Such vitality and strength. And honesty. Quite an intoxicating combination in a woman."

"I wonder how much of you is show and illusion, Mr. Gévaudan? And how much true?"

His eyes widened.

She blushed at the frank nature of her words. "I'm sorry. I tend to speak my mind before I think over the consequences. Well, you did say you valued my honesty," she added.

He appeared thoughtful, as if trying to decide something, and finally spoke. "Please, call me Oscar. I'll be wounded if you don't."

"You're avoiding my question, Oscar."

He raised his hands in mock surrender, then dropped them. "How much of me is illusion? In all probability everything you see, or believe me to be, Miss Perkins."

Sarah nodded, surprised at his answer.

"Have you heard of Socrates and his men in the dungeon?" Oscar asked.

"Sounds vaguely familiar."

"A most thought-provoking story. One of my favorites. And I do love stories; they offer us more of the truth than truth, don't you think?"

"Interesting way of looking at things."

"The ancient philosophers used stories to uncover and teach deeper meanings. Take the Socrates allegory. Three men are chained in a dungeon from infancy. A window is directly above where they are tethered. The window, at ground level, is on a busy street with people walking past, talking. Life going by. All the three men see are shadows cast on the opposite wall from the window and all they hear are the filtered, faraway whispers of voices. They think these shadow creatures are reality."

"How awful."

"Oh, it gets infinitely worse, as all stories tend to do. One of the prisoners escapes, goes up. Talks to human beings, feels the sun on his skin, the breeze in his hair." He leaned closer. "I like to think he makes tender, passionate love to a woman."

She hoped he didn't see the shiver running through her. Oscar Gévaudan performed, playing her like a tightly strung harp. And, strangely, she didn't mind.

"At any rate, the prisoner experiences life in all its three-dimensional, colorful, sweaty, incredible glory. Tragically, he's recaptured and taken back down and chained to the wall. He tells his comrades of his adventures, but they have no reference point, no basis for understanding."

"That is completely preposterous. Such a thing could not happen."

"The story is an allegory, Miss Sarah. As he tells his friends, they do not believe him. They label him insane. To them, the shadows are reality." He touched her chin, stroked her jaw with his finger. At his touch, tingles cascaded through her. "The point is, who can say what reality and illusion really are?" he whispered. "That is always the question, isn't it? What is real?"

He took her face in his hands and brushed his lips across hers. A feeling started deep, shimmering up and right into the center of her chest. He closed the imperceptible distance between them, slipped his arms down and pulled her to him. Beneath cashmere and silk and glimmer, she felt the man of flesh and blood. He kissed her. Bolts shot through her. Everything melted away except Oscar Gévaudan and his taste, his heat, his essence.

Suddenly, he broke contact and stepped back, granting her his mocking look.

"Indeed, who is to say what is real and what is not?"

Dizzy and off-balance, she gasped. A trick? This kiss was one of his tricks? Fury rose along with shame, hot and prickly. She considered pushing him back to watch the spinning paddle wheel pulverize him.

He smiled, amused, like he read her very thoughts.

"Nice night for a stroll," Jeremy's voice intruded. She whirled around.

"Ah. Mister Pilot," Oscar said, his voice edged with a touch of mockery.

Jeremy glared for a moment, anger radiating off him in waves.

"I can't help but notice, you aren't such a big man without your tiger," the pilot finally said.

Oscar's expression filled with mock surprise and horror. "I seem to have upset you, good sir." His smooth voice wrinkled with sarcasm. "I do apologize. I didn't realize I infringed on your territory."

Sarah wedged between them. "Oscar. Jeremy. Just to be certain we all understand each other, allow me to be frank. I am no man's *territory*."

The weight of the last two days settled on her. Toby's flirtation with suicide, boarding new passengers, the party and spectacle of the evening. The tavern murder. Not to forget, Henrietta Jeffries. Everything heaped on her like snow on a tree branch, piling up until she thought she might break. Suddenly, she did feel tired, exhausted even.

"I've had quite enough of this day. I am going up to retire." She took a few steps past the two men, stopped, and turned. Beneath his surface, Jeremy held anger at bay; Oscar, as usual, appeared amused. She decided to leave them both to fend for themselves.

"Good night, gentlemen." She continued up to her cabin.

"I can't believe the mess those people made," Charley said, plucking the last of the confetti off the carpet. They'd tried to sweep it up, but the waiters finally dropped to their knees to pick each piece out. "Why do they need all that glitter and such flyin' around the room?"

"Theatrics," Toby answered, stacking glasses in a pyramid. "All part of the show. And why are you complaining? You missed most of the confetti cleanup."

"Yeah, well draggin' a rich boy's sagging carcass to his bunk ain't my idea of fun, either."

"I guess no matter what, we are the bottom rung on the *Spirit's* social ladder."

Charley smirked and stood, sidling over to the bar to dump his handful of confetti in the bucket Toby had set out. "You sure had your eye up a rung or two this evenin'."

"Hey, Henrietta is a customer. I have to be nice to her."

"No, that singer gal, the little one. The main one. What was her name?"

"In the show? Yum-Yum?" Toby answered, trying to keep all emotion from his voice. Yep, he'd noticed her and knew exactly who Charley meant.

"Yeah, that's it. Yum-Yum. You looked like you wanted to taste her, all right."

"Charley, shut up." He grabbed the bucket and set it on the floor.

"You're red as a boiled beet. You're sweet on her, ain't you?"

"That's ridiculous. I don't even know who she is."

Charley flipped over two glasses from the pyramid Toby just finished stacking. "Hit me, pal."

Toby crinkled his brow. "Hit you? Much as I'd like to—"

"You know what I mean. The captain owes us one."

Toby brought up a bottle, opened it, and splashed amber liquid in the cut-crystal tumbler. "There. Scotch. Not our finest, not our worst, either."

Charley grabbed the glass. "And one for you."

"I'm gonna pass."

"Why? Maybe if you take a hit, you'll find the nerve to ask tasty little treat out for a walk along the moonlit deck. Girls like that kind of thing, you know."

Toby wiped the bar down with a white bar rag. Charley slammed his hand down, stopping the cloth.

"This bar is clean enough. Fact is, ain't a spot on it."

"Time for you to go to bed, Charley."

"Aw, Toby. Come on. I'm jest tryin' to help you out."

"I know."

"You like that girl. Trust me, a quick gulp and you'll be ready to give her a spin. I bet she's awake. Them theater folks are night owls."

"It's going to take a whole lot more than a quick gulp," Toby admitted. "And since when do you know so much about theater people?"

"I been to the theater lots of times," Charlie said, and Toby wasn't sure if the insulted tone in his voice was real or a tease. "I happen to be very cultured. I seen these folks before, and besides, I have my eye on one of them singer gals, too."

"Aha!" Toby proclaimed. "Now the truth comes out."

"It might help us both if we talked to 'em together, you know? Maybe we'll get real lucky and can have a theater party in our room. Two gals is better than one."

"Charley, you're an idiot." Toby shook his head. "Count me out."

"Why? You like girls, don't you?"

No son of mine's gonna be a nancy boy. I'll beat it right out of you and you'll thank me!

Toby grabbed the rag in his fist, pulled. Charley let go, his eyes widening.

"Hey, you turned white as this mop rag. Listen, I didn't mean nothin'. Jest, I seen you in action. No offense, but yore manhood could use some help."

Toby clutched the rag to him as if it might protect him.

"Hey, you all right? Honest, I didn't mean nothin'." Charley's frown held genuine worry.

Toby cleared his throat. "I know. It's okay."

Charley grabbed the bottle and poured a splash in the second glass. He clanked the bottle back down on the bar, and Toby jumped. Amber liquid caught light through the cut glass. Toby remembered the last time, well, the only time he'd indulged.

"I almost gagged when I tried this before."

"Why do you think they call it an acquired taste?" Charley lifted his glass and swallowed. He gritted his teeth and hissed. "Wow, this is good. Warms me right down to my romantic soul."

Toby picked his glass up and sniffed. Remembered how it didn't give him courage, but did help him forget.

Devil's Piss. Don't you ever touch it, boy. I'll kill you, you ever, ever touch it.

Dear Father hated alcohol as much as he hated Toby. Maybe more. He held the glass up to the light, then sniffed the contents a second time.

"It reminds me of Uncle Quentin. He used to smell like this sometimes."

"He used to own this boat, didn't he?"

"Yeah, before you or I came onboard. He died about ten years ago. He liked his drink."

"Smart man," Charley said and took another gulp, emptying his glass. "Hit me."

Toby refilled Charley's glass and lifted his own. Smelled it again.

"You can't drink it through your nose. Come on, Toby, you down that, then let's go find us some theater gals."

"I don't know, Charley."

Charley glanced around. "We don't have all night, it's already pretty late. You won't git in no trouble. No one is in here." He clinked his glass with Toby's. "Here's to pretty women, the reason for our bliss.

May we find ourselves with two tonight, and startin' with a kiss!"

Charlie downed his glass and refilled.

Toby held up his. Stared at it.

Holding his breath, he gulped the liquid down.

Emma climbed the pilothouse steps, knowing in her heart Sarah would stand up here one day on her own. She wouldn't give up her dream; she was Emma's daughter. If she'd taught her children anything, it was that something of value was worth a fight. And Sarah was a fighter.

Briggs stood at the wheel, and Emma never tired of seeing him in here. She understood: the pilothouse for him was like the galley to her. Their other duties were necessary, but this was where the captain's heart stayed.

She topped the steps and pulled herself up to the door. And stopped short. Andrew leaned against the front railing, facing Briggs, and he saw her first. The captain glanced over his shoulder when she opened the door.

"Andrew," Emma said, "I heard a rumor you were onboard, but I thought with all your traveling to meet us, you'd be exhausted and asleep by now."

"I couldn't pass up the opportunity to speak with my old friend." The doctor pushed himself off the rail and came around the wheel. Briggs returned his attention to the river and Andrew hugged her.

"I have to tell you, Emma," Andrew said, "tonight's meal was the best I've enjoyed since the last time I was on this boat."

"Thank you."

No sound from the captain. Silence fell, and not the kind to relax or settle into, but the awkward sound of silence. The pilothouse felt thick with secrets this night. She wondered how to shake them to the surface.

The doctor smiled apologetically.

"I'm sorry, am I interrupting something?" Emma asked.

"Not at all," Andrew answered. "The captain just told me about the plans for this trip. I was eager to hear what other excitement I can look forward to after the incredible performance tonight!" A worn expression settled across his face. "You are right though. I am exhausted and about to retire. Good night to both of you."

"Good night, Andrew," the captain replied, his tone heavy with meaning, although of what, Emma had no idea. She hoped to soon find out.

She waited until the doctor climbed down the steps before she sat on the lazy bench. She watched the captain's profile.

Briggs glanced sideways at her. "Finished with work, can't sleep, or simply wanted to come up and say hello?"

"All of the above."

He looked ahead again. She took the opportunity to give him the once-over. Was it her imagination, or did he seem pale, his shoulders slumped more than usual?

She decided on using a direct approach. "Why is Andrew here on the boat?"

"I invited him. I thought he might enjoy the trip."

She stood and came to his side. "I'll admit, you can be a fair liar. But you aren't telling me the truth. At the very least, you are keeping something from me."

"What makes you think such a thing?"

She softened her voice. "Will. I'm worried about you."

"Have I given you any cause for concern? Other than inviting an old friend onboard for the last trip of the season?"

"You've been a bit tired lately."

He chuckled. "Well, I am getting older."

"Not so old. And next Andrew shows up, unexpected to everyone but you. If there isn't a reason, what is it?"

"Ah, the type of logic only spoken by a woman."

"You won't get an indignant sputter out of me. Nor will you distract me."

"Hmmm. Statements like that used to work." Briggs sighed. "Emma, if I invited Andrew here for a specific reason, isn't it my business? Can't you afford me some privacy?"

"I'm so damned sick of everyone needing their 'privacy' I could scream."

He turned to her, perplexed. "That's quite an interesting comment."

"Oh, Sarah and her test. She insists she can handle her disappointment, but her dreams are crushed. She refuses to share any of her feelings with me in the name of 'privacy.' Now you call in Andrew. If it's simply for the fun of it, why the last minute? Why didn't anyone else know?" She softened her voice. "He's a doctor, Will."

"And a longtime friend. And Sarah, well, this trip is at the end of season and she'll have to pilot throughout the summer the way she always has, with myself or Jeremy with her at the wheel."

"She insists she's giving up."

"Surely you don't believe her. That doesn't sound like our Sarah." He scowled thoughtfully. "Emma, has she revealed any details of what happened that morning?"

"I tried to speak with her, but she invoked her declaration of privacy. I've never seen her like this. She's upset and mad and sad all at once. I don't think she knows how to feel about the entire situation. She swears she's going to walk away."

She watched him digest that. It didn't seem to surprise him. "I think there's more to this business than what's on the surface," he finally said.

"Has she talked to you at all? About the test? About quitting?"

"Not specifically, no. In fact, she's avoided speaking to me about any of it."

"Honestly?" Emma pushed. "Don't keep something from me because you're afraid it might upset me."

He threw her a look of complete innocence. "What do you mean by that?"

"For starters, Andrew onboard."

He scowled. "Emma, I told you—nothing else to it."

"Quentin and his drinking problem."

"And that was ages ago."

"I know, but my point is, you tend to try and protect me. I don't need it."

He chuckled. "Oh, yes, the indomitable, unstoppable Emma. I've met her." He sighed, obviously thinking something over. "You know, every now and again I see him. Quentin."

"What do you mean?"

"Oh, I'll see movement out of the corner of my eye, and I'll think it's him. Then I remember he's gone."

A chill quivered through her. "I have the same experiences sometimes."

"I suppose it's only natural. This boat was him. He became so involved with the plans and details, and insisted on the best materials for the *Spirit*. Oak for the staircase. Beveled glass for the stateroom doors. Mahogany bar. Every piece in this boat reminds me of him, pulses with his personality. I feel he's with us on every trip."

"He loved this boat." Her voice softened. "He loved you."

"He was my dearest friend and companion. For years. I never succeeded in hiding anything from him; he knew me better than anyone ever has, perhaps even better than me, I suppose. When I was so angry at Gage, he made me face the true reason. Mr. Gage was smarter than me, better than me, at least as far as engineering went. Drove me almost to madness."

"So, talk to me." She touched his arm. "You still have a good friend aboard. You don't have to be alone. Tell me what you don't want to admit to yourself."

Briggs' eyes widened, honesty smoothing his features. Then his face hardened. "I asked Andrew to come so I could enjoy his company for our last trip."

Last trip.

She fought against dread filling her, yet it did. And Briggs' words chilled her. She dropped her hand and looked out at the river. Nothing but inky black. The night a heavy blanket all around them. Over them. And she found it getting harder to breathe.

Chapter 11

Jeremy faced Oscar Gévaudan, if that's what his name was. This man was a fake, through and through. If he was French, why did he talk with a put-on English accent? Jeremy guessed that was fake, too. Like every aspect of this ridiculous person standing before him.

"Well, what next, my good man? Fisticuffs?" Gévaudan asked.

Jeremy clenched his fists, wanting to wipe the smirk from his face. He'd seen men like this; they were everywhere. Words and moves calculated for show. Preying on the needs of those weak and needing. Only this man wasn't slippery like an elixir salesman. He glittered like a bright, shiny present under a Christmas tree. All the wrappings enticed, especially for a woman who just lived through the worst disappointment of her life. Sarah didn't need this fraud leading her down a false trail.

Plus, Jeremy admitted to himself, something burned in him, something hot and sour. He didn't like the feeling one bit.

"You can drop your fancy accent and big words. I recognize you for what you are."

"And what, exactly, might that be?"

"A flim-flam man. I've seen your kind before, selling goods not worth a damn. You'd rather play than build a real life, do a real job."

"Ah. Reality. Quite overrated." He smirked. "And you, I suppose, are a *real* man?"

"Closer than you'll ever be."

"This is actually quite fascinating. I'm at a standoff with a Cro-Magnon about to tear my head off, my only crime to enjoy the company of a lovely and, I might add, willing woman."

Jeremy had no idea what a Cro-whatever was, and he didn't care. He wanted this jackass to stay away from Sarah and not hurt her. And, if he were honest with himself, he didn't want Gévaudan around for personal reasons. Very personal.

"Stay away from Sarah. She's a decent woman, something I know you aren't used to. I mean it. Keep away from her."

Oscar answered with his everything-amuses-me grin, then looked beyond Jeremy and his smile grew wider.

"Why, gentlemen, forgive me," Henrietta said, sweeping past Jeremy as she headed for Gévaudan, her gloved hand outstretched. He took it, bowed slightly, and kissed it.

"Lovely Henrietta! What on earth are you doing about at this hour?" Gévaudan straightened, a smug gleam in his eye.

"I can't sleep, and you are to blame, Mr. Gévaudan."

"Now, how is it I've disrupted you? And, please, call me Oscar. When you use my formal name it cuts my heart out."

Jeremy struggled against laughing out loud. This man wasn't just flim-flam; he was a downright clown.

"All the excitement, Oscar," Henrietta answered and giggled. "Your magnificent troupe is more than I could have wished for!"

Gévaudan took her arm and wrapped it around his own. "Well then, some fresh air and a stroll on this moonlit night is precisely what you need." As they brushed past Jeremy, Gévaudan threw him a self-satisfied glance.

Jeremy didn't care. From what he could see, Henrietta Jeffries and Oscar Gévaudan more than deserved each other. He watched them until they were out of sight, Henrietta's laughter echoing down to nothing.

He took a deep breath, glad to be out of such company.

"It does not pay, the attempt to make Oscar angry."

Jeremy spun at the low, throaty voice.

"He does not get angry." A thin reed of a woman slipped from out of the shadows, her eyes almost blackened in with makeup. "All is joke for him."

She took a step closer, her raccoonlike gaze sliding up and down his entire body, appraising every inch. Suddenly, he felt . . . naked? When she came closer and looked up through her blackened lashes, need fisted low in his gut, taking him by surprise. Yet not a surprise. Everything about her promised forbidden, sensual delight.

Long legs, he saw from the scandalous slit up the side of her pale green dress. But that wasn't where his eyes lingered. The front of her skimpy, sleeveless top plunged practically to her waist. Thin fabric stretched over the important parts, not hiding much. He shut his eyes and opened them again. He wasn't hallucinating. She was still there. Unfortunately.

Or fortunately, the grip in his gut reminded him, then traveled lower. She definitely had the wherewithal to fix his needy state. He tried to shake the thought out of his head. Didn't work.

She came closer, and reminded him of Oscar's tiger. Her moves were fluid, graceful. A stalking hunter. "I see you here and there. Watch you. You are big man. Strong too, no?" Her voice chopped with some sort of accent. She moved closer. He swallowed, his throat suddenly dry.

"I am Zelda. You speak?"

He cleared his throat. "Sometimes."

She laughed and the sound shimmied up his spine. She smelled like some exotic spicy flower and, running beneath, a more animal scent. She smelled like sex.

"You must be with the theater group."

"I am." She touched his chest, ran her hand up his shoulder and down his arm. His muscle flexed in response and her eyes lit up. She lifted his hand, traced the calluses. "Mmmm. Hard hands."

And that did it. His hand and arm muscle weren't his only hard parts. This woman wasn't just interested; she was ready. Willing. He wanted to lift her off her feet and take her right here, against the wall.

No. No. No. No.

He'd never dallied with a passenger. No respectable pilot did such a thing. Briggs would be mortified if he found out.

She isn't a passenger, a voice said inside him. She was with the theater. A working girl, and her invitation wasn't lost on him.

"I have private cabin." Her eyes flicked to the path Oscar and Henrietta had just taken. "Must be now."

Now sounded awful good to him. She reached up on her toes and kissed him. He responded, pulling her against him, tasting her, lost in the feel of her. Oh, dear God, everything in him wanted her. Blood raced through him, hot and ready. She bit his lower lip and a prickle of pain shot through him. She nipped his jaw, his neck, and her hand reached down, stroking him.

Lust sizzled up his belly, and his legs trembled. He wanted to throw her to the deck and take her, right here and now. Whoever might see, be damned.

He grabbed her bottom and crushed her into him. She gasped out, made a sound almost like a purr, then lifted his hand to her breast. He felt her heat and the heartbeat beneath.

Then she pulled away, suddenly. He took a step back, disoriented, his breath ragged.

"Sixteen-A," she whispered. "Wait a few moments first. I leave door unlocked." She turned and walked up the steps. Languid. Fluid. He watched her round bottom sashay back and forth, back and forth like a pendulum—mesmerizing, hypnotizing—urging him to follow.

He thought he'd burst right out of his clothing.

He counted to one hundred and gripped the rail when he reached the bottom of the steps. One deck above, she waited. Sixteen-A. He swallowed.

Was he out of his mind? She was seducing him, obviously. Why? Because she liked big men. He wouldn't let her down.

Then he thought of Sarah. He closed his eyes. He wouldn't do this. Such a thing wasn't decent, respectable, or responsible. Briggs would be furious.

Briggs would never find out.

What was so wrong, anyway? She was willing. Wanting. Insisting, actually. Jeremy took the first step up. His body propelled him to follow her. He took the next step.

Waited. This wasn't right. This wasn't him. He was a pilot.

But he was a man. He took the next step. And the next.

Standing before 16A, he hesitated. No. Yes. No. Yes. He was more responsible than this. It had been longer than he wanted to admit. He needed this. He didn't know her, or who she was, or why she came on to him this blatantly.

Maybe she was lonely, too.

Sarah.

He shook his head. This woman wasn't what he wanted. She wasn't Sarah.

Not quite believing what he did next, he headed to his cabin. His cold, empty cabin.

Seems he was responsible after all. And decent. Chivalrous, even, not taking advantage of a lonely woman. Respectable.

"Just my luck," he said and swung the door open to face his empty room. Once he closed the door, he leaned back against it, waiting until his heart slowed. He thought he might have to jump in the river to even begin to cool down.

His thoughts slid to Sarah, in her cabin, alone too.

"What a damned shame." Only no one heard him.

Emma made her way back down to the Texas deck, and in front of their cabin, Gage bent over the rail, watching the inky black river rush by. She approached and touched his back. He straightened, his obsidian eyes holding no emotion, his face, stone. His expression, or lack of one, sliced through her.

"What are you doing up?" She hoped he'd cite work in engineering as the cause for wakefulness, but knew that wasn't his reason. Not with this look on his face.

"I can't sleep. I thought I'd watch the river for a bit."

"Gage, I'm sorry I'm so late. I needed to speak with the captain."

"About?" he asked.

"I wondered why Briggs asked Dr. Brinkstone to join us, but he insists the invitation was issued for Andrew's entertainment only. And I don't believe him."

"I have noticed he's slowin' down, especially the last month or so." Squinting, he searched her face. "What else?"

This man could read her like a schematic. She loved that he knew her so completely, but, sometimes, his devotion could be terribly inconvenient.

"I also wanted to speak with him about Sarah, her giving up over the test. Briggs is a pilot, the one who taught her. He knows what this failure means to her."

Gage nodded and went back to watching the river. "He pry gave you some insight."

"Not really. He's as perplexed about the entire affair as I am."

Every line in Gage's face, every muscle in his body seemed poised for action. She felt energy radiating off him, as if he were prepared for some sort of attack.

"What is it?" she asked. "Pleasant Grove?"

"I feel a noose around my neck every time we pass by." His voice skimmed over the sound of rushing water. She put an arm around him and got as close as she could. This town, the place Gage had almost been hung, the mayor and townsfolk unjustly accusing him of killing one of Jared's victims.

"You didn't die," she said, more of a prayer of thanks than a fact.

"Not for lack of their tryin'. You know, every time we pass here I feel . . . I don't know . . . like I split and part of me went on into a time where I was hanged. Where I faced my end." He swallowed. "I suppose I sound a mite crazy."

"Not at all." She was used to his intuitions, his glimpses into what seemed like other worlds. "But, Gage, it didn't happen in this time."

"And the *Ironwood*." He furrowed his brow. "Blowin' up in front of our very eyes. Any time we travel this part of the river, I hear those cries, smell the burnin'."

September was not only the anniversary of Jared's murderous spree, but also when, ten years ago, a boat racing the *Spirit* blew up, thanks to the ambitious greed of the man in charge of the boat, Captain Yoder. In his obsession to beat Briggs, he'd risked all the men, women, and children onboard the *Ironwood*. He'd lost the bet, and people paid with their lives. A shudder ran through Emma at the memory, the horror of the grand boat exploding and becoming a funeral pyre for so many. The *Spirit* took on the survivors, and it had been one of the grimmest few days of Emma's life. Of all their lives.

"I feel all the lost souls, Emma, every one of them. Look." He pointed to a wisp of white skimming the water. It formed, disappeared. Another materialized. And another.

She'd seen this a rare time or two before. "Briggs says it's a natural phenomenon, river mist," Emma whispered. The shreds darted along the surface, intertwining, twirling. More and more formed and joined in.

"That's what you think they are?"

She trembled and he pulled her close.

"This few miles of the river feels sacred," he said, his voice hushed. "The place where their souls still dance. Their bodies died out on the river in the middle of nowhere and they came home, to Pleasant Grove. Where the *Ironwood* was built. Where her memories live."

Emma settled closer and watched the dance of souls. And prayed they might find some peace, whoever they might be.

We disapprove of smiling when it is a contrived act. Yet falsehood becomes so natural to Us. Our second nature. The Offspring has an easy, charming persona.

We wear the Offspring like a mask. Finally, some use comes from the child.

Our mask can enjoy the parties, people, good food, and ever-flowing Devil's Piss. We would take count of these sins, but there is no need. It will all end in one, glorious moment.

Captain Briggham leads this unholy revelry. He struts about as a cock in a barnyard, impressed with his own arrogance. We would take him down first, but then he won't know, won't see what is to come. We want to experience the moment with him, feel his disbelief, his helplessness, his impotence. We yearn to enjoy when realization comes, see it in his eyes, want him to know it is the end of everything he has built in his lifetime. For this is more important to him than his life. We want him to know We have brought him ruination.

And when We reveal Ourselves, he will.

Until then We smile, bide Our time, and appear as one of them. We walk among them and proceed with Our plans. They do not suspect, so We do this with ease.

We have come into being, not the Offspring and not the Father. We are something far greater and more adept. Something with absolute power over the lives of those so small; they appear as bugs to Us, inconsequential and nothing more, really, than an infestation.

So easily exterminated.

They laugh and dance and drink and make love. They argue and fight and struggle for attention. They eat and tire and sleep and wake.

Soon, all this will be lost. They have no idea of what is about to happen.

However, We like to be fair. We will give them another hint of that which is to come.

Chapter 12

Piles of napkins, shreds of napkins whirled around him. They refused to let him rest.

His monstrous headache wasn't helping the situation any. Toby put the back of his hand to his forehead. What was he, an idiot? Last night. Why did he agree to the first drink with Charley? Or the next? Or the next?

Between Charley and him trying to work up nerve to approach the theater girls, they'd killed off the better part of a bottle of scotch. Now Charley snored on the opposite bunk. Alone. Either they'd struck out with the girls or they hadn't tried. Toby suspected the latter, yet he didn't remember. Anything. He wondered if he'd done something reprehensible, like shred poor, defenseless napkins. The burn in his chest mocked his concern.

He sat up in bed, in his clothes. His stomach lurched. He swung his legs over the bunk, shoes still on his feet. Pathetic.

He'd wanted the drink to help him find the courage to talk to the girl of his dreams, but he knew he had a deeper reason. Jared had hated drink, and Uncle Quentin had loved it. Flawed though the logic was, every gulp of scotch made Toby feel like he chose Uncle Quentin over his father.

Then there was the matter of shutting down that stupid, taunting voice last night, and the scotch did the trick. After his second glass, he didn't hear a whisper from Jared; he even forgot dear Father and his never-ending chest simmer.

Problem was, he'd soon forgotten everything else as well.

He crept out of his room and closed the door as softly as he could, considering the floor moved. A night of scotch and bobbing boat—not a good mix. He gulped in heavy, humid, cool river air. At least that felt better.

So he'd lost a few hours again. He thought. Wasn't sure. His stomach rolled and a chill trembled through him. The napkins. Cripes, if the napkin massacre was the result of his first blackout, what did he do last night? How did he get to bed? Did he stay there? Had he only slept or might there be something hideous to face this morning?

He made his way to the dining pantry in the early morning dark, hoping to find the napkins intact. Flinging open the door seemed like a good idea until it banged against the wall, cracking like a shot. He grabbed his aching head. No one came. The last vestiges of moonlight spilled in through the small window, transforming everything to shades of black. Criminy, it was too dark to see anything.

As he opened the linen closet, he reached in. Felt material. Squares of material. Relief surged through him. The napkins survived his second drunk blackout. Then dread hit. Was anything else in mortal danger? Silverware? Goblets?

This time, he shut the door with great care. Following the sound of rushing water, he made his way down to the paddle wheel. The mist from it wafted around him, cool on his face.

The burn inside reminded him he wasn't truly alone, and he spread his hand over his chest. Why wouldn't this damned parasite leave him alone?

"'Mornin', dear Father," he whispered. "How 'bout we strike a deal? You keep inside for the remainder of this trip, and I'll let you shred all the napkins you want once we're home. If you're a good boy, maybe even an apron or two."

The burn pulsed.

"And a tablecloth?

Pulse.

"I bet I'm the only sap in history to be afraid of napkins," he said. As the shadows of landscape slipped by, he wondered what part of the river they were traveling.

"Runt?"

He turned. "Do you start every day at predawn out here?"

Sarah sighed. "Seems like it. So, you're afraid of napkins? The shredded ones?"

"Oh, you heard that."

She nodded. "What is it, Toby?"

He returned to watching the paddle wheel, mostly to escape her penetrating look.

"Why do they bother you so much? You can trust me." Her voice, gentle and empathetic. She never shied away from his problems, the dark hidden inside him. His rotten soul didn't ever seem to scare her, or cause her to back away.

Tell her about the napkins.

Cripes, he was tired of being afraid, wondering what he'd do next.

"Okay, fine. You want to hear what kind of crazy brother you have?" He didn't face her. Instead, he continued to watch the wheel rotate, water drops misting into a shimmering veil. "I lost a few hours last night. And it wasn't the first time."

Silence. Then, "I don't understand."

"Two days ago, I took a bottle of whiskey with me to the cliff. I'm not sure how much I drank." He spoke slowly and carefully, trying to piece it all together. "It didn't hit me until I came back to the boat.

Before I got to the dining room."

"Oh, Toby." The warmth of her hand touched his back in support, as if she could transfer her strength to him. Her touch encouraged him to go on.

"Charley said he poured hot, black coffee down me and drug me into the head for a cold shower. He left me in our quarters to sleep, but I finally came around." He faced her. "Thing is, I don't remember the hours between the cliff and when I dressed for the dining room."

"Where did you get a bottle of whiskey?"

"Where do you think? I serve behind the bar. I'm not above stealing, you see. Easy enough to slip one in my coat. But, Sarah, don't you understand? Those napkins."

"Are you telling me you shredded them?" Sarah asked. "Why? To get back at Henrietta?"

He threw his hands up, exasperated. "You know, Sis, for such a smart girl you can be really thick when you choose to be." He opened his hands, palms up. "I don't know if I wrecked those napkins or not. I can't remember."

"You won't convince me you destroyed anything on this boat. Such a thing simply isn't in your nature."

"And that's not the end of it," he confessed. "I lost a few hours last night. I have no idea what I did. I can't remember."

He watched her face as she tried to come to grips with the implications.

"I drank last night," he confessed. "Scotch this time."

The color drained out of her face. "Oh, Toby."

Hopelessness bubbled up inside. "I lost time. Hours. God only knows what I might have done. I'm terrified for when everyone wakes up and we figure it out. What if it wasn't just napkins? What if . . . ?" He swiped his hand down his face, rubbed his cheek. "What am I going to do?"

Sarah grabbed his hand and held it. "You are going to do what you do every day. You put on your waiter coat and you work. Work will help you through anything. It's the one thing Mom taught us, and

Gage, too."

He grimaced. "You know I hate work."

"Don't try to distract me. This isn't funny."

"Yeah, I know."

"My guess is nothing happened. If something did, we'll deal with it." She dropped his hand. "Be honest with me. Do you drink often?"

"Naw. The last two days were special."

She sighed. "Toby, please. Uncle Quentin was an alcoholic. It runs in our family."

"As do so many fine qualities." His gave her half a grin. "It's a miracle we are any sort of normal at all. Then again . . ."

She didn't smile in return.

"I guess I owe you a straight answer. No. I never have before the cliff." He looked out at the river and back to her. "The fact that I lost time, don't remember, scares the hell out of me." He stopped, and tried to give her a reassuring smile. "Don't worry, our new napkins are safe. They're the first thing I checked once I came around."

She nodded like she understood the inner workings of an insane man. She already gave him more than he deserved. What if he was deranged? Dangerous? One thing he knew, he was scared.

"Well, no real damage done at any rate," she said softly.

"That we know of."

"The napkin stock recovered. We'll keep our eyes open to see if anything else seems amiss. Toby, promise me you won't drink again."

"Of course I won't. Learned my lesson," he said, trying to give her the one thing he might be able to on this rotten morning. She trusted him, loved him, didn't judge or disapprove. He owed her more than he could ever repay.

"There, then we'll be fine." She squeezed his arm. "I promise."

Tired of the constant weight of his life, he decided there was only one thing for him to do. Set the day back as close to normal as possible.

At least for her.

"I'm sure glad the wedding party is going onshore, considering how terrible I feel. I'm off duty for a few hours. Think I'll spend the morning throwing up."

"That ought to be enough to keep you from drinking."

"I feel pretty awful. I want to go back to bed."

"Well, I'm not so lucky. In fact," she said, nodding to the pilothouse, "I have to go check on timing. I'll be the one leading the revelers off the boat."

"I figured the grandmaster with the tiger would do that. You know, have some magnificent extravaganza planned."

Sarah's eyes lit up, and he was glad to see it. Even his levelheaded sister was caught up in *Le Théatre d'Illusion*.

"You're right," she said, "it's probably more appropriate for me to bring up the rear. I suppose I should talk to Oscar and see what he needs."

"Oscar?"

"The grandmaster with the tiger, as you so charmingly put it. I was on my way to go over the details of today's plan when I saw you back here. I'm sure Mom has a schedule and duty list, and I need to find out who should be where, and when."

"Why don't you just go along and have fun?"

"I enjoy excitement as well as the next person, but I'm the purser. I'm supposed to make sure everything goes as planned, find problems before they happen. How can I do my job if I have no idea what's going on?"

"Is that a real question, or rhetorical?"

She smacked his arm. "Runt, you are such an idiot."

"Yeah, I know." The playfulness usually shared between them felt strained, at least on his part. He wanted to be sure she understood his warning. "Sarah, you are taking me seriously, aren't you? I mean, I know it's hard sometimes, but the hours I can't remember, the wrecked napkins—"

"Toby, they are only napkins. You've promised no more drinking and I trust you. No harm done. See you later. I've got to catch up with the goings-on around here."

He watched her leave.

No harm done.

"Somebody better explain that to the poor napkins."

Jeremy Smith stood at the wheel. Again. The man was becoming a pilothouse fixture. It should be Captain Briggham's watch. Sarah stopped her climb and gripped the stair railing. One thing she didn't like: surprises. She'd had enough for today, and most of the boat wasn't even awake yet.

She didn't want to hear what happened last night after she left Oscar and Jeremy. They'd been like two dogs squaring off over a piece of meat. Jeremy a mastiff and Oscar a poodle. Her lips twitched at the thought as she quietly reversed her climb up the steps.

Jeremy glanced over his shoulder. Saw her. Marvelous. If she didn't go into the pilothouse it would look like she was trying to avoid him.

"Never let it be said Sarah Perkins runs," she said to herself, reversing direction yet again. She finished her climb and swung the door open. "I thought this was the captain's shift."

Jeremy faced her, one hand on the wheel. "Good morning to you, too."

"I'm sorry. Good morning. Now, where is Briggs?"

"I had a nice talk with your boyfriend last night."

"Who?" she asked, all innocence. She actually didn't mind him sounding a bit jealous.

"That silly clown in charge of the circus."

"Oh, Oscar? He's just a friend. And it's a theater, not a circus." She smiled to herself. The memory of Oscar's kiss tingled through her and her cheeks heated up.

Hurt registered on Jeremy's face; then it snapped away. He went back to annoyed and whipped around to look out at the river. She noticed the muscles tense in his arms as his hands gripped the wheel.

"Last night Briggs seemed pretty tired when I took over," Jeremy said without looking at her. "He mentioned he wanted me to cover for him while he breakfasted with Andrew this morning. I told him I'd pull a double to let him sleep in. My bet's on him coming down pretty soon to relieve me." His voice was clipped, all business.

"That's odd," she said. "The captain usually never misses a moment of his shift."

"This has been a long season for him. I think this whole wedding extravaganza and Lionel Jeffries have worn him out," Jeremy admitted.

"I didn't know such a thing was possible. Although you're right, I think. I haven't seen him up here very often this trip. You must be pulling quite a few double shifts."

"He's getting older, Sarah. He doesn't want to slow down and is fighting against it. He's going to have to if he wants to keep up any kind of schedule."

The full meaning of his words hit her. Briggs needed a third pilot, and now, not next year. She'd let him down. Her knees gave out and she sat on the bench, the weight of her failed test refusing to lift or even lighten.

"Don't do that," Jeremy said, his voice soft.

Her head snapped up. "What?"

"Blame yourself. Feel guilty." He shifted his eyes back from her to the river.

"He needed me up and running by now. He needs a third pilot."

"I'm willing to carry the hours he can't. He sure as hell's done enough for me." He paused, brow furrowing with gathered thoughts. "We'll be fine until next year. Just make sure you get to your test on time."

"There isn't going to be a next year."

He jerked his head around to stare at her, almost through her, and

heat radiated until it reached her cheeks. He returned his attention ahead, to the river. "Then you need to tell the captain and make it clear beyond any doubt."

"I knew it. You want me to give up."

"God, Sarah," he sputtered, losing the aloof quality in his voice, "you are the most exasperating woman."

"Admit it. You don't think a woman belongs in the pilothouse."

"It doesn't matter what I think." He shook his head. "The captain has a load of faith in you. Either prove him right or get out of our way."

Anger flashed. "Could you repeat that? Did you honestly say, 'Get out of our way'? I can't imagine I heard correctly."

"Look, you have a duty to the *Spirit,* and if you aren't willing or able to fulfill it, you need to be honest and let the captain know. Don't make him wait another year if you aren't going to even manage to show up to your test on time."

A roar started in her ears. She stood. "Damn it, Jeremy, you don't have the right to talk to me like this. You have no idea what happened."

"No, I don't, because you didn't bother to tell us the truth. The board might have allowed you to take your test if you'd been honest."

"Let me tell you something about honesty. You and your precious board scheduled my test for September 18 on purpose. And it worked. Bravo for you! Your little clique didn't deserve any explanation after setting me up."

"That is absolutely not true. I didn't even remember the anniversary until Briggs reminded me. Stop trying to put your failure on someone else's shoulders. It's obvious you don't take piloting seriously. It's just some way for you to prove something to everyone. You like honesty so much, here's some for you. Your personal agenda is not fair to the captain, or me, or to anyone onboard the *Spirit*."

Anger pulsed down her arms and she clenched her hands until her fingernails dug into her palms. "You wouldn't know the truth if it hit you over the head." She headed for the door before she did something she'd regret.

With one hand still on the pilot wheel, he grabbed her. "Sarah, wait—"

She stomped on his foot.

"Yeow!" he howled, but she got the desired effect. He let her go.

"That will teach you to manhandle me, you ape!"

She turned and ran right into Captain Briggham.

Chapter 13

Charley plopped a towel-covered bowl on the bar. "Heap of sugared lemons, fresh from the galley."

"Thanks. We'd have a riot on our hands if we didn't have these. Passengers go crazy for them. You didn't sneak any, did you?" Toby asked.

"You serious? Even with the sugar, them things make my lips pucker."

"Hey, Charley?" Toby tried to make his voice sound natural. "You sure all we did last night was fall asleep?" He dried and polished bar glasses to a high sheen while they talked.

"Believe me, if we'd got together with them gals, I'd be the first to refresh your memory. We didn't even try to find 'em. You really don't remember?" Charley grabbed a towel and polished silver, starting with the tables nearest to Toby.

"I remember nothing past my second glass of scotch. You sure I didn't get out of bed?"

"I was as passed out as you. Why are you wonderin', anyway?"

"It's weird, knowing I walked around when I don't remember any of it."

"I wouldn't exactly call what you were doin' *walkin'*." Charlie grinned. The smile vanished when he looked at Toby's face. "Don't worry, you ain't used to gettin' drunk, is all. Trust me, there'll be plenty of times you won't want to remember nothin', but you will."

"Not for me. I've had my last drink." He finished the last glass and folded the towel.

"Yeah, right. Hey, you gonna fold up them purty birdies again?" Charley asked, nodding at the bar rag Toby folded.

"Ha ha."

Charley picked up a knife and admired his reflection before he polished it.

"While you're at it, you might want to check your teeth," Toby added.

"Hey, how 'bout them lily flowers you make? Put 'em in the wineglasses." Charley looked up from polishing silverware to bat his eyelashes. "The ladies like those."

"Why don't I take you out back and pound your face in?"

"Like to see you try. 'Course, anythin' on this mug would be an improvement."

"Oh, please." Toby grinned. "Your face causes girls to swoon and you know it."

"A little roughin' up will make me more manly. I'm in need of a young lady to fall in love with me soon. I'm goin' through a dry spell worser than the drought of '03."

The dining room doors flew open, and Lilly entered with a silver tray laden with covered plates, a silver mountain range. "Hey, Tobias, give me some help!"

Already around the bar, he hurried over to take the tray from her hands. "Cripes, Lil, this is heavy."

"Goes into 16A. Standin' order. Breakfast. You need to add a Tom Collins."

Toby carefully lowered the tray to sit at the end of the bar and began mixing the drink. He grabbed the gin, but was light with the shot. Just the thought of a drink made him feel nauseous.

"Hey," Charley said, "you ought to take a sip. Might make you feel better."

Toby didn't think it possible, but his stomach churned with more vehemence. He swallowed nausea back and added lemon juice, a shot of soda, and not to forget the garnish, a sugared lemon. He wedged the drink on the only clear spot on the silver tray. "You want to take it?" Toby asked Charley.

His friend's eyes widened and he shook his head. "Nope, 16A is a theater room, and they's jest about the lousiest tippers we've had. This one is all yours."

Toby hiked the tray on his shoulder headed for 16A—the short way. Every cabin on the boat had entry to the outside deck, with a portal in the wall for passengers to watch the landscape going by if they desired. Each first-class cabin also had a door on this side, opening to the stateroom for easy access. Mostly folks stayed away from using those entrances, probably because the entire room could be seen inside. Not very private.

He wondered what theater person rated a first-class cabin. Most of the players were in the general bunking rooms. Hoping he wouldn't be met by a tiger, he managed to shift the tray to one hand and rap on the door. No sound. Good. At least no tiger. He rapped again.

"Is unlocked." A woman's voice. Low. Throaty. Cripes. He glanced back at Charley, who'd scooted to the other end of the room and busied himself polishing silver on one of the far tables.

Toby swung the door open and the smell of perfume mixed with cigarette smoke hit him. Color draped everywhere: shawls, scarves, material of every hue and tone. Cleopatra's decapitated head stared at him though empty eyes.

He almost dropped the tray, then realized what he saw was a mannequin head on the dresser. Gems sparkled everywhere. Ropes of beads draped the mirror and hung from clothing hooks, giving the impression the room contained a jeweled web. And very fittingly, a spider-woman reclined on the bed.

Both frightening and enticing, she wore a kimono, revealing more of her white legs than was proper. Smooth, alabaster knees rose through the lake of embroidered material. Toby tried not to look. Too late. His cheeks heated up as he focused on her face. She wore heavy eye makeup and sucked on a cigarette through one of those long holders. Wisps of white smoke seeped from her lips and nostrils, floating in the air surrounding her.

"Come in, young man. I not bite."

He gulped and entered, tray first, careful not to trip over the threshold. Setting the silver mountain range on the end of the bed, he noticed the woman was around his mother's age. The makeup creased in her face, making flaws stand out instead of hiding them.

"Hand me drink, please."

She spoke with some sort of foreign accent. Russian? At least she was polite. Toby did as the lady required. "Is this okay for the tray? There's no room on the dresser."

The woman laughed, a deep, satin sound. "Is fine. Cleopatra takes over room, no?"

The delight of recognition lit through him. "Hey, you're the Egyptian woman all those guys carried aboard, aren't you?"

"I am." She reached out her free hand. "Zelda Vashnikoff."

"Oh, that explains your accent. You aren't Egyptian. Russian?"

She answered with a laugh. "And you are? Other than charming and naïve?"

Toby took her hand and, not knowing what else to do, shook it. "Just a waiter."

"No 'just' about you, young man." She looked at him like he was a course on the tray. His collar seemed to close around his neck. "Oh," she continued, "you want tip, don't you?"

"No, thank you, ma'am." A jumble of feelings raced through him, from terror to curiosity to . . . a desire he didn't want to acknowledge. And he didn't want any of them making their way into action. He thought he'd better get the heck out. Now.

"Don't be *jejune*." She rose, gathering her kimono around her legs and walking to the dresser. Despite having a decent education, he wasn't sure what "jejune" meant. He didn't think it was anything good. He also didn't think it was Russian.

She held out a dollar. An enormous tip.

He'd have to step close to her to get it. He reached out, and she pulled the bill back. It rested against the V of skin rimmed by the plunging collar of her kimono.

"I told you, I not bite. Not first, anyway."

If his face got any hotter it might burn right off his head. He took half a step closer and plucked it from her fingers. She laughed when he backed up.

"Thank you, ma'am."

She took a sip of the Tom Collins. "Don't call me ma'am. Makes me feel old."

Toby shrugged. "Okay . . . uh . . . Zelda. Thank you."

She sipped her drink again. "Very good. You make?"

"Yes ma'am—whoops—sorry."

She laughed. If she'd wash the junk off her face, she'd actually be pretty. He returned a tight smile, wanting to get out before anything happened.

"You're cute," she said. "You bring me drinks anytime, Tobias."

Toby backed out of the room, closing the door behind him. Gulping, he whipped around, and Charley stared at him from the far end of the room.

"You were wrong," Toby called and held up the dollar bill. Tucking it in his pocket, he headed for the bar to organize and restock it. He stopped.

He'd never told Zelda his name. How did she know it? Sure, she might have heard someone call out to him, but she stayed in her room. Other than the parade, this was the first time he'd seen her.

Alarm bolted through him. Did he meet her last night and not remember? Had she been toying with him while knowing much more about him than she let on? He didn't know which was creepier: if he'd met her and didn't remember, or if, for whatever reason, she was watching him.

"Cripes." The heat around his collar crept up his neck.

That did it. He was never, ever, ever drinking again.

"I'm glad the two of you are in here together," Briggs said pleasantly, as if he hadn't walked in on the two of them arguing. Or, more to the point, Sarah's attempt to disable the only other pilot onboard.

"Good morning, sir." Jeremy grunted with some pain and returned his eyes to the river.

"I have something I need to discuss with both of you." The captain gestured for Sarah to retake her seat on the lazy bench. Briggs worked himself around the wheel and faced the two of them so Jeremy could see him and the river ahead at the same time. "How's she running?" he asked Jeremy.

The pilot nodded. "Calm and sure. Just the way I like my boats. And my women." He shot a glance over to Sarah. In deference to the captain, Sarah demonstrated monumental control and let his comment pass. "But my foot is killing me," Jeremy added.

"You need to be more careful of where you stick it," she answered. Damn. So much for restraint. Simply wasn't one of her strong points.

"I need something, and I'm imagining it will bring resistance from both of you," the captain said. Sarah and Jeremy snapped their attention back to him. "Jeremy, I realized something at dinner last night. I'd like you to take more of a role in the social situations aboard the *Spirit*."

Jeremy's face registered surprise, then horror. "What?"

"We are an excursion boat. A large part of our function is the show we put on for passengers. And by 'we,' I'm including the working crew—roustabouts to pilots. I've rolled the idea around in my head for a while, and the theater troupe coming aboard solidified my thoughts. We are a show. And I'm not the only one who should be in the limelight."

"Briggs, please tell me this isn't going where I think it is." Jeremy gripped the wheel, his knuckles turning white. Sarah never saw him this uncomfortable. No, make that downright panicked. She tried to keep from smiling.

"Quite honestly, the social aspects of the *Spirit* are expanding, and I need some help. The time in the pilothouse is already split between us. I've decided we need to divide the social responsibilities as well."

Sarah watched as Jeremy's worst nightmare unfolded. Each word the captain spoke etched a deeper line of dismay on Jeremy's face. Couldn't happen to a nicer guy.

"Now, I don't plan to throw you into the current without helping you prepare." He looked pointedly at Sarah. "That's where you come in, my dear."

She dropped her amused grin. A shard of panic shot through her. "What do you mean?" She realized she had leapt to her feet and now stood ramrod straight.

Briggs smiled like he explained something to a small child. "I'd like Jeremy to take on the captain's table at the rehearsal dinner tomorrow night. He's going to need some coaching. And it goes without saying, help at the actual occasion."

She shook her head. Jeremy at least had the good grace to look as dismayed as she felt.

The captain continued. "You are the obvious choice to tutor him, and it does fall under your job description as purser of the *Spirit*."

Sarah and Jeremy both started talking at the same time.

"I wasn't aware there was a job description—"

"Briggs, you can't—"

The captain held up his hand. "Yes, well, I've decided to write up a few guidelines and I've been ruminating on various duties and positions. Emma is so very organized in running the social aspects of the *Spirit*. She's inspired me to clarify crew duties as well. One thing I am striving for is to bring more overlap and backup to each job. Including mine." He frowned. "I have no intention of arguing the point. The captain is a very important social position, and I need help. Jeremy, it's time for you to step up. Which falls in line with your duties and job functions."

"Sir, with all due respect, I'm a pilot. Not a, a . . ." His eyes darted back and forth as he searched for the word. Sarah jumped in to help.

"Lackey?" she offered.

He shot her a searing look. Briggs did as well. She clamped her mouth shut.

Briggs returned his attention to Jeremy. "Jeremy, this announcement brings you quite a bit of good news."

Sarah's stomach clenched. Now what?

"I'm promoting you to first officer starting immediately, and with your promotion comes a multitude of duties, not the least of which are the social ones."

Sarah went from shocked to stunned as silence fell. First officer? Jeremy Smith, First Officer? She tried not to let the despair of seeing her dream crumble reflect on her face.

"Captain," Jeremy managed.

Sarah's face warmed. She clenched her jaw. Tangled emotions overwhelmed her. She struggled not to let anything show. Honestly, she was glad for Jeremy. Really. At least, at some point she might be. Once the shock lifted, the disappointment of her crushed dream dissipated, she would be happy for him. He worked hard and deserved it.

No denying, she was also devastated. This promotion pointed up her failure even more. Especially since she dreamed about serving as Captain Briggham's first officer since coming onboard. She'd imagined herself in a uniform, greeting passengers not as purser, instead as the first officer of the *Spirit*.

A secret dream. A sacred dream.

A stupid, ridiculous dream.

And now, a dream she would never achieve.

She swallowed back tears before they formed. Crying would be wrong for so many reasons. Besides, no matter how insistent the damned tears might be, she never cried in front of anyone. Never. She wasn't about to start with this.

Briggs shook Jeremy's hand. "We'll discuss financial specifics later. I will announce your promotion prior to the dinner hour tomorrow. We'll all have a toast. It will be good to break through all this wedding celebration with such a happy and important announcement from the *Spirit*. Squelch any rumors of us shutting down operation, always a good move before the end of the season."

Sarah gulped back bitter disappointment. "Jeremy, congratulations." She held out her hand, and Jeremy, dazed, grabbed it. Squeezed it. Held on to it. His expression was almost laughable; he obviously wasn't sure whether to be thrilled or appalled. He'd settled for stunned.

"And, Sarah, beginning today you will log twice the hours up here in the pilothouse, whether with me or Jeremy. By this time next year I expect to have the *Spirit* able to run with or without me." He pushed away from the wall, standing straight. "Jeremy, I'll save you the duties of socializing at the picnic if you'd like to stay at the wheel."

"Yes, sir," Jeremy answered, his voice hushed as though lost in thought.

"I'll take her this evening," Briggs said. "Thank you for covering my shift this morning. Well, I'm sure you two have quite a great deal to discuss." Briggs took a few steps to the door of the pilothouse and turned to face them both. "Remember: rehearsal dinner tomorrow night. Announcement then. Congratulations, Jeremy. I expect no less than your best effort. You as well, Sarah."

Sarah waited until Briggs cleared the pilothouse, then realized she still held Jeremy's hand. She flung it from her. "This is awful."

"Thanks," Jeremy said.

She sighed. "I didn't mean your promotion."

His look drilled into her. "Well then," he finally said, "I agree. Only 'awful' isn't strong enough. I'd rather eat a bucket of nails than attend a formal dinner. By the way, my foot is throbbing."

"Good. Touch me again and I'll make sure the other matches."

Now a part of her, a very small, mean, and vindictive part, wished she'd broken his foot.

First Officer Jeremy Smith. Indeed.

Emma watched Briggs make his way down to her. She always enjoyed watching him; his decisive, sure movements exuded confidence and power. Instead of dashing down the steps to the lower deck, however, he descended more carefully than usual. Maybe it was her imagination or because she was looking for something.

"Well, I do believe I just solved your problems and mine," he said, obviously proud of himself.

"Really? Care to let me in on this miracle?"

"I seriously need to cut back on socializing. I'm getting way behind in my reading, and the newest H. G. Wells has just been published. Beginning today, Sarah is going to spend twice the time at the pilot wheel. And I promoted Jeremy to first officer."

"Briggs!" Emma blinked and took a step back in surprise.

"The promotion threw them both into a bit of shock. Oh, and I instructed Sarah to help Jeremy improve his social skills, which should prove to be quite a challenge, even for our Sarah. I'd pay money to watch her teaching young Jeremy which fork to use for dessert. That boy is like a son to me, but sharing a meal with him is rather like dining with a chimpanzee."

Emma laughed. "I doubt it's that bad."

"Worse. I've actually seen him lick his wrist to catch a dribble. I certainly can't let him loose on passengers as he is now."

"Oh, heavens."

Briggs nodded. "We have an image to maintain, every one of us."

"Other than her horror at teaching Jeremy table manners, did Sarah seem agreeable to more hours in the pilothouse?"

"She hardly noticed I threw it in. Those words might sink in later."

"Well, if anyone can keep her from giving up, it's you. She won't listen to me. She discounts any advice I give her," Emma said.

"Although I have no children of my own, I've noticed such is the way with parents and their offspring."

Emma smiled. "Thank you for everything. I don't know what I'd do without you."

"Well, you don't have to wonder. And besides, I did it for myself, really. I'm becoming quite a selfish old cuss."

Emma laughed out loud. "Looks like you are back in complete control."

"Just the way I like it," he said.

She appreciated the captain's continued friendship more than ever this morning. He helped her when she needed help, and never made her feel she was any sort of bother. She knew what a huge support he'd been to Quentin. And he did the same for her.

"Are you ready for the picnic? We land in about twenty minutes," he said.

"All set. We have seven roustys and nine waiters going out for setup when we land. Mr. Gévaudan has a marvelous show planned. The players will actually work around the passengers to make them feel they are part of the performance."

The captain's eyes lit up. "He's doing a version of *A Midsummer Night's Dream*, I hear. With songs."

"Which is supposed to be a secret."

"It is. But there are no secrets kept from the captain, you know."

She laughed. "Only too well."

"I can't wait to see it. Will you be joining us?"

"I have way too much to prepare here for dinner tonight." She saw his warning look. "Don't worry—very light fare after such a heavy midday meal."

"I'm not concerned about that." He stared out to the shore; then his eyes trained back to her. "Emma, you haven't been off the boat in a bit."

A small twinge of anxiety pinched low in her belly. She had way too much to do to consider a minute off the boat. "I've been onshore plenty of times. I went on several shopping trips before we left the city."

"Three times in a month isn't much."

She dropped her head, embarrassed that he'd noticed. "I wasn't aware you kept track. It's just, I have so much work to do . . ."

Gently he lifted her chin and she looked in his eyes. "He's gone, you know. Jared isn't out there."

She pulled away and crossed her arms protectively. Briggs reached out and kept her facing him. She didn't want to look in his eyes, didn't want him to see he was exactly right. Every time the boat landed, every time a crowd gathered, her skin prickled and she felt watched. Trapped. Hunted.

Dear God, would she ever be rid of Jared Perkins?

"There's nothing past the boat that can harm you," the captain said.

"That has nothing to do with why I'm on this boat so much," she lied. "In case you didn't notice, I work upward of sixty hours a week. I don't have time for frivolity."

"And I believe you bury yourself in your work so you don't have to

face what's out there. You don't have to feel or remember."

"You have no room to criticize. You're on this boat more than me."

"I'm not criticizing you, Emma. I wouldn't dream of it. However, I'm beginning to see the error in allowing work to take over everything. I wish I'd gone off on an adventure more often, spent more time enjoying myself. Less time working."

"How can you say that? Look at this business you've built."

"Yet I do wonder what I've missed."

She didn't know how to answer back. What to say. She thought about Andrew.

"Does this new attitude of yours have anything to do with Andrew's visit?"

Briggs laughed. "Only that he's a man who has discovered the finer points of enjoying himself, and I need to take some lessons." He sobered. "Seriously, Emma, work can wait." He took hold of her arms, but this time it was compassion, not insistence, holding her. "And you have done a remarkable job in recovering from Jared and putting a life together for you and Toby and Sarah. You don't have anything to prove—to me or anyone else."

She noticed his feet and realized her head was hanging. She snapped her eyes to his. "Briggs, I do declare, I'm shocked. Your shoes need to be polished."

His rich laughter boomed over her. "See, I told you I was falling behind."

"I've never seen you without every detail perfect." She lowered her voice. "I'll tell you what. I'll accompany you to the picnic if you polish your shoes."

He laughed again. "That's the best offer I've had in awhile. You have a deal." He squeezed her arms, then dropped his hands. "And speaking of falling behind, it's time for me to get back up to the pilothouse and give young Jeremy a break, now he's had some time to digest my announcement. The boy is another who'd work 'round the clock if we let him."

Zelda studied herself in the mirror and began to apply her makeup. Like this, wearing her wig cap and her stark, unaugmented face, she reminded herself of Evelyn, the unremarkable daughter of a farmer and wife of a riverman.

Not to worry; soon she would become Titania, Queen of the Woodland Glade.

She pulled on a golden cascade of curls, flowers intertwined throughout the mountain of locks. She couldn't wait to slip into the sparkling, slightly risqué dress. She loved being watched, men and women both examining her while trying to appear as though they weren't looking at all. Amazing what exotic trappings did for a woman as long as no one got too close.

She was aging, not a good thing for a woman who created her life from beauty and talent. She didn't want to play the mothers. Not even the witches of Macbeth. Or the absolute epitome of awful, being relegated to the chorus. All entertainment, highbrow or not, revolved around youthful beauty. A part like Titania was perfect. A woman still enticing, her beauty coming from both the physical and the wisdom of maturity. A woman who men and magical creatures alike wanted and loved.

"Well, at least that's the way Oscar sees the part." She knew as long as she kept Oscar happy, she would enjoy a starring place in his shows.

She hoped they never came aboard a riverboat again. This place was proving too much for her delicate constitution. And she wasn't able to work up any extra activity, which she found surprising. She imagined the boat to be crawling with bored, desperate men.

She'd try the groom next. They were always willing and panicked before the wedding.

She didn't like the boat. The floating shack reminded her of her deceased husband and the explosion that killed him. He'd burst into a ball of flame much more fiery than his passion had ever been.

A soft rap came from the outside door.

"Come in. I'm dressed."

The door softly opened and someone slipped inside. She saw him in the mirror's reflection as he approached. So, he'd come after all.

"Lock door," she said, in case Oscar might come to her, although this close to a performance he attended to many other matters. Still, it paid to be careful.

His eyes browsed over her, and the effect was good. He sharpened his focus and the air in the cabin thickened with his lust. Suddenly, the boat didn't seem so dismal. It had been decades since she entertained a riverman. They were, she recalled, rough around the edges. Hard hands. Focused, to the point, direct. Fast. Furious. No frivolities. A relief; she got more than enough flair from Oscar.

She looked forward to some plain, down and dirty passion. And these were the best sort of trysts. Nothing to worry about later. No inconvenient attachments.

She rose and spun around. "I wish you'd come earlier, I have little time—"

"All I need's a few minutes." He grabbed her with those big, hard, rough hands and planted his mouth on hers, hands sliding up and ripping her kimono apart.

"Take care . . . the wig . . ."

Heat seared through her and all thoughts of Titania burned away. He pushed her to her bed. Thoughts of age and beauty melted as his calloused hands explored, insisted. All that mattered was hard, unrelenting passion.

She had time for this. She always had time for this.

Chapter 14

Sarah glanced around. Although a few miles away from the spot where they'd land, the crew gathered to disembark. The plan Emma had developed reminded Sarah of a painstakingly choreographed dance. First, the band would begin playing, and the roustys and waiters would forge ahead and transform the plain grove into a marvel for dining. They'd carry picnic blankets, candles, a myriad of cheeses, fruit, finger sandwiches, chocolates, cakes, pies, wine, juices, and the passengers would even enjoy a wait staff.

Oscar wanted everyone settled in the grove before the performers left. He and the actors would lurk in the trees, remaining unseen until the show began.

Sarah figured she'd find Emma down here already in the middle of everything— orchestrating—but her mother was nowhere to be seen. Sarah had the duty rosters, lists, timing, plans. Making sure everything ran smoothly was her job, so she jumped to it.

"Waiters, over here," she called, and three white-jacketed young men joined her. "The roustys are off the boat first; you'll follow. Take as much as you can safely carry."

Some waiters grabbed bundles of checkered tablecloths; others took stacks of picnic baskets. A mountain of boxes and cases were heaped on the deck, all waiting to go ashore. From what Sarah estimated, three trips should do it. And three trips were timed and planned; Emma obviously thought every detail through, as usual. Sarah got a glimpse of her mother coming from the direction of the galley.

Briggs came to Sarah's side and nodded to Emma when she approached. "As you see, my shoes are shined."

Her mom's peach dress glistened in the sunlight. No sign of Emma's apron.

"Mom, you look beautiful. Are you coming, too?"

Emma granted Briggs and Sarah a wry smile. "Yes, I'm getting off the boat. Someone notify the papers."

Briggs leaned closer to Sarah. "As I told your mother earlier, she works too hard."

"Oh, and isn't that a fine statement coming from you?" Emma said.

"Mom, we have everything ready to go."

Oscar appeared at the top of the grand staircase, wearing a morning suit of light tan. His tiger, tight on her leash, led him down the staircase. "Just checking in. Everything on schedule?" he asked, coming off the bottom step.

"To the minute," Sarah answered. "You have a little under an hour before everyone is in place." She backed up. Daisy sat near her feet, seemingly content. Oscar looped her leash around his wrist.

"Perfect." He bowed his head. "Captain. Emma. I do hope you will enjoy our show. We have taken liberties with the Bard. But I think you'll be delighted."

"If it's anything like what we've seen, I have no doubt," the captain answered. "Sarah," he went on, "I think this is the perfect time to put our plan in motion. Why don't you go up to the pilothouse and bring us in?"

Emotions conflicted; she was grateful for the order, yet felt like a student again. She backed away from the group.

"Oh, and Sarah, after that perhaps begin your tutor session with Jeremy. Please feel free to use the office."

She resisted the urge to scream and, keeping her mouth shut, left before she said something she'd regret. She headed to the back of the boat, having to weave her way through passengers. When everyone came out to the decks, the boat was a packed affair.

She climbed the steps up and out of the crowd. On the hurricane deck, the incredibly eclectic troupe waited on the port side, out of sight from disembarking passengers. Sarah glimpsed everything, from faeries to a half-man-half-donkey dressed in a formal suit. She grinned, then saw a creature completely green and hardly dressed at all pad his way from the back of the boat. Barefoot, muscled, the sight of him caused her to take in a sharp breath.

The evil harlequin, as Sarah thought of him now. From his costume, he must be playing Robin Goodfellow, although she thought him terribly miscast. Nothing good about him. His entire body glistened with green paint, leaves covering pertinent parts. He stopped the moment he glimpsed her, his neck muscles flexing like a cobra about to strike. She gulped and continued her climb, chilled despite the sunny day.

When she topped the steps and saw Jeremy at the wheel, relief actually surged through her. Jeremy seemed so . . . normal.

"Briggs wants me to take her in," she said, swinging the door open.

Jeremy gave a curt nod and, without saying a word, moved back.

She stepped up to the wheel. Jeremy's heat radiated along her back as he stayed close behind her. She watched the river ahead, wanting to savor every moment behind the wheel. When Jeremy was this near, she found it difficult to think of anything but him.

"The lazy bench is empty."

"How do I know you are doing everything right if I just sit on the

bench?" His breath tickled her neck and she shivered. Damn. He was close enough he had to see his effect on her.

"Please, Jeremy, back away."

She sensed him move a step back, yet he still stood close behind her. At least she could breathe again.

He pointed ahead. "Right there, past the big willow."

"I know where the grove is. By all rights, I should be taking us in without you breathing down my neck."

He came around to the side and sat on the bench, crossed his arms. Slowly, he stretched out his long legs. "You're in a foul mood."

"And you're in an obnoxious one." She kept her eyes trained on the landing spot and pulled the slowing bell. And he kept his eyes on her. The engine's rumbles backed off by half.

"Don't get too comfortable," she said. "After we're docked, I'm supposed to start your lesson."

"Ha. Not a chance."

"You want me to report that to the captain?"

"I don't need any advice on table manners."

"Not from what I've seen."

He leaned forward. "Look, Sarah, seriously. I don't. I'm perfectly fine if I'm in a social situation. I don't like them, so I keep away."

She rang the gong again and the engines cut. She swung the wheel around, letting the back of the boat catch the current and do the rest of the work for her. The boat turned, and she thrust the gong lever. The engines came to life with a blast, and then cut off. They drifted to the bank, the roustys guiding the boat with their poles.

A gentle bump, and Skunk, along with two other roustys, hopped into the shallow water, ropes in hand. They began securing the boat. The captain moved passengers back as two men cranked the huge chain, swinging the stage across the front to the spot where it would serve as the bridge between boat and shore.

A gust of wind came up and pages from Emma's clipboard blew off, scooting across the deck. She ran to gather them under where the stage swung slowly over. The captain followed her, obviously none too happy that she stooped under a moving stage. Emma shook her head to whatever Briggs was saying, and he bent to help her gather the pages.

Oscar lifted his hand to his eyes to shield them from the sun and caught Sarah's glance. He waved, and she waved back. Jeremy shot off the bench and looked down. Then back to her, squinting with disgust. He stepped close, between her and the window. The expression on his face startled her. She expected to see arrogance. What he revealed couldn't be further from it. Vulnerability? Caution?

"I'll tell you what," she said.

He scowled, a bit too hard. "I can't wait to hear this."

"I'll lay out a place setting. If you can correctly name what utensils to use for what course, we'll consider the lesson accomplished. As long as you promise to follow my lead and not argue during the rehearsal dinner."

His forehead crinkled.

"I can't be any more fair, now, can I?"

"Fine. You go set up your tea party. I'll be there."

Beneath her feet, the boat rocked and a huge boom thundered. Sarah staggered, almost knocked off her feet. Jeremy engulfed her in his arms, shielding her with his body. That's when the roaring began. Deep, guttural, sharp-edged roaring, the sound of Satan himself. Screams rang out.

Her blood chilled as tiny bumps raised across her skin.

"The tiger!" Sarah choked out. More screaming.

Jeremy turned to look, shoving her behind him.

"Damn it, I can't see," she said, trying to work her way around him. "What's going on, Jeremy? What is it? What happened?"

Again the harsh, scraping roar cut through screams.

"Stay back!" he said.

She shoved to his side and saw the aftermath of what had happened.

Theater of Illusion

The stage lay, half on the boat, half off, the railing broken and deck boards warped and cracked beneath it. Right where her mother had been stooping and gathering papers. In two strides Jeremy reached the door. Sarah didn't see the tiger, but it roared again. Her blood curdled in her veins. She followed him to the door.

"Stay up here!" he commanded over his shoulder.

"Not a chance!"

"I said, stay up here!" He turned, and again she faced his massive chest. "The engines aren't completely disengaged; we need a pilot in the pilothouse," he said.

"My mom is down there. Was . . ."

"Goddamn it, Sarah, don't argue," he practically growled. "You are safe up here, and I need you to be on watch. I'm the first officer. This isn't a request; it's an order!" With that pronouncement, he headed down, shutting the door tightly behind him.

Duty eclipsed personal feelings. She had to stay.

She ran to the window, searching for her mother. Surely her mom got out of the way, it was minutes between her papers flying and the stage crashing, wasn't it? Damnation, all Sarah remembered was staring into Jeremy's chest.

Most people were out of sight, under the deck overhang, but she could hear them. Engineers and roustys were crawling around the stage. Good Lord, was someone beneath? And the tiger. Where was the tiger?

She searched frantically for Emma, but didn't see her anywhere.

Where was her mom? Oh, God, her mom.

She pressed the heels of her palms to her eyes and murmured a prayer. A big one.

One thing a person could always count on in a disaster was people acting one of three ways. The ones who jumped in and did what needed to be done, keeping their heads and acting to help everybody, bringing the situation under control. Briggs and Gage gathered engineers around to examine the fallen stage. Emma did her best to calm the crowd of passengers.

People you could count on, Jeremy knew.

Then there were those who, although nothing happened to them personally, acted like it had. That classification covered most of the passengers from what he could see, Henrietta Jeffries being the best example. Her father, Lionel, hugged his trembling, teary daughter to him, insisting everything was fine, while she kept crying out that the wedding would have to be delayed. Although that leap of logic, Jeremy wasn't quite following.

Then there was Oscar Gévaudan. And the tiger.

Oscar moved to the other side of the boat, and the tiger stood on all fours instead of her usual seated position. She looked about ready to spring. Oscar squatted next to her, kept petting her head and speaking soothingly to her, while he glanced around. Was that amusement lighting his eyes?

Amusement?

If Jeremy didn't have his hands full, he'd go over and punch the look right off Flim-Flam's annoying face. Probably a bad idea considering the tiger.

Andrew Brinkstone bolted down the front staircase, bag in hand. "Injuries?"

Briggs shook his head. "No."

"Thank God," Andrew said.

"I'd like you to take a look at my daughter," Jeffries called out. "She is overwrought."

Jeremy shook his head and joined the others examining the stage. Andrew had it right. Thank the good Lord no one had been in the way of the falling stage.

Briggs addressed the crowd of passengers. "Please, everyone, calm down. No injuries, thank heavens. This should only prove to be a minor delay. Return to your cabins or the stateroom; we'll round you up when it's time to disembark."

He approached the group around the stage and lowered his voice. "The stage seems to be in one piece."

Gage stood. "It is, although we'd better test it before we let any passengers go over it. Can't say the same for the deck, though."

"If we have rain, we might get into a problem."

Gage squinted thoughtfully. "We can seal 'er up while everyone is havin' lunch."

"We kin get the stage up and over without the pulley, Captain," Skunk said, and other roustys nodded. "We'll send Jeremy here over it first. If it'll hold him, it'll hold anyone."

A few roustys laughed and Jeremy smiled. A little humor made for a nice relief.

"We need somethin' to cordon it off," Gage added. "Make sure no one trips."

"All right then, we have our next steps. Mr. Gage, I want to know exactly what happened. I'll expect a full report. Complete with a plan to be sure this never happens again."

Gage's dark eyes were unreadable. "Yes, sir." He stooped and picked up the chain snaked across the deck. This close up, Jeremy thought it sure looked thick. Gage began inspecting each link, step by step heading for the pulley mechanism.

"Why the hell doesn't anyone leave?" Briggs asked under his breath.

"This is the most excitement these people have seen since the theater came onboard," Jeremy answered. "And everyone loves a disaster." Most of the passengers were still milling about, watching. But one— no, two—were gone. Flim-Flam and his tiger.

Emma walked through the crowd, talking, smiling, reassuring. Jeremy's tension dissipated until he looked back over at the stage and the wrecked deck. This situation might have easily been a disaster. Especially with a tiger around. Miraculously, the beast hadn't ripped off anyone's head.

He planned on suggesting to Briggs the tiger stay locked up next chance he got.

"Captain." Gage spoke low and evenly, but Jeremy whipped around at the urgency in his tone. As Briggs approached, Jeremy did, too. Gage stood. He'd been kneeling by the pulley mechanism housing the chain. He jerked his head, gesturing for them to step away from everyone to the far side of the deck.

"One of the links was notched. That's what broke the chain."

"Notched?" the captain asked. "How?"

Gage held two pieces out. They were twisted and Jeremy clearly saw where the pieces had broken apart.

"Look here, on this side."

Briggs and Jeremy moved in, Briggs squinting. Scrape marks marred the chain's surface.

"How did you even see that?" Jeremy asked.

"I was lookin' for it. No chance the chain broke on its own. I go over every inch of this boat startin' forty-eight hours before we pull out. Chain was fine then. This weren't no accident," Gage answered. "Someone did this on purpose."

The captain looked at Gage. "Are you sure?"

Gage nodded.

"What the hell?" the captain asked. "Sabotage?"

"No question," Gage said, "and just enough to weaken the chain. No way of tellin' exactly when the accident might occur, but most likely at some point when the stage swung into place or got hoisted back up."

"If it had fallen when the roustys were guiding it—"

"We'd have us some bad injuries. The way we do it is safe as can be," Gage said, "but not foolproof."

Well," the captain said, "it seems fools aren't our problem. Who might have the knowledge to do this?"

Gage scrunched his face in concentration. "Any engineer, someone with industrial experience. Farm experience. Anyone who worked on a boat."

"And that means just about anyone in the whole crew could be our culprit," Jeremy finished.

Gage studied the dissipating crowd. "A whole lot of passengers, too."

Briggs scowled in thought. "Why? What was the desired result?"

"Someone want someone dead?" Jeremy asked.

"No," the captain said, "nothing so specific. The result of this kind of interference is too general."

"Someone wanted to shake up this trip, anyway," Gage said.

"They've done more than that," Briggs said. "They've shaken up the captain. And they aren't going to much like the result. Because when I find out who did this, there'll be more than hell to pay." He crossed his arms. "They will have to face me."

She was going to kill him. That was all there was to it.

From below, cries and voices rose in confusion. Sarah tried to calm the growing hysteria in her, but the hum of panic expanded, finally reaching her hands. She grasped them together to keep them from trembling. The only thing she could do was stand by and watch. She hadn't felt so helpless since holding seven-year-old Toby while he cried himself to sleep in a strange bed, away from home.

Gage, Briggs, Jeremy, and roustys ran about. She didn't see her mom. Surely, if someone had been injured beneath the stage, they'd have called Andrew. Men gathered around the downed structure, examining it. Why didn't Jeremy come up and tell her something? How could he leave her up here, not knowing?

Surely her mother was fine. Surely. Surely.

She struggled to keep calm, but damn it, she should be down there! Panic and frustration mixed until it took over and burst from her. She ripped her hands apart and smacked a palm against the window pane, and the sting brought tears to her eyes. She backed away from the window before she did major damage.

Frustration and fear raged through her. Trapped. Powerless to help. Her mom. Her mom. She turned and slammed her fist on the desk. Where the hell was Jeremy? Where was her mother?

She opened her mouth and screamed from her gut, deep, primal frustration, and despair.

Jeremy opened the door. "That was attractive."

She spun around. "My mother! Where is my mother?"

"She's fine, Sarah; she wasn't anywhere near—"

"How dare you leave me up here! Where have you been?" She stalked over to him. "Why didn't you come up? I've just about worn the floor down—"

"Hey, your mother is fine; no one was hurt."

"—and you have to be the most irresponsible, thoughtless—" she stopped, wrapping her arms around herself. Her voice dropped, barely above a whisper. "My mom is okay. My mom is okay."

Jeremy gripped her arms. "Everyone is fine. The stage fell. No one was injured."

She fisted her hands, then stretched them out, dropping her head into them. God, no, not tears. Please, anything but tears. She hated them, hated showing such weakness. She couldn't help it. First terrified, now relieved, she just couldn't handle everything coursing through her. She dragged in a ragged breath. Trembles shook loose.

Jeremy's arms surrounded her. She gripped his shirt in her fists. A few tears leaked out, and she did her best to stop them. They dripped

down her cheeks. Damn it all, anyway.

"Everything is okay. Shhh . . ."

She pushed him away. "God, I hate this."

"Yeah, how dare you do such a reprehensible thing?" he asked, and smiled. Which caused another drop to run down her cheek. He wrapped his arms around her again, pulling her close. "There is absolutely nothing wrong with tears. You were scared for your mom. You're right, I should have come up here sooner. I'm sorry. Everything happened so fast."

She stood, stiff in his arms.

"Sarah, let me help you. Let go. Just for a moment. There's nothing wrong with leaning on someone. That's why our crew is strong. We help each other out. Just let me hold you."

She found it easy to let the strength in his arms take over for her. Allow her a few minutes. His warm embrace calmed her, stopped her shivering. His heart drummed in his chest, and hers followed suit, beat in rhythm with his. Why did he have to feel so damned good? At least her tears stopped; she'd only allowed a few to escape. Not so bad.

"There is no weakness in a woman's tears." Jeremy spoke in tones so soft she almost didn't recognize his voice. "Fact is, I've seen the strongest women I know cry. Your mother. My mom. Now you. Tears don't mean a woman is weak."

"When have you seen my mother cry?" she asked.

His voice rumbled in his chest. "When Quentin died. I remember she was almost inconsolable. But she didn't hide away. She went on, doing what she needed to, and, in my way of thinking she proved how strong and honest she was, to show her feelings for him like that. She wasn't ashamed or afraid of her emotion." He paused. "And my mom, after my pa died, she had her hands full trying to keep us from starving. She tried to figure out how to support all us kids without the benefit of a husband to help her."

She looked up into his face. "You don't talk about your mother very much."

"She used to cry at night. I'd hear her when I came home. She missed me, hated that I had to work and be away from the family. Especially since I was so young. I was her little boy and she wanted me home with her. Life didn't work out that way for us." No longing, no self-pity in his voice. Just fact.

Sarah slid her arms around his waist and hugged him, and this time, not for her benefit. For his. She thought about her own mother, leaving her and Toby behind at the farm. Perhaps it was her mother's best choice at the time.

"She doesn't shed many tears now that I'm a grown man," Jeremy continued. "She's mostly proud, I think." He chuckled. "Annoyed I haven't found a wife yet, settled down." His voice dropped. "Sarah, I realize how important a mother is. I'm sorry. I should have come up right away and told you Emma was fine."

"I admit I panicked," she said, stepping away from his warm embrace. "Thanks, Jeremy."

"Anytime."

"I should go down." She swiped her face with her hands.

He pulled out his kerchief and handed it to her. "Freshly laundered."

Laughter wobbled out, and she brushed away the remnants of her tears.

"You know," he said, "you aren't so bad when you act like a girl."

"And you aren't so bad when you aren't pontificating."

He shook his head. "I don't even know what that means."

"Lecturing. Acting like you do everything right. Telling me what I've done wrong."

"Me? I do that?"

She finished with his kerchief and folded it. "Sometimes. Okay, all the time."

He reached out to take the piece of cloth. She shook her head.

"Oh, come on now, you have to give it back."

"I'll wash it first."

"It holds something pretty rare." He snatched it from her hand. "Sarah Perkins' tears. I'd say this kerchief is worth its weight in gold. I'm gonna save it forever."

She laughed softly. "You're an idiot."

"Yeah, I've heard." He tucked the cloth in his back pocket. "Now this is the Sarah I'm used to seeing."

"I'd better get down there—"

"No, you stay up here," he said. "Briggs is planning to lift the stage manually and they need all the brawn they can get. I know you're a woman and can do anything and so on, but I'd be willing to bet my life I can lift more than you."

She couldn't come up with a suitable answer for that one.

"I'll come back up when we're finished. Briggs doesn't want to take the boilers down all the way; we aren't going to stay but a few hours."

"So the picnic is still on?" she asked.

"I guess it is. The captain wants to test the stage first. Looks like it will be fine; mostly the deck is damaged. And the rail is smashed."

"What happened? How did it fall?"

A strange look crossed Jeremy's face. "I don't think anyone is sure. Gage is checking everything out," he answered, not meeting her eyes.

"Jeremy, what aren't you telling me?"

His lips pressed into a thin line.

"Don't keep something from me—not now," Sarah said. "If I were down there, which I should be, I'd be privy to everything going on."

"True." He hesitated, then forged ahead. "I guess you'll find out soon enough. Keep it to yourself. Gage thinks someone tampered with the chain."

"What? On purpose?"

Jeremy nodded.

"That doesn't make any—" Thoughts whirled through her mind

and cut off her words. The implications of such a thing were horrendous. Someone onboard? Or before they'd left Sterling City? Was Gage sure? She had a thousand questions. Hopefully, she'd have a chance to barrage Gage and the captain with them later.

"I'll be back up soon as I can. You keep watch." He opened the door.

"Jeremy?"

He turned.

"Keep the kerchief between you and me."

He twisted his lips in an obvious attempt not to smile. "Oh, I'm going to require a little more motivation for that. We'll discuss it when I come back up." He stepped out. "And Sarah? I meant what I said. It's nice when you admit you have feelings and act like a girl."

She took off her shoe and pitched it at him, but it bounced on the door. He wore a grin. So did she. And damn, if she didn't feel better.

Now they know. We are here. We left a clue, a huge one. The first engineer is smart enough to figure it out. They talk amongst themselves in whispers and toss glances of concern. Soon those looks will be horror. Disbelief. And We will enjoy.

The pieces are in place. Our plans, started with the smallest shred of napkin, roll forward, gaining momentum. Like an avalanche, Our revenge will bury all. And while they struggle to understand, We will go about unremarkable and unnoticed and launch Our final offense, realize Our dream. The end of the Spirit.

This is simple: spreading panic and dismay. Almost too easy. Child's play. We grow stronger with each accomplishment.

She is next. The woman who promised to love, honor, obey, but then left Us. She will come into Our waiting arms. Her journey has come to an end. The whore in town was merely warm-up, practice, scales to the overture soon to begin and, next, crescendo into Our grand finale. We have decided the instrument to deliver her fate.

Our very hands.

Not for her the sickness that will soon envelop the others. Not for her a fast, fiery, cleansing explosion to leave her dead before she knows she is gone. No, she left Us once, so quickly We didn't realize until too late. And she was gone. She broke Our heart.

Now she will leave Us at a time of Our choosing. Slowly, her life will drain away under Our hands, feeling Our agony, looking into Our eyes. And then Our tears will drip on her Judas face and she will know her betrayal of Us was her undoing.

Our time is here. As is the Spirit's. *As is hers.*

There is no song but this. The music will be sweet. We have waited so long.

Chapter 15

Jeremy's feet ached. No two ways about it: standing in water with socks and boots was about as miserable a time as any. Every rousty stood in the river. Above them, engineers waited for the order to lift the stage. Even an apparent social order could be seen within the crew: roustys wet and standing below, engineers dry and up on the deck. And the captain, watching over them all. Jeremy regretted his decision to join the men thigh deep in the water. He wondered what he'd been thinking.

They all watched as Gage and his top engineer, Peabody, removed the railing in preparation to move the stage down far enough to clear the damaged deck.

"Just about there," Gage said, voice straining with the pressure he applied to his wrench. The bolt gave way, and the post fell over with a *thunk*.

"We only have to go a few feet to the south," Jeremy said.

"Ready, Captain!" Gage swung backward over the side, dropping down and holding on with his hands. Then he let go, splashing into the river, and took a place along the line of roustys. "We have to do this careful, no point in gettin' any injuries now. Be sure you're out of the way when it slides down. We'll let it hit the bank and then lift it."

The men in the river moved back.

"One . . . two . . . three!" Briggs, standing on the deck, counted off. Muscles strained as the engineers lifted. Then the end of the stage slid off the boat as men backed away. It thudded against the bank, their end dropping into the river. A splash, and mud covered Skunk.

"Shit!" he yelled.

Laughing, they swarmed around, and this time Jeremy counted off as he gripped the stage. "Okay, ready? One . . . two . . . three . . . lift."

Fire seared through his arms and his muscles screamed out; then the thing was up, over his shoulder. The engineers lifted their end, and pain shot through Jeremy's back with the new weight. He gritted his teeth. They all shuffled aft, and every muscle in him protested. The stage was damned heavy.

"Clear! Down!" the captain called.

The stage clanged into place. Briggs immediately stomped onto it while the roustys backed away a few feet. The captain hopped. Up and down. Up and down.

"Appears sound," Briggs said. "How does it look from down there?"

"Hard as Jeremy's head," Gage shouted, which brought scattered laughter from the men.

"All right, roustys, back up on deck. We have a picnic to unload. Jeremy, Gage, I want you to keep down there. Watch for any signs of trouble."

The two men did as ordered and stood in the river looking at each other as the roustys clambered up the bank. Jeremy wondered if Gage's feet were squishing around in his boots like his were as they stood guard. The roustys tromped over the stage. The structure held up fine.

"How long do you think we'll have to stay down here?"

"Make yourself comfortable," Gage answered. "We have more cargo to unload, crew, and passengers."

"Comfortable? Not much of a chance there." Jeremy stretched, trying to work the kink out of his back. "My feet will be blistered by the time everyone makes it off the boat. I hate getting my boots wet."

Gage shot him half a grin.

Once the first group of roustys and waiters disembarked, their arms loaded with picnic fare, the two men scrambled out of the river and up the bank to walk over the stage themselves. While they waited for the roustys to return, Jeremy helped Gage and Peabody pull up some deck and nail down temporary planks.

Jeremy's feet slogged around in his socks and boots. Was there anything worse than sopping wet feet? No point in changing socks or pants. They resumed their place under the stage each time the roustys came and went.

Finally, the band played ragtime again, the signal to hop back in the river.

"Sometimes this job isn't much fun," Jeremy said. Voices rose, chatting and laughing around strains of bouncing music. Everything was back to normal.

"Thought any more about the cause?" Jeremy asked, speaking low. "Or the culprit?"

Gage shook his head. "Let's not talk about it yet."

Great. Standing in water and nothing to do except watch the stage vibrate with footsteps. He might as well think about Sarah in his arms. That ought to warm him enough. Good thing his feet were so damned clammy; otherwise his body might start embarrassing him.

And her tears. Only a few. They didn't make him uneasy or nervous. With all his sisters, he'd dealt with plenty of female emotions over the years. He didn't like to see Sarah upset, but didn't mind getting a glimpse of her softer side. He wanted to fix things for her and hold her until she felt right again. And for a few moments, she'd allowed him to do just that. God, was he falling in love with her? No, couldn't be. Sure, he cared for her. They'd practically grown up together. Maybe he did love her, like one of his sisters anyway.

And that was a big, fat lie. He wasn't sure how he felt about Sarah Perkins. One thing he did know, it wasn't brotherly affection.

Jeremy watched the last of the passengers head for the grove. "Finally," he said. "I think we're done."

"Nope," Gage said. "We wait a few minutes. Next the theater folks disembark.

"Oh, Christ, this is taking forever."

"I can get Skunk to take your place if you're too uncomfortable. No need for our pilot to be sloppin' around in the river."

Jeremy got embarrassed at his own whining. "Not necessary. Besides, Briggs wanted you and me down here."

"We're the ones he trusts most."

"Yeah, lucky us."

Gage smiled.

The captain leaned over the railing. "You gentlemen enjoying yourselves?"

"Yep, this river is as muddy as it is wet. My feets is enjoyin' every minute," Gage replied.

"Some people pay big money to soak in mud. There's a place in Colorado where the hot mud will cure about any ache or pain," Briggs said.

"Yeah, well, this isn't exactly hot," Jeremy said.

"A few more moments. Mr. Gévaudan insists that the passengers be out of sight before the actors go ashore. I assume the stage is doing fine from down there?"

"Yup." Gage nodded.

"All right, then." He disappeared as the sound of his footsteps retreated across the deck.

"Who would pay to sit in mud?" Jeremy asked.

"Rich folks. From what I've seen, they'll pay for just about any silliness."

"Including Flim-Flam and his tiger."

Gage snickered. "Don't get me wrong, I love workin' on this boat. But I'd like to go back to when we actually carried food and people up-and downriver. We had a real purpose then. We weren't just a movin' hotel for the rich," he said. Jeremy heard the longing in his voice. "Although Quentin would have loved all this finery and entertainment."

"I was just a kid, but I remember the man loved good times."

Gage eyes grew distant, like he saw something beyond the bottom of the boat. "That he did."

More tromping. The theater troupe. Jeremy saw fringes of skirts, heard the clomping of boots. The troupe spoke in quiet murmurs. He guessed they were working now. He wondered if the Russian woman had ever cooled down. He hoped she wouldn't notice him down here, standing in mud.

"Come along, Daisy, nothing to be frightened of. This bridge will hold you, angel. The big, strong men waiting in the river will make sure we are safe."

Flim-Flam, coaxing his tiger over the stage. Once across, Oscar broke from the group and smiled at the two men standing in the muck.

"Thank you, gentlemen, for insuring our safety. I have only the deepest appreciation for the working class, and never more so than at this moment." He did a mocking little bow, turned, and rejoined his group.

"I'm really starting to hate that guy," Jeremy said under his breath.

Gage tried to clamp down on his erupting smile, and Jeremy realized he'd spoken louder than intended.

The captain strode over the stage. "Gentlemen, thank you for your attention. I trust all was steady?"

"As the river current," Gage answered.

"I'm heading for the picnic, Jeremy. Although the boat is moored, please, if you would keep to the pilothouse until I return."

"Yes, sir."

"Feel free to change your pants and boots first."

Jeremy shot Briggs a wry grin, and the captain headed for the grove.

Gage pulled himself out of the river and scrambled up the muddy bank. Jeremy followed, his boots slipping in the mud. He righted himself with his hand and finished the climb up the bank. He stood, wiping his muddy hand on his pants.

Lush trees, bushes, and curtains of vines swallowed up just about all of the theater troupe. Briggs caught up with Flim-Flam, the two men speaking in low tones. A sour feeling twisted Jeremy's gut. He pushed it aside, refusing to be jealous of such a silly, pompous cretin.

The last actor, a woman, paused before entering the trees. Long, gold curls glittered in sunlight, her dress almost painted on.

"Jesus, Mary, and Joseph," Jeremy muttered. He'd recognize that bottom anywhere.

She turned. Smiled at Jeremy. His stomach dropped to his toes.

"You know her?" Gage asked, and Jeremy jumped.

"Not really."

She continued on. Gage glanced sideways at Jeremy, his look unreadable, and then headed across the stage.

Jeremy followed.

Meet me, to the north and south of the glade,
walk just a bit, I will wait in the shade,
and take you to heaven, my love.

Zelda folded and tucked the note in the bosom of her dress. Poetry. Simple verse, yes. Nevertheless, who would guess such a rough working man wrote poetry? She imagined his calloused hands holding a pen, broad shoulders bent over paper, writing expressive prose.

She quivered, glad this was a short trip. She could easily fall in love. Her body tingled with excitement and satisfaction all at once. She shouldn't do it, she knew, shouldn't risk meeting him, right here under Oscar's nose. A good chance of exposure, of being caught. The very thing that made the challenge sweet.

The efficient boatwoman, Emma, kept track of passengers, but not the theater cast. And not the crew. Supposedly, they were here doing a job and did not need to be looked after, which made the timing perfect for a woodland tryst.

Making love, naked in the woods, breeze on bare bodies in the wild, with Oscar a few meager steps away. Madness. Which was exactly why she wanted to do it.

"Ill met by moonlight, proud Titania."

Her cue.

She floated into the center of the glade, delivering her lines with her usual brilliance. She spoke, mesmerizing passengers sitting on checkered cloths around the rim of the glade, food piled high, wine flowing freely. Oscar stood against a tree, Daisy at his feet, his eyes riveted upon her. She raised her arms.

"Then I must be thy lady: but I know when thou hast stolen away from fairy land." Ah, but she loved Shakespeare.

Faeries tripped around her, twirling, jumping, singing. Zelda wasn't sure she approved of melding the Bard with songs and music, but *Le Théâtre d'Illusion* was Oscar's creation, and he determined the world needed not another circus, nor another theater company, but a "theater extravaganza." So that's what his troupe delivered.

A small, young woman—Zelda hardly remembered her name—playing the fairy Peaseblossom, flipped over and over, landing on her feet. Robin Goodfellow tossed five flaming torches in the air, catching them and sending them back up again, his green muscles glinting in shafts of sunlight. The crowd applauded and delighted laughter flitted up into the trees. Quite pedestrian, this group. They didn't know

Shakespeare turned in his grave every time Oscar bastardized him.

Standing back a bit, the efficient boatwoman kept glancing at her clipboard, frowning. Something must not be perfect in her mundane life. Zelda remembered those days of endless details, paying no attention to what was important. What mattered. Like one's beauty or the enjoyment of lovers.

She delivered her lines with all the seductive enchantment she could manage. No point in allowing little Peaseblossom or Robin Goodfellow to upstage her. She may not have flaming torches, but she was Zelda Vashnikoff and possessed something much better. The look, sound, and feel of forbidden fantasies.

She finished her lines and circled, making sure everyone saw her from every side. Such a shame they wore costumes. Zelda much preferred the bathhouse production when three young men had painted flowers and a forest on her naked body. Performing in the nude. These boat people would be scandalized forever.

"*Not for thy fairy kingdom. Fairies, away! We shall chide downright, if I longer stay.*" She caressed her lines with her voice, her body. Oscar wanted to take her right here; she could tell from the way he watched her. She enchanted them all.

She felt a bit sore from the morning with her rough boatman. He'd been relentless and fast, driving her with crude persistence to the heights, again and again. He'd taken her on the bed, against the wall, on the floor. Her backside still smarted a bit.

So young. Strong. Virile. She planned to wear him out, here amongst the trees. And perhaps Oscar later, to fulfill her more refined tastes. Such a good day. One of her best, the scent of lovers mixed on her skin.

She spoke again, walking around the circle of the glade, past the wedding party. She didn't see the spoiled girl bride with flaming hair. Curious. Perhaps she had a tryst all her own. For the girl's sake, Zelda certainly hoped so.

She delivered the remainder of her lines with sensual aplomb and the time came she dreaded: mingling with the audience. She hated listening to these people, pretending they were the least bit interesting; but she was an actress and played her part well.

The groom-to-be locked his attention on her and headed her way, no sign of his bride.

"You were wonderful, Miss Titania," he said, never taking his eyes off her thinly covered breasts. She would enjoy deflowering a groom on the eve of his wedding, but, alas, she had more than enough men who wanted her, needed her. Still, adding this boy to the list might be fun. She decided to give him a thrill. She held out her hand and he took it, brushing his lips across the back.

"My sincerest thanks to you, sir," she said. Covering his hand with both of hers, she pulled it close, making sure his knuckles brushed her breast. His eyes grew wide. She bowed her head slightly and, delivering an enchanting smile, dropped his hand.

He swallowed. Collecting these men—so easy. Hardly a challenge at all.

She worked her way to the edge of the glade and watched for a moment to sneak away from the group, difficult given how everyone became mesmerized with her. Finally, she slipped into the woods, unnoticed. She walked only a few yards in, when a voice stopped her.

"Going for a walk, my dear?" Oscar asked. "You'd best not be long. We head back to the boat in a little over an hour. And after such an exhausting performance, you'll need time for lunch."

She spun. Her blood tickled through her. Was he following her? Did her waiting lover see? She walked backward, luring him farther in.

"You watched me. I hoped you to follow."

His eyes glistened, his desire clear. The afternoon became complex. And exciting. Oscar backed her against a tree and hooked a finger, pulling her dress from her shoulders. The note fluttered out.

"What's this?"

She caught the paper in her palm. "My lines. In case I forget."

He looked at her, questioning, which forced her to think fast. She shrugged her dress from her shoulders, allowing the material to drop to her waist. She slid one hand down to his pants, unfastening, while the other hand crunched the paper into a tiny ball. His eyes darkened. She planted her mouth on his, intent on distraction.

It worked. She draped her arms around his neck and flicked the tiny ball of paper behind him. Such a shame. Such a lovely poem. She wanted it for a keepsake. Ah, well.

He grabbed her arms, and with one hand, pinned her wrists to the tree above her head. Lowering his head he kissed her shoulders, bit them.

She cried out, "Now, Oscar. I want you now."

He bent his head lower, kissed her bared breasts. She arched into him, a moan escaping her lips. He nipped. Just hard enough. She cried out.

Oh, God, her boat lover must be watching from the trees somewhere. Excitement beyond belief. Oscar let her hands go and raised her skirt. He discovered she wore nothing beneath.

"Ready for someone?" He touched her, toyed.

She took in a ragged breath. "You, Oscar. For you."

He pushed her against the tree. She grabbed his shoulders and wrapped a leg around him. He drove inside her, held there, and looked in her eyes. Let loose, then drove into her again. And again. His thrusts became harder, more insistent.

Heaven, the feel of air on her skin, her breasts bared, her Oscar taking her right here, out in the open. Another lover watching. Perhaps even other eyes, someone from the picnic out here, seeing them. Maybe the spoiled Henrietta. Take notes, little bride, she thought; then sensation swirled through her and logical thought burst.

He came, quickly, a disappointment. He must have read frustration in her eyes.

"Only time for one quick knee-trembler. The others will be looking for us." He backed away and fastened his pants. "I will make it up to you tonight, my queen," he said with a sly smile. "I pledge to spend hours pleasuring you."

"I look forward to such." She pulled up the shoulders of her dress, covering herself again. "I look good?"

He took her hand and kissed it. "Always. No one will guess. I'll go back first; you come a few moments later. Wouldn't do to begin gossip. These Midwesterners are so . . ."

"*Jejune,*" she finished for him.

He started to leave, but paused. "Eight o'clock. When most of these people are suitably drunk. We'll have plenty of time then."

At least his feet and legs were dry. Jeremy would never risk slopping mud in the captain's pristine pilothouse.

A few folks straggled back, but most were still in the grove. Jeremy knew Emma had everything under control; nothing ever got past her and her clipboard. Although his duty was up here, he would have liked to see at least part of the play. And not because of interest in theater. That Russian woman was lodged in his head.

Well, a few other places, too.

Briggs came out of the trees, heading for the boat, returning early, which surprised Jeremy. Briggs loved the *Spirit's* social functions, and as much as he hated to admit it, from the few glimpses he'd seen, Flim-Flam put on a good show.

The captain walked at a clipped pace, but he wasn't moving with his usual vigor. In fact, he seemed a little out of breath. Jeremy hadn't recalled seeing such a thing before. Briggs stomped over the stage, and Jeremy figured he was in for some more mud-sloshing time.

Minutes stretched, and it soon became apparent Briggs wasn't coming straight up. Curious. The captain always at least checked in when he returned to the boat, whether his shift started or not. After a time, his head appeared as he climbed the steps. He opened the door, his skin waxy—pale and with a sheen of sweat. He immediately sat on the lazy bench. Again, curious.

"Captain, are you feeling okay?"

Briggs' hand went to his gut. "Just some indigestion." He put a fist to his mouth as a small belch rose. "The show was incredible. I'm sorry you missed it."

"I'd rather be up here, honestly."

"Well, don't get used to it. I'm going to have to begin sending you in my stead or I'll die of rich man's disease. Too much of the good life."

Jeremy laughed, his heart not behind the sound. The captain's decline in health the last month was seriously beginning to worry him.

Briggs patted his pants pockets. "Oh, damn it all, I left my glasses somewhere."

"Your room?"

"No, I used them to read the playbill Oscar passed around. Then I took them off. Set them on a nearby stump. Damn." Briggs stood. "I could hope Emma will see them and bring them back, but they are my only pair. I need them to read the maps."

"You can navigate the river with your eyes closed."

"Yes, well, still and all, they are an expensive accessory. Much as I hate to admit needing them to read, I just began Zane Grey's *Spirit of the Border*. Riveting. About the Ohio Valley, you know."

"You can't put that off till we get back. I'll fetch them for you."

"But I remember right where they are."

"Tell me which side of the grove the stump is at."

Briggs looked thoughtful. "Actually, I think it is the only stump in the grove. Must have been a huge, ancient tree. Shame someone cut it down. It's on the far west side."

Jeremy headed for the door. "I'll be back before you realize I'm gone."

"Take your time. Talk with some of the passengers. You haven't come out much this trip, and it will be good for you to get to know a few people before the rehearsal dinner."

The last thing Jeremy wanted to do was mingle with anyone from the wedding party or theater. However, an order was an order. And he needed some brisk exercise.

He set off to retrieve the captain's spectacles.

Zelda watched until Oscar was out of sight. She walked even farther into the woods, still feeling Oscar on her skin, the brush of his lips, his scent. She raised her arms, stretched, and spun around.

Not a sound, only the wind in the leaves. Yet she knew someone watched, sensed him. Just couldn't pinpoint where. A slight rustle. She turned again; the sound could have come from anywhere.

One way to snag a man.

She dropped the shoulders of her dress. Her nipples hardened in the breeze, sensitive after Oscar's mouth had worked its magic. Sunlight fell across her breasts, a lovely and unusual sensation. Really, clothing was such a bother. She read about a movement in Germany, where people insisted the human body was neither obscene nor a sin, and they advocated going about in the altogether. A perfect existence for her. She might have to go to Germany sometime soon, before everything on her fell too far.

Still no sign of her boatman. His feelings might be hurt; perhaps he thought himself cuckolded. She would probably never make it to Germany, not with the theater's schedule. Why not begin her own movement?

She slipped out of her dress completely, standing there in the woods, wearing nothing except glittering hair falling to her waist. She opened her arms in sacrifice.

"I am here for you. Come to me, my love," she said out loud, and shut her eyes, letting her head fall back.

He came up behind her. She lowered her arms, waiting to feel his hands on her skin.

"Whore!"

She spun and a fist knocked her off her feet. The weight of him pressed down on her. His hand went around her throat.

"You know me, whore. Don't you? Don't you? Look at me close."

She looked into his face, not believing who she saw. Not him. God, not him.

She tried to cry out—he was hurting her—then tried to plead. No sound came. She clawed at his arms, his face, but he didn't let go.

He grinned, his weight on her, holding her with one hand. He was killing her. She grasped his arm with both hands. Her strength fluttered, a butterfly compared to his steel. She reached for his face. Her hand implored, begged.

He held up a pair of spectacles. Spectacles? She fixated on them as the edges of her sight grew dim. A ray of sun caught them, beaming white light all around. He placed them in her frantic hand, and she clutched them.

A leaf from the tree above came loose and slowly drifted down, down, swirling into the edges of black with a grace only angels possessed. They were here, the angels. One of them, so handsome. Strong. He took her in his arms. Such calm. Such peace. Finally.

Chapter 16

Toby topped the crystal pyramid with the last glass. The bar was again in perfect order. Charley opened the door to the stateroom, rushing in with a bucket.

"I'm almost done, Charley."

"Me too. I jest got all the stains off the outside deck." He drew in a breath.

"Hey, slow down," Toby said.

"I jest wanna be sure I get all them spills cleaned up. Malcolm's been ridin' me lately, and I need this job. Some of them stains is gonna need another treatment or two. That red wine's a booger."

"I wondered where my bucket went. Who absconded with it. Criminy. Can't find good help nowadays."

Charley grinned. "I thought you didn't need it."

"Well, you thought wrong."

"I'll make it up to you. What can I do?"

Toby pointed to a wine stain on the carpet.

Charlie groaned and dropped to his knees. "Can't those people figure out how to get a wineglass to their big, yappin' maws? Thank the good Lord and all that's holy they're off the boat for a few hours."

"No kidding," Toby agreed. "Glad they got the stage back in order so they could get everyone off."

"I can't take much more. Them people might be rich, but they's mean as a bunch of hornets smacked out of their nest. You'd think they'd be nicer, all the liquid fire they drink."

"Well, judging by the amount of stains, not much is making it to their 'big, yappin' maws' as you put it." Toby sighed. Besides, liquid fire made people crankier, far as he could tell. Drinking made folks do crazy things.

Emma must have known they'd all need a break and some space from each other when she suggested the picnic at the turnaround point. A small group, including Toby and Charley, were charged with boat cleanup and setup for the buffet dinner tonight. Forty-eight hours and they'd be home free. Tomorrow night, the rehearsal dinner and party, followed by an elegant wedding aboard the boat at sunrise the next morning. Then this bunch of demanding rich folks would finally disembark for good and they could all relax.

"I'm right there with you, Charley. I can't wait for everyone to get off the boat so we can get back home and put her away for the winter." At the end of the season, the *Spirit* went into dock and the real work began. Although Toby did enjoy performing magic tricks and making passengers laugh with his silly antics, the façade he wore weighed heavily and caring for the boat always made him feel like he was restoring his soul, too. He needed some time off more than the *Spirit* did.

"You think Briggs will hire me on again next season?"

"I don't see why not," Toby answered. "We've been booked solid all year and if I'm not mistaken, we're close to capacity for next. I can't imagine we aren't profitable. We must be making good money, especially with this wedding extravaganza."

Charley snorted. "I guess it's worth it, then. Panderin' to all these ridiculous types."

"Two more days to go after tonight. Dinner tomorrow night and then the wedding."

"I'd jump off a cliff afore I'd marry that shrew," Charlie said.

Toby jolted at the mention of a cliff. Then he thought about Henrietta and her upcoming wedding. Felt sorry for her. "Aw, she's not so bad sometimes."

Charley's eyes just about bulged out of his head. "You kiddin' me?"

"When she lets her guard down, she's okay. She has her own set of problems. It's tough to keep up a face to show the world, and I've seen Henrietta's slip. She's getting married for everyone except herself. Pretending to be the happy bride is hard on her."

No one knew better than he did. His face-to-the-world was sprouting more holes than a shot-up tin can, and he needed to close them up tight, lest something hideous escape.

Charley shook his head. "I don't understand half a what you is mutterin' about, and I don't think I agree with much of it. She's a mean ol' bitch."

Toby whipped his head around. "Hush, Charley. Someone might hear you."

Charley glanced around, too. "Hey! Here comes one a them actor gals," he said. "I thought they was all off the boat. And us, without time to down a scotch."

Through the glass door a vision approached. Toby's stomach dropped. He'd recognize her anywhere, even though he'd never seen her out from under the costumes and makeup she donned to perform. The first time he saw her, she came aboard the boat, a flitting, dancing fairy and next, the sweet, exotic Yum-Yum. Nothing she played was as lovely or wonderful as the real girl swinging open the stateroom door.

Her blonde hair was piled high, and sparkly combs held the curling mass. But those eyes, blue and slightly upturned, dark lashes rimming, were almost all he could see. They were huge, expanding. Her eyes became his world and his heart stuttered in his chest. She was beautiful beyond belief.

"Hey, that ain't Tasty-Treat, is it? Lord, have mercy, I do believe it is."

"Oh, please, hush up, Charley," he said, his eyes never leaving the sunny girl heading their way.

She smiled so prettily, Toby thought he might melt. He gulped, preparing to do his best and not be a fool. Although he didn't hold out much hope. His tongue tied in a million knots.

"Hello, gentlemen. How are you today?" she asked as she passed Charley, her voice rich and glittery all at once, like fine brandy poured in a cut-glass chalice. Charley followed her, staring like a man seeing a woman for the first time.

"Jest fine, Miss. Yore show last night was wonderful."

"Thank you. I love Gilbert and Sullivan, don't you?"

Charley gulped. "Yes'm. He's a crackerjack, that one."

If Toby weren't so nervous, he'd have laughed.

Then she trained her wide, blue eyes on Toby. Again, the sensation of melting. Her tiny stature and porcelain skin beneath a cloud of blonde hair made her look like an angel from another world, something fragile and beautiful and completely beyond his reach. He was a no-consequence waiter on a boat. Still, her smile for him sparkled. Her eyes lit up; she was such a good actress.

"I'm glad I have the day off. I've been anxious to come down. I don't believe we've been formally introduced. I'm Lucy." She hopped up on a stool.

"Top of the morning to you, Miss Lucy," he said, his voice cracking. "But, actually, it's pretty much afternoon." God, he sounded like the village idiot, even to himself.

She giggled. "True, but I just woke up. Do you have a name, Mr. Top-of-the-Morning?"

"Charley!" The waiter stuck his hand out and Lucy took it. Toby thought about shaking a soda-water bottle and aiming it at his friend.

"Hello, Charley. I've seen you around. Nice to meet you."

"Don't you have some tables to polish?" Toby asked. Charley scowled and Toby threw a bar rag at him. "I see a particularly filthy one about three rows down."

Lucy gave him a knowing look. "And your name? I hate to call you Sir Barkeep."

"Tobias. Perkins. But you can call me anything you want." Cripes, could he sound any more idiotic?

"May I ask for a glass of lemonade?" Her question floated, quiet, shy. "The way you make it, with the fizzies? I enjoyed one last night."

"I shouldn't be serving you before the dinner hour, Miss Lucy, especially fizzy lemonade," he said with mock sternness. He wanted to hit himself. What a stupid thing to say. He smiled, trying to cover his awkwardness. "But for such a talented performer . . . anything." God, the more he talked the stupider he sounded. *Never mind Charley,* he thought, *somebody shut me up!*

To distract her from his idiotic babbling, he grabbed a glass and flung it up in the air, and another and another until they made a rotating, twirling circle of crystal. As each glass came into his left hand he tapped it on the bar so rhythm shot through the room, making it appear the glasses danced to percussion. Lucy laughed and clapped her hands. He replaced them one by one and, whirling around, caught the final glass behind his back and flipped it over. He grabbed a pitcher and poured golden liquid. He topped the drink off with soda water, pushed a sugared lemon slice on the rim, and slid the glass to her.

"That was wonderful! No one has ever made me laugh this early in the day," she said, casting her eyes down. A blush began to color her cheeks, and even though it was obviously embarrassment for his silly performance, he loved the way the glow made her porcelain skin come alive.

She was lovely. He'd never seen any girl as fragile and beautiful as this one.

He was grateful for the mahogany barrier between them. She didn't see his knees wobble. To his dismay—delight—whatever was making his insides churn—her tiny pink lips pursed together and she watched him while she sipped her drink. Blood pounded through him until he thought he might pass out altogether.

In the back of the room, Charley winked and then flipped the bar towel he'd been using over his shoulder. He proved to be the best friend in the world and silently headed for the door.

Panic, low and shimmering, rose from Toby's knees to clench his gut. What would he say? What should he do? He changed his mind, wishing he'd been nicer to Charley, despite the male competition. He needed help. Bad.

Charley turned to give a quick wave. Toby tried to communicate desperation and jerked his head, hopefully imperceptibly, at Lucy. Charley smiled and backed out the door.

"What is so interesting over my shoulder, Tobias?" Lucy asked, clearly amused.

"Uh, um . . ." Brilliant. In another minute, he'd be slobbering.

"Where did you learn to juggle?"

He shrugged, his tongue feeling like a lead weight. "Here and there."

"And your magic tricks?"

"Same." Then she repeated with him, "Here and there." He laughed. "I guess I'm not so eloquent, huh?"

"You should consider performing for a living. You're a natural."

"I already get paid to be polite and listen when people tell me their troubles over a glass of rum. That's true performing for a living."

She looked down at her drink.

Panic tumbled through him. "Oh, no, no, I didn't mean you!"

"I know." She sipped. "I'm sorry our stay is ending so soon. I've really enjoyed this wonderful ship." She set her lemonade back on the bar, scooting the lemon along the edge of the glass.

He was about to blurt out "boat!" to correct her. Thank heavens he managed to gulp it down before it came out.

She continued. "And I've enjoyed meeting everyone. Meeting you, Sir Tobias the Barkeep."

His brain whirled, trying to think of something to say, something witty, charming, funny, to make her remember him forever. This was probably his only chance to say anything to her, anything at all. Nothing came to him. Not even something stupid.

He turned—seeming to mop the bar behind him but actually frantically searching for words—and hoped she didn't see him blushing in the mirror's reflection. Eyes lowered, he couldn't think. His mind stretched out, a great, frozen wasteland, offering nothing. He swiped the bar with his rag and knocked over a bottle. Gin sloshed over the bar, soaking his coat sleeves.

"Oh, cripes!" He grabbed and righted the stupid thing, his ears burning. *Dumb. Dumb. Dumb. Dumb.*

He mopped the alcohol up with his rag and wrung it out over his bucket, never once looking back at her. He didn't want to see whatever expression might be on her face. He went back to mopping up his spill.

The door swung open and relief flooded through him when he looked up in the mirror, seeing the reverse of the stateroom behind him. Charley?

Nope. Henrietta Jeffries.

Toby's relief curdled.

Henrietta had a brief moment of excitement, maybe even friendliness on her face. She saw Lucy and surprise filled her expression. She narrowed her eyes, resembling a thundercloud about to burst. Even her dimples disappeared in a scowl.

What was she doing here during a picnic off the boat in her honor? And why was she furious? She fisted her hands and planted them on her hips.

"You. *Boy.*" Her voice shot through the stateroom like a ricochet of buckshot.

In the mirror Lucy's expression darkened, and Toby whirled around, hoping to get rid of this mess before it careened out of control. Even though he wasn't positive what kind of a mess this might be, he was pretty sure he stood smack-dab in the middle of something bad.

Henrietta strode to the bar.

"Miss Henrietta, shouldn't you be frolicking about at your picnic?" Lucy asked sweetly. Yet the tone wasn't quite right—kind of like the garnish perched on her glass. Sugar over the bitter, sour taste of pure lemon.

Uh oh, Toby thought.

Henrietta tilted her head, swishing her hand around as if warding off a pest. "Is there a gnat flying about in here? Because something of no consequence seems to be buzzing about."

"What can I do for you, Miss Jeffries?" Toby asked quickly, but not fast enough. Lucy scowled and slid off her stool, bumping into Henrietta. The heiress gasped and fell back, grabbing the actress. Lucy stumbled and lost her balance. Lemonade flew through the air. The two women landed on the floor, in a heap.

The crystal glass smashed into the bar, shattering. Glass flew in tiny sparkles, everywhere. The sound unfroze Tobias, and he ran around the bar to see the two girls rolling and screaming and pulling each other's hair.

"Ladies! Ladies!" He didn't know what else to say.

Charley came rushing in. "Holy Mother of God!" he yelled, winding his way through tables. He reached down to grab one of the young women. Which one he aimed for wasn't clear. Henrietta bit his ankle and he yelped like a wounded pup. Toby didn't know what to do. He grabbed the pitcher of lemonade and poured the contents over the rolling tangle of female, hoping to startle them into stopping.

Charley, hopping around on one foot, slipped in the puddle and landed on top of the two women. Toby extended a hand to help his friend, and Charley pulled him into the mêlée. Before he realized what was happening, he was sticky, wet, and rolling on the floor with Henrietta Jeffries, Lucy, and Charley.

Toby jumped up and grabbed the soda bottle from the bar. "Stop or I'll fire!" No response other than more screeching and hair pulling. Charley started laughing. Laughing! Toby aimed, depressed the lever, and a stream of fizzy water spurted out over all three. Lucy and Henrietta flung their hands up to protect themselves from the onslaught, and as quickly as it began, it ended.

Panic pushed laughter out; then Toby found the whole thing so damned funny. His giggle turned genuine. Henrietta Jeffries, heiress and bride, rolling on the floor in lemonade. Not to forget fizzy water, his secret lemonade ingredient, and him, nervous he'd do something stupid and embarrass himself in front of Lucy. Something stupid? What could be more idiotic than dumping a pitcher of lemonade on a bratty heiress and the most beautiful girl in the world? A girl he was trying to impress.

He was the king of dunces. He laughed. And laughed.

Henrietta stared at him, astounded, squeezing out tears of pure outrage. Or perhaps her face was wet with lemonade or fizzy water. Or both. She wailed like a drunk coyote. Charley mimicked her, howling like there was a full moon hanging from the ceiling. They almost harmonized. Toby aimed at his friend and fired a shot of soda water.

Lucy shook her head like she just woke from a dream. She sat up and a grin broke out on her face, too. Charley stopped howling and started laughing. Henrietta wailed one more time, her cry ending in giggles. Toby couldn't get any air, he laughed so hard. His knees lost any remaining strength, and he plopped down to sit on the floor.

Henrietta's arm wrapped protectively around her middle. "You should have seen yourself," she said to no one in particular.

"You bit me on the ankle," Charley managed to get out.

No longer able to hold himself upright, Toby lay back on the floor and watched the ornamentation where the arches met the ceiling, supporting the structure amidst swirls of sculpted vines and lush, hanging bunches of grapes.

"You nit," Lucy managed between laughs.

"You pulled my hair," Henrietta accused, but her voice was, for the first time Toby had ever heard, good-natured. "I spent hours on this hairstyle."

"You shouldn't have bothered," Lucy said. "What did you use, an eggbeater?"

Toby sat up in time to see Henrietta's laughter fade. Her face crumpled into a look of real upset. She put her head in her hands.

Charley, Lucy, and Toby looked at each other at a complete loss.

Lucy touched Henrietta's shoulder. "Henrietta?"

The debutante raised her head. "Nothing, I'm fine." She glanced around. "Tobias Perkins, you've made an absolute disaster of this place. I daresay the captain will have your hide."

"Me?" Toby said and grinned. "At least I've graduated from 'boy' status into a human being with a name. Thanks for that much."

"Don't get too used to it." Henrietta looked down at the wet Persian carpet. "I suppose I've been a tad horrible this trip, haven't I?"

Silence followed.

"Henrietta, why are you irritable?" Lucy finally asked. "This week has been all for you and your wedding and you've been miserable with every detail."

"Have I really been that bad?"

The three nodded at once.

"Worse," Charley said with great earnestness. "You been like a demon from hell."

"Maybe that's what I feel like this wedding is," Henrietta continued, her voice dropping to a whisper. "Hell. And I can't stop it from claiming me."

A voice boomed through the silence. "What is the meaning of this?"

Lionel Jeffries stood in the doorway, Captain Briggham behind him, glaring directly at Tobias. He knew that look. The captain demanded a response. Toby glanced around at the three others, wet, bedraggled, sticky; Henrietta's up-done hairstyle tilting to one side, and the spreading wet on the brocade carpet.

"Uh—just some fun?" he answered.

The two men in the doorway looked anything but amused.

Toby and Charley sat on the deck before the front office, drying off but sticky. Uncomfortable. Kind of like the situation, Toby thought.

While the two boys sat there, sticking to their chairs, voices and strains of laughter floated up as passengers returned from the picnic. They were straggling in a few at a time, which saved him the humiliation of having his mother up here. She'd be down below checking her list, making sure all the passengers boarded.

Not so with his sister. The air around her reeked with disappointment. So troubled. So worried. He wanted to tell the captain not to bother with any punishment. The look on Sarah's face was more than enough.

She leaned against the rail, shaking her head. "What were you two thinking?"

Toby shrugged in response. He hadn't thought. He'd simply reacted and, well, had fun. And all things considered, the "Great Fighting Girl Tangle" had ended up just fine. Not without its surprises.

Not so funny now. Everyone was all serious, like something awful had happened. It wasn't like a stage had crashed to the deck or anything. Only damage, some lemonade on the carpet. Not even as bad as a glass of spilled wine, in his opinion.

"I thought the picnic took place off the boat. Everyone sure seems to be wandering around here," Toby said.

"When Mr. Jeffries discovered Henrietta missing, he returned to the *Spirit,* and he and the captain looked for her," Sarah answered. "I doubt they dreamed they'd find her rolling around on the stateroom floor with the two of you."

Toby wanted to point out Jeffries shouldn't be surprised, seeing the misery Henrietta's impending nuptials caused her. That should be his concern, not a couple of wet waiters.

Lionel Jeffries' voice boomed from the captain's office. Toby suddenly felt the life Henrietta had, the choices forced upon her. He sure wouldn't want to go up against her father's will. *What is it with fathers anyway?* he wondered, rubbing his chest.

The wall muffled the captain's voice, but his words leaked out. "Lionel, I promise you, I'll attend to Tobias and Charley. You have my complete and sincere apology. Nothing of this sort will happen again.

Charley slid down in his chair.

Money. It made all the difference. If Jeffries wasn't a paying customer, the captain would have laid the man out by now. And if Jeffries wasn't a millionaire captain of industry, his daughter might have the freedom to make her own choice. None of them had an option other than to make the millionaire happy. And all because of money.

"I should be in there," Sarah said. "I'm the one who is supposed to smooth everyone's ruffled feathers." She glared at Toby and Charley. "Although 'ruffled' hardly seems to cover the situation. Were you two out of your minds?"

"I'm gonna get sacked," Charley said mournfully.

Toby leaned forward. "No, you won't. No real harm done. Besides, that's the first time I've seen Henrietta laugh since she came aboard. She needed some fun."

"You two managed to eclipse a crashing stage," Sarah said.

"What ever got into you boys?" Emma asked, coming up the steps. Oh, well, so much for his mother being otherwise occupied. "I can't believe what I'm hearing. This day has been an absolute nightmare! The mangled stage, a picnic with a missing guest of honor! And to discover she's back here, in the stateroom, rolling around on the floor with my son?"

"Mom—" Toby began. Sarah moved between, blocking him from his mother's view.

"You don't have to worry; everything is under control," Sarah said.

"You have a strange understanding of *under control*," Emma replied.

Toby stood and peered at his mom over Sarah's shoulder. "Mom, I can explain everything—"

Lionel Jeffries interrupted Toby's explanation and burst from the office, glared at Toby and Charley, his dark goatee trembling with rage. Toby was surprised facial hair could show so much emotion. Jeffries spun and stalked down the corridor away from them. The strength drained out of Toby's legs and he sat back down. Much as he'd reassured Charley, he was afraid they were in for trouble.

Briggs emerged, his face dark as a storm. He stared hard at the two young men. "I assume you boys heard the dressing down I endured in your name?"

"Captain, I . . ." Toby found himself without words. He decided to use an honest approach. "Captain, Charley and I both apologize. It happened so quick. We got carried away and ended up having some fun."

"Fun? The bride, not to mention daughter of the man paying ten thousand-plus dollars for an unforgettable wedding, is found wallowing on the floor with two of my deckhands, and it was just *some fun*?"

"Well, Mr. Jeffries wanted *unforgettable*, and we just delivered." The words slipped out before Toby could stop them. The captain's glare pushed more from him. "And Henrietta did enjoy it; I mean, we kind of talked and she dropped her fake, snotty act, and—"

"Fake?" Sarah snorted. "Hardly."

The captain glanced at his purser before returning to his study of the two offenders sitting before him. "If I didn't know better, I'd swear you boys had been drinking."

Guilt bolted through Toby, although he hadn't touched a drop. His cheeks heated. The color drained out of Sarah's face.

"No, sir," Charley denied emphatically.

Toby's focus swung to Briggs. "Captain, what can we do to fix everything?"

Charley's head bobbed in agreement.

Briggs looked up to the sky. "At last they come to their senses." He returned his attention to the sticky duo on the deck chairs. "You may start by cleaning yourselves up, then the stateroom, and when you are presentable, both of you will deliver a formal apology to Mr. Jeffries and Miss Henrietta. We'll see how far that goes to repair the damage done today. Dismissed." He turned to Sarah. "Sarah, please ask Mr. Gévaudan to have his young diva do the same. Perhaps we can salvage this disaster." Briggs relaxed his stance. "I've done all the apologizing I'm going to do, and I've already done too much. Leaves a nasty taste in my mouth." He turned, seemed to think better of it, and whipped around. "I do not need any more trouble from anyone. What the hell is happening to this crew?" He stalked off.

"The captain has serious matters on his mind," Emma said, "and the last thing he needed was a ridiculous situation like this one." She clutched her clipboard. "I don't have any more time for this, I have to finish re-boarding everyone from the picnic." She took a few steps down and looked back. "Tobias, I expect better of you for the remainder of this trip."

When they were alone, Sarah's eyes implored. "Please tell me you two haven't been drinking." Although addressing them both, she looked straight at Toby.

He shook his head. "I swear. No."

"No ma'am," Charley said, sounding like a contrite kid. Which pretty much described each of them at the moment.

She leaned in and sniffed. "Then why do I smell it?"

Toby shrugged. "I work behind a bar." He recalled his clumsiness in front of Lucy. "I knocked over a bottle and spilled some gin on my coat."

"We been moppin' up wine all morning, Miss Sarah," Charley added, his earnestness amplified.

She looked at Toby, hard. "I'll do what I can to smooth this over, Runt." But he could read it in her eyes; she didn't believe him. Thought he'd been drinking. Sarah continued, disappointment and worry sharp in her expression. "Both of you, go clean yourselves up. And try your best to keep out of trouble."

Dear Father flared, and Toby wanted to shrink into nothing.

Chapter 17

Drinking. Hiding it. Lying about it. Like Uncle Quentin.

Sarah paced the length of the boat three full times, passing Gage, Peabody, and two other engineers repairing the deck. Finally, she stopped to watch them work.

She didn't know what to do. Toby was in deep, deep trouble. She'd failed him, but she'd deal with that later. For now the most important focus was how to best help him.

Frightened her inaction might make everything worse, Sarah decided, for the first time in her life, she needed help. Gage was the one person on the boat she did trust, who might understand. He also knew how to keep his mouth shut. She needed him.

He always sensed when someone watched him, and sure enough . . . He put down his hammer and turned. "Sarah?"

She came to him. "Hey, Gage. I wonder, do you have a minute?"

"For you, more than that." He stood.

"I need to talk to you somewhere private. Really private."

He frowned in thought. "The captain's dinin' room."

She followed him up to the Texas deck. Gage unlocked the door and lit the lamps. Prisms danced across the room from the chandelier; rich wood paneling surrounded them. She ran her hand along the table, polished to a high sheen. She loved it in here. The calm, the serenity helped soothe her anxiety.

"This really should get more use. It's lovely."

"Yeah, tell that to Briggs. He guards this room like a secret." Gage shut the door and faced her, crossing his arms. "Why do I get the feelin' you got trouble, Sarah-girl?"

She tried to smile, but a wry expression twisted her face and her brow furrowed. He waited for her to speak. Two sides fought in her, both wanting the same outcome. Toby's well-being, perhaps even his life was at stake.

Her brother might have sworn he and Charley hadn't been drinking, despite the fact she smelled it on them both. And the crashing of the stage brought the entire situation into very serious focus.

"I'm not sure how to start." She wondered how she could form her question without breaking all her promises. Without giving Toby away.

Gage pulled a dining chair to face one of the armchairs in the corner. He sat on it and patted the seat across from him. "Sit. I got a feelin' this might take awhile."

She was grateful to have him in her life. She knew she could trust him, but what she needed to tell him might put him in a bad situation with the captain, Emma, perhaps even his conscience.

And don't forget your little brother, who trusts you to look out for him.

That's why she was here, she insisted to herself. Toby trusted her to do what was best. She sat down. Sighed. Ran her fingers through the front of her hair.

He grabbed both her hands in his and leaned his elbows on his knees. "Tell me. Just spit it out."

"Gage, I know I can trust you, but can I *trust you*?"

He shot her a perplexed look.

"Will you keep this to yourself no matter what, even if you think you need to tell the captain or Mom? I'm desperate for advice, and I don't know where to turn. I need some information and you are the only one I can trust to give it to me without judging or going off your head."

His brow furrowed. "I'll tell you what. I won't take no action or say a word until I talk it through with you."

"And we agree? If I don't . . ." What was she doing? What was she asking?

"Sarah, tell me." He squeezed her hands. "Hey, I'm on your side. Always."

"I don't want to put you in a difficult position."

"Let me worry about my position."

"Do you have any leads on the chain?"

He dropped her hands and sat up, surprised and confused.

"Oh, Jeremy filled me in." She rushed to defend him. "He knew you or the captain would tell me anyway, and he thought I'd be able to keep a lookout, or perhaps I'd seen something."

Gage nodded.

"Gage, I'm part of the executive team."

"I know, Sarah. I just didn't realize anyone told you. Once I examined the housin', I saw the notch marks." He hiked his shoulders. "No ideas, really, on who might have done it. Not even sure it was on purpose, although sure seems someone tampered with the chain. Have you seen anyone fool around the mechanism who shouldn't be?"

She shook her head. "No, but . . ."

"Sarah, you'd better tell me. Now."

"It's not that I have any information; I just have a question." She closed her eyes. Now or forever hold her peace. So to speak. She opened her eyes and met Gage's. "You spent so much time with Toby in engineering when he was younger. You taught him so much. Is there any way he has the knowledge to sabotage the chain?"

Gage sat back in his chair as if she smacked him in the chest. He obviously struggled with her words. "I'm not sure what I expected, but that wasn't it."

"I realize I'm shocking you. I'm sorry."

"Toby?" His voice rang, incredulous.

"Would he know how to do something like that?"

"Sarah, what are you sayin'? Toby?"

The concern in his face did it. It all spilled from her. From the cliff to his drinking and blackouts, to the napkins, to her constant worry over her brother, to his suicide attempt four years ago too, and, finally, to Emma not knowing the specifics of any of it.

Gage pulled out a kerchief, and that's when she realized tears ran down her cheeks. His face registered nothing the entire time she talked, except compassion.

He sat back in his chair. "That's a mighty big load you been carryin' Sarah-girl."

"Please, please don't tell Mom. She has enough to worry about."

"Sarah, she's your ma and Toby's, too."

"Toby and I have managed fine all these years without her."

"What I'm hearin' ain't nowhere close to you and Toby managin' fine. You two are hidin' things from your ma, and she needs to know." He took her hands again. "Ain't no way you and Toby should be carryin' this alone."

"So what about the chain? Do you think he could have done it?"

Gage sat back again. "I doubt it. Toby was just about the worst kid workin' with tools I'd ever seen. And add to it, him bein' drunk and notchin' that chain? I don't think so."

"You doubt it. Is it possible?"

"Sure, anythin' is. But probable? Nope."

Relief tumbled through her.

"Sarah, there's a problem wide as the river here, whether Toby notched the chain or not. You're talkin' about someone in big trouble. He's tried killin' hisself?"

"He promised me he wouldn't anymore."

"And drinkin'?"

"He swore no more drinking either." She realized how weak her words sounded.

Gage's face grew sad. "Yeah, someone promised the same to me. Again and again. And his blood runs through Toby's veins."

"Uncle Quentin."

Gage nodded. "My guess is whatever demons are drivin' Toby to drink are also behind his attempt to end his own life."

"He promised me he wouldn't do either again."

"Boy's makin' lots of promises."

"I'm scared, Gage."

They stood and he gathered her in his arms. She held tight. "Don't worry so much. You ain't alone nomore. We'll figure this out."

"Please don't tell Mom."

He dropped his arms and scooted the chair back into its spot at the table. "She has to know, Sarah. I'd like to spend some time with Toby before we bring her into this." He hesitated. "We're a family, Sarah. All of us. That's how folks get through serious trouble. And that's what we got us a bunch of here."

"But—"

"Sarah, I don't want no argument. Toby needs all the help he can get. Your ma and I love him as much as you do, whether you see it or not. You know I'm speakin' God's honest truth."

She nodded. "I think I wanted you to help me tell Mom, somewhere underneath all this. I never know how to talk to her. Gage, I don't want to upset Toby any more than he needs to be. He's so fragile. He carries guilt for everything Jared did."

"That's the first thing we need to straighten out. He didn't have nothin' to do with that man's evil."

"He doesn't see it that way. He thinks he carries some sort of legacy; he's afraid he'll get angry and out of control and do something terrible."

"That's ridiculous. That boy don't never get mad."

"I know. But it frightens him so. He hides it behind jokes and juggling, but the fear is constantly there. Trust me."

"Oh, I do. And, Sarah, it seems to me you spend a whole bunch of time tryin' not to upset your ma or Toby." He put a hand on the small of her back and opened the door. When they stepped out onto the deck, he relocked the door. "You did the right thing, tellin' me."

"I sure hope so, Gage."

"Now we gotta figure out how to break this to your ma."

Latest disaster averted. Lemonade spill gone. Another party. Dinner and a thunderous Lionel Jeffries had arrived.

Behind the bar Toby mixed drinks and grinned—rather sardonically, he realized—but did not have time to juggle or perform any magic tricks. So much for tips.

An array of buffet food was piled high on tables down the center of the stateroom. Roasted turkey and fresh croissants, potatoes, scalloped onions, apple and cranberry salad. People milled about, drinking, eating, laughing, and the wall of people constantly broke to spew customers to the bar.

The best part about the jovial ruckus—no time to think. Make that *dwell*. And the *Spirit* headed back to Sterling City, a relief. Toby would be glad to see the end of this trip.

Voices rose above the band playing in full ragtime swing, the steady vibration of the engines running beneath. The members of the theater troupe dressed as what passed as normal for them, eclectic glamour mingling with the wedding party. The theater folks appeared to be having the time of their lives. Toby wondered which took more acting, their shows or the smiles and conversation of this evening.

He caught no glimpse of the Russian woman, but no surprise. She mostly kept to her room, which he found to be a relief. She scared and excited him, all at once. But more than welcome, he caught a glimpse of Lucy, beyond beautiful in a light blue beaded dress, her cloud of curls held with a few sparkling ribbons. She didn't show any sign of the Great Lemonade Fiasco of the afternoon and held to Oscar Gévaudan's arm. Eyes followed them; people gathered around them. The handsome couple didn't seem at all like common people.

Royalty, Toby thought. The two of them, charming, poised, sparkling. Just like royalty. He tried not to let his lovesick gaze follow Lucy around the room, but it was hard. He stole a few glances at her. She, on the other hand, never tossed a look his way. And after he'd showered and cleaned up.

Even Henrietta had recovered and wove around, speaking and laughing with everyone. Except the sound of her voice revealed strain, at least to him. Her eyes sought him out every so often, like he was, somehow, a lifeline. And there, on the face of a woman seemingly heading to her own execution, he saw genuine delight break through every time she caught his eye.

Apparently, she thought they were friends. And maybe, Toby thought, they were. At the beginning stages, anyway. But after this trip, she'd forget him. That was the way it worked on the riverboat. Just like the theater people would leave and never look back. Lucy, gone for good. Henrietta too. Neither giving him a second thought.

Probably for the best. No one in their right mind would get involved with him for any length of time. His family didn't have a choice. With that thought, the dark crowded in. A kernel of worry sprouted.

Grew. Again.

Forget lemonade fiascos. He had bigger problems.

Since the accident, rumors rippled through the crew. The stage didn't fall on its own. Either innocent or intentional, someone's hand played a part, gossip insisted.

His own fears came. Did the event have anything to do with him and his missing hours?

"'Course not," he murmured. He wasn't an engineer, didn't work near the housing or the stage. He didn't even know enough to cause any mischief of that magnitude.

Did he?

When he'd first come onboard the *Spirit*, Gage took Toby under his wing, showed him around engineering. Taught him . . . stuff. Toby had no inclination or talent for any of it, and Gage's engineering lessons ended when he realized Toby wasn't interested. Instead, they'd built models together. As they worked, Gage told him stories of what it was like to work on the boats years ago when they'd carried cargo, people, and animals. Toby kept the miniature model of the *Spirit*—his favorite—on the shelf above his pillow. He could build models. But he didn't have the wherewithal to cause the stage to fall.

"An accident," he reassured himself.

"Talking to yourself again?"

He looked up. "Speak of the devil," he said to Henrietta.

"I've been called worse, believe me." She rolled her eyes with extreme drama. "Can I have one of your fizzy lemonades? Only this time, I think I'll drink it instead of wear it."

"Coming right up."

"You didn't get into much trouble, did you? I told Daddy it was all in fun."

"Yeah, my story, too," he said, shaking a jigger of his secret-recipe lemon sludge.

"Hey, do me a favor."

"The great and powerful Henrietta Jeffries needs a favor from lowly me? The *boy*?"

She had the grace to look sheepish. "Yeah, sorry. How many times are you going to make me apologize?"

"Oh, twenty more times ought to do it." He poured his lemon sludge into a glass.

"Fine. I need you to do something for me."

"Out with it." He blasted a shot of soda water into the drink.

"Forget what I said about marriage in general, would you? And mine in particular." She lowered her voice and leaned closer, over the bar. "I do not need any more trouble. I just have to get through the next two days."

"Marriage? What marriage?" He stirred the drink and topped it off with a sugared lemon.

"That's what I'd like to know." She sounded defeated. "Honestly, between you and me, I need to buckle down and act like the wife of a millionaire. It's my fate, empty though it may be. Like your fate is to serve drinks and juggle."

"Now you are depressing me." He slid the drink to her, across the bar. "I guess we all have our loads to bear. It won't be so bad. You'll be able to travel, do anything. You're rich."

"In money anyway." She reached out to take the glass. Toby put his hand on hers.

"Cheer up, Henrietta. A miserable marriage is nothing new. Look at the good part. The wedding is going to be great. And pretty soon you'll have babies. You can revolve your world around them, and you'll be fine. Happy."

A sad smile followed. She gripped his hand. "Thanks. You know, you really are nice."

"You've said that once already on this trip. You're starting to get mushy."

Her sad smile broke into a giggle. Billy the Buffoon spewed out of the crowd and slid up next to her. "What do you have to discuss with my beautiful bride with such intimacy? Your foreheads are practically touching."

Toby pulled his hand back. He liked this guy better when he ignored everyone. He thought about honoring Billy with a mock salute, but figured he was in enough trouble. "What can I get you?"

Billy the Buffoon glared.

Uh-oh. Time for a distraction. Toby flipped a glass in the air. And another. Then another. As they circled and caught the light, people around the bar turned to watch. A few applauded.

"What will it be, sir?" Toby asked. "Your wish is my command."

"Gin and tonic."

Toby plopped two of the spinning glasses back into the pyramid, thunking the final one in front, close to where it landed. Henrietta giggled while he mixed the drink.

"You like to show off, don't you?"

"Billy!" Henrietta admonished.

"I'm nothing more than the hired entertainment," Toby said. Much as he wanted to throw the drink in the idiot's face, he merely smiled and shoved the glass across the bar.

"You call that entertainment?" Billy picked up the drink and hooked his arm around Henrietta's neck, pulling her away from the bar. The two disappeared into the crowd.

"No," Toby said softly, "I call *you* entertainment, Billy the Buffoon." Then he saw movement out of the corner of his eye, close to the bar. He jerked his head sideways to see who'd heard his smart-aleck comment.

Oscar Gévaudan, *sans* Lucy, leaned on the bar, his eyes shining with merriment.

"You are the most entertaining bartender on this ship."

"Boat. And since I'm the only bartender, I guess I won't take that as a compliment."

"Oh, please do." Oscar's eyes narrowed. "Have you ever considered a career in theater?"

"What makes you think this job isn't?"

Oscar's grin widened. "My boy, I sense a very bright future for you. We do need to talk. You don't want to be a bartender forever, do you?"

A tiny spot ignited in his chest, reminding him he had much larger issues and more to worry about than juggling or bartending. Or Oscar Gévaudan, or Henrietta, Lucy, Billy the Buffoon, any of them.

As his face smiled at Oscar, the flaming kernel of worry sprouted into a full-fledged inferno. Toby didn't let any of it show.

Finally, Sarah's last charge stumbled to bed. Perhaps late, but at least, for the night, she was free. Only one place she wanted to go.

This time, when Sarah came into the pilothouse, Jeremy didn't scowl as usual. His face eased into a delighted and slightly shy smile. "Hey, what are you doing up this late?"

She nodded out the front window. "The moonlight looks beautiful on the water." She enjoyed her truce with him. One thing in her life not getting worse. "You might recall, Briggs ordered me to put in twice the time up here, and since most of the passengers are bedded down"—she tried to keep from grinning—"I'm reporting to fulfill my part of the bargain, that is, if I can pry your hands off of the wheel."

Without hesitation, he moved back and gestured for her to step up. "Be my guest. I've been up here the whole trip, feels like."

"You practically have." Warmth radiated where his hands were moments before. This time, she didn't mind him close behind her. "By the way, you missed your tea party," she said over her shoulder.

"Men don't have tea parties." His voice brushed her ear.

"One does. Look in the mirror and you'll recognize him."

He moved in closer her and she felt his heat along her back. Those darned tingles started again. She didn't fight them. Time to be honest with herself. She liked the way he made her feel. That is, when he wasn't goading her to anger.

"I figured, with all the excitement, you cancelled," he said. "Besides, I was busy lifting the stage and moving it around. You know, he-man stuff. No time for tea parties. I'll keep eating with my paws."

She laughed, gently. "Did you get any time at all to sleep?"

"A couple of hours this afternoon."

She piloted a few minutes in comfortable silence, the engine's hum the only sound. He rested his hand on her shoulder. She decided to let him keep it there and watched the moonlight ripple on water. Maybe it wasn't the worst thing, piloting under Jeremy's eye. Still, she longed for the time she'd be up here on her own. Responsible for everyone and everything.

She stopped herself short, before she moved into the competitive, frustrated stage where she railed against the unfairness of such an antiquated male-dominated system.

Jeremy broke the quiet. "This feels good."

"Me at the wheel? Of course it does," she said.

"No, us." He squeezed her shoulder. "Like friends. You aren't ripping my head off over anything."

"You haven't said anything idiotic or offensive."

He chuckled. They traveled another mile in comfortable silence.

"So tell me more about your mom."

He dropped his hand, and the spot on her shoulder cooled. He moved to the side, sitting on the lazy bench. "Not much to tell. Dad dropped dead, my mom and sisters almost starved, I started working on the riverboat, everything came out okay. End of story."

She decided to try another tactic. "I remember hearing your father actually died on the boat. What happened?"

"You've heard."

"Not from you."

Jeremy seemed to consider. "He was playing cards and toppled over. Fine one minute, gone the next. I was no more than ten feet away and didn't have any idea what happened. I felt sort of, I don't know, an upset in the air. Like something was wrong. The roustys started shouting." His eyes were focused on the memory, far from them in years. He spoke again, speaking in a hush, like everything had just transpired. "This group huddled around him. He lay on the deck, stretched out, his fingers curled up. I'll never forget those fingers. Like he was trying to hold on to something, but nothing was there."

An ache of empathy twisted through her.

"I was just a kid, and I got scared and ran to him, wanted him to wake up and make the world right like he always did. I guess, on some level, I knew he was gone." His voice hardened. "He was dead before I reached him."

He'd never opened up and shared this much with her.

"That must have been awful for you."

"I don't know. Life. Never know what it's gonna do." He looked up and out the front window at the moon glow, then back at her. "Gage gave me a job, although at that point I wasn't much good to him. But that's Gage. Took me under his wing. He's a good man, Sarah.

"No argument there."

"See. There are decent men in the world. If you give us a chance."

"And that is called pontificating."

"Huh?"

"You saying things to teach me a lesson, or make a point. I liked you much better when you were being open and honest."

This time the silence falling between them wasn't comfortable. Sarah decided to break it. "Everything with your father happened before we came on the boat."

"Yeah, ancient history."

"It must have been hard, torn away from your family."

He hiked his shoulders. "I was used to it. Me and Dad on the boat. My mom and sisters tending the home fire. Worked for us."

She wondered how different she'd be with a more traditional upbringing. A silly, stray thought. She wouldn't be who she was, and her strength came from the difficulties in her past. Yes, she'd erected a pretty impenetrable defense. Still, she wouldn't trade herself for anything. Warts and all.

Below, Andrew moved into a pool of light on the main deck. He squinted up at the pilothouse and Sarah waved. In the lamplight, his face resembled a mask, his cherubic expression drawn.

"Andrew's on his way up."

Jeremy stood and watched the doctor climb. "Something's wrong." He opened the door and they heard the doctor's footsteps, finally his head coming into view.

"I hoped this was the captain's shift."

Jeremy shook his head. "Not until later tonight."

"I have to find him and he's not in his quarters."

"Have you tried the stateroom?"

"First place I looked."

Sarah piped up. "The galley. He spends time down there with my mother sometimes."

"Good, I'll try there." He turned to leave.

"Andrew, what is it?" Jeremy asked.

He sighed. "You'll hear sooner or later. I have three very sick people in my cabin. I need a room for an infirmary."

"Three?" Dread rose from low in her belly and fisted in her chest. "Heavens, Andrew, what is it?"

"I'm not sure yet. Let's hope they were served something rotten and this isn't anything worse." He paused. "I've heard of a recent outbreak of cholera on the East Coast, although I'm simply running possibilities through my mind. We need to proceed with the utmost caution. The symptoms came on quite suddenly for the three and are fairly severe."

"I'm coming with you." Sarah looked at Jeremy. "I can't pilot now. We're in trouble. If it's just a bad meal, Mom is going to be—"

Jeremy grabbed the wheel. "Sarah, you don't have to explain. You have more important matters. Go ahead."

She always seemed to have something more important than piloting. So be it. Her mother and the captain were going to need her.

She followed Andrew down.

Chapter 18

Emma placed a mug of broth down in front of Briggs. She didn't like the way he looked, not one bit. He leaned slightly over the counter, resembling deflated bread dough, both in color and demeanor.

"Sip that. It will help."

He shook his head. "Emma, I need to get back to my room." His voice ground out around a clenched jaw. "This is—" He grabbed his gut. She dashed, but before she made it around the counter, he toppled.

She knelt beside him, shock jolting her. Captain William Briggham? Toppled and on the floor? She glanced up at the window in the door, praying to see someone. They were alone. She had to go get help.

"No," he gasped, as if he read her mind, "just help me up."

She grabbed his shoulders and, as gently as possible, lifted him to a sitting position, against the cabinets. He pulled his knees up, biting back a moan.

Now he frightened her. He never showed pain. "Will, I need to get the doctor."

"Damn it, I won't have anyone see me on the floor," he hissed between his teeth. "Help me to my room. Then you can summon the doctor."

Damn his pride anyway, she thought, and hooked his arm around her neck. She rose, dragging him to his feet. His knees buckled.

"We're not going to make it. I'm going to set you down and fetch Andrew."

He grabbed the counter with his free hand. "Damn it all, woman, I will be fine! Now stop yammering and get me to my room!"

Never, since she'd known him, had he spoken to her in such a way. He must be in terrible pain. They took a few steps to the door when he coughed. He dropped to his knees, retching, and pulled her down with him.

"Oh," was all Emma managed. She scrambled and grabbed a bucket from under the counter, slid it to him, then rushed to the sink to soak a rag. She kneeled and pressed the cloth to his forehead, holding him while he retched. His body shuddered and lurched with his sickness. She held on and spoke soothing words, just as she did with her children when they'd been sick.

When he paused and gasped, she gently helped him back to lean against the cabinets. He groaned and turned a shade of yellowish gray, his breath chuffing out in pants.

"I'm going to get Andrew," she insisted as the door behind her creaked open.

"No need." Andrew stooped and tilted the captain's chin up. Sarah slipped in and stood behind the doctor.

"How long has he been like this?" Andrew asked.

"He came to the galley about fifteen minutes ago, looking for something to settle his stomach. He was in pain."

"How severe?"

"With the captain it's hard to say. Until a few moments ago he managed it. Then it got pretty bad. Andrew, I've been worried about his being run down for a while now," Emma explained, "though he hasn't been sick like this."

"We have a much bigger problem." Andrew gazed directly at her. "There are three others with similar symptoms in my quarters."

Fear jolted her as she focused on listening to him.

"We need to set up an infirmary, Mom, right away," Sarah said.

"The passenger deck will be the best place. Dragging people up and down steps will be kept to a minimum," Emma said, locking onto something useful to do.

"The stateroom comes to mind," Andrew suggested. "Passengers' cabins open into it."

"But that's where we serve meals. Where will we have the rehearsal dinner?"

"Emma, I need to be honest with you. At this point I doubt there will be a rehearsal dinner. Or wedding. I have three others in my cabin, sick. This is four. Hopefully it's something from breakfast or lunch, and all they did was eat something bad." He returned his attention to Briggs. "Although a difficult enough scenario, alternatives are much worse."

Emma's own stomach churned, but not for any outside reason. The food they prepared made passengers sick? Made Will sick? Andrew's implication struck her.

"*Hopefully* bad food?"

"We have some sort of gastric distress outbreak on our hands." His voice grew grim. "Why, I can only guess. The symptoms appear quite severe."

She closed her eyes. It was the food. It had to be, if sickness came on this suddenly. Dear Lord, she'd made everyone aboard the *Spirit* sick. Her daughter's arm wrapped around her shoulders.

"Mom, it will be okay."

Emma opened her eyes, looked at the captain. His eyes glossed over; he stared at nothing. His breath came in short chops, mouth hanging slack. He'd aged decades in the last few minutes. She'd done this to him? Done this to others?

She jerked past the guilt threatening to overwhelm her. The captain and the others needed her to keep on task. "We'll set up in the stateroom."

Andrew softened his voice. "Emma, I'm a doctor. I always look for the worst that might happen. With any luck, we'll move the few who are ill out before morning and you can serve your rehearsal dinner." His voice rang empty, like he didn't believe his own words.

Emma didn't believe them either.

Bad food or sickness, this felt like they were at the beginning of something terrible. Three more people had stumbled out of their quarters, seeking help. Seven patients lay on the stateroom floor, one retching violently. The sound echoed off the walls, and Emma wondered how this could happen. Hours before, the room had been filled with mountains of mouthwatering food, an endless array of tasty libations, the air filled with strains of music, and beautiful people dressed to impress, laughing, moving about with ease.

Toby and Sarah set up makeshift beds in the stateroom, mostly blankets and sheets on the floor. Mattresses when they had them. Latticework scrolled up the arches above them, framing them as they worked. The huge mahogany bar sat in judgment, mocking the people lying on the floor.

Charley fetched water and cleaned up after the sick. His usual good humor had turned as serious as Emma had ever seen. Janine did laundry without being told, gathering soiled towels and blankets. They all kept glancing over at Briggs, expecting him to rise up and take control.

Not this time.

Emma leaned back until she heard her back crack into place. Good. Now she could keep going. With a cool rag, she mopped the face of a woman passenger, Dolores, she thought. The woman had vomited for over an hour, finally stopped, and now moaned. Andrew told Emma to keep the patients as clean and cooled off as possible, and to try to get them to drink something.

"Andrew, she threw up the water I gave her."

"Dab a moist rag on her lips, give her a few drops," he said over his shoulder, then sat back on his heels. "Emma, I apologize, I'm certain you know this, but make sure the cloth you use is fresh."

Emma bit back her retort. After all, she might be responsible for this entire disaster. She nodded instead.

"Help me, Toby. I need to get some more blankets," Sarah's voice instructed her brother. No surprise, her daughter wasn't upset or worried, but took the disaster in stride.

Toby rose to his feet. "Where are we going to get all these blankets?"

"Janine is gathering bedding from the sick quarters," Emma said. "She'll launder them, so coordinate with her." They'd already taken the thin mattresses from the bunks of the ill. There wasn't much else they could do.

Sarah stood. "Doctor, what do you think about going door-to-door? Shouldn't we let everyone know?"

Andrew knelt next to Briggs, taking his temperature. Dread weighed heavily on Emma. The possibility she made all these people sick. But more than anything, she hated seeing the captain incapacitated. He'd always been a constant in her life, a strong and reliable source.

"If this is an epidemic outbreak," Andrew said, "our going out and about will hasten the spread. I ought to quarantine this room, although I'm not sure that's practical."

"Besides," Toby added, "it's four in the morning. Most people will be asleep."

"What if someone is in their cabin and can't get help?" Emma asked.

"True. And, honestly, if this is an outbreak, no one will be completely safe who is on the boat." Andrew nodded at Toby and Sarah. "Why don't you two go ahead. Emma and I will keep going in here.

Tell people to stay in their rooms unless they need to use the facilities. And instruct them to limit all unnecessary contact. We'll do our best to contain whatever this is."

"Speaking of facilities, Toby and I will start there. Might be some of the sick made their way to the head," Sarah said.

"Ugh." Toby grimaced. "That's enough to curl my gut."

"Inform people of how it starts," Andrew instructed. "Nausea, abdominal pain, dizziness. If they have any of those symptoms, even slightly, get them down here."

"If many more are sick, we'll need to recruit some more help." Emma went through names of crew in her mind. "And I'll need to consult the passenger manifest, to see if there are any more doctors or nurses aboard." She shook her head. "I don't recall there are any. I'll double-check."

"I'm fairly certain there are no other doctors aboard," Andrew said. "However, it won't hurt to make sure."

Gage opened the stateroom doors, his face grim. "I heard there's trouble up here." Concern filled his eyes. "Em, what's goin' on?"

"You might want to stay back, Gage. I'm not sure what we're dealing with yet." Andrew stood. "Gastric distress. I'm hoping it's a case of bad food, but it might be something worse. I don't know exactly."

Gage tore his eyes from Emma, and she watched his gaze roam over the people on the floor, to Toby, Sarah, and Charley. The buckets set up. Andrew and the captain. Then back to her.

"Whatever it is we're facin', I'm in." Gage stepped in the room and the door closed behind him. He gestured to Briggs. "How is he?"

"He's sick as a dog," Briggs barked from the floor. Which made Emma feel better; at least he was still cranky. Much preferable to moaning and quiet.

"Toby and I are on our way out to let everyone know what is happening," Sarah said. "Make sure no one else is ill in their quarters."

"I'll come, too." Charley jumped to his feet. "I jest about got everythin' cleaned up."

"We're gonna need more help, especially if we have to get people in here," Gage said. "I'll go round up some others."

"Make sure they volunteer, and they realize the risks—we don't know what we're dealing with," Andrew said. "I won't blame anyone for staying away."

"Doc, don't worry about that. We're all part of the *Spirit's* crew. Besides, this ain't such a big boat. No place to hide from this kinda thing. Whatever it is."

"Emma." The doctor gestured to a man three people down, who wasn't moving. She rose to her feet and rushed to him. Knelt beside him, as did Andrew.

"He's breathing," Emma said.

"Let's cool him down."

Lilly burst through the door. "Oh, Jesus, Mary, and Joseph, what's goin' on?" She glanced around. "What can I do?"

"Lil, you might not want to be in here." Andrew said. "We aren't sure what's caused these people to be sick and it might be catching."

"Shoot, Andy, you obviously ain't been part of a crew before. We're in this together." She strode over to him. "Give me some orders."

"We could use a few glasses of soda water actually," Andrew said, nodding to the bar.

"Comin' right up." Lilly sprinted to the bar.

"And please make a quarantine sign for the door," Andrew continued. "I'm getting tired of sounding out the warning."

Lilly carried two glasses of water. "One sign comin' up. Jest tell me how to spell whatever it was you said." She set the glasses down on the floor next to Emma.

The doors again opened. This time, Toby and Gage drug an unconscious man—at least Emma hoped he was unconscious and not dead—through the door. "Found him on the deck outside," Gage said. "And there's another one right behind us. I got a rousty down, too."

"Oh God," Emma whispered.

Charley and Sarah came in, doing their best to hold up a moaning Henrietta Jeffries.

"Well, one thing's for certain." Lil said, coming back with two more glasses of sparkling water. "There won't be a wedding on this boat anytime soon."

Danny burst into the pilothouse. "Doc says we need to stop in Pleasant Grove. They's a doc in town he's friends with who might help, and he says . . . uh . . ."

"Slow down, take a deep breath, and you'll remember," Jeremy said.

"Oh, yeah, Sterling City's hospital is closest."

"Does he realize Sterling City is two more days after Pleasant Grove?"

Danny sighed heavily and turned to make another run.

Andrew couldn't wander far from the sick, Jeremy wasn't able to leave the pilothouse, and Sarah had her hands full in the stateroom. They set up the best way to communicate: this kid running back and forth. The doctor made sure Danny kept on the other side of the stateroom door, calling out brief requests and information.

"Hold on, Danny," Jeremy said. "You don't need to run and tell him. Andrew's familiar with how far out we are, I'm sure. I'm just thinking out loud."

Still breathing heavily, Danny flopped on the lazy bench, his eyes huge and scared. Jeremy didn't blame the boy for being frightened. They didn't know what they faced. Jeremy preferred his opposition to be out in the open, come at him head-on. Sickness snuck around, striking unseen.

Thank God the kid hadn't taken ill. But things were looking pretty grim, spiraling out of control. Last Jeremy heard, the list of the fallen had climbed to about twenty. He focused, intent on getting to Pleasant Grove and fast, engines running to full. As long as he kept steady, Gage and he would get them there in one piece.

The pilothouse door flew open. Jeremy jerked around and Danny jumped to his feet.

Oscar Gévaudan. Just what he didn't need.

"Turn this boat around!"

"Right." Jeremy returned his attention to the river. He didn't even want to hear what Flim-Flam might have to say.

"I mean it. One of my people is missing."

"Did you check the stateroom?"

"Of course I did!"

"I saw you jest lookin' through the window," Danny piped in.

Jeremy gritted his teeth. "Here's an idea, Oscar. Go inside and get a proper look."

"I can see perfectly well from the door and I'm telling you, she isn't in there."

"I've got a boat full of sick people and we're heading for Pleasant Grove."

"Your simian brain apparently can't process logic with the ability of us humans. Let me make my situation clear. One of my troupe didn't come back from the picnic. Ergo, you must turn this boat about to fetch her."

Jeremy gripped the wheel. He would not punch this man. He would not punch this man.

"Who's missin'?" Danny asked. "It ain't the tiger, is it?"

"No, Daisy is fine. One of my actresses is missing."

"So you didn't make sure your troupe all came back from the grove," Jeremy observed.

"They're adults. Unlike the way you people treat your passengers,

I find no need to be their nursemaid."

"Yeah, that's worked out pretty good, hasn't it?" Jeremy let Oscar sputter, then said, "How can you be sure she's missing when you won't even go into the stateroom and look? This boat is one step away from chaos. My simian brain has no plan in it other than full steam ahead."

"Zelda Vashnikoff. No one has seen her since the picnic."

Jeremy's brow crinkled. The heated-up Russian lady? Great. She was probably in someone's cabin right now, making some man really happy. "Have you looked everywhere? Asked around? Checked all the cabins? Maybe she's with someone."

Flim-Flam missed the implication, his usually amused expression creased with worry. "We had an . . . er . . . appointment. She wasn't in her cabin then. I thought it odd, but not terribly so. She does tend to forget scheduling at times. You know. Actresses."

Appointment. Right. Jeremy did know. That woman was most likely spread over someone's bed. He admonished himself for such an unkind thought. He was getting tired, still sore from lifting the stage, and a boat of sick people under his feet were counting on him to get them to help.

Oscar sat on the lazy bench next to Danny. The kid just about slid off the other end trying to make room.

"This trip is a disaster. Zelda is missing; my cast is in the dining room retching with wild abandon."

"Keep your wits about you." Jeremy said. "You're their leader. It's up to you to keep a level head."

A look of annoyance spread over Flim-Flam's face. "Oh, no. I'm not responsible for any of this. You and this damned boat—"

"This is a tough situation; it doesn't matter how it came to be. We all need to pull together and do whatever we can."

"The captain would listen to me, but he is completely incapacitated, which leaves me with you." Flim-Flam jumped to his feet. "I'm done discussing the situation. I demand you turn this boat around. Now."

"I'm in command now, and Pleasant Grove is the only place this boat is heading. There is another doctor in the town and Andrew thinks, if nothing else, the man will come aboard to help. Beyond is Sterling City and a hospital. And that's the way we're going."

"Damn you! Turn the boat! Now!" Oscar roared.

Jeremy had never heard the man raise his voice. He didn't even blink. When he spoke, he kept his voice calm, even easy.

"Danny, go down and get Sarah up here. Tell her we need a roustabout or two as well."

Danny jumped up. Oscar stepped in the boy's way.

"Oscar, step aside," Jeremy said calmly.

"What are you about?" Oscar narrowed his eyes. "Why summon the roustabouts?"

"I'm going to have them drag your worthless ass out of my pilothouse unless you sit down and calm down."

"No!" Oscar yelled and actually stamped his feet in the beginnings of a full-out tantrum.

"That does it," Jeremy said. "Sit, or I'll take care of you myself, right now."

"You can't let go of the wheel." Oscar didn't sound convinced.

Jeremy clamped the wheel bridle in place, let go, and turned. Oscar squealed, jumped out of Danny's way, and plopped down on the bench. "Fine. I'll behave. You don't need more muscle up here. I can barely survive the chest-pounding show you put on."

Jeremy actually snickered. The man was annoying, but sometimes pretty funny, too.

"Danny, just fetch Sarah, please." He smiled. "It will be my pleasure to take care of Mr. Gévaudan myself."

Danny scooted down the steps and Jeremy unclamped the bridle.

"Now, step one—we make sure your actress is truly missing."

Oscar sighed theatrically. "What do I have to do to prove it to you?"

"This isn't some sort of game. The well-being of everyone, including Zelda, is at stake. You haven't convinced me she's really missing. You haven't searched thoroughly yourself."

"I have, too! Step one should be to turn the boat around."

This was like arguing with a petulant child. "I told you," Jeremy said, "I'm not doing anything until we are sure your actress isn't aboard, and then we will send help back to her once we reach Pleasant Grove."

"You idiot, she'll be lost." Oscar jumped to his feet. "Likely as not she's wandering around in the dark right now. Freezing. Her costume was skimpy."

"Yeah, it was. A woman has no business parading around like that."

"Spare me your outdated Midwestern morality. And don't be a hypocrite. I watched you ogle every curve on her."

"Hard not to. And you're not fooling me. You plan it that way."

Oscar sat back down on the bench. "If only I hadn't left her alone out there. I should have insisted she come with me."

"At the grove? She wasn't alone; there were plenty of people around."

"No, in the woods. A little ways in. Poor thing doesn't have any sense of direction."

"You left her in the woods?" Jeremy had a good idea of what business the randy Russian woman and Flim-Flam might conduct in the seclusion of bushes and trees. Things were starting to add up.

Oscar looked like he'd been caught with his pants down. "She needed to relieve herself. I left her to her privacy."

"Right. And her 'appointment' with you this evening?"

"I'm not sure that's any of your business, Mr. Cro-Magnon."

"My compliments. Nice job of taking care of your woman."

"Ah, precisely the kind of caveman sort of sentiment I'd expect from you."

Sarah opened the door. "Looks like I'm getting here just in time."

Oscar jumped to his feet. "Sarah! I'm relieved you are here, my dear. At last, someone who can talk some sense into this gorilla. Please explain to him that we must turn the boat around."

"Oscar, we can't do that. We have twenty sick people below; we have to get them to help. Andrew is the only doctor onboard, and thank God he's here, or we'd really be in trouble."

"One of his ladies is missing," Jeremy said. "I thought you might get someone to take a look around, check cabins."

"We already did a cabin-to-cabin search for anyone sick. Maybe I saw her." She returned her attention to Flim-Flam. "Who is missing?"

"Zelda Vashnikoff. Titania."

"Oh, the older actress."

"It would wound her to hear you refer to her in such a manner. She's seasoned."

Sarah took Flim-Flam's hand. Jealousy curdled through Jeremy, and he didn't like any of it—the jackass touching Sarah or the fact that it bothered him.

"Oscar, come with me. We need to leave Jeremy alone so he can do his job. I'll help you find her. I'm sure she's onboard."

"I'm sure she's not."

"Then we'll figure it out. Come along." She paused. "Jeremy, are you doing all right up here? Will you need me to come up so you can get some rest?"

"I'm fine to make Pleasant Grove. Thanks anyway."

Sarah ushered Flim-Flam out and gave a final glance to Jeremy. He returned what he hoped was a grateful look.

He turned back to the river. Thanks to Gage running the engines at capacity, they should make Pleasant Grove by about daybreak. No hospital. At least there was a small clinic and another doctor, one Andrew knew and worked with before.

A boat full of sick people and a missing randy Russian beauty. She

could be anywhere. But only one place for the sick folks to get the help they needed.

Jeremy focused on the river and the path ahead.

Emma walked through the field of sick, moaning people and headed to the bar in the back of the stateroom. A group gathered around the window of the front door. Whenever anyone from the stateroom walked outside, the people backed away, shouting out questions, desperate for updates. However, none were desperate enough to get near those working with the sick.

If anyone she loved were ill, nothing would keep her from their side.

Gage joined Emma at the bar. "Doin' all right?"

"Good as I can be considering I've made this many people ill."

"We don't know that."

She shrugged. "Fairly obvious."

"Not at all. That's the frustration of all this."

"You know the strangest part?"

He shook his head.

"I can't help this feeling of *déjà vu*."

"And that means?"

"French term. Something unpleasantly familiar. I can't help feeling odd—like I've been here before."

"When the *Ironwood* blew up," Gage said, "and when we brought aboard all those injured people in pain."

"That's right. I guess I try not to think of that time at all." The awful memory tumbled through her. "Hard to ignore when we travel over the very spots."

Emma turned and looked in the huge mirror behind the bar. The room's reflection stretched out behind her, seeming like another place. Another time. An alternative to this life.

"I was thinkin' about the *Ironwood* again, too," Gage agreed. "I have this feelin' there's somethin'—I don't know."

"What?" She tore herself away from the room in the mirror to look at him.

"Connected?"

"That's because of *déjà vu*. The feeling it gives you, even though events are new."

"Somehow, that don't seem right. Somethin' . . ." She watched as his eyes drifted off into thought with his voice. She knew he saw wisps of visions. Long ago, she learned to trust his intuition.

She shifted her attention away from Gage and to the corner, where Andrew knelt beside one of the sick. The doctor caught her eye and jerked his head, signaling for Emma to join him. He mouthed "bring Gage" to her over the moans of the sick.

"Andrew needs us."

He nodded and followed her.

The form beside Andrew wasn't moving. At all.

As they approached the doctor, numbness crept through her fingers and worked its way up her arms and into her chest. A roar started in her ears. The man, one of the bridegroom's young friends, lay sheet-white. Still.

Emma sank to her knees next to Andrew. "Oh, no. No."

Andrew nodded. "I'm afraid he died a few moments ago."

Never mind *déjà vu*. Emma experienced the sensation of existing outside of her body. She dropped her face into her hands. Gage kneeled down and put his arm around her.

"I've killed someone," she whispered.

"That ain't true," Gage said.

She lowered her hands and looked at the lifeless young man. Faced what she'd done.

"Gage," Andrew began, "we need a morgue. Someplace we can

take him . . ." He paused, looking apologetic, then continued ". . . and perhaps others. We'll need a place with easy access."

"Most room is in engineerin'. The back, with the throttle. The only other choice is up by the boilers, and I don't reckon we want dead bodies in the heat."

"I don't reckon we do," Andrew said softly. "No place else?"

"We off-loaded them before, durin' the *Ironwood* tragedy," Gage said. "We left them on the bank and someone came back for them."

A crease appeared between Andrew's eyes. "No, we can't do that, not without knowing what's caused this."

Emma flinched. Gage gripped her hand tighter.

"Besides," Andrew said, "we can't take the time to land and off-load them. With the *Ironwood*, there were many more dead."

"We don't know how many this will be." Emma's voice sounded distant, even to herself.

"We could stack them in the dead man's cabin." Gage's voice echoed with thought.

"If we need more room, it means more have died—"

"Which means we'll have more cabins," Gage said.

"Please!" Emma's voice trembled. "Stop talking about them like they are objects. These are people. People." She swallowed hard, trying to come to grips with the horror of her part in this nightmare. "Dear God, I do hope this stops before the entire boat is . . ."

Gage squeezed her shoulder. "Hold on. Keep the faith, Em." He gestured to the dead man and looked at the doctor. "Do you know who this boy was?"

"Not really. He hadn't been able to speak since he came down," Andrew answered.

"Then I'll find out. And notify his kin, if they are onboard."

Emma fought the urge to wail. She clenched her jaw, keeping tears away.

He helped her to her feet, held his arm around her. "Emma, you did not do this. I am sure of it."

She wished she shared his faith. A man was dead. What if she was responsible?

A locomotive, when it first rolls out of the station, moves slowly. Creeps. Once it begins, it picks up speed. Moves faster. Steam belches, fogs around, a portent of the power that the large, rumbling beast harnesses within. Faster and faster still the thing moves.

As it picks up speed, it becomes more difficult for the behemoth to come to a stop. And indeed, after a bit of forward momentum, it cannot stop. Or be stopped.

An unseen engineer stokes the fire, giving the train power to forge ahead. If something gets in its way, it slams into the offending object, crushing it, flinging it aside as if it were the most inconsequential of objects.

The mighty fall before the locomotive; the lesser are swept away. And it keeps going. Moving. Forward. Sweeping aside all in its path.

And so it is. Nothing compares to the power of the train.

And so it has become with Our revenge. And Our hate.

It is tenacious in power, relentless in motion, sure of the final destination.

Chapter 19

The bell sounded twice, and engines dropped to half. They were here. Again. This time, stopping.

Emma sat back on her knees. Unsettled hardly described her feeling every time they neared Pleasant Grove. Jittery, shaken, upset. Overwhelmed. She pushed shreds of anxiety aside, although try as she might, these feelings hung thick in the air, permeated her soul.

The people in this town had almost lynched Gage. And now Pleasant Grove was their best hope.

"Someone walking over my grave, I think they call it," she murmured, then checked to make sure she hadn't disturbed her patient, Captain William Briggham. He slept, uneasily, but he was alive, his breathing less ragged. She lightly touched his forehead; the fever was diminished. He reminded her of corn left on the stalk too long, its insides withered and almost gone, the remaining husk paper thin, crumpled, and weak. He'd grown ancient in one day, his life essence stolen.

She fought against folding under the weight of guilt, but this load was a heavy one.

The engines dropped off to idle mode. The sound of the door opening drew her eyes to the front of the stateroom. Gage entered, heading for her and the captain. Emma rose to meet him.

"We've arrived," he said, his black eyes sharp.

Emma took in a deep breath, held it, and slowly let it out. "Let's hope stopping here does us some good."

"I wholeheartedly agree," Andrew said, joining them. "Time for me to depart, soon anyway. I told Jeremy I'd meet him on the deck at dawn."

"Glad it's you and not me goin' ashore," Gage said.

Andrew nodded sympathetically.

"Looks like we're early," Emma said.

"Jeremy asked us to push the engines to their edge. I got coal heavers who are glad for a rest finally."

"Let's hope we've arrived in time," Andrew said. "Now to see if there's any help for us here. Do you have the list, Emma?"

She pulled a sheet of paper from her pocket and handed it to him.

"Thank you. I'm glad you're this organized; it helps me a great deal."

Gage pressed his lips together. "Andrew, good luck. Anythin' you need while you're gone?"

"Do your best to keep everyone alive for a while, and I'll do my best to bring back help."

The doctor picked up his satchel and left.

"Nothin' important for me in engineerin' now we're here," Gage said. "Can I help?"

She allowed a tired smile to surface. "Why don't you get some sleep? I have a feeling once we get going again, you and Jeremy will have your hands full."

"You talk like there won't be no help for us here."

"What do you think?"

"I don't hold out much hope." He rubbed his neck like he felt the brush of a hangman's noose. On impulse, she wrapped her arms

around him, and he returned the embrace. "We'll get through all this, Em. We been through worse."

Perhaps, but she'd never been the cause before.

Emma let go of him, attempted a smile of reassurance. "I'm going to go check on Toby."

Walking along the rows, she stopped near Henrietta Jeffries and Toby.

Emma knelt down beside her son. "How is she doing?"

"She finally stopped retching. She's sleeping on and off. When she wakes, she doesn't seem to recognize me."

Emma put a hand on his shoulder.

Toby continued, "I feel so sorry for her, Mom. Her father hasn't come in at all; he's just glanced in the window a few times. And that woman they pay to help Henrietta. Adele, I think? She isn't here either. Henrietta's all alone."

Emma was so very proud of him and Sarah both. They hadn't hesitated. Quite the opposite, they jumped in to help wherever needed. Despite their difficult beginning in life, she'd raised good, strong people, with caring, empathetic hearts.

"Henrietta has you. You're doing a wonderful job, Toby."

"I thought more passengers would help. I guess they're afraid of catching whatever it is."

"Fear is a difficult thing to overcome." She gave her son a look of encouragement. "And your help is more than enough. You have a very good bedside manner."

His sweet, blue eyes looked up at her, and she wished she could do something, anything to soften the worry she saw in them.

"You and Henrietta are becoming friends, aren't you?"

"Well, you don't have a lemonade fight with just anyone."

She summoned a smile and rubbed his back, then rose to resume checking on patients. As she continued her walk between the rows of makeshift beds, she wondered how many of these people would live through the next day. Who would they carry into the cabin of the dead? And how many people, now healthy, might join them in the stateroom infirmary?

She tried not to let guilt overtake her, but a voice nagged. *She did this. She did this.*

"Why can't we pull in?" Danny asked, peering out the window as Jeremy and a rousty rowed the doctor in the yawl. Over Danny's shoulder, Sarah watched the small boat head to the bank. She'd been left at the wheel of a running riverboat without a pilot license. A testament to how grim the situation was getting.

"We're being careful. We have no idea what made everyone sick. Or if it's catching. They'll probably insist on keeping us in quarantine," she answered.

"What does that mean?"

"They won't let us onshore until everyone is well." *Or dead.* She pushed the thought out of her head. "If they do quarantine us, we'll have to stay out here and no one will be allowed off the boat. Hopefully someone will volunteer to bring supplies to us."

And if we're really lucky, another doctor. Andrew went the entire night without sleep; fatigue had lined his usually pleasant face. The *Spirit* was at the mercy of the small town, and Pleasant Grove possessed the deserved reputation as the least friendly stop along the river. This was, after all, where Gage had almost been hanged, accused of killing one of Jared's victims—actually, Danny's mother—years ago.

Not exactly Sarah's favorite place. Probably not Gage's either.

"Do you remember living here at all?" Sarah asked.

Danny shrugged. "Not really. I jest remember the dragon." *Dragon.* His label for Jared Perkins, the man who murdered his mother. God, would they ever get away from the echoes of his violence?

"He was scary," Danny said, "but Gage got me away, and that's what counts."

"And you are exactly right." She gave him a quick hug and he pushed out of her arms.

"Yeck."

"Sorry." Finally, a genuine smile emerged from her.

She watched the men row closer to shore. Their best emissaries. If Andrew and Jeremy couldn't make the case for help, no one could.

Out of the corner of her eye she sensed movement from the deck below. A burst of alarm raced through her every time someone climbed the steps. The news was never good. She glanced over to see Oscar making his way up.

No anxiety, but her shoulders drooped with fatigue. She knew exactly what he wanted. The entire boat, outside the stateroom, knew his demands. She was tired of having this discussion with him. He opened the door, looking terrible. His usually jovial, amused demeanor went dark, his eyes hollowed out from a night of missing sleep and worry, she supposed. He seemed positively wilted.

"I need to get off. Is there another one of those little boats I can take?"

She shook her head. "Oscar, we aren't allowed—"

"Damnation, Sarah." His voice rose and Danny's eyes grew round. "I've given up on any help from you in turning the boat around. At least let me off this rubbish scow so I can go back to search for Zelda myself."

"Danny, will you go ask Lilly for a pitcher of water? We need one up here."

Danny sighed heavily. He gave Oscar a forlorn glance. Then back to her. "Yes, ma'am."

Oscar glared until Danny left.

"Jeremy will talk to the sheriff and have him organize a search for her."

"Oh, yes, I have no doubt finding a wayward actress will be first on the sheriff's list. If Cro-Magnon even remembers to mention it."

"Despite what you might believe, the well-being of all passengers is a priority for him, for all of the crew. He wants to help you and Zelda."

"Oh, don't bother with all your placating words. I've seen the care you people take. Half the boat is sick. A few are dead. You do your jobs, oh, so very well."

She counted to ten before she answered. "Jeremy will be sure the sheriff organizes a party, or sends word downriver to look."

"No one cares about us. Ever. People are happy we come to bring some light into their dull, dreary lives, but make no mistake. I know what they really think. We are carnival folk. Considered outside the realm of decency. Not quite human. Same social status as animals grazing in the fields. Wait—make that one rung beneath."

"Oscar, that is not at all true. Look at the reception you've enjoyed on this boat. You and your actors are treated like royalty." She paused to bring her voice under control. "And you are the last person who should head a search. People familiar with the area, who know how to track in the woods, will do much better, and on their own. You will only slow them down." This time when she paused, she thought about how difficult it was to stand by, waiting for someone else to act. "Sometimes the best you can do is keep out of the way."

"She'll be frightened, she might even be sick. She did consume the swill this boat calls food. It will be the death of us all!"

Sarah bristled, but choked back her defensive remarks. Oscar was upset and this was no time to run her mouth. She planned to keep her temper and her wits about her. No matter how sorely she might be tested.

"Trust me, Oscar. Jeremy will relate how important it is to find her. They will start looking right away and—"

"I do not need to hear that one more time!" he shouted. "I've listened to enough of your soothing words, your golden tones meant to manipulate calm! No one out there will help us! Never mind strangers, not even you or your pet gorilla give a damn!"

"Oscar, calm down!"

"Bah!" He raised his hand to strike her. She jerked back with alarm, and he lowered his hand and scrubbed it down his face. "Sarah, I apologize," he said, his voice sheepish. "My passions do carry me away."

She whipped her attention back to watch out the window before she said something she'd regret. She concentrated on watching the boat land and the small town sprawling up the side of the hills. Mostly small houses, a few businesses, and some people beginning to come out. The Pleasant Grove morning had begun.

The arrival of the yawl caused some attention. People pointed and a few drew near. Jeremy and Andrew made their way up the brick landing, to the main street of the town, while the rousty stayed with the small boat. They stopped and Jeremy gestured as he called out to a man. She couldn't hear what Jeremy said, but the man backed away.

She experienced a strange sensation, like she were an observer to life, and not really part of it, and the *Spirit* traveled on the outskirts of reality.

Oscar slid into her line of vision. He trained his chocolate-brown eyes on her—huge, warm, pleading—and she felt sorry for him. He was frightened. They all were.

"Please forgive me," he said softly, his tones low and smooth. He took her hand. "I am beside myself, lovely Sarah. Not at all at my best."

"None of us are, which is why we must work even harder to be calm." When he released her hand she put it to his cheek. "You are worried about Zelda, and that is quite a testament to you, as her friend and employer. Trust me, we are doing everything we can. Jeremy will take care of it. You can rely on him, Oscar." She stopped, thinking how she could trust him, too. "If I know him, he'll have a search party forming at this very moment."

He took her hand from his face and opened it. "You have much more faith in the Cro-Magnon creature than I do." He traced the lines on her palm and sent a shiver through her. "I am sorry. I've been difficult. I am just so worried. Zelda is special; she's delicate." His voice etched with sadness. "Except when she is in her prima donna mode, then she is a force to be reckoned with."

Sarah smiled, she hoped, reassuringly. She squeezed his hand. "We will find her, Oscar. Safe and none the worse for wear. I'm sure of it."

"You shouldn't be here." Although several yards away, the mayor took a few steps back, holding a kerchief over his nose and mouth with a pudgy hand. His gold pinky ring twinkled in the sunlight, so tight it must be cutting off his circulation.

"There's been no indication of any risk of contagion," Andrew said. The mayor didn't drop his kerchief, which suited Jeremy just fine. He didn't want to see any more of the man's sneering face.

Beside the rotund mayor, a tall, thin minister stood. Dressed in black from head to toe, white hair and close-cropped beard glistening in the morning sun. Both men kept their distance—about ten feet away from the men of the *Spirit*. Every time Jeremy or Andrew took a step forward, the mayor took one back. If the situation weren't so grave, Jeremy would run to the pompous official, throw his arms around the man, and give him a big, fat kiss.

On second thought, not if his life depended on it. Lack of sleep was obviously getting to him.

"Please, Mayor," Andrew said, "we aren't sure this is any sort of epidemic. People have the symptoms of acute gastric illness most likely caused by something served on the boat. We are keeping our distance for caution's sake."

"Get out of this town! Get out now! No, your boat may not land. We have no help to give you." He puffed out his vested barrel chest, and buttons strained. The minister had the good grace to look ashamed. He kept his eyes downcast as the mayor spoke. The fat man continued through his handkerchief, "You'd best be on your way to Sterling City, where there is a hospital."

"We are about thirty-six hours at full speed from there," Jeremy said, "but we have passengers who won't make it that far. And Doc here is without a night of sleep already."

"Please," Andrew again pleaded, "we are desperate for help."

The mayor made no move to reply. They were prepared for this kind of reception, but facing a complete standoff made Jeremy's gut tighten. He wanted to launch into this jackass and force him to do right.

"Fine. Then all I ask is that you carry this note to Dr. Elliot." Andrew held out a folded slip of paper. "It's a request for him to come aboard and assist. Also, I have a list of medical supplies we need." He stood still for a few seconds. When it became obvious neither the mayor nor the minister was going to take the paper, he set it on the ground, placing a small rock on top. "If the doctor can spare them," he finished and straightened.

"Take that filthy thing with you," the mayor said through his kerchief, his rheumy eyes like small, runny raisins in a mound of gray pudding. "No one will dare touch it."

"Then let it lie here; ask the doc to come and fetch it. He'll help, I'm sure of it."

"I'll kick it into the river! You'll leave nothing behind!"

Andrew's usual gentle, convivial manner wore away with each hour, and it now appeared altogether gone. He glared at the mayor, the angriest Jeremy had ever seen him.

"Tell me, Mayor," Andrew said, "how is your daughter? I hear she recovered quite nicely from her pneumonia last winter. I trust she is well?"

The mayor turned red as a choking drunk and dropped his attention to his feet. "She's fine. I appreciated everything you and Doc

Elliot did for her.

"Yes, quite an epidemic. Over ten people, I recall. I also remember taking turns with you, holding your daughter upright night after night. Thank heavens good, caring people surrounded her. People more worried for her than themselves. She would surely have died otherwise. That's the thing about the sick. They are always someone's daughter, or sister, or wife, or father, or son. Someone's loved one."

"I did pay you for your service," the mayor mumbled.

"Raspberry jelly. All you could afford at the time. Or so you said." Andrew's voice was tinged with sarcasm. "Not what I usually charge for weeks of sleepless nights and bedside doctoring, but who keeps track of that sort of thing?"

The minister finally broke his silence. "God keeps track."

In the moment of quiet Jeremy opted not to say anything. Nothing like righteous indignation. Andrew was doing fine without him.

"I intend to pay you in full, Doctor. I will make good on that debt." The mayor's words came out timid and small. "But make no mistake," he continued, his voice rising, "your boat will not land in our town!"

A younger man, walking down from the town, finally came up behind the mayor. The sheriff, Jeremy surmised from his badge. He guessed the blond man might be the same sheriff from the days when Gage was almost hanged. Lawmen did tend to keep around river towns, make their permanent homes in the small communities. Jeremy planned to use guilt if he could work it in. It seemed to do well enough for Andrew.

"No closer!" The mayor grabbed the young man, keeping him back. The sheriff planted his feet and crossed his arms.

"We can't say for certain what we are up against," Andrew said. "I have a boat of one hundred forty or so people, about twenty of whom are sick. Some sort of acute gastric illness. We are in extremely dire straits and anything you can do will be seen as more than kindness."

"I'm sorry, Doc," the sheriff replied, "but we can't let you land. Not until we know for certain there is nothing catching. We can't take the risk. Go back to your yawl and get offshore now."

Andrew gestured to the pieces of paper on the ground. "I've listed requests. I'd appreciate it if you'd look at them."

"We aren't touching those!"

"You don't need to," Andrew said. "Just please tell the doctor they're here waiting for him."

Jeremy resisted the urge to run forward and poke the mayor right in his fat belly. Instead, he said, "One of our passengers is missing. We landed about sixty miles down at the grove beyond where Rambling Creek lets out. We off-loaded for a picnic. The passenger, a woman, never returned to the boat."

"Good heavens, your incompetent crew lost a passenger?" The mayor's indignation was not the least bit appropriate, as far as Jeremy was concerned.

"Tell me about the missing woman," the sheriff said.

Jeremy related the details of the picnic in the grove and gave a description of Zelda Vashnikoff.

"Well, we can assure you of one thing. We'll send a party down there right away to search."

"She may be a carrier, too!" the mayor puffed.

"In that case," the sheriff said, his voice tight, "we can't let her wander around. Who knows where she may end up? We need to contain whatever this is."

"The owner of the theater group has offered a reward," Jeremy said. Suddenly all eyes snapped to him. "Five hundred dollars for her safe return."

The number fell between the men, and the mayor's piggy eyes finally sparked with some interest.

"And Sheriff, Mayor," Jeremy decided to add, "Gage sends his best. I'm sure you remember? The innocent engineer you came close to hanging?"

The mayor sniffed loudly through his handkerchief.

The sheriff nodded. "We'll look for your actress. We owe the *Spirit* at least that much."

"Thanks."

"I do have to ask you to go straight to your yawl and return. And no one is allowed off your boat. I'm sorry we can't do more."

"We appreciate any help, Sheriff," Andrew said.

"And please send our best to Mr. Gage. We regret that happenin' in our town's history," the sheriff called after them.

Andrew's shoulders slumped. Jeremy patted his back. The bright, morning light mocked the two men. They walked in the dirt street, down to the river.

"Good job, Doc. Hopefully the guilt will do its trick. Did you really sit up with his daughter?"

Andrew nodded. "She took terribly ill, but she made it. Influenza spread through town, and for several it became pneumonia. We suffered no fatalities—a miracle. Doc Elliot has called me to town several times to help, last winter the latest instance. I certainly hope he's more inclined to consider our pleas."

"He will, if he's anything like you," Jeremy said.

"By the way, I didn't realize Oscar Gévaudan offered a reward."

"He didn't. I thought I'd improvise."

Andrew glanced sideways at Jeremy.

"I figure when they find her, he'll be so damned happy, he'll be glad to fork it over."

"And if they find her and he doesn't pay?" Andrew asked.

"I guess that'll be Oscar's problem. As I hear tell, this town isn't too happy when it comes to disappointing the powers that be. Just as soon string a man up as listen to his story." Jeremy shrugged. "I imagine

Oscar will come up with the money."

Despite the serious circumstances, a shadow of a smile crossed Andrew's face. Jeremy put his hand on the doctor's shoulder. Andrew's drawn face reflected their grim situation.

"Hold on, Doc. We'll manage."

They boarded the yawl and Jeremy and the rousty pushed off. Jeremy glanced behind as he dipped the oars into the river. Despite the white glow of the boat in gentle morning sun, he shuddered.

For the first time in his life, the *Spirit* looked like a boat of the damned.

"This is an outrage!" Oscar's voice thundered over the deck. The roustys securing the yawl back to the *Spirit* ignored him.

"They are sending a search party to look for her," Jeremy insisted. "It's the one thing we got them to promise."

"It is obvious they are only paying lip service to you, but I wouldn't expect a gorilla to pick up on any intricacies of communication."

That did it. Too much frustration for one morning. A bolt of anger shot through Jeremy and he grabbed Oscar by the throat and pushed him against the mast.

"You call me that one more time, or make any reference to a caveman, and I'll show you just how rough the jungle can be on a flim-flam excuse of a dandy."

"Jeremy." Andrew's voice, from behind.

He let go and Oscar sputtered. Jeremy didn't care; he'd suffered enough of the bastard. He was sick and tired of unimportant men blustering, pushing him around. He headed for the steps, and he and Andrew climbed to the second deck. Flim-Flam had the good sense not to follow.

"This is where I get off." Andrew headed for the stateroom.

"Hold on. How long do you want me to wait for word from Doc Elliott?"

"I'm sure we'll hear shortly. I can't imagine they will deny us supplies. Let's say two hours."

"We can make Sterling City in a little less than two days."

"If it's the best we can do . . ."

"Andrew, I'll give it everything we've got, and then some."

"I know. Jeremy, thank you."

The men shook hands and Jeremy continued up to the pilothouse. He didn't mind the weight and responsibility, but not being able to jump in and fix everything with his hands and his will was just about more than he could handle.

"I take it the meeting didn't go well," Sarah said when he entered the pilothouse.

"How do you figure?"

"You aren't very good at hiding your feelings."

He thought of all the complicated, confusing feelings he hid from Sarah and laughed sadly. "I need practice, I guess. Where's Danny?"

"I sent him down to the galley. Oscar has been incorrigible."

"Big surprise, although you don't need to tell me. He practically jumped all over me when we got back."

"So they won't help us?"

"Actually, I can't blame them," Jeremy said. "They are right. If this is something contagious, we do need to contain it here, protect against it spreading."

"Why is it you are always so logical?"

He thought about saying because he was a man. Then kept it to himself.

Sarah continued, "And if you say anything like it's because you're a man, you'd do best to move your foot out of my way."

"When did you start reading my mind?"

"As I said, you aren't good at hiding your feelings."

He balled his fists, then stretched them out. He'd never experienced such frustration. He had to do something. These people, this boat was too precious to lose to anything, let alone something as indiscriminate as an illness.

He never thought he'd see the day when Briggs fell. Jeremy worried Sarah might catch whatever it was, or Gage, or Danny. Toby. Charley. Any of them could be next. Whatever made everyone sick didn't choose based on any reason.

He gathered Sarah in his arms.

She looked into his eyes. "What is this about?"

"For once in your life, keep quiet. Let me hold you. Sarah, I just need to hold you."

Her eyes softened with understanding. Grew dark. She dropped her gaze to his mouth, and sent a spiral of fire through him. He brushed his lips across hers, wanting to kiss her, but not daring. For a hundred reasons.

She took care of his dilemma, spread a hand on either side of his face, pulled him to her, and kissed him.

Every worry and fear drained away, if only for a moment. He pulled her so close he could feel every part of her, and deepened the kiss. Desire worked its way through him and his body responded to her. She had to notice, too. She snuggled closer to him, and a moan escaped him, low, deep.

She pulled back, rubbing his lips with her thumb. "Well," she said.

"Well," he answered.

"This is much better than arguing."

"Or you stamping on my foot." This time he kissed her, slow, soft, exploring. Needing.

The kiss ended and she drew back. "Jeremy. What now?"

He let her go. "We wait for word from the doctor in town."

"I meant about us."

He sighed. "Honestly, I'm not sure. I've been waiting a long while to kiss you, and this felt like the right time."

They looked at each other for a minute, and he wasn't sure what to say.

"Sarah, anything could happen here. I want you to know I'd like more time. With you. Things are tangled up between us. We've been everything from best friends to adversaries. But I feel something different now. Something important. I'd like to figure things out with you."

"Oh, dear God, no!"

Surprise, followed by hurt, bolted through him. Then he realized she was looking past him. He whipped around just in time to see Oscar Gévaudan jump overboard.

Chapter 20

If Tobias Perkins never saw another person vomit, it would be fine with him.

One look down at Lucy, and he instantly regretted his unkind thought. These people couldn't help what happened to them. He was a cad to even think such a thing.

Glancing from Lucy to Henrietta, he wasn't sure which made him feel worse. Lucy lying on a mattress, her porcelain skin waxy, beauty sharpened by her tragic state. Like a fragile, broken bird, the illness bound her to the ground instead of where she belonged, soaring to the heights. Or Henrietta, lying across the room. He wasn't spending near as much time by her side, and he was a double cad for it. She was his friend. He actually liked Henrietta.

But Lucy, Toby thought as he looked down at her fragile form, he adored.

Then the nagging feeling persisted. Was he somehow responsible for all this? After all, he felt responsible for everything that went wrong on this boat, so why not add this to his list of problems? Besides, when a drunk missed hours, who knew what might happen?

As Lucy slept, her breathing became more even than it had been in hours. Across the room, Henrietta squirmed. He decided to attend to her; he hadn't been over there in a while.

He dropped to his knees beside her, and pushed back damp, red hair. She trembled, and he tucked the blanket tighter around her shoulders. She gazed up at him, no recognition in her eyes. She'd been violently ill for several hours now, but calmed down awhile ago, which he hoped was a good sign.

Three people were dead. Thank God Lucy or Henrietta wasn't one of them.

A silhouette appeared in the beveled glass of the stateroom door, the broad shoulders and stern bearing of Lionel Jeffries. Toby gestured for Mr. Jeffries to enter, to come to his daughter's side. The man stood, still as stone, observing Toby with his daughter.

"Get in here, you . . ." Toby let his voice die. If it were him, lying on a mattress, his mother, sister, Gage, all of them would be by his side. Henrietta was not only this man's daughter, but a bride. Her wedding was the reason everyone was on the boat. Yet no one came to hold her hand. Not a single person in the bridal party. Not her groom. Not even her father.

Toby smiled sadly at Henrietta. "Not quite the fairy-tale wedding, is it?"

When he looked up again, the silhouette disappeared. Morning sun bleached a spot on the floor where Mr. Jeffries' shadow had been cast moments before.

And not a sign of Billy the Buffoon. That guy wasn't even peeking in the door.

"Henrietta?" Toby whispered softly, smoothing her heated skin with a cool cloth. "Henrietta?"

No acknowledgment.

"That's it, Toby, keep talking to her, saying her name." The doctor dropped on the other side of her. He picked up her thin wrist to take

her pulse, and Toby thought any pressure might snap it. "Saying her name is like a lifeline. If she grabs it, we'll have a chance of bringing her back." Andrew patted him on the shoulder. "Keep at it. We'll get these people through this."

"I hear you didn't have much luck in town."

"Who knows? The next hour will tell." Andrew rose, moving on to the next bed.

Toby returned his attention to his charge. "Henrietta?"

Her eyelids fluttered and her eyes slid to him, finally focusing through the glassy gaze.

"Henrietta?"

"Boy?" Just a whisper, but her humor was a song that hummed through his heart.

"Hey, you're awake."

She swallowed. "What's happened?"

"Some sort of outbreak. We aren't sure. You were one of the first we brought in."

"Oh." She swallowed again. "Water?"

He dabbed a small cloth in a glass and moistened her cracked lips. "Doc says not too much at first. Don't want to start you vomiting again."

She closed her eyes for a moment. "Toby?" she asked. He leaned forward. "No juggling? Could use a laugh."

"Naw, I'm moving on to my new career in medicine. I've been told I have quite the bedside manner."

The shadow of a smile playing on her tired lips just about broke his heart. Then she frowned. "How many?"

"Sick? About twenty at first. The number has gone down," he said before he caught himself. She didn't pick up on his blunder, so he didn't have to report people dying. She drifted to sleep. He thought she might be okay. He needed her to be okay. A realization struck him.

Toby studied Henrietta's face. She really was pretty, when she wasn't ordering people around. This woman on the mattress seemed so weak and helpless. So unlike the blustering Henrietta he'd come to . . . like?

Had he done this? In his drunken state he might not be able to drop a stage, but make people sick? Yeah, probably.

"My fault," Henrietta whispered.

For a moment he thought she read his mind. He leaned closer. "I thought you were asleep."

"My fault," she repeated. "This. My fault."

"Everyone getting sick?"

She nodded.

"Why do you say that?"

"Didn't . . . want to get married."

Although it seemed insane, was this her last confession? "You made everyone sick so you wouldn't have to get married?"

"No." She paused. "Idiot. A miracle. I prayed for one."

He surveyed the rows of sick people, a few still retching. Others knelt beside the ill, doing what they could. A sour smell hung in the air. Here and there, prayers whispered above the sounds of illness.

"Trust me, Henrietta, this is no miracle."

Her hand brushed his. "My father?"

Toby's heart lurched for her.

"Sick?" she asked.

"Nothing to worry about there, he's fine."

"Oh." She closed her eyes. A tear leaked down her cheek.

Gently, very gently, Toby swiped it away. He took her hand. So cold. So small. He sighed and sat back on his feet, watching her eyes open again.

"You're a nice man, Toby Perkins."

A commotion caused him to whip his head around. Andrew knelt next to Lucy. Toby dropped Henrietta's hand and dashed over, falling to Andrew's side.

Lucy didn't move.

"Doc?"

Andrew sat back and shook his head.

Lucy's glassy eyes stared up at the ceiling.

Panic speared through him and Toby lunged forward, grabbing Lucy and shaking her shoulders. Her head lolled around on her neck, her eyes open, gazing nowhere.

"Oh, God," Toby whispered, his voice rising to a squeak.

Andrew pushed Toby away from the body and gently brushed his hand over Lucy's face to close her eyes. A roar filled Toby's ears, and he sat back, numbness spreading through him. He held her hand, rubbed it, as if the action might bring her back to life.

"Lucy?" he asked again, his voice small and lost in the huge room. "Lucy?"

"Toby, here," his mom's voice sounded in his ear, but he didn't respond. He was trapped, pulled down deep inside a sorrow so thick he couldn't come to the surface. Not even to speak.

Someone pulled him away and he let go of Lucy's hand. It fell back to the mattress curled slightly, like she was reaching for someone. For anyone. For him.

Arms encircled him, held him, rocked him. His mom. His mom. God, his mom. He turned and she folded him in her embrace.

"My poor baby. I'm sorry, my poor baby," she said softly, soothing him.

Lucy. Nobody's baby. And she'd died without knowing how very much he loved her.

Oscar's face seemed to float above water, his coattails drifting behind. His hat swirled downriver. Oscar's intent face bobbed toward the bank.

Jeremy considered going in after him, but hesitated. The water here was deep enough for a man to drown in, and he didn't want to lose control and hold Flim-Flam under until some sense came to the man. Sarah might never forgive him if he killed the silly clown.

"Oscar! Get back here!" Jeremy roared. Roustys surrounded him.

"What the hell is he doin'?" one asked.

"Trying to get to town. If I have to go in, I'm gonna drown him." He meant what he said up in the pilothouse. Part of his responsibility, he realized, was to keep this thing from spreading on land. "What an idiot!"

A crowd gathered on the bank to gawk at the boat, and a man pointed at the floating Flim-Flam and started shouting. A few people broke from the crowd to run up into town.

Great. This only meant trouble.

"Oh, Holy Mother of God." Jeremy pulled off his boots. His other pair wasn't dry yet, and he saw he had no choice but to go in after the fool.

"Damn it all," he said and yelled, "Oscar! Get the hell back here!"

Flim-Flam ignored him, face continuing to bob away from the boat.

"If I have to come in after you, I'm going to drown your worthless ass!"

Still no response. Jeremy sighed and jumped in. His feet hit the bottom; he was neck deep. Ahead, Oscar's head bobbed above the surface. Jeremy decided it would be the quickest to swim to him. Oscar apparently tippy-toed on the river bottom to get to shore.

Jeremy caught up to him in a few seconds. Flim-Flam flapped his soaked arms and splashed around. Jeremy grabbed him by the collar.

"Let me go, you simian beast!"

"I warned you!" He dunked Oscar, counted to three, and brought him back to the surface. Oscar squealed and splashed around in the water, and Jeremy could hardly see.

"Calm down, now!" He dunked him under again, counted to three, and pulled him up.

"Let go!" Oscar gasped.

"Calm down, or you're going under again."

Oscar's arms slowed down. Jeremy headed to the boat, pulling Oscar behind him, which started Oscar flapping again.

"Let go of me, you gorilla!"

"Listen to me—" Jeremy cut his words off when something zinged past his ear and splashed behind him. Jeremy whipped his head around.

Several men stood onshore, rifles aimed.

Oscar screamed like a girl. Jeremy pulled him around and threw Oscar in the water between him and the boat. "Get back to the boat! Now!"

"I can't swim," Oscar said, his voice breaking.

"Oh, for the love of God." Jeremy grabbed him around the waist and picked him up, careful to keep Oscar shielded with his body. "Stop wriggling!" Another zing and Oscar obeyed, going slack.

"They seriously can't be shooting?"

"No, those are just really fast bugs," Jeremy answered between gritted teeth.

The water helped him carry Oscar. Roustys gathered at the edge of the boat, and Gage came out, waving his arms.

"Don't shoot!" Gage yelled at the bank, and the roustys joined the chorus, waving and hollering.

"Why are they shooting at us?" Oscar gasped out, along with a mouthful of river.

"For God's sake, do you even have a brain? I have never, in all my born days, seen anything as stupid—"

A slam shoved Jeremy forward; then heat spread over his back. Then pain. He lost his grip on Oscar. The edges of his vision grayed. His fingers numbed.

He'd been shot. Saving Flim-Flam. What a stupid way to die.

Then relief. At least he'd kissed Sarah. At least he'd accomplished that much.

Why hadn't he told her . . . ?

Chapter 21

"Please, please let Jeremy be okay. Please, don't take him. Not now." Sarah opened her eyes and resumed pacing the floor of the pilothouse. Her feet struck up a rhythm. Waiting and pacing, pacing and waiting. She was going to lose her mind. Stuck up here with Jeremy somewhere below—what? Fighting for his life? Dead?

Incredulous did not begin to cover the way she felt. Townsfolk, shooting from the bank? Had the world gone insane? Her hands trembled and she gripped them together. For years, all she wanted was to be the only one in the pilothouse, and now here she was, trapped in it.

"Take care what you wish for," she whispered, her dream fulfilled at the cost of Jeremy and the captain.

As she kept watch, seconds stretched into minutes stretched into hours. Hours and hours. She glanced at Jeremy's watch up on the front windowsill. No, only a half an hour since Gage and the roustabouts pulled Oscar and a bleeding Jeremy aboard.

A wagon clacked down to the riverfront. The driver pulled the horse to a stop near a willow tree where a small rowboat pulled its line taut, swaying and bobbing in the river's current. Two men hopped out and pulled the boat closer to heap the wagon's contents into the small craft.

Supplies. Well, good. Shooting Jeremy activated enough town guilt to get a little help.

One man, tall and quite thin, climbed out of the wagon. Hair trimmed neat and dressed in a suit, while the others wore simple work clothes, he looked out of place. Once the boat was ready, the tall, suit-clad man shook hands with the others and got in, rowing toward the *Spirit*. His spectacles gave him an intelligent air, but she didn't want to build her hopes up.

"Oh, what the hell. You'd better be Doc Elliott."

He did a terrible job of rowing; the current threatened to sweep him and his supplies down river at any moment. His boat finally bumped into the *Spirit*, and he threw a line to the group of roustys. He passed a sack and crate over, and to Sarah's relief, grabbed a rousty's hand and stepped up on deck. Doc Elliott after all.

The doctor passed under and out of her line of sight. She remembered Jeremy's words to her, how hard it was to stay in the pilothouse when it was your job, when you were given no other choice. She never felt so alone. No Jeremy to argue with or tell her what to do, no captain to guide her. Their absence made the pilothouse a lonely place indeed.

She nodded to herself and accepted her duty. She'd waited so long, and although the job didn't come the way she imagined, it had come all the same.

Gage's head popped into view as he headed her way, climbing awful slow, like a man carrying a burden. A bolt of fear hit her gut. Jeremy. Dread settled around her heart as she watched Gage approach, and she steeled herself for bad news.

He opened the door. "Jeremy's holdin' his own. Took a shoulder shot, lost a good bit of blood, but he's strong and stubborn. Those are the doc's words, not mine."

Relief tumbled through her. She closed her eyes.

"It's okay, Sarah-girl. Things is lookin' up. Doc Elliot's onboard, here to help. He's goin' all the way with us to Sterling City."

Her eyes flew open and her anger spiked. "Did the doctor have any explanation for why they kept shooting once Jeremy headed to the boat? Do they have an excuse for that one?"

"The doc came here to help, and he wasn't among the shootin' folks. You're right, what happened down there was wrong. Pleasant Grove tends to kill first, find out later." He hiked his shoulders. "Strange town."

She put a hand to her forehead. "I'm sorry. I'm not angry with you or the doctor. I don't know what is wrong with me."

"You're goin' on just about no sleep, you're stuck up here, scairt for Jeremy. I'd say you deserve a moment of mad."

"So he's all right? Honestly?"

"Andrew don't want to say he's out of danger, but you know Jeremy." Gage smiled his half grin. "Like tryin' to take down a bull elephant. At first he caused a heap of trouble, wanted to get up here and pilot, but when he tried to get past Andrew and collapsed, it became pretty clear he better start listenin'."

The edges of her relief frayed. "He collapsed?"

Gage nodded. "It was enough to convince him he was in a bad way. Doc calmed him down long enough to get him stitched up. His shoulder is wrapped and the bleedin' stopped. Bullet went clean through. Long as there's no infection, he'll hold his own. But he's out of commission for a while." He paused. "Sarah, there's somethin' else."

She didn't like the sound of his voice, or the look on his face. "What now?"

"That pretty little actress. The one Toby got in all the trouble over. Lucy."

A sick feeling curdled in her stomach.

"She died about a half hour ago."

"Oh, God." Suddenly tired, Sarah sat on the lazy bench. A weight settled heavy in her chest. "Oh, no."

"Yeah, situation's pretty bad. That Oscar fella's devastated." Gage sat beside her and put an arm around her.

Sarah pushed her hair back. "Toby?"

"He's takin' it pretty hard. Your ma is with him."

"I have to go to him."

Gage shook his head. "You can't, Sarah. It's time for us to git. Your place is right up here. He'll be fine. Your ma is tendin' to him."

"Gage—"

"It's not up to you to take him through every bump in his life."

"He needs me," she insisted.

"We need you more."

The truth. Not the easiest thing to face. "This is a nightmare."

"And, unfortunately, it's up to you, and only you, to get us home."

"I shouldn't, Gage. I'm not a licensed pilot." Even as she spoke the words, she knew it was time. Her time. Sarah stood. "I guess I'm all we've got."

"We're lucky to have you. You are a pilot all right, Sarah-girl." Gage stood and squeezed her shoulder. "Don't need a bunch of old men to tell you so."

"I remember you telling me as much only a few days ago."

"You'd best listen to me from now on. I'm always right." His face grew serious. "You think you can do this? Stay awake for two days?"

"Absolutely. Tell Mom to start brewing coffee."

"I'll be down in engineerin', on the throttle the whole time you're up here. I'll make sure the boat does what you need it to."

"Gage, you don't have to do that."

"Sure, I do," he said, "and it's my honor to stand behind such a pilot. I am proud of you, Sarah. You are an amazin' young woman." He grabbed the door, swung it open, and turned to her. "Now git us home."

She stepped up to pilot the *Spirit of the River*.

First, blood. Next, pestilence. And finally? Explosion. Then, a rain of fire.

So poetic.

Throughout history there have been many such occurrences. Take, for instance, ancient times. The lost city of Pompeii. Those inhabitants knew what it was like for God to turn his blazing glare down on their city and incinerate them all.

Then modern times, disaster a scant three years ago. The great mining explosion in Pennsylvania, killing two hundred forty workers when fire burned through the tunnels. So many lost lives. Fate, unrelenting in its delivery.

And Minneapolis, a flour mill, of all mundane things. Who would have thought flour could explode and cause the death of eight people? How did their families feel, their loved ones destroyed by so comic an ending?

And then there are riverboats.

The explosion of the Eagle, *taking thirty-six lives and forever scarring the engineer of the* Spirit.

The Ironwood, *a beautiful, majestic riverboat, the finest and best on the river. Captain Archibald Yoder died with others that night, over a hundred lost. The man who is responsible for the demise of the* Ironwood, *the jealous coward who caused such pain and suffering, still walks this earth. Admired. Revered. Loved.*

That man will pay.

Briggham humiliated Captain Yoder, smashed his memory to pieces, caused the Yoder name to be so marred those of the bloodline are shunned. Ostracized. The humiliation grew until We hide Our name. None will take it up again. We are forced to skulk about, denying Our birthright. This man destroyed not only Captain Yoder, but the Yoder family, Our identity; he ruined Us all, piece by piece. Took everything away, Our lives, Our name, Our existence. What was left of Our family.

Nothing remains. Nothing.

And so it shall be for William Briggham.

He hangs on to life by the barest of threads. We are glad for this. Others see him as We do, weak, groveling, humiliated as he should be every day of his life. The illness was merely the beginning, the taste of what is to come.

We have much more in store for him than wallowing in his own sickness. We will finish, putting in place the final pieces of Our revenge.

And William Briggham will feel Our exquisite wrath when his world explodes and the ravage of fire rains down upon him and destroys his Spirit.

"It's time," Andrew said, his voice soft and laced with kindness. He stood, compassion radiating from him like the warmth of a fire on a frigid night. "Would you like some help?"

"No, I can take care of her." Toby wrapped Lucy's sheet around her body and gently lifted her. She almost weighed nothing. Like a fragile bird. This bird would never fly, never soar again. Her wings had been clipped and her time was past. "Can we take her somewhere else besides that morgue cabin? Those beds are . . . being used . . . and I don't want her on the floor. She would hate that."

Andrew glanced down at his clipboard, and flipped to the list Emma had provided him.

"Cabin 7A." He let go of the papers and they flopped back down into place. "It belongs to Bradley Johnson, the second to pass. You're right, Toby, no need to put anyone on the floor yet. We can afford everyone the dignity of a bed."

Toby followed the doctor. He swallowed against the thickness of tears in his throat. He knew men weren't supposed to cry, but they kept pushing and insisting, these tears for the dead.

Andrew opened the cabin door and Toby carried Lucy inside. He laid his most precious charge on the bunk, arranging the sheet around her. She looked peaceful, like she was only sleeping.

He'd heard Oscar Gévaudan was beside himself. First, one missing actress, now one dead. Still, he hadn't come in to see Lucy, not before she died, nor after.

And Toby hadn't been by her side either. She'd passed away alone.

He smoothed back her hair. Her most incredible golden hair.

"It's difficult to lose a patient." The doctor spoke softly, almost in a hush. "We did everything we could. She simply wasn't strong enough to make it through."

"Sure doesn't seem fair."

"Fairness plays no part in anything like this."

"How do you stand it, being a doctor?"

Andrew's brow crinkled in thought. "Well, for every one I lose, I'm able to help a quantity of others. I try not to dwell on this part of it. Everyone has their time. I do what I can when they are here and need me, and then I have to let go. Just like you do now."

"She looks like she's only sleeping,. She's really gone, I guess," Toby said, his voice wobbling. "I should have spent more time with her."

"It's difficult not to sink into regrets, but you mustn't." Andrew's words brushed through the silent cabin. "The only way to get through pain this deep, Toby, is to keep moving forward. You have another patient who needs you now."

Once he and Andrew returned to the stateroom, Toby immediately checked on Henrietta, still sleeping. More importantly, breathing. Skinny but tough, she was getting better. Briggs, pale, sat propped against the wall. He refused to stay down. His feisty insistence was good to see, although the captain looked decades older and kept dozing off, reminding Toby of a doddering old man. Sickness leveled everyone, making the strong weak and killing the weakest.

The burn flared in Toby's chest.

"Like you did," he whispered. "Preyed on the weak. Guess that's why you've chosen me. I'm not strong enough to fight you."

He kept walking until he reached the bar. He needed a couple of moments. He hunched down and sat on the floor behind mahogany, hidden from view. Tears burned behind his eyes, insisting on emerging. He tucked his legs up and wrapped his arms around them, laying his face to his knees. No sobs, no crying out, he just let tears spill of their own accord. He didn't have to be embarrassed. No one could see him.

He mourned Lucy. For the time he didn't spend with her the last few moments of her life. For the songs she'd never sing, the lines she'd never recite. Even for Oscar, although he hadn't shown his face. The time would come when the grandmaster would regret not being at Lucy's side, and he wouldn't be able to change the circumstances. He'd have to live with guilt and regret. Toby knew exactly how such a thing felt.

Was any punishment worse?

When he was empty of every tear in him, he didn't feel better, as conventional wisdom insisted. He felt spent. Before him, the shelves under the bar resembled staring eyes. All watching him. The cubbies, lined with liquor bottles of all shapes and sizes, mocked him.

The bottles reminded him of easier times, parties, and celebration. His lemon sludge ingredients recalled the lemonade fight, in this very room, just a day ago. With Henrietta. And Lucy. Her beautiful laughter, sparkling through spraying soda water and sticky lemonade. A moment so far away it might as well be years past. He couldn't ever talk to her again. Serve her one of his special lemon fizzies. Lucy had loved his lemonade.

His heart went cold.

She drank so much of it.

Vance McIntyre, Bradley Johnson, and Lucy, the three people who'd died. He'd served them all glass after glass. They were all dead.

Henrietta. Yes, lemonade. Yes, sick.

Joseph Meyers, Dolores Keef, P.J. Phillips. Each drank gin with lemonade. Each one sick, lying on the stateroom floor. Who else? Who else?

Panic clawed through him, drying any remaining tears.

Wait—it couldn't be the lemonade. The captain didn't drink any. Did he?

"Not the lemonade, not the lemonade," he murmured, and realized he'd started to rock back and forth. He hugged his legs tighter, willing himself to stop shaking. Oh, my God, what if he did something? What if this really was all his fault?

He rose to his knees and began rifling around in the cubby, his hands trembling. Lemons, sugar. His fingers bumped an unfamiliar item, way in the back. He pulled it out. Froze.

Uncle Quentin's tin. The strong man tin. What was it doing here?

He popped open the lid. White powder lined the bottom. What was this? He kept aspirin in here, and they'd been just about gone. How did it turn to powder? And so much?

He refastened the lid, slid the tin back in the cubby, pushing it far, far to the rear, and thought of his lost hours. And lemon fizzies.

The dead girl in 7A.

Hands trembling, he reached in again, dragging out the box. It was too dangerous to leave in here. Someone might find it. He stuffed it in his pocket, grabbed a bottle of scotch, and tucked it under his jacket. No one would stop him. People tended to turn away from people in mourning. He rose. Walking through the stateroom, he clutched his coat around him. He was right. No one even glanced his way.

Chapter 22

Emma grabbed the tray of cookies, sure they weren't lethal. "I'm heading up to the pilothouse if anyone needs to find me."

"Tell Sarah to keep up the good work," Lilly called, her usually bouncing voice dragging with fatigue. Emma made certain of all the food coming out of the galley now. She tasted every single dish, and waited an hour or two before serving it to anyone else. If she didn't get sick, they served the dish. At this rate, she would weigh three hundred pounds by the time they arrived home, but at least if anyone else fell ill, it would be her. Even though she tasted all the food, she couldn't taste anything. Eating was difficult when guilt gripped you by the throat.

Gladys and Lil made small dishes, snacks really. People weren't eating very much, most completely skipping any sort of food. And who could blame them? No one else had fallen sick. Obviously something served at the picnic made people ill. Andrew had plenty of help since the passengers had realized they were safe from any sort of contagious epidemic.

Emma lifted her skirt with her free hand and climbed the first bank of steps, passing the stateroom. Through the window, Andrew and Doctor Elliot cared for their patients, almost every bed hidden from view with the family clustered around. She continued climbing to the pilothouse and her daughter, trying not to dwell on the part she or her staff might have played in this tragedy. It would do no one any good if she collapsed in misery. She had to keep going until they were all safely to Sterling City. Then, whatever there was to face, she'd face.

The bank rushed past, the boat just about racing. Her daughter and Gage kept their pace steady, fast, and sure.

Emma opened the door. Danny slept on the lazy bench while Sarah stood at the pilot wheel. She gripped the massive wheel, so huge half of it was beneath the floor. Although the steering was helped along by some sort of steam rig, as Gage explained it, enormous strength was needed to guide the boat. Sarah didn't even seem tired, her shoulders and back straight and strong. Despite Emma's sadness and worry, pride flashed through her. Her daughter was born to pilot a boat.

Sarah glanced back at her. "It is entirely possible for a person to stay awake for two days." She held the wheel. "I'm two-thirds of the way there. I'll make it."

"I'm sure of it." Emma set the tray on the desk behind Sarah, and took the lid off the coffee pot.

"I've never gone this long without sleep. It's not so hard. Sometimes I feel fine and full of energy; other times I'm ready to keel over and pass out for a year."

"You can sleep all you want once we land. You don't have far to go." She poured thick, dark coffee into a mug and took it over to her daughter. She'd made it extra strong.

"Rip Van Winkle's got nothing on me. I even think I've cut several hours off the trip." She bridled the wheel and took the cup from Emma. "This smells like heaven."

"I also brought you some of Lilly's butter cookies."

Danny's eyes popped open and he sat up. "Cookies?"

"I brought enough for you, too, Danny."

He ran over and, along with Sarah, plucked one from the tray.

"Thanks, Mom," Sarah said. She took a sip of coffee and set the mug on the ledge next to Jeremy's watch. She unbridled the wheel, taking it again under her control. "Can you spare a few minutes, give me an update?"

Emma sat down on the lazy bench, exhaustion making her feel strange, sort of outside of her body. "Don't worry. I tasted everything a few hours ago."

"Oh, Mom."

"What else can I do? I'm going to try everything before anyone touches it." A wry grin twisted Emma's face. "So far the only danger is in getting fat. I'm constantly nibbling."

Sarah shook her head. "I'm sure it wasn't the food."

"What else could it be?"

"I don't know. None of this feels right."

"That's fer sure!" Danny piped up, a cookie muffling his words.

"Danny, why don't you go down and—"

"You don't need to make no reason up, Sarah. I'm gettin' used to leavin' so you grown-ups can talk." He stamped his way to the door. "You better not eat all them cookies, Sarah Perkins!"

Emma actually smiled, but the expression settled, heavy and sad. Like her.

Sarah kept her voice low. "Mom, are you all right?"

"I've killed three people. And made seventeen horribly sick."

"We don't know for certain what this is, and if bad food was involved, it's not as if you prepare every dish yourself."

"I'm responsible for everything people eat." Emma stood and came to Sarah's side. "I can't shirk away from that."

"Don't borrow trouble."

"No one else fell sick after the initial few hours. If it was something else, others would be taking ill."

"We don't know anything for certain." Sarah hesitated. "How is Jeremy doing?"

The door creaked open. "He's doing fine!"

The two women swung around. Jeremy entered the pilothouse, and behind him, Danny.

"Jeremy! You are not supposed to be on your feet!" Emma insisted.

He sat down on the lazy bench, almost as white as the shirt he'd managed to drape over his shoulders. The garment tilted on his large frame, like an askew cape. He'd closed one button, not matching up to the buttonhole. No socks or boots. At least he'd managed the nuances of his pants.

He leaned his head back and closed his eyes. "I'll be damned if I spend another second in my quarters."

"You're not going to do anyone much good, bleeding to death up here," Sarah said.

His eyes snapped open and he looked at her. "I figured I could watch over Danny's shoulder and give you a couple hours of sleep."

"I'm not leaving the pilothouse."

"I happen to have Andrew's approval for this," he answered.

"You do?" Sarah asked. "I find that fairly difficult to believe."

"Would I lie to you?" he said, his voice teasing. Then Jeremy's face became serious. "Sarah, you will need to be clearheaded to navigate into the docks. You'll need a couple hours of sleep so we don't add a sunken boat to this mess. Andrew gave me a limit up here of two hours. You'd better make the most of it. You've already wasted thirty seconds by arguing with me."

"Besides," Danny said, "now I can help for real! This is an easy part of the river, anyhow."

"Makes perfect sense," Emma added, hoping her daughter would relinquish the wheel.

"Sarah, we're a crew," Jeremy said softly. "Accept our help. It will only make you a better and more capable pilot."

Danny came forward, and Sarah took a step back, turning the wheel over to Danny.

"Thank you," she said to Jeremy. Sarah leaned over him as he slumped back on the lazy bench, and Emma watched her unbutton his shirt. "Let me fix this for you so you don't look like a drunk who just rolled out of a tavern."

As he sat straighter, his eyes warmed and he and Sarah shared an intimate moment as if they were the only two in the room. Emma sensed the energy between them and wondered what it meant. At the wheel, Danny scrunched his face and waggled his tongue. Neither Sarah nor Jeremy noticed.

"Next time, get someone to help you dress," Sarah said. "Aren't your feet cold? Can I bring you up some socks?"

"Nope. Git. And don't worry. Hand me your coffee and I'll take care of it."

Sarah passed him the mug. "I'll be back in two hours." Her voice softened and she brushed back his hair. "Jeremy, thank you."

His hint of a smile was only for Sarah. The intimacy between the two struck Emma, and she knew what she was seeing. When did her daughter and Jeremy Smith fall in love? Did they realize it yet? And how did Emma not see it coming?

"Come on, Mom." Sarah opened the door and they made their way down the steps to the Texas deck. "He looks fairly good, don't you think?"

She enjoyed the buoyancy in her daughter's voice. "He does."

"Although he's going to need someone to help him dress next time. Can't have our first officer running around barefoot." She stopped in front of her cabin door. "I'm actually looking forward to a quick nap. Are you going to do the same?"

"I'm going to check on a few things first," Emma said.

"Mom, you need sleep, too. You seem exhausted."

"I'll be fine. I have been stealing naps here and there, not up all night like you. Have a good rest."

Once Sarah entered her room, Emma went to the only place she wanted to go. The place she needed to go. She walked the length of the boat, circling around until she came to the familiar wood door with the eagle door knocker. She pulled her key out and unlocked the room.

She lit only one lamp and closed the door. She didn't bother with the rest of the lights; she wanted dark. She lifted the teapot and brought it over to the table, sat down before it, and placed her hands over the top of it. She wasn't sure why she felt closer to Quentin when she touched this teapot; she just did.

Except now. Only cold stone and silver chilled her palms.

"I don't know if you are really here or not. I certainly hope so. I need you."

She wished she possessed magical powers, could bring her uncle back for a few minutes. Although the room felt empty, she kept talking.

"Quentin, I killed three people. I don't know how I can live with this." She strained to listen, but saw and heard nothing. The room seemed desolate, not like before when she felt Quentin's presence. She knew her memories made him seem close. So why didn't she feel him now?

She sat back in the chair. Conjured up Quentin's face. His laughing blue eyes. Her head nodded, and yanked her back to consciousness. Her daughter was right, she was exhausted. She laid her arms on the table and lowered her head. Closed her eyes. Thought of Quentin, settled in a chair on the deck, a quilt wrapped around him . . .

Emma jerked awake and lifted her cheek from wood. Where was she?

Quentin's teapot sat in front of her. That's right. She came to the captain's dining room for a few moments of peace, then tried to feel Quentin's presence. What a fool. There were no such things as ghosts.

Just hopeful memories. And she'd wasted time here, when someone needed her, somewhere.

What time was it? How long did she doze?

"Enough of this foolishness. I have work to do."

She stood and left, started to shut the door. She lingered for a moment, hoping she might feel something, run back in, find some answers. Except there were none. Nothing to do except face the world. She finally closed the door and pulled her key out to lock it.

Behind her, a roar. She jumped and spun around, slamming her back against the door.

Oscar stood, his eyes burning, accented by dark circles. The huge tiger sat at his feet. "I have been looking all over for you. We have a score to settle."

"Mr. Gévaudan!"

"Not another word, you! Not a sound from the woman who destroyed my life! You've taken so much from me, you and this damnable boat." His voice, usually light, airy, slightly humorous, slithered with something dark and angry. "It's time we have a discussion, Emma Perkins. Just you and I."

The tiger growled, low in its throat.

Toby slammed the door to his cabin. Leaned against it. What was he going to do?

The tin. White powder. What was it? And how the heck did his tin, from his room, end up under the bar, with something in it he didn't recognize? Why didn't he remember?

Somehow, he knew, just knew, the little box had something to do with everyone being sick. He felt it in his heart. The burn blossomed in his chest, big then small, big then small, almost with a heartbeat all its own.

"Criminy, not now." He thumped on his chest.

He pulled the tin from his pocket. Maybe he should taste some of the powder. What was the worst that might happen? He'd get sick and die.

So what?

He hopped up on his bunk and set the small box down next to him. He flipped the tin open. Jumping off a cliff was one thing. Vomiting and diarrhea-ing to death was quite another. He'd watched people do that for twenty-four hours, and he wasn't anxious to join their ranks.

"Cripes, what a coward," he said to himself, snapping the tin closed. Especially if he caused all this.

Sarah would know what to do, but she was stuck up in the pilothouse. Everyone in the stateroom depended on her. Mom. He'd go to Mom. He hopped off his bunk. She was worried it was the food making people sick. This might be a relief to her.

Nope. If he'd done something, it would be worse for her than if she did it herself. Moms were like that.

The door swung open. Charley looked startled for a moment; then he relaxed. "It's you. I'm worn out. Thought I'd git in a quick nap. You, too?"

Toby paused for a moment, gathering his thoughts. "Charley, what would you do if you weren't sure you were in deep trouble or not?"

His friend paused with his jacket removed halfway, studied Toby, and continued to shrug his jacket off. "That question don't make no sense. Either you're in trouble, or not."

"What if I was drinking and I don't remember?"

Charley tossed the jacket, and it caught on a hook. "Lookit that! I git it every time." He jumped up on his bunk and untied his shoe. "You mean when you was drunk and can't remember? What do you think you did?" His eyes widened, huge. "Oh Jesus-in-a-bucket! You knocked someone up?"

"No, you dolt."

"I didn't think so."

"Hey, what's that supposed to mean?"

Charley tossed his shoe to the floor. "Nothin'. You're shy, that's all. And kinda inexperienced. And pretty silly. Gals usually go for—"

"Yeah, thanks, that's enough." He let a moment go by and Charley studied him.

"Toby, what's wrong?"

"What if I destroyed something? Like those napkins? I don't remember a few hours that day. What if I'm the one who cut them up?"

"Jest a bunch of napkins. We got more, so it turned out okay." Charlie took off his other shoe, then lay back on his bunk. "I think you worry too much."

"What if I did something worse?"

"Toby, you're torn up. Your pretty gal died, and you been with sick folks the last day. I'm startin' to feel less than my happy self, and you tend to git gloomy even when nothin's happenin'. You jest need to relax and forget ever'thin' for a while."

Charley was right. As usual. He needed to forget.

"Think this will fix me?" Toby pulled out the bottle of scotch.

A grin spread across Charley's face. "Now you're talkin'." He jumped off his bunk and grabbed two glasses from the washbasin. "These'll work."

Toby poured for both of them. They clinked glasses.

Charley raised his. "Here's to the sick, may they get well. Here's to the dead, Lord keep 'em outta hell."

"You are quite the poet."

They both tossed back their drinks.

"You think that theater feller might hire me on as a writer?" Charley asked.

Toby refilled their glasses. "Not a chance."

They tossed that one back. Then another. And another.

Toby lost count as the world went fuzzy. Guilt receded, didn't seem so important. Even the burn tapered down. And he relaxed. Didn't hurt. Didn't care. He lay back on his bunk. Slowly drifted off.

He dreamt of a drowned minister with rotting, shredded skin. The thing chased him with a tin spilling white powder and tattered napkins flying from his rotting corpse.

The zombie minister's eyes were his own.

"Mr. Gévaudan, I am so sorry." Emma pushed her back to the door.

"You are sorry? *Sorry?*" His voice rose as the last word came out, almost a scream. Again a growl from the tiger. "I have lost two of my dearest, closest friends, nay, my family, and you are *sorry?*"

She flinched. "I don't know what else to say. Except don't give up hope on Miss Vashnikoff. We'll arrive at Sterling City soon, and I'm sure we'll have news of her well-being."

The grumble grew until it became a constant sound.

"Easy, girl," he said, reaching down to where the leash fastened onto the tiger's rhinestone collar. "She's in concert with my feelings, you know. She has been quite upset by my overwhelming despair."

"Mr. Gévaudan."

"Oscar. Please. You must call me Oscar," he said, his voice smooth as silk. His eyes hardened. "We are on the most intimate of terms, are we not? You killed my dear Lucy. Your minions refused to go back and help my precious Zelda." He toyed with the clasp. "What, no 'I'm sorry' again?"

"You're upset, Mr.—Oscar."

"How very sweet of you to notice."

She nodded to his hand, still on the clasp. "What do you mean to do?"

"I know what my heart tells me. And the world certainly won't miss one drab, uninteresting cook on a boat."

Anger flashed through her. She stood away from the door. "I understand you have suffered a terrible loss, but that gives you no right to threaten me this way."

He patted Daisy's head. "Why do you think I'm threatening you? You must be feeling vulnerable with all your 'men-folk' disabled. Aren't around to protect you now, are they?"

"I don't need any 'men-folk' to protect me. And you toying with the leash as if you are about to set your tiger on me? What do you call that if not a threat?"

"A little fun? You owe me at least a few minutes of entertainment."

She stared at him. "Mr. Gévaudan, you are sick."

"So I've been told."

"I am going to go past you, and return to the stateroom where there are scores of ill people to take care of, none of whom have seen even a glimpse of you."

Anguish shot through his eyes before he narrowed them.

"I am a lawyer, Mrs. Perkins. Ah, I see Sarah didn't reveal that piece of business, did she? By the time I am through, I will own your boat. I plan to take the *Spirit* much farther than your dull mind ever could. You'll fade away into mediocrity, where you belong. You'll wallow in exquisite misery, because I will turn this into a waterfront theater and use my fame to remind you and everyone what your pathetic excuse of a business did to these people. Why, that will be my first heart-wrenching performance, *Death on a Riverboat*. Try to keep your head up while that plays, Mrs. Perkins! Your fate will be well deserved. And this is more than a threat."

"You are a mean little man," she answered.

A glimmer of respect edged his haunted eyes. "So there is some of your daughter's gumption in you after all."

"Step aside, Mr. Gévaudan."

"Make me."

Emma thought of two children on a playground, facing each other down. She glared at him. "I said step aside."

He simply glared back. She took one step forward. The tiger growled. Every fiber in her screamed to run. Instead, she calmly walked purposefully around Oscar and his tiger, heading for the steps.

Claws gouging down her back.

Didn't happen.

Teeth sinking into the back of her neck.

Nope.

She kept her pace even, made it to the steps, and turned. Oscar and Daisy watched her. Oscar tipped his hat.

"Congratulations, Mrs. Perkins. I didn't think you had it in you. Enjoy the last few hours on your boat. The moment we hit Sterling City, your entire business will be mine."

She decided in favor of letting him have the last word. And the tiger might have had something to do with her final decision.

Arrogance. The most destructive force there is.

Arrogance to rebuild a town where hurricanes level every building and kill thousands. Arrogance to live on land where earthquakes, year after year, destroy cities and take countless lives. Arrogance to leave the sanctuary of the Spirit *open, trusting no one will harm what is inside.*

The teapot is first. Such a sweet little thing. It shatters with only one drop, but the dragon's head continues to stare up at Us. We smash it under Our boot.

The china in the server. Here the destruction is such a simple matter.

In danger of discovery, We move fast. Surely someone will hear Us? But the Spirit *is enfolded in its own tragedies and despair, thanks to Us. No one comes.*

Theater of Illusion

Our hammer makes short work of the table. Our knife finishes the upholstery, shredding, and We enjoy the feel of soft stuffing as We gut the chairs. It falls to the floor, a lush, deep snowstorm. We rip, tear, slash, crush, mangle, smash. Laugh. The sanctuary ceases to be.

We destroy the heart before the body, and this feels so very good.

Chapter 23

Jeremy snapped awake when the door creaked. Damn, he'd fallen asleep, and with a boy at the wheel.

"I see I'm up here just in time." Sarah approached.

"I only drifted off for a minute."

"Yeah," Danny insisted. "He's been watchin' me like a hawk. I'd holler if I needed him."

"Thanks for defending me, kid, but I can fight my own battles." Jeremy shifted his weight and a bolt of pain shot through his shoulder. He winced and tried to hide the expression. He realized Sarah saw it when her brow crinkled with concern.

"You need to get back to bed," she said softly. She came to sit beside him, put her arm low, around his back. "Can I help you up?"

"I'm not some doddering old man," he snapped.

"No, you are a mighty, brave warrior fallen in the heat of battle." Danny sniggered.

"You've been shot," Sarah continued. "I'd say you've earned some help." The smile he gave her was weak at best. "If you're the one doing the helping, I guess I'll take you up on it."

When they rose, he was actually glad for her steadying arm. The worst part of this whole business wasn't how bad he hurt, but the dizziness. He could hardly believe he wasn't able to pilot. Good sense told him he'd make a wreck of himself and everything if he tried. That was the thing about piloting. Duty made you choose what was right and best for the crew and passengers, despite pride. And his was not easy to get around.

"Thanks," he said.

"You are welcome." She kept her arm around him. Whether to steady him or help him, didn't matter. She touched him with tenderness and it felt so damned good. "Danny, can you help Jeremy back down to his quarters? I'm ready to step up."

She dropped her arm, and he immediately missed her touch. When had he let her in this far? He was about to issue some snappy retort when she stepped up and her stature at the wheel stopped him. She reminded him of the old Sarah, the one before the test. So strong and proud. He'd once thought she didn't really belong at the wheel of a boat. He'd been wrong. She had proved it to him and, obviously, to herself.

Something opened in him at that moment, something that went beyond enjoying her touch, or laughing at her jokes, or wanting to see her, thinking of her at all hours, at odd times of the day. He felt something expansive, inclusive, huge. Overwhelming.

Shock jolted through him. He was in love with her. Oh, God. Now what?

She glanced to him, raised an eyebrow. "Anything wrong?"

"No," he said, his voice soft. "I was admiring you, standing at the wheel of the *Spirit*. And it's all yours. You're right, Sarah. You belong exactly here."

Her eyes sparkled with perhaps just a bit of gratitude.

"Oh, yeck!" Danny said, and Sarah and Jeremy both laughed.

"Come on, kid. Get me down to my cabin in one piece." When they reached the door, Danny darted down first. Jeremy paused, looked back. Sarah's eyes were on the river, but she glanced back to him.

He gave her a quick nod. "I'd say good luck, but you don't need it. You are perfectly capable of bringing us home."

He'd done it again. Lost a few hours.

And Toby was pretty sure his sick feeling, the throwing up and pounding headache, was a result of scotch, not the illness on the boat.

He pinched the tin with his thumb and finger. Leaned his elbows on the rail. The river below rushed by, the paddle wheel pounding with a furiousness he had never seen.

"It's your fault, isn't it?" he asked, looking at the strong man on the cover. "You made everyone sick, didn't you? Oh, you might have used my hands, but you did it, dear Father. You."

Would be a shame if he dropped the tin, it sank to the bottom of the river, contents never to be known. He would be safe. He could forget.

On the other hand, he was pretty sure he couldn't.

He'd decided to finish what he began before the boat left Sterling City, what he didn't have the guts to do back then. If he'd jumped a week ago, three people would still be alive. Including his beautiful Lucy.

He wouldn't have long to live with all this guilt; they were almost home, and this time he'd do it. Leave a note confessing to everything. Go to the cliff. Jump. He couldn't let his mom take the blame for any of this. Much as it might destroy her for the time being, Gage and Sarah would help her through. Once he and dear Father were out of way, everyone he loved could get on with their lives. Everyone would be safe.

The other deaths, Vance McIntyre and Bradley Johnson, were bad enough. But he'd killed his precious Lucy. He simply could not live with this in his heart.

He briefly thought about confessing and allowing the authorities do the job, but dismissed it as a bad idea. He'd heard about hangings. Sometimes it took the condemned almost fifteen minutes to die. They called it the dance of death for a reason. And Toby wasn't in the mood for a dance of any kind.

Yep, leaping off a cliff. Much easier. Quick.

He thought about Lucy. Saw her eyes. Heard her laugh, like crystal sparkling in sunlight. Like her . . . fragile, glittery, beautiful beyond reason. He had to pay for what he'd done.

The answer was simple. He turned, fully prepared to complete his task.

They were almost here. Home. The stacks bellowed their approach. Beyond the next bend, a glow reflected off low-hanging clouds, a smear of gray against the black night.

Sarah's first solo piloting was about to come to an end. She brought them back safe, and it was all that mattered. Strange. She imagined, for so many years, the triumph, praise, celebration of this moment. All she felt was a sense of relief.

In reality the only licensed pilots aboard were sick or wounded. Sarah Perkins: the last one standing. Points of some sort, she thought. Even Danny was down, sleeping on the lazy bench. He'd stuck with her the entire time, dozing and eating up here. Great kid. He'd make a wonderful pilot himself someday.

She tightened her grip on the wheel and focused ahead. Her eyes burned, her shoulders and arms ached, but she didn't have far to go. As they rounded the bend, the lights of the city reflected on water. She pulled the bell twice and three decks below, Gage throttled back.

They'd made record time, pushed the boat to its limit, and nothing had exploded.

More of the city came into view. The docks swarmed with lights, hand-carried lanterns by the way they shifted and wobbled. Obviously, Pleasant Grove telegraphed ahead, and Sterling City was prepared to keep them in quarantine. She made out a handful of police and recognized the chief standing in the front of the group. At 3:00 a.m., such a late hour?

She brought the *Spirit* in only one time before, piloting through the docked boats to their landing. Briggs had stood at her shoulder. She was sure she could do this, but she missed the presence of the captain's watchful eye at this moment more than ever. She pulled the stopping bell.

The engines dropped as the *Spirit* drifted closer. Three decks below, Gage stayed right with her.

Roustabouts lined up with their poles on deck, ready to guide the boat in, or push off if she drifted too close. She lugged the wheel to the right. Her arm muscles screamed and through enormous effort, she felt the rudders turn the back of the boat. Not too far, or the current would pull them completely around.

When they were a few feet to straightening, she gonged once to signal Gage to change directions. She paused and rang twice. Instantaneously, a burst of power. Danny blinked awake and bolted upright.

She pulled the stopping bell. Power cut, and they began the drift. Perfect.

The boat slid only inches from the dock, the roustys guiding. Ropes flew over the group of men and lanterns, and they began to secure the *Spirit*. She snapped the bridle over the wheel, her final duty as the pilot of the *Spirit of the River*. Finally. They were home.

Surprisingly, two officers jumped aboard.

Engines dropped down, almost silent. Her stint as pilot had ended, but the night was far from over.

"Danny,"

"I'll stay here, sir!" he said and saluted.

She resisted the urge to ruffle his hair as she darted past him. She lifted her skirts and tore down the steps.

On the main deck, the two policemen flanked the chief of police, who spoke in low tones to Emma and Gage.

"What's going on?" Sarah asked. Her mother's face was exhausted, and the concern surrounding her was palpable.

"The actress. Zelda Vashnikoff," Emma said, her voice deflated. "They found her in the woods back at the grove. Murdered."

"What?" Sarah asked, although she heard just fine. With Emma's announcement, the situation deteriorated from bad to worse. "Does Oscar know?"

Gage shook his head. "Not yet. Haven't seen him; he's pry asleep."

"Oh, Lord, this is awful," Sarah said. Then she remembered. Wasn't Oscar the last one to see the woman? At least, that's what Jeremy told her. She was too tired to follow any lines of logic. She crinkled her forehead. "This doesn't make any sense . . ." Her voice trailed off. "Who would murder her? Why?"

"Both good questions," the police chief said, "and before the *Spirit* departed, another woman was murdered here." His shrewd, dark eyes watched each of them, darting from face to face.

"I remember hearing about it when I went to go to the mercantile," Sarah answered, "and by the way, what are you doing onboard? I thought we'd be in quarantine."

"Given the murder in town and the murder of the actress, we are fairly sure foul play is involved with everyone on the boat becoming sick," the chief explained. "I don't believe in coincidences." Tall, with a deep, commanding voice, the man was obviously in charge.

"Plus, we get paid double for hazard duty," one of the uniformed officers added. The chief shot him a dirty look.

"So you think the tavern murder has something to do with all this?" Sarah asked.

"The Blue Grass waitress smothered in mud, the actress, strangled. First two murders in years. Our job is to find out if they are related, isn't it?" the chief answered. "Other than those going to the hospital, I want everyone to remain onboard. We'll release people as we interview them."

Sarah nodded. "That will put everyone in a lovely mood."

"Sheriff Thompson filled us in on the symptoms you've been dealing with. He said they are similar to cholera, food sickness, and various poisons. We're going to question everyone and do a thorough search of the boat and belongings as people disembark. We aren't ruling anything out at this point. How many have died?"

"Three." Emma said quietly, her voice steady. "We have seventeen sick. I'm not sure if Pleasant Grove informed you or not; one man is wounded. Shot. Can we get them all to the hospital?"

"We have four wagons rounded up; we'll take three in each. Most serious first. And, if you'll hand over your passenger and crew manifest." He paused. "I'm sorry to hear Briggs is down. I'd hoped to run the investigation through him." He looked pointedly at Gage. "You in charge here?"

Emma stepped forward. "I am. Emma Perkins. Captain Briggham and I own the boat."

"I'll go round up Jeremy," Sarah said.

"He's our first officer," Emma said, "the man they shot in Pleasant Grove."

"I'll want to speak with him right off, if he's able." The chief looked chagrinned. "Sheriff Thompson did fill me in. Unfortunate incident."

"Especially if you happen to be Jeremy," Sarah said. "Do you want me to tell Oscar about Zelda, Mom?"

"I will take care of breaking the news to him," the chief said. "You can all relax. We are in charge from here on out."

Strange, stepping back, but Sarah was tired enough to give up her control. Which meant she must actually be exhausted.

She headed up the steps to the officers' quarters, fatigue blurring the edges of her thinking. Given the circumstances, she wondered how long it might be before she got any sleep.

Emma led the chief up the steps. "You can use the office. That might be the best place. There are two desks, and your officers can set up there."

"It will do quite nicely, Mrs. Perkins. I appreciate your cooperation."

They came to the top of the steps. The captain's dining room door stood ajar. Confusion furrowed her brow; then she remembered the last time she'd been up here she was intimidated by a tiger.

"Oh," was all she said. She rushed forward, an uneasy feeling building inside. The door swung open easily, and she reached for the lamp. It wasn't there, but light from the lantern on deck revealed chaos inside. The chief came up behind her, his lantern held high. She pushed the button to illuminate the chandelier.

Prisms of light danced over devastation.

She faced so much the last few days: people falling ill, guilt at her part in it, a murdered actress. She'd held up through it all. Somehow, this deliberate destruction of the most precious place on the boat speared through her, the final burden making the load too heavy to bear.

"Good Lord," the chief said.

Quentin's delicate teapot, shattered, lay on a slashed Persian carpet. Emma dropped to her knees. The dragon's neck was bent, its tongue snapped off. The tail was broken in two pieces. She picked them up. Held them in her cupped palms. Someone had demolished what was left of Quentin. The last of his possessions, destroyed.

She lowered her head and let her tears fall.

Sarah knocked on his door, hoping Jeremy was awake. No answer. She swung the door open.

He stood next to his bed, his hair ruffled, his eyes bleary with sleep. And not a shred of clothing on him, the sling and bandages his only cover. He grabbed a blanket with his good hand and held it in front of him.

"Sarah!" he managed.

She backed out and slammed the door. Laughter bubbled up. From embarrassment. Hers, she figured. He'd looked anything but embarrassed. He looked . . . good. Her giggles had nothing to do with what she'd seen, but her flaming cheeks did. He'd been on his feet, held up by tree-trunk legs. Muscular. Powerful. His big frame was even more impressive without clothing.

She heard him shuffling around on the other side of the door, and she clapped her hand over her mouth, trying to stop the bubbles. Lord, seeing her laughing would infuriate him.

"Jeremy," she said once she decided she could speak without giggling, "I came to help you get dressed. The police are onboard. May I come in?"

"No!" Like a shot, roaring through the door.

More shuffling. She clamped down on her grin. And saw him in her mind, naked as the day he was born. She should be ashamed at her thoughts, mainly that she'd love to feel his huge shoulders and arms pull her in, that powerful body next to her, against her, his skin touching hers. Feel his heat envelop her . . . She shook her head to clear it. This was no time for a fantasy. She must be giddy from no sleep.

He swung the door open, wearing nothing other than pants and his sling. "You ever hear of knocking?"

"I did, but you didn't answer! You ever hear of a lock?" She came close and he moved aside, allowing her in. "I came to help you dress. I had no idea you slept in the altogether."

"You never asked." He cocked an eyebrow.

"Wipe that expression off your face. You look like a wolf."

He sat on his bunk. "I've been shot, I haven't seen you for hours, and this is what you have to say to me?" His sitting brought them face-to-face.

She came close, and moved right in against him, resting her hands on his thighs. Heat rolled off his skin.

She met his eyes. "How are you?"

"Glad to see you. Obviously." He grew serious. "You did a beautiful job of bringing us home. Like I knew you could."

"Thank you."

"In fact, knowing you were up in the pilothouse helped me listen to Andrew and follow his orders. I'm going to the board the moment this is over and insist they license you."

She stepped back. "The last thing I need is your help, you arrogant jackass."

"Now what did I say?" he asked, exasperated. "I figured you'd be glad."

"Then you are an idiot."

"Well, no argument there."

"In the first place, if you believed in me, you should have shown some of this forthright attitude when the board wouldn't even let me take my test. But, no, you were too busy chiding me for being late. In the second place, I don't need any interference from you to get my license. I'll get it on my own. In the third place—"

He cut off her next sentence by pulling her in with his good arm and kissing her before any more words tumbled out. He slid his hand down her back and pulled her right up against him. She thought of him without his clothes; she couldn't help herself. His hand dropped farther, and she shivered, her whole body responding to his touch.

"That's more like it," he murmured against her lips. A small moan came from the back of her throat. She placed her palms against his bare chest and felt his heart beating strong beneath muscle and skin. Oh, heavens, she could get into trouble with this man.

She pulled back. This was not the right time to lose her head. "Jeremy, the police are here. They found Zelda in the woods near the grove. Murdered."

His eyes went from liquid dark to incredulous. "You're not serious."

"I wish I weren't. With that in mind, they are searching the boat. Questioning everyone before they disembark. They want to talk with you as soon as you can manage. Then we need to get you to the hospital."

"I do not need a hospital."

She put her hand to his cheek, caressed his lips with her thumb. "I think Andrew might argue with you there, and he is in charge."

She backed up when he hopped off the bunk. "Well, then, you'd better help me get on a shirt. And socks. And my boots. I definitely can't manage my boots." He pulled a shirt from the small closet. "Murdered? How?"

"Strangled, the police chief said. No more information, though. I get the impression they are the ones who will be asking all the questions. The chief seems fairly competent."

"Never met the man, but Briggs has mentioned they socialize. Here, help me put on this damned shirt."

She moved behind him and lifted the garment up his arm and over his hurt shoulder. She came to the front to button him up and replace the sling. He watched her, seeming like he intended to say something. He remained silent.

"Does it hurt?" she asked.

He smiled. "I wondered when you were ever going to ask." He pulled her to him. "Sarah. We have some things to make clear between

us. You are a wonderful pilot. You stepped up when you needed to, and the River Board wasn't fair to you. I'm breaking every rule there is, but I want you to know, I tried to talk them into rescheduling the test when you were late. They refused, and majority rules."

"You stood up for me?"

"Of course I did. I'm not your enemy; I never have been."

"I've fought my way for everything." She dropped her eyes. "Sometimes it's hard to stop."

"You can trust me. I'm on your side." He tilted her chin up until she met his eyes. "And in case you didn't notice, what we have is becoming much more than friendship."

"Oh, believe me, I've noticed. Do you want that?"

"Yes," he answered. "Do you?"

"Absolutely." She paused. "I have another question."

"Okay."

"You aren't the least bit embarrassed I saw you naked, are you?"

He pressed his lips into a line, but the grin beneath was apparent, the gleam in his eye speaking volumes.

"You know, you really are incredibly arrogant," she said.

"And you have a miserable temper." He let his grin rise to the surface. "But at least we know what we are getting into now, don't we?"

She took his good hand in hers. "Come along, first things first. We need to get you up to the office to speak with the police. Then on to the hospital. I want you healthy as fast as you can manage."

"Oh, don't worry. I'm ready for you anytime."

Now it was her turn to cock an eyebrow. "I sincerely doubt it." She saw a pinpoint of red on his shirt. "Jeremy, what is that?" She undid his top few buttons and looked at the bandages beneath. "You're bleeding again."

"Hmmm. Not surprised. You kissed the stitches right out of me."

"This isn't funny."

"It's fine, Sarah. Just a little blood."

"Drop the bravery act and come along. First stop has changed. We're heading for Andrew and the stateroom. Try not to fall over on our way down. You're way too heavy for me to catch."

"Don't worry, no he-man stuff. You're doing fine without me."

If he hadn't already been bleeding, she would have given him a good whack.

Toby wanted to say good-bye to Henrietta, but he'd only had time to write one note, to his mom. He grasped the pillowcase under his jacket. Monkey Bear, the tin, and one of the models he'd made with Gage. His favorite one. The miniature *Spirit of the River* with toothpick Captain Briggham in the pilothouse. He'd wanted to be buried with these treasures, but his body might never be found. Next best thing: take them all with him, over the cliff.

The front of the deck teemed with people. This ought to be easy enough, Toby thought, with all the activity. Lionel Jeffries even helped by throwing a fit. He wanted off the boat to accompany Henrietta to the hospital. Toby wondered where all this bluster was when his daughter lay sick on the stateroom floor. She sure could have used some concern then.

The police patrolled the entire side of the boat against the dock. Lamps flickered everywhere, light and shadows shifting. Surely he could find a way off the boat.

Of course. The one place the Perkinses always went when they needed to think.

The majestic paddle wheel sat still, its buckets and planks a network of dripping opportunity. He secured the bag in his belt and climbed up. The wet, slippery wood made it difficult, but not impossible to climb—like being on a big playground. He pulled himself over and up, watching the water below. No one even glanced back here.

He took care not to crush the bag; he didn't want the model boat to splinter to pieces. Which, he supposed was silly, since he planned to dive off a cliff with it in his arms. The burn in his chest pulsed, reminding him of the seriousness of his task.

He had to get to the cliff before more people died.

It only took him a few minutes to wriggle through the paddle wheel. When he reached the edge, as quietly as possible, he hopped down on the dock. They were off-loading patients. He heard the new doctor's voice calling out instructions.

Toby crept along to the back of the dock where a tug was moored. Deserted. He scrambled over it and from there he climbed over to the next dock.

Surrounded by mostly dark, he slipped from shadow to shadow, farther away from the life he'd made into such a shambles, and closer to his destiny.

Chapter 24

"I'm not going to go first, Andrew," Jeremy insisted.

The doctor held his list. The worst off to go to the hospital. Two roustabouts stood by to usher Jeremy down to the hospital wagon. Bleeding or not, Jeremy wasn't about to take one of those precious spaces. He was perfectly comfortable here on the floor, sitting against the bar.

"May I remind you I'm the doctor, and I decide who goes when, based on condition. I am not going to stitch you up again," Andrew said. "You are pushing yourself entirely too hard."

"Get the passengers to safety first. Period. Besides, I'm fine."

"Ah. And when did you get your medical degree?"

"Look, I've stayed down here like you asked so you could keep an eye on me."

"Jeremy, that bullet took more out of you than you are willing to admit. Do you need another collapse to convince you? Perhaps I can stitch you up yet again. How much blood do you have to lose before you'll listen to me?"

"I'm doing fine, and besides, the police want to talk to me and they haven't yet."

"Here to remedy that," the police chief said, striding into the stateroom.

"See, Doc," Jeremy said, "I'll stay good and quiet while I talk to the nice policeman"

"Chief Inspector Wilcox," the chief corrected, pulling a chair over. He towered above Jeremy, forcing him to look up from the floor.

Jeremy smiled tightly. "First Officer Smith."

"Is there anywhere we can have more privacy to talk?" the chief asked, apparently not amused.

"I'd like to keep him in here," Andrew said, "because he has a habit of wandering around, doing whatever he damn well pleases and saying he has my blessing. Which he does not."

"Sarah needed a couple hours of rest to pilot us to the dock safely. She did. I am fine. I guess that makes me right."

"Remind me to tell you who my worst patient has been to date. Ah, you don't need to ask. You're winning. Hands down."

"Gentlemen?" Chief Wilcox interrupted.

Lionel Jeffries burst through the front door. "I demand to know why my daughter is not being taken to the hospital right now."

"Daddy—" Henrietta called from the center of the room.

"Because she's recovering and out of danger," Andrew barked. Jeffries ignored the doctor, heading straight for his daughter.

"Doc," Jeremy said quietly, "why don't you send Henrietta in my place with the first group? That way I can talk to the chief, and you'll get Lionel Jeffries off the boat."

Andrew opened his mouth to answer when Jeffries rose to his feet. "Who is in charge? I demand to know who is in charge!"

With a long, labored sigh of surrender, Andrew stood and gestured to the two roustys who had come to help Jeremy to the wagons. "Take this young lady next, please." He gave a curt nod and headed for Henrietta.

Jeremy looked up, returning his attention to the police chief. "So, are we far enough back for your privacy needs?"

"Suit yourself. I was asking in consideration of you, First Officer Smith."

Jeremy crinkled his brow. "Why would I care about privacy?"

"Fine. We can talk here. Tell me how well you knew the murdered woman, Zelda Vashnikoff."

"Not at all."

"I've heard the opposite, First Officer Smith."

"Okay, you can skip the title and the condescending tone. I don't lie. I said I didn't know her at all, which means *I didn't know her at all.*"

"So you deny having intimate relations with her on the deck the first night of this voyage?"

Andrew, who had been returning to them, stopped in his tracks.

"Uh . . . well. It wasn't like that."

"Then perhaps you could tell me what it was like," the chief prompted.

Andrew turned away and began directing the next group of roustys.

Jeremy decided the best way to handle the situation was complete, honest truth. "She kissed me. I'd never seen her before, well, other than when the circus parade boarded the boat. I watched from the pilothouse, which is pretty far up. That night I came down on deck, and she came out of the shadows. We spoke a little, and she kissed me."

The police chief's brow furrowed. His tone was skeptical. "How fortunate for you."

"Not really," Jeremy answered. "Look, as far-fetched as it sounds, she came on to me."

"From what we hear, you practically, um, took her right on deck."

"I did no such thing. Who told you this?"

"It doesn't matter."

"It does to me."

An officer burst through the front door with Skunk, and the two men trotted back to where Jeremy and the police chief sat.

300

"Ah. Well," the chief said. "We'll get this sorted out now, First Officer Smith."

Skunk didn't look like he'd come very willingly. In fact, guilt flushed his face. "I'm sorry, Jeremy, they made me tell."

"What?" Jeremy's neck stiffened, like bands of iron. "Skunk, what do you have to do with any of this?"

"I had to tell them the truth."

Jeremy narrowed his eyes. "What truth?"

That I saw you kissin' and gropin' that Russian gal, and practically humpin' her on deck. Sorry, Miss Sarah."

Jeremy sat straight up and whipped around. With his movement, pain lanced through his neck and shoulder, but it was nothing compared to what bolted through his chest.

Sarah, who must have come in through the back door, stood frozen, her face white with shock. "I'm sorry, I didn't realize you were . . ." She backed away.

"I imagine you'd like that privacy now?" the chief asked.

"Sarah, I can explain. Wait, this is crazy."

Thank God she stopped.

"The first night them theater folks was here," Skunk continued and Jeremy whipped his head back around to glare at Skunk. His look of warning didn't shut the man up. "I never seen nothin' like it, her half-nekkid body up agin' your'n. I didn't want you to get in trouble for humpin' a gal on deck; you know what the cap'n would have to say 'bout that. I was glad when you two headed to her cabin finally."

"I did not go to her cabin!" Jeremy said through clenched teeth.

"You did! You trailed right after her!" Skunk insisted. "I saw you."

Jeremy gulped. "Skunk, shut up!" This was getting out of hand.

"What happened after you 'practically humped' then 'trailed' to the cabin of the woman you didn't know, First Officer Smith?" the police chief asked, his voice level.

"Nothing!"

"So you deny you went to her cabin?"

"No, I . . . look, I did go to her cabin, but—"

Jeremy heard the back door to the stateroom slam shut and glanced back. Sarah was gone. He let himself fall back against the bar and closed his eyes. For the first time, he felt every nuance of his condition: he was tired, sick, and felt like he'd been shot. Only not in the shoulder, but right through the heart.

"First Officer Smith?"

Jeremy opened his eyes and fought the urge to rip the inquisitive and slightly smug look off the police chief's face. "What?"

"Let me ask you one more question. We spoke to the captain, and he was able to answer part of my question." He held up a pair of smashed spectacles. "Explain to me how, after Captain Briggham sent you to fetch these at the picnic where Miss Vashnikoff was murdered, they ended up gripped in the dead woman's hand?"

Sarah couldn't believe she wasted tears on Jeremy Smith. Or let him kiss her. She rubbed her fist across her mouth. And touch her, he'd touched her! In places she never should have allowed. He'd done that and more with the actress, apparently the way he operated with women. And she fell for his seductive words, had been lured by his intimate touch. Sarah was right every time she called him an arrogant jackass; he was that and much worse.

She stormed out of the stateroom, ducking through the back doors. Raising the heel of her hand, she smacked her forehead.

"Stupid, stupid, stupid!" Once, twice, the third time she stopped.

How could she have been such an idiot to trust him? How did she fall for such an obvious ploy? Why, he probably let her walk in and see him naked on purpose, figuring she wouldn't be able to keep her hands off him.

Arrogant didn't begin to describe the bastard.

Oh, she didn't believe he'd killed the Russian woman, not for one moment. But he'd confessed to kissing her. And groping her? Going to her cabin? Sarah put her hands over her ears to block the memory of Skunk's words. It didn't work. . . . *her half-nekkid body up agin' your'n. I didn't want you to get in trouble for humpin' a gal on deck . . .*

She kicked the wall, and instantly regretted it when pain reverberated up her leg. She'd been right all along. Men were rutting pigs. All of them. She hated them. Every last one. She would never forget this. Never.

"Sarah-girl, thank God I found you."

Whirling around, she almost launched herself into Gage. She focused on him. Gage. Put her hand to her forehead. Took one deep breath. Two. There were a few decent men in the world, and Gage was proof, she reminded herself.

His black eyes were fraught with anxiety. "Sarah, we need you. Come with me."

"What's wrong?"

"Your ma. She's tryin' to find Toby."

Icy fingers gripped her guts, pushing away every shred of anger. "What do you mean? He's missing?"

"He's got to be around somewheres; the police ain't lettin' no one off the boat until they're questioned. But Emma's in his room. She found a half-drunk bottle of scotch and two glasses."

"Oh, no."

Gage nodded. "She's fit to be tied."

Sarah followed Gage to Toby's cabin, putting Jeremy Smith and his piggish behavior to the back of her mind. She didn't have any more time to waste on him.

Emma stopped pacing when they entered the cabin. Her face was pallid with fury and etched with fear. She raised the bottle gripped in her hand. "Do you know anything about this?"

"Mom, calm down—"

"Don't tell me to calm down. Do you know about this?"

"I was handling it," Sarah answered.

"Your brother is nowhere to be found, he's been drinking in his cabin, hiding it, and you are *handling it*?"

"Em, Sarah's right, you do need to calm down," Gage cut in. "Hysterics ain't gonna solve nothin'."

Even though Emma snapped her angry, hurt glance to Gage, it cut through Sarah's own heart. "Mom, please listen. Toby has gotten drunk a few times, but he knows he has a problem. Gage and I were going to tell you as soon as we got the boat—"

Emma glared at Gage. "You knew?"

Damn. Sarah clamped her mouth shut.

Gage nodded. Emma's mouth dropped open. "Have you all gone mad?"

"How could we tell you in the middle of all this?" Sarah asked.

"He's my son! My son is in trouble and you don't bother to tell me?"

"We did the best we knew how, Em. It's a tough situation. We decided we'd deal with it once we came home and got back to normal—"

"I don't understand either of you!" Disbelief sharpened in Emma's eyes. "How could you keep this from me when Toby is in this much trouble?"

Sarah felt it, a rip somewhere in her center. Her life, everything she held so tightly, spiraling out of control. Jeremy, Toby, her mother. She'd had enough of everything.

"Mom, calm down. Right now!"

Emma and Gage's eyes trained on Sarah.

"You had no idea the difficulties *your son* has struggled with, because too much was happening, and you were too involved with the boat to even see he has problems at all."

"Nothing is more important than my son!"

"Oh, really? Toby's problems are right there, in plain view, if you take the time to look."

Pain then anger bolted through Emma's eyes. "You keep things from me, refuse to talk to me no matter how many questions I ask, you demand I allow you and Toby *privacy,* and now you tell me I don't take the time to see? How dare you!"

"Here's how. I've been his mother and sister both since you left us. I had to keep him in one piece, and I did. While you were off gallivanting on this boat having a grand old time, Toby and I did the best we could."

"Having a grand old time?" Emma asked, her voice tinged with despair. "Do you not remember your father? He came after me! I left you two to protect you."

"He could have come after us just as easily—"

"Jared didn't give a damn what happened to you, Sarah. Or Toby. It was me he wanted." Emma's face drained of even more color, except for a pinpoint of red spotting each cheek. "You and Toby were a weapon to use against me. I left because I thought it would keep you and Toby truly safe! It was the only way I knew to protect you." Angry, hurt tears glittered in her mother's eyes. Her face was strained with shock.

Sarah couldn't stop. "And we tried to protect you the best way we knew how, by acting like our lives were fine. Well, here's a revelation for you, Mom. They aren't. Yes, Toby has a drinking problem! Yes, he carries around guilt for everything our father ever did. Yes, I'm disgusted and appalled by men. Yes, we aren't perfect. And we'll attend to it all. Stop making the situation worse!"

Emma dropped the bottle on the bed and turned away. Sarah saw her shoulders shake. Her mother was crying. And Sarah realized she was crying, too.

"Em, Sarah—"

The walls closed in and she needed to get out. Sarah whirled around, ripped the door open, and stalked out into the morning light.

She wasn't sure where she'd go. One thing she did know, she had to get away from her mother and out of that room.

Gage's arms wrapped around her. Furious and brokenhearted all at once, Emma turned and pushed him away. "How could you not tell me?"

"Em, I only found out yesterday. When do you think I coulda told you? While people were dyin'? While you were already consumed with guilt, just tryin' to keep a hold?"

She felt completely betrayed. And Gage, of all people. "How can I ever trust you again?"

Anguish pierced his black eyes. "You're angry. When you calm down, you'll see I didn't have much of a choice."

"I will never forgive you for this."

Gage swallowed. "Yes, you will, Em. Of course you're upset. Sarah is, too. This ain't the end of the world."

"He's my son, Gage. My son."

"Maybe you need to face what's really upsettin' you." He paused. "Your son is in trouble. It ain't that you didn't know, or I knew before you that's got you all torn up. You watched the same demon jest about kill Quentin. You're scairt for Toby. And you don't know what to do."

God, he was right.

Everything broke. Everything. Her tears changed to sobs. Then Gage was there, his arms around her. He held her tight, and she cried into his shoulder. He gripped her tighter.

"We'll get through this, Em. It seems like a big mess now, but Toby will be fine. Sarah, too. They're good kids."

She made a shambles of her life, of her children's lives, yet this man stood by her, comforted her, helped her. She wrapped her arms around him and held on for dear life.

"Don't let go," she whispered.

"I never will."

She waited a few minutes until she stopped shaking and then gently pulled away from him, standing on her own and swiping her cheeks. "We have to find him. That's the first step."

"You're right."

"I hope Sarah will forgive me."

"Em, she's been through so much. One step at a time. One kid at a time. Toby's first. He's in a heap of trouble. Then we'll work on Sarah. You won't have to do this alone."

"Oh, God, Gage. You are absolutely right. I'm terrified for him."

"I know." He nodded. "I am too. We have to believe he'll be okay. You and I can get him through this."

A knock thundered at the door. "Mrs. Perkins?" the chief's voice came through.

"Oh, God," Emma whispered. Gage handed her a kerchief and she swiped her face and nose. She raised her voice. "I can't talk right now."

"Mrs. Perkins, I think you'd better take a look at this. One of my officers found a note addressed to you when he searched the bar. It's from your son."

Chapter 25

Up on the Texas deck, Sarah walked the boat, heels clicking against wood in a purposeful rhythm, suggesting she was headed somewhere. Important. In truth, she traveled in circles. Circles, circles. She kept close to the walls and as far from the rails as possible. Even though the boat was practically empty of passengers and patients, she didn't want to risk being seen, not like this.

Her hair had come loose, cascading over her shoulders, unraveled, just like her life. She raked her fingers through it. Wanted to kick and punch the wall.

She thought she might explode.

During her third pass on the port side, she heard Andrew organizing the final wagon of patients going to the hospital. She stopped when she recognized Jeremy grumbling below, and flattened herself against the wall.

She recognized Chief Wilcox's deep voice. "Don't leave the hospital, First Officer Smith."

"Go to hell," Jeremy's voice gritted out. He must be clenching his teeth.

"I'm sending an officer to accompany you. And since Briggs thinks so highly of you, I'm going to give you some advice. Find yourself a lawyer."

She listened to a few moments of shuffling and footsteps.

"Jackass," Jeremy said.

"He's just doing his job." Andrew's voice drifted up. "Jeremy, if you're smart, you'll keep your mouth shut. And he's right, you need a lawyer."

"I didn't have a damned thing to do with that woman."

"Other than kiss her. And go to her cabin."

"Oh, Christ, not you, too, Andrew. She threw herself all over me. Was I slow to back off? Regrettably, yes. Did I go to her cabin? Yes, but I stopped at her door. I didn't go in. Doesn't that count for anything?"

"I'm sure you're telling the truth, but that was quite a look on Sarah's face."

Heat prickled her cheeks at the sound of her name.

"You think I'll ever forget it?" Jeremy sounded like she felt. Brokenhearted. "I feel like the biggest ass in the world."

"I believe Sarah might agree with you on that account."

Tears stung behind her eyes.

Was Jeremy being honest about what happened between him and Zelda? Or just trying to protect himself from an arrest? A lone tear escaped and trickled down her cheek as she tried to think straight and reason it all out. She was just too tired. God, she knew one thing. She wished so much for Jeremy to be telling the truth, the desire became an ache deep within her.

Another tear leaked out. Damn. She knew where she needed to go. Something was about to break inside her, and when it did, she wouldn't be able to control herself. She'd be damned if she let anyone see her in such a state.

All remaining activity now took place on the lowest deck. She headed up to the pilothouse. No one would look for her there.

First things first. Jeremy made his plans to get out of this place. He didn't plan to stay long at all. Escaping shouldn't be too difficult, he thought, analyzing the hospital room. Tall windows in the back, total of five beds, including his, complete with patients. The captain's bed was empty at the moment. Most likely Andrew placed him next to Briggs on purpose.

Jeremy wasn't about to wait around and get hauled off to jail. He hadn't killed the Russian woman. Someone on the boat did. Which meant one thing.

The *Spirit* was in danger. He didn't yet know from who or why, but his entire body thrummed with alert, his senses sharpened. He'd been lying around too damned long. Time to take some action. Of what type, he wasn't sure, except for one aspect—he was getting out of this wretched hospital.

And he had to fix things with Sarah. He wasn't about to lose her.

An orderly wheeled Briggs into the room in a wheelchair. Jeremy's heart felt even heavier at how worn the captain appeared. He should be worrying about his pending murder charge, but somehow seeing Briggs slumped, an orderly pushing him about, was the worst possible outcome of the nightmare of Henrietta's wedding cruise.

Then again, the memory of Sarah's face, the look of betrayal, shot through him. God, he'd botched up the best thing in his life. And so completely. Damn it all anyway. He was an idiot. And an ass. And everything in between.

He was sure he could fix the rift. He just had to get to her.

Two men lifted Briggs back to the bed and covered him. Chief Wilcox had asked Briggs to identify the Russian actress; apparently Oscar was too beside himself to be of any use to anyone. No surprise there.

Jeremy waited until the orderlies left to ask his question. "Was it Zelda?"

"You know, I didn't realize it until they put the wig back on. No makeup, and without the wig, she looked completely different. Damnedest thing, though, she seemed very familiar."

"Really?"

Briggs leaned up on his elbow. "I'd swear I knew her."

"Are you sure it wasn't just seeing her like that? Maybe she looked like somebody else but still resembled Zelda? I don't think I'd recognize her if I saw her on the street without all her trappings."

Briggs shook his head. "I swear, I've known her. That has to be fairly significant, don't you think?"

Jeremy shrugged. "It would be nice if the police found the real explanation for her murder and got off my back."

"I've warned you about dallying with the passengers. I'm actually quite appalled at your behavior. Having an affair with a passenger is not what I meant by taking more responsibility in the social arena."

"Briggs, I—"

"Let me finish, Jeremy. You can't get the reputation of a womanizing pilot. Men will keep their wives and daughters far away from the *Spirit*."

Jeremy's shoulders slumped. "Probably a mute point anyway, since it looks like I'm going to be arrested any moment."

"Moot point," Briggs corrected. "There is an officer sitting at the door, you know."

"I saw him." Jeremy flopped back, and got rewarded by a stab through his shoulder. Damn, his wound was getting tiresome. "You know, Briggs, she came on to me. Gave me an open invitation. I didn't take her up on it. I've never seen a woman so heated up. She was looking for anyone."

"And found trouble in the grove." The captain sighed and leaned back. "The world is full of predators, unfortunately."

"I think she was lonely," Jeremy said. "What happened to her is pretty sad. I got the feeling she needed someone to make her . . . I don't know . . . feel special. Cared for."

"How did she get my spectacles?" Briggs asked.

"How should I know? I told you, I couldn't find them. By the time I got there, they'd been removed."

"You have to admit, that in itself looks fairly bad for you," Briggs said. "I apologize for involving you in any way. I had no idea at the time the police questioned me you'd been seen with her in a compromising state."

Jeremy sighed. "Oh, for Christ's sake. It was only a kiss, and not my idea."

They sat for a few moments in silence.

"You know, Briggs, it's likely someone on our boat, passenger or crew, killed her."

"My vote is passenger. We don't know what those theater people were about. Many of them are fairly strange. No one on my crew is responsible."

"Your loyalty is admirable, Captain, but something doesn't feel right. Especially since your spectacles ended up in her hand. Like someone tried to make you look guilty."

"That clue points directly to you."

"You and I were the only ones who knew I was going back for them. You must be the target."

Briggs' eyes widened in surprise. "Damn it all, boy, you're right. If I weren't so shaky I'd have thought of that myself."

Jeremy clamped down on an amused smile. "Yes, sir. You would have."

"So someone is after me. Who on earth might that be? Why?" He sunk deep into thought and settled back into his pillow.

Jeremy's thoughts circled as the captain relaxed and his breathing slowed.

"Damnation, that's it!" Briggs suddenly bolted upright and swung his legs over the bed.

Jeremy jolted; he'd thought the captain drifted off again. "What is it, Briggs?"

"I know who that woman is!"

A suicide note? Toby admitting he was responsible for making everyone onboard sick? The world tilted and nothing made sense. Emma shook her head.

"Are you sure you have no idea where he'd go?" the chief asked.

"She's already told you," Gage said, his arm around her, his thumb hooked in her skirt waistband. He wasn't holding her up, but holding her back from launching herself past this man and ripping the world apart to find her son.

"My son has threatened to end his life. Don't you think, if I had any inkling of where he is, I'd tell you?"

The police chief's eyes drilled into her. "Briggs insisted I can trust you completely, but when it comes to mothers and children, I don't assume anything. And we can't find your daughter."

"You ain't much of a police chief, are you?" Gage asked. "She must be onboard; she was with us ten minutes ago."

The chief narrowed his eyes. "I understand you are upset, but we must find your boy, Mrs. Perkins."

"And I agree with you."

"Somehow, I am skeptical. When we find him, his future will be grim. Killing three passengers makes him the second mass murderer in Sterling City's history."

"Toby? A mass murderer?" If the situation weren't dire, Emma might have laughed.

"The first was his father," the chief said.

"Tobias is nothing like Jared," Emma said. "My son juggles. Makes jokes. He folds napkins into shapes. He's the gentlest, kindest young man in the world."

"That means nothing. What lies beneath, that's what we need to get at. Mrs. Perkins. Your son has confessed. We have it in writing."

"For some reason he feels responsible for what has happened here, but I assure you, he's wrong. He wouldn't hurt anyone. Such a thing simply isn't in him."

"We'll see when we find him."

"He was devastated when Lucy died. He would never do anything to hurt her. To hurt anyone," Emma said.

"Em." Gage dropped his arm and took her hand. Clenched it. Once. Twice. "Why don't we let the chief do his job?" He swung his gaze to the chief. "Please, find our boy. We've given you all we know."

"I've got my officers scouring the city."

"What can we do to help?" Gage asked.

"Stay on the boat. Or if you leave, tell one of the officers where you'll be."

Gage squeezed Emma's hand again, a signal to keep quiet. She kept her mouth shut. Defending Toby here would do no good anyway.

"We'll be right here," Gage said with complete sincerity.

The chief and his officer left. They listened until the men's footsteps and voices faded, and Emma's knees gave out. She sat on the bed. The boat was just about empty. Andrew and Dr. Elliott were gone with the patients. The police had proceeded methodically, questioning people and releasing them. Most of the passengers were off-loaded.

Her son. Dear God, where was her son?

"The best way off the boat is the paddle wheel," Gage said, low. "No one will see us. I figure that's the way Toby got off the boat with all the police and passengers on the dock."

Hope bolted through her. "What?"

"Em, I know exactly where he is. He's tried this before." She jumped to her feet. He grabbed her shoulders. "We have to wait a few minutes, be sure we don't arouse suspicion. They'll stop or follow us if they see us." He pulled her to him. "Don't worry. We're gonna save our son." He let go and took her hand. "You think you can climb through the wheel?"

"To help Toby? I can do anything."

She had herself a good cry. Sometimes, it was just what a girl needed. Sarah felt much better, but the feeling dissipated when she came down from the pilothouse and walked the Texas deck. The boat seemed deserted. She checked Toby's quarters. A bottle lay on the bed, its contents soaked into the mattress, a reminder of the argument with her mother. The room smelled like a gin mill. Gage and her mother were nowhere to be found. Even if she wanted to mend some fences, she couldn't.

She walked down to the next deck. The stateroom was strewn with blankets and beds, water glasses and other leftover bits of Andrew's makeshift infirmary. The elegant room smelled sour, a remnant of the recent sickness that had inhabited it.

And no one in the cabins. Not even police. They must have finished interviewing and searching. Even the dead bodies were gone.

The *Spirit* felt like an apparition, a ghost of itself. The boat never felt this empty, even in the down months. Toby, her mother and Gage, or Jeremy and the captain were always around. But this was different. She thought she might actually be completely alone.

The boat echoed with quiet.

"Toby? Mom?" she called out. Water lapped around the edges of the *Spirit*. From beyond the docks, the city sounded miles away. "Gage?"

She descended the grand oak staircase and walked around to engineering, the clack of her heels a solitary sound. The boilers threw off some warmth; they'd only been down for a few hours.

Piles of coal were heaped in the coal bins. Shovels leaned against the bins. The deck looked like all the engineers and roustabouts had simply disappeared.

Damned eerie.

Something didn't look right. Some sort of webbing trailed around the floor? She kneeled down. Dirt? Grit? Did something spill during the police search? When she rose, she pinpointed bundles heaped around the edges of the engines. That wasn't right either.

She took a few steps closer to the engines. Peered into the dark. "Gage?"

The sound of shuffling rushed from behind her. She turned.

Charley, grinning. A strange glimmer in his eye. What on earth? He was filthy, and holding a shovel.

"Sorry, Sarah."

She jerked her arm up, but not in time to stop the swinging metal. The shovel hit her and the world exploded, then faded to black.

Chapter 26

"Damnation, that's it!" Briggs suddenly bolted upright and swung his legs over the bed.

Jeremy jolted. He'd thought the captain drifted off again. "What is it, Briggs?"

"I know who that woman is!"

Andrew, leaning over another patient, straightened and strode over to them. "I'm tired of fighting with you," he said, pointing at the captain's legs. "Get back under the covers."

"Hush, Andrew." Jeremy sat up straighter, alarmed at the intensity on Briggs' face. "Who, Captain?"

Briggs scowled but kept his voice low. "Andrew, Jeremy, it took me a bit, but I finally remember where I've seen the woman before. Years ago. She was married to Archibald Yoder."

Jeremy's mouth dropped open. "*The* Archibald Yoder? The captain who blew his boat to smithereens during our race?"

"It's exactly where I've seen her." He looked at both men. "Although she wasn't Russian then. And she didn't dress quite the same."

His gaze drifted off to a memory. "Of course, no wigs. No cosmetics." He focused back to Jeremy. "No wonder I didn't recognize her. The few times I did see his wife, she was a tad on the dowdy side."

Zelda dowdy? And Yoder's wife? A sinking feeling pulled on Jeremy, and he wondered if the illness hadn't rattled the captain's brain.

"Will," Andrew said his voice gentle and humoring, "you must be mistaken."

Briggs shook his head. "I never forget a face. Although hers was quite hidden by her various masks. Damnation, Yoder's wife . . ."

"If it's true . . ." Jeremy's voice trailed off.

"Of course it's true!" Briggs demanded. "I may have spent the last few days retching, but I'm none the worse for wear, make no mistake!"

"Then what the hell does it mean? Yoder?" Jeremy asked, his head reeling.

"Nothing," Andrew said. "It means she used to live here. So what?"

"I disagree, Andrew." Briggs grimaced. "Yoder was pigheaded. "I'd leave it to him to refuse to keep to his grave, where he belongs.

"Oh, yes! He's risen from the dead to avenge his wounded pride," Andrew said in a theatrical voice. Then he grew serious. "Captain, I must insist you lie back down and stop this fanciful musing. It's doing you no good."

"Wait." Jeremy leaned forward. "Captain, didn't you say Charley McCoy was the one who recommended the theater to you?"

Briggs nodded. "He did. Surprised me. Charley doesn't seem to be the theater-going type, but there is a bit of circus extravaganza involved and—"

"So," Jeremy reasoned, "Zelda, from the theater Charley recommended, is dead. People on our boat where Charley works got sick. Charley is one person who bridges both the boat and the theater."

"How?" Andrew said. "Just because he saw them . . ."

"No, there's a connection," Jeremy said. "Might be nothing, but worth checking out, anyway."

"Boy, you're right," Briggs said. "I've got to get to my boat."

"Absolutely not!" Andrew crossed his arms. "I'm getting tired of trying to keep you two in your beds!"

The captain ignored Andrew's sputtering. "Jeremy, there has to be something to this. Even though the evidence all points to you, we know you didn't do it."

"We don't have any other ideas," Jeremy reasoned. "And I don't like the fact the *Spirit* is sitting in dock, no one aboard."

"Worth a check, no question," Briggs said.

"Why is no one listening to me?" Andrew interjected.

"Because," Jeremy answered, "if we don't figure out what's happening, I'll be swinging at the end of a rope in the near future. Then it won't matter how many stitches I tear out of my shoulder, will it?"

Andrew's eyebrows rose.

"Captain, maybe Andrew is right. This whole thing might have nothing to do with Yoder," Jeremy said. "Maybe that's a coincidence, his wife coming back. That woman was looking to bed down with anyone, and it makes more sense someone got rough." He cleared his throat. "I've heard—ah—there's a way of intimacy that involves choking near to death while two people . . . you know . . ."

Briggs scrutinized Jeremy. "I must say, your vast knowledge in the area of bizarre sexual practices is a tad unsettling. Especially considering the pending charges against you and your behavior."

Jeremy's face heated up. "I just hear things."

"Indeed," Briggs said. "Well, one thing I've learned, gentlemen, is that there is no such thing as a coincidence. If there appears to be even a slight connection, it's worth a look." He stared pointedly at Andrew. "I have to get back to the boat and speak with Charley. I'll know if he's telling me the truth or not." The captain's voice hardened. "And I want no argument from you, Doctor. I am, at least, still a free man.

And I'm going to my boat."

A resigned look spread over Andrew's face. "Fine. But I'm going with you. Someone will have to drag your inert form back here."

Briggs nodded. "Get my clothes, if you would, please. Glad to have you onboard instead of arguing with me."

"Oh, the shame of it all." Andrew pulled the captain's pants and shirt from the cabinet. "A doctor wanting what is best for his patient."

"What's best is to let me get back to my boat."

"Grab my clothes, too," Jeremy said. "I'm going with you."

"There is a guard outside, and they won't allow you to leave," Briggs said.

"I'm not under arrest yet."

"Matter of time. Besides, I do not need police chasing us down, interfering. You have no choice, Jeremy. You'll have to stay here." Briggs shifted closer. "But, trust me, I'll get to the truth."

"You both belong in bed," Andrew said, kneeling to help Briggs with his socks. "At least one of my patients will receive adequate care. The other . . ." He shrugged. "Well, it appears there's not much I can do about your wild-goose chase."

Jeremy leaned back and worked on looking resigned. He didn't care if there were officers in the hall, keeping watch. He'd be damned if he'd stay back and let Briggs have all the fun.

But best to let the captain get a head start.

They stopped a few yards back. Emma's sweet baby boy sat at the edge of Lost Soul's Cliff. Relief and horror tumbled through her all at once. She found him. And he was in terrible trouble.

She glanced over to Gage, also out of breath, and she gulped in air, trying to resume some semblance of normal. If she came up behind Toby gasping, if they startled him, he might go over. Dear God, she couldn't believe he sat at the edge of a cliff. Her mind raced in a thousand different directions, and then mired to a stop, paralyzed. She wasn't able to think straight, and they had no room for error.

"You scoot up on the right side of him; I'll scoot to the left," Gage whispered. "We can talk him down from this."

"What if we startle him and he jumps? Or falls?"

"He won't, Emma. Long as we stay calm."

Toby's shoulders slumped with the weight of the unimagined. Although she was sure Toby would never, ever harm anyone, she didn't care if he'd poisoned the whole boat. She did not want him to die. She'd take his place, if possible. The sickness was her fault. She had to convince him of it.

"Toby?" Gage called out softly. Toby's shoulders tensed. "Toby, it's me and your ma. We're gonna come closer."

"No!"

Gage nodded to her. She shook her head, not sure they should approach yet. He nodded again, insisting. They walked slowly until they were a few feet away. Gage motioned for Emma to sit, and he did, too. Toby held his Monkey Bear and the miniature *Spirit* he and Gage made when he was a boy. An ache squeezed through her chest.

"Scoot on back here, Toby," Gage said. "This is no way to solve anythin'."

"I didn't even hide the letter good enough. You weren't supposed to find it until later. When this was over. Cripes! I can't do anything right."

Her heart broke at the anguish in his voice. Gage scooted closer and she followed.

Toby whipped his head around, swaying. His eyes caught Emma's.

"No, Mom!" With his cry, he lost his balance.

Briggs and Andrew had been gone about ten minutes, although it felt more like an hour. The other three patients in the room slept. The officer sat in the hallway, facing in. He was almost nodding off. This would be easy.

Jeremy pretended to sleep and waited for his chance. In truth, he was just about jumping out of his skin. He only needed a minor distraction in the hall or the cop to doze off, which the man was close to doing. These hallway officers were no match for him.

But the waiting was killing him.

He wondered what was happening, and it upset him to think Charley might be involved at all. He really liked the kid.

Jeremy closed his eyes partway, looking through slits. The officer came close to sleeping, but not yet. A commotion in the hall woke the cop up, and he jumped to his feet. Damn.

But then another officer blocked the view; they were changing places. A bolt of excitement charged through him. Now or never.

Jeremy slipped out of bed—fully clothed, boots and all—and sprinted to the window. He'd only have a second before the cop noticed. He planned to be long gone by the time someone raised the alarm.

Jeremy pulled himself up, over the sill and out, his shoulder screaming. He was probably popping stitches, but didn't care. Patching him up would give the doc something to do.

His feet landed on pavement, and he ran. He dodged down a side street. If they were quick they might follow. They'd look for him on the main street sprawling through the center of town and down to the river landing. He planned to stay out of sight until he made the docks.

And it might be advantageous, police swarming the boat. Just in case.

A woman gave Jeremy a quizzical stare as he hurried by. He stopped and ducked into an alley to catch his breath. He kept moving, but dizziness swayed his vision. Brick scraped his palm when he reached out to steady himself. Sweat trickled down his back, and not the good kind. The sickly, weak kind. Damn. This run would normally be nothing for him.

Fear pushed his heart to race, and if he weren't dashing to the boat, the pounding in his chest might drive him crazy. He didn't know where Sarah might be. If she was aboard, Jeremy wasn't sure how he'd convince her to leave. He'd probably have to throw her over his injured shoulder and drag her off.

Whatever was going on, the *Spirit* didn't feel safe. The unknown sharpened his senses.

He stumbled on a jagged street brick, caught himself before he fell. He didn't stop. He needed to keep moving forward. He assumed the *Spirit* was in trouble and the police were looking for him. The worst possible scenario on all fronts. Thinking this way kept him wary and alert.

He started running again.

Over the buildings the *Spirit* rose, moored out on the last dock. Morning light bounced off the beautiful boat as she sat, majestic and peaceful. Going in from the back dock, keeping low and out of sight was his best option. He glanced around for the captain and Andrew. He saw no one anywhere near the *Spirit*.

He was the first one here after all.

Horror froze Emma. Toby caught and righted himself.

She breathed again. Her son had almost gone over because of her. "Toby, I want to come and be with you," Emma said, trying to keep fear from infusing her words.

"No, Mom. Please." His voice trembled, and she knew he was crying. Oh, God, she wanted to grab him, hold him in her arms. He was hurting so bad.

"She'll stay back," Gage promised, motioning her to do so. He put his fingers to his lips, signaling her to keep quiet.

She was upsetting Toby, the last thing he needed. For the second time in her life, she knew keeping back and away was best for her child. It just about broke her, but she stayed right where she sat.

"Let me come up there, Toby," Gage said. "I'd like to talk with you. I promise that's all we'll do. Talk."

Her son didn't respond.

Gage glanced back to her. Emma put every ounce of faith she possessed in him. Gage scooted to the edge of the cliff and swung his legs over. She clasped her hands, muttered a quick prayer, and stayed put, watching as the two men she loved beyond reason dangled their legs over a deadly drop.

"Quite a view from up here," Gage said.

"You know the worst part?" Toby said, his voice wobbly. "I can't ever do it. I should be floating downriver by now, but I get too scared. I'm such a stupid coward."

"Toby, you can face what life has to throw at you. You're no coward." He paused. "Givin' up and takin' your life before it's your time, leavin' everyone who loves you behind, that's not the way to do things."

"I killed all those people, Gage. Me and dear Father."

"Dear Father? What do you mean?"

"Jared. He's inside me. I see his eyes, looking back at me in the mirror. I can feel him; he's this burn in my chest. He won't leave me alone. If I don't go over with him, who knows what else he'll do? What he'll make me do."

Emma willed herself to make no sound. She couldn't believe Jared was still ruining their lives. Why wouldn't he stay dead? She closed her eyes.

God, save my son. I swear, I'll do anything, I'll never allow Jared in our lives again. I'll put him in the past. I promise. Just save my son.

"Jared is gone," Gage said, "and all his evil is buried in the grave with him. Leave him there, right where he belongs." He paused. "Toby, there ain't a piece of that man in you."

324

"How can you say that? Look at me! I look exactly like him."

"I am lookin' at you, and I see Tobias Perkins. A funny kid who is growin' into a fine, gentle, kind young man. A man I'd be proud to call my own son."

Tears burned Emma's eyes.

Gage continued. "You are my son, Toby. You're more mine than you ever were his. Look at what's in your hands."

Toby bowed his head, looking down. "Our model."

"Makin' that together? Those were some of the best times of my life."

Toby glanced sideways at Gage. "Come on, I was hopeless."

Emma glimpsed Gage's half smile as he shifted to face her son. "You might have been a mite clumsy at fixin' or mechanics, but you loved buildin' models. You are good with your hands, good at makin' things. Look at all them napkin sculptures. Our models. You make beautiful things, Toby. Fun things."

"Useless things."

"Don't you ever say that. Makin' beauty and joy is the finest anyone can do for this world. There's more than enough ugliness in it."

A breeze rustled through the trees, leaves hushing the morning.

"Your model of the *Spirit* there," Gage said. "The only reason I didn't ask to have it is because you were so proud of it. I figured you should keep it. But it means everythin' to me, Toby. Every time I see it, I remember how you wanted to spend the time with me. Wanted to make me happy and proud of you. You struggled at first, puttin' it together. But you never gave up."

Toby set the rickety model carefully beside him. When he spoke, it was so soft Emma hardly heard it. "But I killed all those people, Gage."

"Toby, no." Gage paused and Emma prayed. "I would bet my life you didn't. Your letter said you don't remember doin' none of it."

"It was me. When I drink, I can't remember, and I do terrible things."

"How do you know?" Gage asked. "You pass out from drinkin',

that's all. Ain't that unusual. And you're afraid. I'll help you, son. I love you. Your ma loves you. Don't leave us."

"The tin. The powder in my tin. I explained it in the note."

"You said yourself you don't have any idea what's in it. You're makin' a lot of jumps in logic here, Toby."

"I feel this burn, all the time. It's him, Gage. Inside me. And it's up to me to end it."

Gage paused, and the leaves rustling sounded like a death rattle.

"Don't make your ma see you go over. You can't do that to her."

"Aw, cripes."

Emma flinched at the anguish in his voice.

"Toby, you're nothin' like Jared. I know, in my heart of hearts, you didn't have nothin' to do with any of this. Trust me, son. Now, come on. Scoot back. Trust me."

Toby shook his head. "I can't."

Her son's voice sounded unsure of what to do, and at that moment, Emma knew they had a chance.

"Toby, you can," Gage said quietly. "Come back. Whatever it is you have to face, we'll do it together. You ain't alone."

Emma felt she held her breath forever.

"How come you always make sense?" Toby asked.

"'Cause I know a good man when I see one. There are too few in the world. Don't take one away."

Toby stared at Gage. Time froze.

He scooted back. Gage did, too.

Emma put her hand on her stomach and let out her breath. She ached with anxiety, but relief never felt so sweet.

Black. Clanging. Sarah's head throbbed and consciousness wobbled.

Something sticky and wet oozed in her hair. Blood? Her face lay against wood. A floor? She tried to move and agony bolted through her head. Her arms ached and her hands were numb. She whimpered.

"Ah, you're comin' to."

Charley's voice. Then she remembered. He'd hit her with a shovel. Her arms. She couldn't move them. Or her legs. Rope bit into her wrists and ankles. She opened her eyes to boots on the floor, every breath shooting thorough her with searing, red pain.

"Charley?"

"You know, I wasn't sure how to get the captain back here so's I could finish the job, and then you waltz right into my plans. I owe you my sincerest thanks." His feet moved, and he pushed her with the toe of one boot, rocking her back. Pain shot through her head and she bit against crying out. "And by the way, I'd like to thank you for pushin' Toby around so much. You bossed him and took care of his problems. You did a fine job of makin' him into a mama's boy. Or sister's boy, I guess. Made it easy for me to dupe him into thinkin' this is all his fault."

"What—?" She choked on her question. Nausea flooded her body.

"I guess I smacked you awful hard. Glad I didn't kill you, though. Wasn't thinkin' straight. I need you alive for a mite longer."

Nothing made sense to her throbbing head except one thing. She was in big trouble.

"No tellin' how long it'll be till someone comes back. We may have ourselves a long wait, or short. Make yourself comfortable."

His boots thunked away. Her eyes grew more used to the dark and the flashes in her eyes subdued. She saw what he'd packed around the engines. Explosives. She recognized bundles of dynamite and heaps of black powder.

Big trouble? More like catastrophe.

"Charley?" she managed.

Footsteps approached. He squatted down.

"What? Why?" she asked.

"Full of questions, ain't you? You might have a chance to find out before you're blown to bits. And if not . . ." He shrugged. "Well, once we get to the hereafter we'll know everythin', right?" He rose and walked away.

Suddenly, Jeremy and the Russian woman, her mother, Toby's drinking, every problem shrank to less than disaster. She hoped she'd live long enough to deal with them again.

Her mind whirled, and it felt like half her brain didn't work. Her thinking shot around, scattered and fragmented. She focused on what was clear.

She was incapacitated, her thoughts rattled at best, her hands and feet bound.

Charley meant to kill her and blow up the *Spirit*.

The captain was his main target.

So what to do? She tried to focus through the searing inside her head. Her first problem. Getting out of the ropes. She tried to pick at the binding, but her hands were numb. Movement caused pain to shoot up her arms and shoulders.

"Ah, just in time. Howdy, Captain!"

She shifted and saw Charley, a dark blurry figure against the bright sun falling over the port-side deck. Beyond, Sarah knew, the dock.

"Don't come any closer. If you do I'm gonna blow this boat to kingdom come!" Charley's voice remained good-natured, almost happy.

"Charley, what is the meaning of this?" the captain's voice called, sounding far, as if it came from the dock.

The captain was here. Oh, God, and in danger. He would die with them. Then anger ignited inside her. No one was going to die. She refused to lie here like a trussed-up animal waiting for slaughter.

Sarah twisted and scooted in the direction of the tool shelf. If she could get something in her hands to cut the rope. Maybe someone left something down on the ground. Gage insisted on engineering being

perfect; every tool had a place. Of course, nothing on the floor.

"Me and Pa, we been waitin', Captain. We're all ready for you. Oh, I got to tell you, Sarah's back here. Got her tied down so she won't cause us no trouble."

"Don't count on it," she muttered quietly. Her anger felt familiar. Good.

Then Charley's voice changed, dropped deep. "We intend to blow this garbage scow of a boat off the river, and if you don't want the girl to be on it, We suggest you step right up and take her place, Briggham. That is, if there is any nerve left in you!"

Charley spoke in the voice of another man. A chill slithered down her spine. He was possessed or insane. Either way, catastrophe didn't do justice to the situation either.

This was horrifying. And she didn't see a way out.

Chapter 27

Jeremy climbed up the side of the boat, sopping wet. Pink stained his shirt. He must be bleeding again. He was going to give Andrew hell about his sloppy stitches. Damn things refused to stay in.

He rolled on the boat, face up in the sun for a second. Strength leached out of him into the deck. Fighting the urge to drift off to sleep, he flopped over and raised to all fours, shaking his head like a wet dog. He needed to keep clear. The cool river helped, the sun beat on his back, felt good. Too good. He didn't have time to stop and enjoy the warmth.

Someone was yelling from inside the boat. A deep voice, one sounding vaguely familiar and different, all at once. The voice stopped, and Jeremy experienced a strange sensation, the silence of death wrapping around the boat. Life sounded far away, ghostly strains echoed from the city.

The whole moment seemed eerie and like a dream. A very bad one.

He wasn't sure what he faced and needed to be as quiet as possible. He sat back and pulled off his boots. Not easy to manage, but urgency drove him. He bit back a grunt when his shoulder screamed with pain. He dare not make a sound until he assessed the situation completely.

Yelling again. He gently laid his boots on the deck and rose again to all fours, creeping up to the starboard side wall. Hugging the wall, he crept as close as he dared to the hallway leading to engineering. He figured whoever was hollering, they yelled to someone on the dock; the voice carried away from him.

"We intend to blow this garbage scow of a boat off the river, and if you don't want the girl to be on it, We suggest you step right up and take her place, Briggham. That is, if there is any nerve left in you!"

Well, that message was clear enough. The captain was here. And someone had captured a woman on the boat, and she was in trouble. Jeremy wanted to charge in, but pushed his feelings aside. He could not allow emotion to get in his way and meddle with his thinking.

He fell back to his pilot's training. First things first. Assess the situation. Then formulate the plan. Next, proceed and do what needed to be done. No matter what that might be.

He scooted up to get an idea of what circumstances waited at the end of the hall. The entrance to engineering was dark and murky. He didn't want anyone catching a glimpse of him, but he needed to see what was happening.

Slowly, he edged to the hallway opening, and peeked around, only allowing the smallest part of his face to show. Just enough to see out of one eye. Squinting against the sunlight pouring over his shoulders, he didn't see much. In the dark murk of engineering, a bundle lay, something heaped on the floor near the doorway at the end of the hall.

It moved. Unwrapped. A woman. He'd recognize her anywhere. Sarah.

He pulled back, holding himself from charging in to save her. If he acted on emotion, it might mean the end. He balled his fists, took a deep breath. He needed to think this through.

"Charley, please. You don't need to do this." The captain's voice wafted through the boat. Jesus, that other voice was Charley's? Sure didn't sound like the kid.

A thought hit him, sharpening his urgency to a hot point. What if the cops came on the scene or were here, and charged the boat? Jeremy trusted the captain and Andrew, but he sure as hell didn't have much faith in the police. Especially the arrogant chief. He needed to get Sarah out of danger before any of the bumbling cops arrived or God only knew what might happen.

He couldn't see a way down the hall without alerting Charley.

Jeremy ducked back when footsteps crossed engineering and came his way.

Sarah scooted a little farther, got close to the wall, and then flopped over.

And in the doorway, near the floor, a miracle. She glimpsed a flash of Jeremy's face.

He disappeared. He was there. She was going to be fine. He was—

Her back shot through with sharp pain and although she tried to keep the cry in, it erupted from her. The bastard had kicked her.

"What in the hell do you think you are doing?" Charley growled.

He dragged her to her feet. She clamped her teeth together, agony shooting through her back. He pulled her off balance, dragging her over to the sunlight side of the boat, her shins and knees stinging as skin scraped off on wood. He dropped her on the deck. Little bastard possessed the strength of the insane.

She blinked, not able to see. Tears swam in her eyes from the bright sun. He stooped down and slid her along the floor, pushing her out in the light, keeping behind the wall himself. Then he pulled her back. Wood tore her blouse and scraped her back.

"Now, you see? We will trade, Captain. Her for you. We care nothing for this girl. It's you We want. It's you Our revenge seeks."

What the hell? We? Our? What was he talking about? No one else was here. He grabbed her feet, dragging her back into the dark through the web of powder on the floor. She saw it laced around the boilers, leading to the coal, the cords of wood. He'd rigged it to blow the boat up from anywhere in engineering. Powder gritted on her face and through her hair, stuck in her scraped off skin.

"You don't have to do this!" Briggs called. "Charley, come out and talk to me. I won't harm you, I promise."

"Harm Us? Briggham, you killed Us. Destroyed the Yoder name. Murdered Our future. It's time to face your sins!" Charley roared. Cold ice gripped Sarah. It sounded like Satan himself possessed the boy. Through her haze of pain, she tried to understand. Yoder? What did Yoder have to do with any of this?

She tried to think, to grab on to an idea, but everything was happening so fast.

"Charley, you are not your father." The captain's voice again, but unsure; as if he guessed.

Charley chuckled, only the sound was hollow and mean. "The boy was useless, We are finally together, Father and Son."

"You know the destruction of the *Ironwood* wasn't my fault," Briggs called out, "just as all this isn't your fault."

"You kilt him, Cap'n," Charley called, his voice rising to normal and escalating higher. "You kilt my daddy." Now he sounded like a boy, the sweet, sorrowful voice causing Sarah's blood to run cold.

Charley pulled a candle from his pocket.

Gunpowder, explosives, insane man, candle. Definitely not good. She wriggled, looking around for something, anything. There must be an answer. If Charley blew up the *Spirit*, Jeremy would be killed, too. She would not die like this; she would not allow Jeremy to die.

"Your father loved to shift the blame. I knew him, Charley." A pause. "And you didn't have a chance. I see that now." The captain's voice lowered. "Charley, you killed your mother, didn't you?"

"We exterminated another whore from the face of the earth," the deep voice snarled. "She will not be missed." Every time Charley's voice deepened he used pronouns. *We. Us.* As if more than one person lived inside his body.

Sarah tried to understand the information. Charley was Yoder's son? Captain Yoder from the *Ironwood*? And Charley killed his mother? The tavern waitress? Zelda? One of the passengers who died? She thought he'd been an orphan, at least that's what Toby told her.

Charley's voice rang out again. His normal voice. "The farm hands came to call and she put me in a closet, locked me in, stuck a chair in front of the door. But I'd hear." His voice trembled. "She forgot sometimes, left me in there all day." He again broke into the high pitch of a child. "It's hot in here, Mommy, please," he cried.

She knew, in that instant, the hollow hurt inside him. The neglect, the abuse of a child. Even though he'd murdered people, even if he ended up killing her, she felt sadness and regret for the life he'd been forced to live.

"Oh, Charley," she said.

This time his foot found her gut, and her breath wailed out with his kick.

"Charley, stop it! I can't allow you to harm her!" Briggs called out.

She tried to take in air, but he'd kicked the breath out of her.

"Then come and get her, Briggham. Her for you."

Sarah gasped finally. And moaned. Oh, God, she had to get them out of this, needed to clear her head. She couldn't think. She was only reacting to pain and fear and it made her crazy, this helplessness.

Still grasping the candle, he grabbed her feet and dragged her farther into the dark center of engineering. He stooped down. With sunlight blazing behind him and in the dark, she didn't see any of his features. Probably for the best, not to be able to see his face. He was already scaring the hell out of her with all these voices spewing from him. Not to mention the surrounding gunpowder and explosives. She didn't need any more fear; it just got in the way.

"We'll see what kind of man he is now, won't We, Miss Sarah Perkins? We have to hand it to you. You've given Us all the leverage We need. Even if he doesn't die, he'll never get over watching Us go up in flames. With you at Our feet."

Charley rose and pulled matches from his pocket.

The maniac lit a match. Lit a candle, blew the match out. Jeremy saw gunpowder strewn around the floor.

"We've lit the flame, Briggham. Not much time for you to decide. Hero or coward?"

Sarah wriggled at Charley's feet. The kid's back was to him now, but he held the damn candle. Jeremy never felt so useless and impotent in his life. His boat, Sarah, and the captain all in trouble of the worst kind, and here he was, hiding. Almost cowering. But if he charged, he'd blow them all to kingdom come. He clenched his fists and his teeth, held himself back from acting without thinking. In truth, the urge coursed through him to tear the entire deck apart.

Sarah continued to wriggle, and Charley kicked her in the gut. She curled around his foot and her groan of agony wrenched through Jeremy. Every muscle and cord in his neck strained; he thought one might pop right out. He bit back the roar of rage pushing to erupt and lowered his forehead to the floor. Counted to three.

He was close to breaking, and Sarah needed him to keep his head.

Charley kicked again, and her sharp intake of air cracked with misery.

Oh, the hell with it. Jeremy couldn't keep back; Charley was beating the woman he loved to death, one kick at a time. He rose to his feet and gripped the edge of the doorway, ready to charge.

And everything changed.

From the port side, the captain's silhouette moved into view. "Let her go, and I'll do whatever you say."

Now or never. Jeremy slid around the corner and into the hall, keeping flat to the wall. He couldn't make out details on the captain's face, but hoped he'd hide any reaction if he saw Jeremy. He trusted Briggs in any situation. The captain would know what to do. He took a step closer.

"Come on in, Captain. We'll let you do the honor of untying her. We won't do a thing until she's off the boat, unless you try to engage your pathetic brand of heroics. Don't be wary, Captain. Join Us."

"How can I trust you?"

"The same way We will trust you." Charley chuckled low. "You don't care much for this, do you, Captain? Everything in Our hands."

Jeremy took another step. Sarah, facing him, caught his eyes and hers widened with hope. All he needed. He gave her a quick nod and crept forward.

"I've been sick for days. You saw me, Charley. I'm not able to do you any harm . . ." The captain's voice trailed off, then came back stronger. "Although I'd love to kick your wretched ass, Yoder. You coward. Hiding behind your son. A boy. You disgust me!"

Jeremy realized the captain must see him and was trying to distract Charley. He took a step closer. No going back now.

Charley began to tremble. "What did you dare say to Us?"

"That you are a useless excuse of man. You always were."

Jeremy took another step. Only a few feet more.

"Hiding behind a boy and a woman! A woman! And holding a candle like it's Christmas or May Day. You're a travesty to the river! You don't deserve to be a pilot, let alone captain!"

Another step. So close. Almost there.

"A joke!"

Charley's head jerked sideways. He saw Jeremy. Sarah reared up and bit him on the knee. Charley howled and the candle slipped from his fingers, dropping to the deck.

Jeremy, with a prayer and his hands outstretched, dove.

Time slowed to a crawl, and every second passed as a year. Jeremy hit the deck, slid toward the dropping candle.

The candle landed in his palms.

Charley kicked Sarah in rage. Again.

Jeremy snuffed the flame, then rose to his feet and lunged at Charley, knocking him down. The two men rolled. Jeremy straddled Charley and pinned him to the deck by the neck. His wounded shoulder screamed. He ignored the pain and punched Charley in the face. Hands pulled at him and somewhere within his haze of rage he thought it might be Briggs, but Jeremy didn't care. He tightened his grip on Charley. Punched again. Blood spurted. Jeremy roared and hit him. Again. And again.

More hands grabbed, but didn't stop him. He hit Charley again.

It took four police officers, a police chief, and one weakened captain to keep Jeremy from killing Charley McCoy with his bare hands.

Chapter 28

"I hear his face changed to Yoder's!" a rousty called out when Jeremy passed. As the crew returned to the boat, rumors of what transpired flew from one person to the next, inflating and becoming more dramatic with each telling.

Jeremy hadn't stayed in the hospital very long. No longer under guard, it was an easy thing to sneak out. He was sure Andrew was beside himself, poor fellow. Well, the doctor could cluck around the captain all he wanted. Jeremy needed to settle a score.

He glanced around the deck, targeted his quarry. Skunk didn't see him coming.

He used his good arm to pin the roustabout to the jackstaff. The man's face bulged red.

"Time for the truth, Skunk. All of it."

"I don't know what yore talkin' on," Skunk whined.

"Bullshit. You gave more details about my encounter with Zelda than I even remember. Exaggerated, if I remember correctly. Which I do." He tightened his grip. "Tell me the truth, Skunk. We got to get this clear or there will be no peace between us."

Skunk gagged. "Jest let go."

Jeremy shook his head. "Not on your life."

"I cain't tell you nuthin'!"

Jeremy gripped harder. Skunk choked, and Jeremy held the rousty for a second. He loosened his grip to let the man talk.

"I am in no mood, Skunk. I watched Sarah get practically beaten to death. She'll be in the hospital God only knows how long, and I'd like to kill someone. You'll do just fine."

"Ifin' I tell, will it stay betwixt gentlemen?"

"It would if there were any gentlemen around here. You've proven you aren't one, and I'm about to throttle you, so I'm clearly not one either. Now tell me."

"If I do, you'll forgive me?"

Jeremy squeezed. He wasn't going to kill Skunk, and both of them knew it. But he'd make the man hurt. Bullet hole in his shoulder or not. He let his grip relax enough for the red in Skunk's face to come back down to an uncomfortable shade of pink.

"Okay," Skunk said. "I was the one bangin' her. I knew if police found out and took me in for questioning, my wife would kill me fer sure."

Jeremy let go. "You have got to be kidding me. You? Did the woman have no sense of smell?"

"She liked me," he said with a tinge of wounded pride. "She liked my rough, manly ways. What she said, anyway."

"God. Poor woman. Although she was married to Yoder and was consorting with Oscar Gévaudan. I guess she didn't have much taste."

"I ought to take umbrage at that there insult."

Jeremy narrowed his eyes. "Oh, really. You interested in discussing *umbrage*?"

Skunk groaned. "Jest don't tell my wife."

"Skunk, why? Don't you love your wife?"

"Sure I do, but a man's got needs. We're away for weeks at a time. That actress said she liked my furry body rubbin' agin' hers."

"That's enough!" Jeremy roared. Any more and he might take after all those sick people in the stateroom and start puking uncontrollably.

"I'll make you a deal," Skunk said. "Let's not discuss none of this ever again."

Jeremy plunged his hands in his pockets. "Yeah, that seems like the best thing to do."

"Uh, Jeremy?"

He glared at Skunk.

"Yore shirt. It's gettin' red."

He looked down at his shoulder. Damn it all anyway.

"I still don't believe it." Toby sat up in his bunk. Gage sat at the foot of his bed; his mom stood next to it. His whole mind and body had been numb for several hours, and he couldn't grasp what was going on. He couldn't raise the strength to get out of bed and felt like a shell, the life in him gone for good.

"It was Charley," Emma said. "Yoder's wife left home, and Yoder got stuck with a toddler. He shipped Charley off to live with his aunt. She's on her way here to make sure Charley is really Yoder's son, but the police are pretty sure."

Gage shook his head. "Charley hid everythin', Toby. His feelin's, his hurt, his pain. His name. His anger grew and took over until it was natural to be someone he wasn't."

"He's Yoder's son?" Even saying it didn't feel right. His best friend? Killed all those people? Killed Lucy?

"He was just a little boy when the *Ironwood* exploded. His aunt said he ran away when he heard, and they never saw him again. We don't know what happened to him between then and the time he came to the *Spirit*," Emma explained. "A lot can happen in ten years."

Gage stared off for a second. "Mustn't have been good, to break the boy like that."

"Charley?" Nothing made sense anymore. "But this stuff in the bottom of my tin," Toby said.

"He must have put it there, while you were passed out," Emma said. "The police are having it analyzed. They think it's some sort of poison."

"Arsenic, most likely, Andrew thinks." Gage sighed. "No smell or taste. Symptoms match."

"Mom, what's going to happen to him?"

Emma and Gage exchanged a glance. "He's not well, Toby," Gage said. "One minute he talks like he's Yoder, the next like him, and sometimes like a little boy. He's at the jailhouse, locked up. The best he can hope for is an asylum. The worst . . . well. Your ma hired a lawyer to help him."

"You said his mom left him?" Toby asked, and instantly regretted his question when a flash of sorrow echoed over his mother's face. She slowly nodded.

"The police figure he tracked her down," Gage explained, "and found her with the theater company. He urged Briggs to bring them to the *Spirit*. When they were hired for Henrietta's weddin' and came onboard, it pushed him over. His two most painful memories collided. The boy couldn't handle everythin' ragin' inside."

"Pushed him over, huh?" Toby shook his head, thinking of the cliff. "It could have been me." He looked directly into his mother's eyes. "If you hadn't come back." He glanced up at Monkey Bear on the shelf, remembered tearing the toy apart when his seven-year-old soul could no longer keep the growing and monstrous anger hidden within. And Monkey Bear was no more, until his mother brought him the toy, resurrected. She fixed it, sewed it up, closed the wounds. And brought Monkey Bear home with her when she returned.

"And you too, Gage," Toby continued, his eyes sliding to the model of the *Spirit*. "I had both of you, and Sarah. Poor Charley didn't have anyone."

He lay back down, wanting to crawl under the covers and never come out.

Gage grabbed his foot and wiggled it. "Hey, kid, you been moonin' around in here long enough. Time to come out and git some fresh air."

"I'll get up in a bit."

Again, a look passed between his mom and Gage.

"We are going to see your sister in the hospital," Emma said. "She'd love a visit from you, I'm sure."

"Could pry use a good dose of all of us," Gage added. "Charley beat the bejesus out of her. Seein' you might perk her up some."

Toby sat up. "Oh, cripes." He recognized when he was being manipulated, still, he knew they just wanted the best for him. "Okay. I'll get dressed."

Gage looked at him. "We have a lot to talk about."

"Yeah, yeah, I know. No more drinking," Toby said.

Emma's voice grew stern. "We don't want you to hide it from us anymore, Toby. We're asking you not to hide anything."

"Easy for you to say," Toby murmured.

"No, it's not," Gage said. "We know you have problems, Toby. Hell, we all do. But that's what families are for, to help a person get through the rough times."

Toby shrugged. "You two want to leave so I can get dressed? Don't worry. No hidden bottles in here."

His mother nodded and turned to leave. Gage rose to follow.

"Quentin used to hide 'em in his shoes." Gage glanced back to Toby. "I know your cabin's clean, 'cause I searched before we brought you back."

Toby sighed. "I suppose I won't have any privacy anymore."

"You'll have enough," his mother said.

"Hey, Gage? I was wondering. Want to build a model of Sterling City? You know, for the boat. I was thinking a panorama would be sort of fun for kids onboard."

Gage smiled his half grin. "We can put it in the captain's dining room. After we clean up everything that's broke in there, it'll pry be empty. Never got much use anyhow. I'll build a table."

"Yeah!"

"Hey," Gage said, "we can order some figures from Henry Dobson's Mercantile. You know, a tiger and circus performers."

"For the landing and boat." Toby brightened. "That's a good idea, Gage."

When the door closed, Toby hopped out of bed. He grabbed a glass of water and the pills Andrew gave him for his "gastric-distress burn." He needed to be in top form to see his sister. She'd probably want to kick his butt around her hospital bed. At least, he sure hoped so.

She opened her eyes when the side of her bed shifted with weight.

"Mom."

Emma smoothed back Sarah's hair. "Oh, sweetheart."

"I'm okay, Mom."

A wistful smile crossed her mother's face. "No, you aren't. I don't want you to pretend with me ever again."

Toby sat down in the chair opposite her, while Gage stood behind Emma.

"Hey, Sis, don't worry. I just got the same lecture and lived through it."

Emma glanced disapprovingly at Toby, and he snickered. Gage just shook his head.

Suddenly Sarah felt exhausted. "Mom, the things I said . . ."

"I needed to hear." Emma kissed Sarah's forehead. "I needed to know how you feel. I don't ever want you to keep anything from me again. You and Toby are my life. I love you, Sarah."

A tear leaked out. "Me, too. Mom, I'm so sorry."

Emma shook her head. "You don't ever have to be sorry with me. I'm your mother."

"Hey, you have another visitor," Gage said. "We'd better scoot. Don't want to wear her out," he added.

Emma and Toby rose, and Sarah saw Jeremy filling the doorway. As Gage passed, he nodded to the pilot, as if the two were in cahoots. If she could think straight, she might figure out what it meant. She didn't have the energy to pursue her curiosity.

Damn, that whack with the shovel must have been harder than she thought.

Jeremy sat carefully on her bed; it sagged with his weight. He took her hand, his face clenched with anger and worry. She never saw such an expression on him before.

"Oh, God, Sarah." He gently touched her cheek—the unbruised side.

"It's much worse than it looks . . . wait . . . I mean, worse than it feels . . . I mean—"

"It hurts like hell."

"That'll do," she said.

"I'd love to get my hands on him."

"He's got all the problems in the world, Jeremy. Did you hear him? It was awful."

"Well, it's over."

She tried to smile. The right side of her face shot through with serious agony. His fingers gently caressed her left cheek, and his face drained of anger. Went to regret.

"Help me sit up."

He put his arm behind her and gently lifted her, propped pillows behind her. Smoothed back her hair from her face. And she watched as

his face broke. He gently pulled her to him, gathering her in his huge, warm arms. His heart beat, sure and steady, against her chest.

"I almost lost you," he said into her ear, his voice hushed with emotion.

"You didn't. That's what counts."

His arms wrapped tighter, gently. She wanted to stay here forever, safe, warm, protected.

"Every time he dragged you, or dumped you, or kicked you, I wanted to rush in and rip him apart. But I knew that would be the end of you. I've never been so—"

"Hush. It's over. You did everything just right."

He let loose to look into her face. "I am never going to forget what that felt like, thinking I'd lose you." He kissed her forehead and folded her in his arms again. "I'm never going to let you go."

"I'm afraid you're going to have to. I can't breathe."

He set her gently back against her pillows, no humor in his face. She hated seeing him like this.

"I was teasing you," she said. "I'm fine."

"Sarah, I'm sorry."

"For what? You saved my life."

"If you hadn't bitten him, we'd have been blown to pieces."

"Took all of us. You, me, the captain. Like a famous pilot once told me, accepting help makes a person stronger. Hard lesson to learn, when one is bullheaded." She smiled, trying to show him she was fine, but an ache clenched at her face. Most likely, her expression was more of a grimace.

He looked down, took her hand. "I meant I'm sorry I hurt you. What happened with Zelda."

"Oh, heavens. That feels years away."

"Can you ever forgive me?"

She wanted to hold out the moment, tease him, but he seemed so serious. Almost tortured. "You are certain you only kissed her?"

Annoyance rose in him, and she was glad to see it. "To be precise, she kissed me. Once. And just so we're clear, that's all that transpired between us. Took me by surprise. And it happened back when you were still shoving me against walls and stamping on my foot."

Well, he'd recovered nicely. "Oh, the whole thing is my fault?"

He puffed out an exasperated sigh. "That's not what I meant at all." He lowered his voice. "But I want you to know, if you decide to give me another chance, I will never, ever betray you." Again the tortured look took over his expression. "I'd die first."

She placed her hand on the side of his face. "Relax, Jeremy. I believe you. It was just a kiss. If you recall, I got one of those theater kisses, too. They really don't mean much, do they?"

He lowered his head and brushed her lips with his. She pulled him closer and kissed him, and still he was careful, as if she were delicate and might break at any moment. With the pain pounding in her head, she was glad he was so tender.

"Now *that* is a kiss," she whispered. "Jeremy, I love you."

He jolted. "Hey, I was about to say that."

She chuckled. "Ah, but you didn't. I win. I'd say I definitely have the most courage."

"No argument there." He took her hand from his face, spread it open, and kissed her palm. "Will you marry me?"

Now it was her turn to jolt. "What?"

"Aha. I win."

Shock grew into indignation. "You proposed to me to win?"

"Absolutely. And if you say yes and agree to be my wife, then yeah, I'd say I'm definitely the big winner."

The man's train was as silly as him. Jeremy approached the long, garishly painted thing, wondering which part of it housed Oscar Gévaudan. He realized it wasn't a challenge to figure out at all. The show-off part.

The caboose was not only splattered with loud colors and whimsically rendered ballerinas, medieval and exotic figures, and decorative scrolling; a painted tiger roared, its open mouth the back doorway. No doubt Oscar Gévaudan lived inside.

Affirming Jeremy's hunch, the grandmaster emerged from the mouth of the tiger. He looked a bit worn. No top hat, but glints of gold wove through his beige jacket and pants, and caught the morning sun.

"Well, I thought I must be hallucinating," Oscar said. "They've let you out of your cage for the day?"

Jeremy approached the back steps. "Can we talk?"

Oscar drew back, surprised. "You wish an audience with me? I'm shocked, Mr. Cro-Magnon."

"Yeah, I bet."

"Well, I see you are partially incapacitated," he said, nodding to Jeremy's arm. Or lack of one; it was bound beneath his shirt. Andrew had taped Jeremy's arm across his body, swearing it was the only way he'd get the pilot to heal.

Oscar looked him up and down. "I suppose I'm safe enough with you trussed up like a Christmas goose. Come in." He gestured to the door.

Jeremy climbed up the steps.

"You'd better duck," Oscar said, "I'd hate to see you brain yourself on my doorstep."

Jeremy bent and stepped into the most bizarre room he'd ever encountered. Tasseled lamps, walls lined with red velvet, chairs and sofa tufted in every color imaginable. Doorways were draped with strands of gold and silver, and every window in the caboose sparkled with stained glass. From the inside with light coming through, Jeremy could make out the scenes. Various positions in lovemaking.

"You are one strange little bastard."

"I've heard. Have a seat, if you think you won't break one of my chairs," Oscar said. "And if you are expecting any sort of cooperation from me, I suggest you change your tack. Insults won't get you very far."

Jeremy carefully lowered himself on a tufted, blue brocade chair, letting his weight settle a little at a time. When he was sure it wouldn't collapse beneath him, he relaxed. "Where's your tiger?"

"Daisy has her own room."

Jeremy studied the grandmaster. Oscar didn't wear the smug, snappy, slightly amused expression he once did. He seemed older and definitely sadder.

"Oscar, I'm sorry for all your loss. Lucy, Zelda."

Oscar's eyes reflected hurt, then grew round and sad. "I miss them both so much."

"I'm sure you do. Grief is a hard thing."

"What do you know about it?" Oscar snapped.

Jeremy thought of his father, Quentin. "A fair amount, although I never have lost a woman I love. I can't pretend to know how much that hurts."

"You know," Oscar said, "you aren't half bad when you act like a human being. I never did have the chance to thank you for saving my life. I realize you put yourself between the bullets and me. I am grateful."

Jeremy nodded. "Where are you off to next?"

"We're going to try the West Coast. San Francisco. I'm tired of winters. I much prefer outdoor venues. And I hear California is rife with opportunity."

Jeremy leaned forward. "I have a favor to ask."

"Ah, and we finally get to it."

"Not for me, for Sarah."

"How is she?"

"She's back on the boat. Doing well. She's a strong woman."

"No argument. And you are one lucky man. She could do much better than you."

Jeremy smiled. "Yeah, I know."

Oscar sat back. "So how can I help our lovely Sarah?"

"She wants, more than anything, to get her river pilot's license."

Oscar jerked his head, confused. "She doesn't have one? She drove all the way back."

"We had extenuating circumstances." Jeremy explained about the test she'd taken several times, and the River Board's unfair prejudices. Finally, he ended by telling Oscar the board scheduled her test on September 18 in hopes of distracting her.

"So, what is it you'd like me to do?"

"I understand you are a lawyer."

Oscar's eyes lit with understanding. "Ah."

"I was wondering, before I take this any further, if we have any recourse to have the test rescheduled."

"There's always recourse. Whether it works or not is the question. I imagine a lawsuit like this would have next to no merit in court."

Jeremy stood. "Okay, thanks for hearing me out."

"Wait. That doesn't mean we can't sue anyway." A devilish grin broke across the grandmaster's face.

"What's the point?"

"Well, many times defendants will settle out of court before a thing gets expensive. Since we aren't talking about money, just a reschedule of the test, I'd be willing to bet I could bluster about and push them into acquiescing. Threaten all sorts of dire consequences. Make them believe we can ruin them. After all, if nothing else, I am a master of illusion."

"No argument from me." Jeremy paused. "Oscar, I'd sure appreciate it."

"I won't be doing it for you."

Jeremy nodded. "I understand."

"I can't guarantee Sarah will get her license, though."

"One step at a time. I just want her to be able to take the test."

Oscar stood. "When can you convene this board of yours?"

"Tonight?"

"I'll be there."

Jeremy smiled. "Make sure you bring your tiger."

October 31, 1910 (one month later)

Jeremy and Sarah stopped at the stage of the *Lamport*. The rickety boat took on a certain rough dignity this morning. She actually appreciated the fact that it wasn't perfect. Jeremy let go of her hand and pulled out his pocket watch. "Five minutes early."

"And I suppose you'd like to take credit for my being punctual this time around?" Sarah challenged.

"Not at all."

"I'm teasing." She smiled up at him. "Thank you for this."

He shrugged. "Least I could do. Actually, most of the credit goes to Oscar. He's the one who scared the board half to death. Daisy managed to do her share, too."

They laughed together, and then the seriousness of the situation settled on her shoulders.

"Jeremy, would you mind if I took a few minutes down here alone? You know, to gather my thoughts."

He glanced at her, skeptical.

"Oh, please. Don't tell me you think I might run?"

"I know better." He paused, studied her. "You want to walk in there on your own."

"Finally! You understand me."

He shook his head. "I'm sure I'll spend the rest of my life trying to figure you out. I'd say good luck, but you don't need it. You did it, Sarah. Saved the *Spirit*. Got another chance at your test."

"Hardly by myself. I was never alone."

"Between me and your family, I doubt you'll ever be, even if you wanted to. I'll see you upstairs."

He climbed the steps, finally disappearing into the pilothouse and she looked around. Amazingly, she wasn't nervous at all.

"I guess after you've piloted through a shooting, a poisoning, and a near boat explosion, this is not such a huge affair." She climbed the steps.

When she opened the door to the pilothouse, they all turned, the giant, ancient, many-headed turtle. And Jeremy, his arms crossed, leaned against the desk. Just when she thought she'd seen every expression he had, a new one broke on his face. Pride. For her.

She stepped up to the pilot wheel. "I'm ready."

One More Moment

Check it out! There is a new section on the Medallion Press Web site called "One More Moment." Have you ever gotten to the end of a book and just been crushed that it's over? Aching to know if the star-crossed lovers ever got married? Had kids? With this new section of our Web site, you won't have to wonder anymore! "One More Moment" provides an extension of your favorite book so you can discover what happens after the story.

medallionpress.com

Passion's Blood
Cherif Fortin & Lynn Sanders

Lady Leanna is a flame-haired beauty loved by her betrothed, Prince Emric, desired by his loathsome brother, Prince Bran. Although in love with Emric, Leanna has still not made her peace with the knowledge that this arrangement was forced upon her.

Prince Emric, noble and courageous, rides to war, ignorant of his brother's dark treachery.

In a net of betrayal and violence, the young lovers must preserve their faith, and Leanna must keep Emric alive with her love and the magical powers she herself does not fully understand . . .

ISBN# 978-160542062-2
Hardcover Adult / Illustrated Romantic Masterpiece
US $25.95 / CDN $28.95
AVAILABLE NOW

There Be Dragons
Heather Graham

Nico d'Or was a kind and gentle man who lived in the age of dragons. Through a simple twist of fate, Nico married the lovely Princess Elisia, and the couple were blessed with a beautiful daughter, Marina. Would they live happily ever after?

Well, not quite. The neighbor's wife, Geovana, was neither sweet nor lovely, but a devious sorceress who spent her time casting dreadful spells, devising vile tricks, and mixing powerful potions with eye of newt and the horn of a toad.

Geovana used one of her favorite spells—strategically hurling rocks through windows to smash into the heads of her victims—tragically killing both Nico and Elisia, and leaving the beautiful Marina all alone. To make matters worse, Geovana became Marina's guardian and, greedy for power, arranged a marriage between Marina and her own evil son, Carlo Baristo.

But Marina was in love with someone else. And as Christmas Day approached, Marina was faced with a terrible choice: save her land and her people, or follow her heart and believe in the magic of Christmas and true love.

ISBN# 978-160542071-4
Hardcover Adult / Illustrated Romantic Masterpiece
US $25.95 / CDN $28.95
AVAILABLE NOW
www.theoriginalheathergraham.com

THE PRICE OF SANCTUARY

GAYLON GREER

Shelby Cervosier murdered three men in self-defense. Brutally beaten and raped by her captors, she does what any woman would do: kill or die. To avoid manslaughter charges, one involving a sadistic immigration officer, Shelby cooperates with the Caribbean Basin Task Force, a sleazy undercover government agency. In exchange for legal amnesty and political asylum in the United States, she completes a treacherous mission in Haiti. Now the agent who hired her wants her dead. Facing a contract on her life, Shelby flees with her younger sister, Carmen, to find safe haven in America with two assassins in close pursuit.

Hank Pekins accepts the contract. Like any competent killer-for-hire, he captures Shelby and escorts her . . . to his farm in a remote part of Colorado? That wasn't part of the deal. A killer kills. A paid assassin doesn't protect an illegal immigrant and turn her into his lover.

In a coldhearted profession where ruthlessness rules and emotions obscure an annihilator's judgment, passion has no clout at the critical moment the job must be executed. But Hank knows that his own days are numbered. Money cannot buy human life. Especially not the life of the woman he adores beyond reason.

The second assassin loves no one. Vlad, known as The Impaler, intends to complete his assignment. First, he will torture Shelby in his trademark style, and then he will kill her. No one, not even Hank, will stand in this psychopath's way. For Shelby Cervosier, what will be *The Price Of Sanctuary*?

ISBN# 978-160542058-5
Hardcover / Thriller
US $24.95 / CDN $27.95
AVAILABLE NOW
www.gaylongreer.com

First, there is a River

Kathy Steffen

A family conceals a cruel secret.

Emma Perkins' life appears idyllic. Her husband, Jared, is a hardworking farmer and a dependable neighbor. But Emma knows intimately the brutality prowling beneath her husband's facade. When he sends their children away, Emma's life unravels.

A woman seeks her spirit.

Deep in despair, Emma seeks refuge aboard her uncle's riverboat, the *Spirit of the River*. She travels through a new world filled with colorful characters: captains, mates, the rich, the working class, moonshiners, prostitutes, and Gage-the Spirit's reclusive engineer. Scarred for life from a riverboat explosion, Gage's insight into heartache draws him to Emma, and as they heal together, they form a deep and unbreakable bond. Emma learns to trust that anything is possible, including reclaiming her children and facing her husband.

A man seeks revenge.

Jared Perkins makes a journey of his own. Determined to bring his wife home and teach her the lesson of her life, Jared secretly follows the Spirit. His rage burns cold as he plans his revenge for everyone on board.

Against the immense power of the river, the journey of the *Spirit* will change the course of their lives forever.

ISBN# 978-193281593-1

Trade Paperback / Historical Fiction

US $14.95 / CDN $18.95

AVAILABLE NOW

www.kathysteffen.com

Jasper Mountain
Kathy Steffen

Two lost souls struggle to find their way in the unforgiving West of 1873 . . .

Jack Buchanan, a worker at the Jasper Mining Company, is sure of his place in the outside world, but has lost his faith, hope, and heart to the tragedy of a fire.

Foreign born and raised, Milena Shabanov flees from a home she loves to the strange and barbaric America. A Romani blessed with "the sight," she is content in the company of visions and spirit oracles, but finds herself lost and alone in a brutal mining town with little use for women.

Surrounded by inhumane working conditions at the mine, senseless death, and overwhelming greed, miners begin disappearing and the officers of the mine don't care.

Tempers flare and Jack must decide where he stands: with the officers and mining president—Victor Creely—to whom Jack owes his life, or with the miners, whose lives are worth less to the company than pack animals. Milena, sensing deep despair and death in a mining town infested with restless spirits, searches for answers to the workers' disappearances. But she can't trust anyone, especially not Jack Buchanan, a man haunted by his own past.

ISBN# 978-193383658-4
Trade Paperback / Historical Fiction
US $15.95 / CDN $17.95
AVAILABLE NOW
www.kathysteffen.com

*** 2009 BENJAMIN FRANKLIN FINALIST
IN THE HISTORICAL CATEGORY***

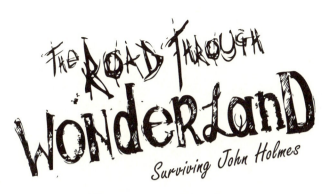

Dawn Schiller

The Road Through Wonderland is Dawn Schiller's chilling account of the childhood that molded her so perfectly to fall for the seduction of "the king of porn," John Holmes, and the bizarre twist of fate that brought them together. With painstaking honesty, Dawn uncovers the truth of her relationship with John, her father figure-turned-forbidden lover who hid her away from his porn movie world and welcomed her into his family along with his wife.

Within these pages, Dawn reveals the perilous road John led her down—from drugs and addiction to beatings, arrests, forced prostitution, and being sold to the drug underworld. Surviving the horrific Wonderland murders, this young innocent entered protective custody, ran from the FBI, endured a heart-wrenching escape from John, and ultimately turned him in to the police.

This is the true story of one of the most infamous of public figures and a young girl's struggle to survive unthinkable abuse. Readers will be left shaken but clutching to real hope at the end of this dark journey on *The Road Through Wonderland*.

Also check out the movie *Wonderland* (Lions Gate Entertainment, 2003) for a look into the past of Dawn Schiller and the Wonderland Murders.

ISBN# 978-160542083-7
Trade Paperback / Autobiography
US $15.95 / CDN $17.95
AVAILABLE NOW
www.theroadthroughwonderland.com

From *New York Times* best-selling author

Shannon Drake
Emerald Embrace

"... a brilliant testament to Drake's versatility."
—*Publisher's Weekly* Starred Review

Devastated over the premature death of her dearest friend, Mary, Lady Martise St. James ventures to foreboding Castle Creeghan in the Scottish Highlands to dispel rumors surrounding the young woman's demise and retrieve a lost emerald. Beneath the stones of this aging mansion lurks a family crypt filled with sinister secrets. Locked within this threatening vault is the answer to the most dangerous question, and the promise of the most horrifying death.

Amid jaded suspicion, underlying threats, and the dreaded approach of All Hallow's Eve in 1865, Martise encounters a witch's coven and meets Lord Bruce Creeghan, the love of her friend's life. Mysterious, yet passionate, Mary's husband elicits a deep desire and a profound fear in the core of her soul. He knows ... something. And it's up to Martise to reveal what he hides from her prying intrusion.

Lord Creeghan wards off the invasion of his private fortress, yet he cannot resist his magnetic attraction to the beautiful sleuth. As strong as the inevitable pull toward the catacomb beneath their bed, an overwhelming obsession propels them into disheveled sheets of unquenchable hunger and lust. While savoring an affair that cannot be denied, Martise must discover whether her lover is a ruthless murderer or a guardian angel.

ILLUSTRATED BY YEVGENIYA YERETSKAYA

ISBN# 978-160542082-0
Mass Market Paperback / Historical Romance
US $7.95 / CDN $8.95

AVAILABLE NOW
www.theoriginalheathergraham.com

BACK IN PRINT AFTER 19 YEARS!

MEDALLION
P R E S S

Be in the know on the latest
Medallion Press news by becoming a Medallion Press
Insider!

As an Insider you'll receive:

· Our FREE expanded monthly newsletter, giving you more insight into Medallion Press

· Advanced press releases and breaking news

· Greater access to all your favorite Medallion authors

Joining is easy. Just visit our Web site at
www.medallionpress.com and click on the Medallion Press
Insider tab.

medallionpress.com

MEDALLION
P R E S S

Want to know what's going on with
your favorite author or what new releases
are coming from Medallion Press?

Now you can receive breaking news,
updates, and more from Medallion Press
straight to your cell phone, e-mail, instant messenger, or Facebook!

Sign up now at www.twitter.com/MedallionPress to stay on top of all
the happenings in and
around Medallion Press.

For more information
about other great titles from
Medallion Press, visit

medallionpress.com